A **JAK**

THE
CHAMELEON

RON McMANUS

BAY BEACH
BOOKS

Published by Bay Beach Books
Edited, designed, and distributed by Bublish, Inc.

ISBN: 978-1-6470437-5-9 (Paperback)
ISBN: 978-1-6470437-4-2 (eBook)

To my sister
Judith McManus Armfield

ACRONYMS AND ABBREVIATIONS

CBP: Customs and Border Protection

CCTV: Closed Circuit Television

CIA: Central Intelligence Agency

CO: Commanding Officer

DCM: Deputy Chief of Mission at the US Embassy

DGK: Dera Ghazi Khan

DIA: Defense Intelligence Agency

EOD: Explosive Ordnance Disposal (US)

EOD&S: Explosive Ordnance Disposal and Search (UK)

FBI: Federal Bureau of Investigation

HMRC: Her Majesty's Revenue and Customs

ISI: Pakistan's Inter-Services Intelligence

JeM: Jaish-e-Mohammed (Army of Mohammed)

JSOC: Joint Special Operations Command

LeT: Lashkar-e-Taiba (Army of the Good or Army of the Pure)

MIT: Massachusetts Institute of Technology

MI5: Military Intelligence, Section 5 (the United Kingdom's Security Service)

MI6: Military Intelligence, Section 6 (the United Kingdom's Secret Intelligence Service)

PAL: Passive Active Link

PNS: Pakistan Naval Station

POTUS: President of the United States

RHIB: Rigid-Hulled Inflatable Boat

RPG: Rocket-Propelled Grenade

SOS: International Distress Call

SPD: Strategic Plans Division

TEU: Twenty-Foot Equivalent Unit (size of a standard intermodal cargo container)

TS/SCI: Top Secret/Sensitive Compartmented Information

UKBA: United Kingdom Border Agency

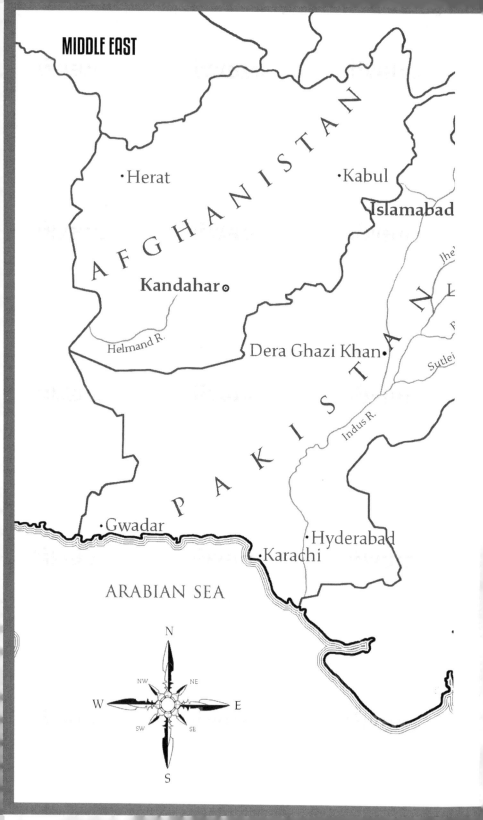

MIDDLE EAST

AFGHANISTAN

·Herat

·Kabul

Islamabad

Kandahar⊙

Helmand R.

Dera Ghazi Khan·

Jhe'

Sutlej

Indus R.

PAKISTAN

L

·Gwadar

·Hyderabad
·Karachi

ARABIAN SEA

N
NW   NE
W   E
SW   SE
S

Line of Control

Pakistani-administered Kashmir

Area occupied by China, claimed by India

KASHMIR

⊙ **Srinagar**

Indian-administered Kashmir

CHINA

Jhelum R.

Chenab R.

Lahore

Ravi R.

·Amritsar

R.

NEPAL

Ganges R.

New Delhi ⊙ Delhi

Yamuna R.

Agra·

·Kanpur

Lucknow·

I N D I A

·Ahmadabad

1

JOINT SPECIAL OPERATIONS COMMAND
FORT BELVOIR, FAIRFAX COUNTY, VIRGINIA

Jake Palmer leaned closer to the computer screen, shaking his head at the document staring back at him. The US Department of State was advising nonessential personnel of the United States Embassy and all US government agencies in Pakistan to leave the country.

He sat back in his chair, sighing. The warning came as no surprise—the decades-long tension between Pakistan and India had now escalated to the boiling point. The Pakistan-backed terrorist group Jaish-e-Mohammed, or JeM—meaning Army of Mohammed—had attacked an army camp in India, killing over fifty soldiers. And, more recently, assassins had murdered Deepak Chandra, an outspoken activist for peace and editor-in-chief of a Srinagar, India, newspaper—along with his two police bodyguards. India was gathering its forces and war seemed inevitable. The evacuation order cautioned that, if war were declared, the use of nuclear weapons by one or both sides could not be ruled out. State Department advisories often required some interpretation and the ability to read between the lines in order to understand their purpose and meaning. Not this one. Earlier intelligence reports had forewarned that an evacuation of Americans was possible. For months, both government- and nongovernment-employed US citizens had been packing up and either going home or relocating to another foreign assignment.

Palmer hit the print icon. The printer beside his desk whirred to life, spitting out a copy of the communiqué. *Why am I even here?* He didn't need to look any further than himself for the answer to that question. Being an independent investigative consultant had been a good ride. He'd had the ability to handpick his cases and had no boss, no deadlines, no employees to manage. He'd made enough money to live in comfort and put some aside. Yet he had given it all up to serve his country once again. Now, here he sat, shuffling papers.

With a printed copy of the official State Department communiqué in his hand, Palmer stormed down the hall. The director's secretary glanced up from her computer screen only long enough to see who it was. She nodded her head in the direction he was walking. He never broke stride. When he entered, he held up the communiqué. "When am—"

"Your final security clearance came through, and you have your assignment," the director interrupted. "Pack your bags."

"Where am I going?"

"Islamabad, Pakistan."

Palmer stopped in his tracks, taking a moment to collect his thoughts. John "Fast Ball" Benson had thrown him a changeup, a pitch he was not expecting. Palmer smiled.

Benson had spent his entire career in service to his country. After graduating from West Point, he'd served in Army Intelligence. Then, after he left the military, he went to the Central Intelligence Agency, the National Security Agency, and now Joint Special Operations Command. Approaching sixty, his size and shape had shifted significantly from the framed photograph on the wall behind his desk that was of him pitching in an Army-Navy game—a game Navy won 8–2 according to the attached plaque. His gray hair was cut high and tight, the hairline receding like the ebb tide, and he had swelled by perhaps forty pounds, most of which hung from his belly—too much time sitting and too little exercise.

"I hear Islamabad is beautiful this time of the year," Benson said with a wide grin.

"You heard wrong."

Palmer's transition to his current role had begun after a couple of his high-profile cases captured the attention of the media. Although he largely avoided the press, that didn't change the fact that some people were watching and taking notice. Among them was Benson, a senior member of the US Joint Special Operations Command at Fort Belvoir in Fairfax County, Virginia, near Washington, DC. While offering Palmer the job, Benson had smartly gone right for Palmer's soft spot, appealing to his sense of patriotism and duty. The country needed his experience and unique skills. Knowing little about the specifics of the potential assignment, Palmer agreed on one condition—he was to be brought on board as an independent contractor, not a full-time employee. JSOC agreed, with the understanding that Palmer would only commit to a two-year hitch.

Palmer reported to a JSOC unit at Fort Belvoir so secret that the name of the group often changed. It had been called Field Operations Group, Intelligence Support Activity, Mission Support Activity, the Activity, Gray Fox, and most recently, Task Force Orange, or simply Orange. Officially, the group's responsibility was to gather actionable intelligence for elite special operations groups under JSOC's command, including the Air Force's 24th Special Tactics Squadron, the Army's Delta Force, and the Naval Special Warfare Development Group or DEVGRU, better known as SEAL Team Six. Unofficially, Orange's remit was much broader and involved a wide range of other activities, such as hostage rescue. When Palmer signed on, he was told he would be assigned to the Middle East or South Asia, nothing more.

At first, the buzz of working there and the anticipation of what he might be doing kept him interested and enthusiastic. Palmer now found himself stuck behind a desk, reviewing low-level analyst's reports from South Asia on the Pakistan-India conflict. He had been assigned an interim security clearance while awaiting the top secret, sensitive compartmented information (TS/SCI) security clearance needed by individuals who required access to specific data, hardware, and certain controlled-access areas related to their roles.

Palmer understood the delay but had grown impatient. He was the new guy who hadn't yet paid his dues. He didn't care that he was the new guy. He'd paid his dues in the past, just not to this organization. And it wasn't as though he'd accepted the role in Orange to make friends. He was there to do a job and would carry it out to the best of his ability.

Benson pointed at the paper that Palmer was holding. "You'll be one of the few nonmilitary personnel going into Pakistan. Everyone else is getting the hell out. Are you fired up?"

Palmer took a moment and sat down. "Don't get me wrong. I'm eager to go, and after reading this Department of State advisory, I'm not surprised. But why me? You can't swing a cat by the tail on an Islamabad street without hitting a CIA officer or some other US intelligence operative."

Benson laughed. "You're right about that. And, yes, others in the region have a similar remit. Thing is, Palmer, we need a fresh perspective, and you're it. I was told to get you in the field as quickly as possible. You're a former Navy SEAL, corporate regulatory attorney, and you have an impressive resume as an investigative consultant, having broken up a terrorist cell in Virginia and busted a global counterfeit medicine and money laundering operation. Except for your security clearance and some intel training—both of which you now have—you were ready when you arrived. Meanwhile, I've reached an agreement with the top brass on your assignment. Your base of operations will be the US Embassy complex in Islamabad."

2

LONDON
UK SECRET INTELLIGENCE SERVICE, MI6

Fiona Isabella Collins buttoned up her Mackintosh raincoat and picked up her pace. The walk from Britain's MI6 headquarters at Vauxhall Cross to the tube stop would take only a few minutes. There she would catch the Victoria Line to her flat near Clapham Common. On a nice day, when she had time, she walked home. Problem was, she seldom had time. Every minute of her day was precious.

Since starting her job at MI6, she commuted into London but quickly learned that neither driving nor taking the train was ideal. So, she rented her house in the peaceful Kent village of Sevenoaks Weald to an elderly couple and used the money to offset the rent for her London flat. She had inherited the house from her parents and cherished her memories of growing up there. However, one particularly bad memory still haunted her, often sinking its teeth so deeply into her dreams that she'd wake thrashing from a dead sleep. It'd been years since she'd been abducted from her home, but the fear was still fresh, and perhaps it always would be. She owed her life to Jake Palmer, a man with whom she had since fallen in love. Palmer had rescued her, killing her murderous abductor with his bare hands.

It had been almost a year since she had seen him. She had turned up at his condominium in Philadelphia to break the news she was leaving B&A Pharmaceuticals and accepting a job with MI6 as an intelligence analyst, working in London. Because she was fluent in Italian, she was told she would also spend time in Rome. She knew Palmer was concerned for her safety, but he had supported her decision anyway.

The transition from the head of a corporate auditing function to an intelligence analyst had challenged her. Now, ten months into the job, she was beginning to get the hang of it. Stressful, yes. Information and recommendations made by the analysts saved lives, but in other cases cost lives. She was putting in ten- to twelve-hour days, often working on weekends.

Her current assignment was working with a senior analyst to help analyze intelligence data related to the Pakistan-India conflict. The situation there was heating up, and the UK was eager to enhance its relationship with Pakistan. Almost everyone was optimistic that the planned China-Pakistan Economic Corridor would boost Pakistan's economy and, in doing so, provide huge opportunities for UK business. Pakistanis made up almost 2 percent of the UK's population. Last year, the UK had signed an agreement with Pakistan regarding enhanced security counterterrorism, organized crime, and border security. On the other hand, India called Pakistan "Terroristan," a label the American president latched onto when he declared Pakistan a state sponsor of terrorism. It all made for a complex political and economic environment, one in which the gathering and analysis of intelligence was a top priority.

On a personal level, Collins had little to no social life. On occasion, she would meet coworkers for drinks; however, she considered that more of a networking opportunity than a relaxed social setting. It was during one of those gatherings that she met a senior MI6 staff member. He recognized her potential and soon became her mentor. At his suggestion, Collins enrolled as a part-time student at King's College London's Centre for Science and Security Studies, taking courses in intelligence and counterterrorism. At the moment, she was not working toward a specific degree, though at some point she might do so. For now, she was just interested in learning as much as she could about the work she was doing. When she wasn't working or studying, she was reading from a long list of books on subjects related to those topics.

Approval of her security clearance had taken longer than expected—probably because of her recent history with Palmer. The two of them had been involved in an operation that prevented a US aircraft carrier from being destroyed by a terrorist cell in Virginia and broke up a counterfeit medicine and money laundering operation that was funneling money to terrorists. Although Palmer had managed to keep his name out of the news, Britain's media had thrust her into the spotlight. The *Daily Mail* nicknamed her "Britain's female Bond," and the *Guardian* called her "Fantastic Fiona." The B&A Pharmaceuticals executives were not pleased. Yes, they showed public support, saying all the right things, but behind closed doors, they gave her an ultimatum— to either stop her unauthorized exploits with Jake Palmer or leave. She was so upset that the same day, on a total whim while having lunch at her desk, she went to the MI6 website and discovered an opening for an intelligence analyst. She applied and was offered the position. The very things that were negatives to her B&A managers were positives to those who interviewed her at MI6.

By the time Collins got to Vauxhall Underground Station, it had begun to rain. It was half-past seven, and the station was less crowded than at the peak of rush hour. She got on the car, not bothering to sit for the short, nonstop ride to Stockwell Station, where she jumped off and took the Northern Line to Clapham Common. Before she stepped out of the station, she pulled the hood of her coat over her head. The foul weather matched her mood. She was tired and needed to see Palmer. He had called her earlier that day and asked if she had the weekend free. If so, he wanted to stop over in London to see her before traveling on to Islamabad. He said he wanted to talk to her about something face-to-face. *How long can we keep this up? It's not fair to me or him. What type of relationship can survive this? Maybe that's why he wants to see me. Is this the end of the line for us?*

3

LAKE VIEW PARK
ISLAMABAD, PAKISTAN

The Pakistani Inter-Services Intelligence officer went by the name Aaliyah. She was, by anyone's standards, an attractive, intelligent woman—an agent provocateur. She was also an enigma. Being one of a select group of women serving in ISI gave her an advantage over her male colleagues. Those who doubted her mental and physical toughness often suffered the consequences.

On the surface, Pakistan's ISI served as the country's military intelligence agency, gathering, processing, and analyzing intelligence data related to national security, similar to the role of other national intelligence services, such as the US's CIA and Israel's Mossad. However, since the 1990s, its role and influence in Pakistan had grown to the point that it was considered one of the most powerful and feared intel agencies in the world.

ISI recruited foreign assets, sometimes called agents, using a variety of methods employed by intelligence agencies worldwide. Some assets were reluctant to cooperate at first. They turned over information they believed was not critical to their home country's interest and would not result in loss of their countrymen's lives. By doing so, they rationalized their behavior. Although they were still betraying their country, they felt less guilty about it.

One American asset that Aaliyah recruited had access to the names of US Embassy personnel who were entering and leaving the country, as well as information on Pakistani assets recruited by US operatives. An ISI talent spotter had identified him and turned his name over to Aaliyah, who made initial contact. It took months for her to gain the American's confidence and ask him for information. He became angry and refused to cooperate, saying he would never betray his country. However, when Aaliyah laid out the compromising evidence against him and threatened to pass it along to the embassy, the American's anger waned. He saw no way out. The consequences of not cooperating were dire, including certain dismissal from his position and possible imprisonment.

Aaliyah's prearranged early morning meeting with the asset was at Lake View Park. The park had a large promenade with a view of Rawal Lake, a reservoir built on the Korang River, which ran from the Margalla Hills north of Islamabad. The usually crowded promenade was nearly empty. Only a few people were there in the cool freshness of the morning—mothers pushing baby strollers or joggers getting their daily exercise before going to work. She stood next to a rail at the water's edge, gazing out at the birds flying over the tranquil water. A few minutes later, her asset sauntered up and leaned against the rail, close enough to talk with her at a normal level but not close enough as to appear they were together.

"What do you have for me today?" asked Aaliyah.

Without looking at her, he reached over and handed her a piece of paper.

Aaliyah took a minute to review the handwritten list of names. Beside each name was a job title and reporting date.

"Any of these noteworthy, or is it another useless list of new administrative assistants?"

The asset put his finger on a man's name, paused, and then moved down the list, stopping on a second name, a woman's. The woman was listed as an information technology specialist and had recently reported for duty. The man was listed as a security specialist and was scheduled to report in a couple of days.

"What are their true assignments?" Aaliyah asked.

"I believe they are members of a highly classified joint special operations intelligence group."

Aaliyah turned her palms up and tilted her head. "Interesting, but I'm still not seeing anything unique. The Americans routinely rotate intelligence or military men and women in and out of the embassy complex. They assign them to seemingly unremarkable jobs with nondescript titles. What is their mission? What's special about them?"

"Officially, they will take over management of some assets, including mine. You remember I'm being reassigned, don't you?"

"Of course. So, they will be like you and me, recruiters and handlers of foreign agents?"

"That's probably a cover. Their real mission or assignment is top secret."

"It must be difficult for you, an intelligence officer for the US and a foreign agent for Pakistan—a double agent."

"Painfully so."

Aaliyah studied the list, focusing primarily on the names of the man and woman. This was indeed valuable intel. At a minimum, ISI would monitor their movements. "At last, you have given me information I can send up the line without being embarrassed by how useless it is. I doubt anything will come of it, but once they are both in the country and you have a sense of their role, let's get back together."

★ 11 ★

"No. That's all you're getting from me. I'm quitting."

Aaliyah inched closer to him until their shoulders were almost touching, "No, you're not. You know what will happen if you quit."

"The same as what happened to those men who I told you were providing information to the US. Most of them have gone missing."

The asset had previously given Aaliyah the names of several Pakistanis, some of whom worked at military facilities and were providing the US with information related to Pakistan's nuclear weapons program. ISI rounded them up and interrogated them. No one ever heard from them again.

"We questioned them and released them from government service. One, I think, was imprisoned. The rest have gone into hiding, like witness protection. The most recent name you gave me is still around, isn't he?"

"Gone into hiding? They're dead, aren't they? You know what? That's it. I don't care what you do to me or what you tell anyone. You've already ruined my life. It's not worth the guilt and stress. I'm done."

Aaliyah had had assets threaten to quit in the past. It was part of the process of recruiting and handling foreign assets. Most came back after a sleepless night of chewing over the consequences of walking away, and almost all of those became more cooperative as a result. She would give him a day or two and see how he handled it.

"No. You're not quitting," Aaliyah repeated, with a smile that would melt away any man's resistance, and took another step toward him, their arms now touching. "I want you to do something for me. When those two are on board, invite them to go along with you on a meeting with your new asset. Let me know when and where that will be. We would like to see this secret special operations duo."

The asset shook his head hard as if to shake himself out of a trance. "No. I'm finished with this and with you," he said, stepping away from her and storming off.

Aaliyah adjusted her dupatta, bringing the scarf closer to her brow, and watched him leave. What a shame. She had grown to like this one. He had no wife or children to threaten. If he carried through and quit, he would be eliminated by an ISI assassin before he left the country. She might have him eliminated anyway rather than risk him flipping once he was safely home in the US. All she had to do was put in a request, as easy as ordering paper for the office printer.

4

CLAPHAM, GREATER LONDON

Palmer arrived at London's Heathrow Airport on a busy Friday morning and went straight to Collins's flat. She had left a key for him with an elderly neighbor. Once inside, he recognized some of the furnishings that had been in her house in Sevenoaks Weald. Although it was much smaller than her house, it still very much looked, smelled, and felt like her. He picked up a framed photograph of them taken at his father's wedding in New York. Beside it sat a framed selfie of them at a restaurant in Positano, Italy. He felt the beginnings of a smile. They had shared some fun times. Although their relationship had lasted years, the total time they had actually spent face-to-face with each other was probably less than a few months. Still, he felt completely committed to her. They needed to talk.

After a cup of black coffee, he changed shoes and went for a long walk to clear the cobwebs that had begun cluttering his mind after the overnight flight. On his way across Clapham Common, he came across a drum-shaped, concrete rotunda near the mounds on the grassy expanse. He had driven by the common in the past but had never paid much attention to the mounds or to the concrete rotunda. When he approached it, he learned from a guide that it was the entrance to a massive World War II shelter that had only recently been refurbished and opened for tours. His curiosity got the best of him. The shelter, a hundred feet below ground, was made up of one thousand three hundred tunnels, creating an underground village that could house up to eight thousand people during the air raids and the feared Nazi invasion of England. Following the war, the shelter was converted to a secure document storage facility. It was a fascinating journey into the past, a reminder that there is no end to wars, only the manner in which they are fought. Einstein said it best: "I know not with what weapons WWIII will be fought, but WWIV will be fought with sticks and stones."

Palmer continued his walk and found a sandwich shop where he ate a late lunch. He was eager to see Collins, wishing she had taken the day off. It had been over a year since they were last together—the longest absence since they'd first met. In the past, time apart truly had made their hearts grow fonder. Now, for the first time, he realized that they had drifted apart. Both had new jobs and were so immersed in them that they had begun neglecting each other. Did she still love him? Did he still love her? He could only speak for himself, and he did indeed love her. But perhaps the intensity of that love had waned. Would this short visit reignite that fire or would it only confirm what he feared—that they had moved on? The major stumbling block had always been the reluctance to move to the other's home country to live and work. When she worked for B&A Pharmaceuticals, she could have transferred to their US headquarters but hadn't. Now that she worked for MI6, that was not an option. He'd had more flexibility to relocate when he was an independent investigative consultant. Why had he not moved then? Now that he worked for JSOC, he had less flexibility.

Palmer's phone vibrated in his pocket. A text from Collins.

Running late. Should be home by 5. I'll make it up to you. Promise.

Palmer thought a moment and, using his slow, index finger approach, replied. *Finish what you need to do. Meanwhile I'll think of ways you can make it up to me.*

At six, after periodic text updates, Collins arrived. Palmer met her at the door and embraced her. Even after a day at work and a ride on the underground, she smelled wonderful. Collins broke free from their embrace in a way that seemed to him to be a little abrupt. Maybe she was just tired or tense from work.

"How was your flight?" she asked.

"When you fly on the government's dollar, you fly economy, but I'm not complaining. How was your day at MI6?"

"Extremely busy and mentally challenging. I finally feel like I'm contributing instead of asking a thousand questions a day like a pain-in-the-ass trainee."

"You're a quick study. I'm sure they've already recognized your ability and potential."

"I hope so. For the first time in my life, I believe I'm contributing to the greater good while serving my country. It's difficult to describe. Working for B&A, I felt good about what the company did—discovering and developing new medicines for those who need them—but there was always the ugly commercial component."

"I get it. In the US, when men grow old, they don't parade around in hats that have a company logo on them. They wear hats that proudly show how they served and what war they fought in. It doesn't matter whether they were only in the service for a short period of time or they retired after thirty years in the military, because in the end, having served their country was more important to them and a source of pride."

"I see it in the UK as well, although baseball caps aren't a thing here."

"We have a lot to catch up on. Any quiet restaurants nearby where we go can for dinner?" Palmer asked.

"There's one I think you'd enjoy," Collins said. "I'll ring them and book a table. Then I'll get ready while you have a drink. There's a surprise for you in the cabinet," she added, pointing to a cupboard under the window in the living room.

"Don't take too long."

"I'll just be a few minutes."

Palmer opened the cabinet and found an unopened bottle of eighteen-year-old Glenmorangie with a light-blue bow on it. *A woman after my own heart.* He grabbed a couple of glasses, opened the bottle, and poured a couple of fingers. Taking a sip, he relocated to the sofa, savoring his drink until Collins returned, wearing a short red dress that hugged her curves and exposed her well-shaped legs. She snuggled in close beside him and took his glass, drinking what little remained.

"I'm not a whisky drinker, but that's brilliant."

He poured a small amount in a glass for Collins and a bit more in his. "Not what I had in mind when you said you'd make it up to me, but I love it."

The whisky seemed to melt away their initial awkwardness. They talked for a while about everything from Palmer's family to Collins's move to London.

"Let's have another and skip dinner," Palmer suggested.

"If I weren't starving, I'd be good with that. I worked through lunch and this is going straight to my head," she replied, holding the glass up to the light before finishing it off. "Maybe I'm a whisky drinker after all."

They took a taxi to a gastropub, an upscale pub with excellent food. The pub was full but not overly crowded, humming with subdued laughter and conversation. Because Collins had made a reservation, they only endured a short wait before being seated.

"I wish you could stay longer," Collins confessed.

"Me too. I have to report the day after tomorrow. That doesn't leave us much time. I feel like I'm back in the military."

"Well, you sort of are, aren't you?"

"I guess so. My job isn't running missions and engaging the enemy in combat, and I don't anticipate I'll be shooting anyone or that anyone will be shooting at me in the near future. It's calmer—relatively speaking. Of course, nothing in Pakistan is totally relaxed or safe."

"Do you know anyone there?"

"Not really. I may run into some guys I served with. I remember a friendly Pakistani naval officer. We participated in some joint training exercises. I respected his dedication. Been years since I last saw him. Maybe I'll look him up while I'm there, if he's still around."

"I'm working on Pakistan as well. I'm afraid I can't share any of it with you."

"Same here. JSOC wouldn't be happy if they found out I was collaborating with a foreign intelligence analyst."

"I wouldn't have known what JSOC was a few months ago. I've learned a lot about special operations," Collins said. "I'm even getting an idea of what your life must have been like when you were on active duty. You've never talked to me about it, and I've never asked. I've seen you do some incredible things. But seriously, a US Navy SEAL? My God. I knew you were my hero, but you're a real hero. Is there anything that frightens you?"

"I'm terrified of losing you."

"Are you?" Collins's eyes locked onto Palmer's as if she were looking deep into his soul. "Our relationship has been on my mind a lot lately. Can we continue like this—seeing each other so infrequently? Our jobs dictate that we may have to see or communicate with each other even less often over the next year or two."

"Would you quit MI6 and move to the US when my JSOC commitment is over?" Palmer asked.

Collins slowly shook her head. "I can't, Jake. This is my home, and I love my job. Would you consider moving to the UK?"

He had asked himself that question on a number of occasions and had come up with a different answer each time. Collins wouldn't move to the US, so a negative response could signal the end of their relationship. In the blink of an eye, it could be over. When Collins took the MI6 job, they'd told her she might be working in Italy for long periods, which was fine with her because her mother was Italian and Collins was fluent in the language. Even if he said he would move to the UK and find work, she might move to Italy or wherever MI6 needed her. His analytical mind considered all the barriers. He rarely acted solely on emotion.

"I would."

"Really?"

"I know we can't continue like this—being with each other only every few months. It's not fair to either of us. I've put my consultancy practice on hold while I work with JSOC. After that, I can set up shop in the UK and Europe. Knowing that, what would you say if I were to propose here and now?"

Collins took a long drink from her glass before responding, followed by a deep, cleansing breath. "I would probably say no because the only difference between being engaged and our current relationship would be a ring on my finger. I can't believe I'm saying this." Collins's lip quivered, and she dabbed at the corners of her eyes.

"Fiona. Don't."

"Let's stop pretending and put a hold on our relationship until you complete your commitment with JSOC. If at that time, you're still willing to live here and still want to take the next step, then you can pop the question. In the meantime, we'll stop communicating with each other. No emails, texts, or phone calls. If there's someone you want to see or go out with while you're there, do it. I'll do the same. I hate it when we go for days or weeks without talking to each other. I wonder what you're doing and why you're not calling. It's stressful. It will be worse when you're in Pakistan."

"I don't like this." His words felt feeble, contrived. But he didn't push. He had feared this. Now here it was. Perhaps she was right.

"I love you, Jake. Perhaps not as much as you love me. I can't really tell because you keep your emotions locked deep inside. As hard as this is, I'm convinced it's best for both of us."

———

Palmer spent the night with Collins, although neither of them slept much. Each time they awoke, they made love, talked for a while, and went back to sleep, their bodies close. They had a pleasant Saturday in London, ending it with an early dinner at a Thai restaurant in Soho and a West End show that evening. In spite of the love that they felt for each other and the affection they shared, their interactions were influenced by the previous night's conversation about their relationship and Collins's decision.

The next morning, Collins drove Palmer to Heathrow well in advance of his departure time. At the curbside drop-off, she got out of the car. They embraced and kissed each other goodbye. Palmer walked toward the terminal, stopping before he went inside to turn and look at her one more time. She was already in her car, pulling away from the curb.

5

UNITED STATES EMBASSY
ISLAMABAD, PAKISTAN

On final approach into Pakistan's capital city, Islamabad, Palmer stared down at the arid countryside. The city seemed larger, but little else appeared to have changed in the years since he'd last been in the region. Politically, however, it had transformed into something else entirely.

After being pushed out of Afghanistan post-9/11, the Taliban had returned to the country, and the Afghan government had asked them to the table. Rumors were that the US was involved in the discussions. Meanwhile, Pakistan was quietly turning a blind eye to terrorist organizations operating not only in Afghanistan and India but on its own soil. To make things worse, many believed Pakistan's Inter-Services Intelligence not only sanctioned their activities but supported them as well.

Over two thousand Americans had lost their lives in this region, and American men and women were still fighting and dying here. If not for a teammate who had come to Palmer's rescue while he was pinned down by Taliban fighters, he would have been among them.

The Islamabad International Airport, which had opened in 2018, was a vast improvement over the aging Benazir Bhutto International Airport he remembered. After going through immigration and customs, Palmer spotted a driver holding up a sign with "Palmer" on it and pushed his way through the crowd.

The United States Embassy was located within the Diplomatic Enclave, which contained numerous other foreign diplomatic missions and housing. The Enclave, surrounded by high walls, barbed wire, and concrete barriers, was not accessible to the general public. Extremists had burned the original US Embassy building to the ground in 1979. In 2015, the new embassy complex within the Enclave was inaugurated. The US Embassy complex was staffed by a large contingent of diplomatic staff as well as intelligence personnel and military officials.

After passing through security at the gate, the driver dropped Palmer and his luggage off at the entrance to the building, where Martin Singleton was waiting. Singleton greeted Palmer as soon as he got out of the car, grabbed a bag, and took him to an office on the third floor. "This will be your office. I've cleared out my personal items since I'm leaving in a few days and won't be around much between now and then. I'd forgotten how time-consuming the logistics of moving can be. You'll have access to all my asset files online. Most of my assets have been working with us for a while now and are self-sufficient. One is still in the process of being recruited. I've informed all of them that I'm leaving and to expect you or your partner to contact them soon."

Palmer looked at the office. "Thanks, but I doubt I'll use it very often. If I'm sitting at a desk, I'm not doing my job."

"Suit yourself," Singleton said with a slight shake of his head. "There's a secure landline in here if you need one. You have an apartment nearby in the Diplomatic Enclave. It's compact but fully furnished and safe. I'll take you there after we meet with General

Reynolds, our station chief. We have some time before the meeting. Would you like to grab some lunch?"

Palmer was hungry and having lunch would provide an opportunity to get to know Singleton before their meeting with Reynolds. Singleton was in his mid-thirties, about five feet, ten inches tall, and had tanned skin, dark hair, a neatly trimmed beard, and brown eyes. He was wearing a long-sleeved, banded-collar shirt and linen trousers. Although clearly a Westerner, his overall appearance and dress were more Pakistani than American. American tourists were easy to spot overseas, whether in London or Islamabad. Clothes were a clear sign, as were the style of shoes, the cut of their hair, and the shape of their eyeglasses.

"What path brought you to Islamabad?" Palmer asked.

"I grew up in Baltimore, then attended Georgetown University. I have an undergraduate degree in foreign service with a specialty in international politics and a master's in security studies. After graduation, I worked in Washington with a consulting firm as a federal contractor. I wasn't there long before they assigned me here as an intelligence analyst. After a couple of years, I felt it was time to make a move and landed a position with JSOC, where I've been for the past four years, working as a human intelligence field officer. I gather human intelligence data on Pakistan's military operations and Islamic terrorist groups—of which there's no shortage. Officially, I'm a special assistant to the deputy ambassador."

"Unofficially, you're a spy."

Singleton cringed. "I consider myself more of a recruiter and handler of human intelligence resources."

"After six years here, you must speak the language," Palmer said.

"I'm fluent in Urdu, and I can get by in Pashto, one of the most common regional languages. How about you?"

"A little Urdu and Arabic. I haven't used either in years."

"You won't have a problem. Along with Urdu, English is one of the national languages of Pakistan. About half the population speaks English as their second language, especially in major cities like Islamabad."

Singleton spoke of his love for Pakistan and Islamabad and said that he couldn't imagine himself anywhere else. He had twice turned down promotions and transfers. He'd believed his ability to recruit foreign sources and gather intelligence in Pakistan had made him invaluable. Now, he realized that it hadn't. He had to decide whether to quit his job and stay in Pakistan or turn the page on this chapter of his life and move on to his new assignment.

Palmer had seen it before. The life of an expat could be truly exciting, challenging, and addictive. A person can't help but put down roots after a couple of years of living abroad, speaking the language, being fully immersed in the culture, and doing a job for which he or she is uniquely qualified. Expats enjoyed a life few could even imagine. Palmer had felt it himself after leaving the Navy and entering law school. Law school was challenging, but going from Navy Special Warfare to corporate attorney was kind of like going two hundred miles an hour in a Formula One car in the Monaco Grand Prix to getting into the family car and driving to the office for a nine-to-five job.

"Are you in a relationship?" Palmer inquired bluntly.

Singleton hesitated, looking into Palmer's eyes for a reaction. "I was in a relationship with a woman I met here."

"Was?"

"Yes—was. I've broken it off." Again, he paused, eyes locked with Palmer's. "You're not the type to ask about this without a reason. You already know, don't you?"

"I'd heard about it." Palmer shrugged. "I also heard she was vetted and cleared."

"I didn't know that, but I'm not surprised. Believe me, I didn't enter into the relationship blindly. At first, I asked myself if she could be a Pakistani operative. Was she using me? It's difficult to trust anyone here, especially a woman who herself might be working for Pakistan's ISI or another foreign government."

"Were you certain she wasn't?" Palmer asked, focusing on what he really wanted to know.

"I was 95 percent certain."

"You still had some doubt then?"

"I have healthy doubt about everyone, including you."

"Five percent?"

"That's the minimum I start with for anyone I don't know," Singleton said. "Maybe 10 percent for you."

"Fair enough. What's the rest of that story?"

"The relationship caught fire, so I informed General Reynolds's predecessor as was required. She and I broke it off about a year ago—too many questioning glances from Pakistanis and from my colleagues. It became a problem for both of us. The cultural and religious differences were great. Not to mention that it cast a cloud on my role here. After only a short break, she called me, and we got back together. Everything was great until she found out I was being transferred. She wasn't willing to move, and I couldn't see her waiting for me to return. I have only a few days before I'm scheduled to fly out. I'm considering quitting and staying in Islamabad, not to be with her but because I love it here. The only problem is the pending war with India. This isn't a safe place to be."

"Believe me, I'm the last person to offer anyone relationship advice. You're going back to the DC area before you're assigned to your new post, right?"

"Yes, and that just adds to the uncertainty of it all."

"Allow me to be blunt. You've been here too long and being somewhere too long is bad for your career. Get over it and move on. You may find that your next assignment is even better than this one. Frequent reassignments are part of the job. Moving from a place you've come to love, leaving friends, and ending relationships." He couldn't help but pause, even briefly, seeing a flash of Fiona's face when they parted at the airport. "It's all very hard. Sometimes, you're glad to move on. Other times, you hate to leave. See where they ultimately assign you. With your experience and language skills, I expect you'll land somewhere in this region."

Singleton nodded. "Thanks for that. How about you? Anyone waiting for you back home?"

"No." Nobody was waiting for him. Not anymore. "Not back home. A few years ago, a British pharmaceutical company contracted me to do some work in Cornwall. I worked with one of their senior auditors. Before the project was completed, we had fallen for each other. She recently left the company and has a government job that takes her back and forth between London and Rome." Palmer was careful not to tell Singleton too much, including Collins's name and that she worked for MI6, for obvious reasons.

Singleton took a deep breath before he responded. "I understand you're under contract. Is this a short visit or do you plan to stay a while?"

"I'll stay as long as it takes to get the job done, even if I have to extend the contract."

"You were blunt with me. May I return the favor?"

"Fire away," Palmer said.

"What are you doing here? Help me understand. You've been in the private sector for years and have returned to a post for which you have little or no experience and at a time when the stakes are extremely high. Meanwhile, I'm being reassigned, against my wishes, to God knows where. I'm one of the most experienced field operatives in Pakistan, and I'm leaving on short notice at the most critical time in the India-Pakistan conflict. I'm supposed to turn everything over to you and your partner and be packed up and gone within a few days. If you ask me, it's bullshit. I've read both of your files. You are way beyond recruiting and managing a group of human intelligence agents. That would be a total waste of your talent. I believe you're here for other reasons. No one admits to knowing what that is. Some of my colleagues suspect the two of you are with Orange."

"I haven't met my partner, so I can only speak for myself. I'm here to do a job just like everyone else. And that job hasn't been well-defined. I wasn't planning to return to government service, and I certainly wasn't eager to come back to this part of the world. Yet here I am. I'll carry out to the best of my ability whatever responsibilities are assigned to me during the time I'm here."

————

After lunch, Singleton met with General Geoffrey Reynolds. He introduced Palmer and was quick to point out that he was a former US Navy SEAL.

"No former about it. Right, Palmer? Once a SEAL, always a SEAL."

"The only easy day was yesterday, sir," Palmer replied, citing the unofficial motto of the Navy SEALs.

Reynolds was one of those career military men who looked the part, whether he was in uniform or in civilian clothes, which Reynolds was wearing that day. He sat erect. His haircut was high and tight. His clothes looked like they'd been pressed just an hour ago, and his eye contact with you left with little doubt about who was in charge.

"I reviewed your military record. Impressive. You were here under much less pleasant circumstances," Reynolds said.

"A few times. Didn't spend much time in Islamabad. My ops were mostly near the Afghanistan-Pakistan border."

"If you don't mind me asking, why did you leave the service before you had your twenty in?" Reynolds asked, referring to the requirement of twenty years of military service before one could retire with a government pension.

"Woke up one day and knew it was time."

Reynolds nodded. "That happens, especially to spec ops warriors. After you left the Navy, you got your law degree and worked as a regulatory attorney for big pharma before becoming an independent investigative consultant."

"It didn't take me long to discover that I wasn't cut out for corporate life. Too much internal politics and BS. Being an investigative consultant gave me the freedom and independence I needed, and the law degree comes in handy every once in a while. But when I was asked to join the Joint Special Operations Command, I couldn't turn it down. I hope I can add some value to your mission."

"I'm counting on it. You're being thrown into the thick of it. Along with your partner, you'll be handling Singleton's assets. Our relationship with Pakistan plummeted after we came in uninvited and killed bin Laden in 2011, and it's getting worse. POTUS has declared Pakistan a state sponsor of terrorism and halted two billion dollars a year in aid."

"That must have pissed them off."

"Indeed. I, for one, was glad to see it. I know you've just arrived and are scheduled to meet your partner. We have a lot to discuss, and there's something I need the two of you to do. Get a good night's sleep. I'll see you and her at 0700 tomorrow to discuss it with you."

"One more thing, General," Singleton said. "One of my new Pakistani recruits, Hakeem Jaffar, has contacted me. He holds an administrative position in the transportation department at the Wah Cantonment Ordnance Complex and nuclear facility. I have arranged to meet him at the end of the week. Although he's provided nothing of use so far, he has the potential to serve as a paid agent. It will be my last day on the job, so it would be a good opportunity for Palmer and his partner to meet him."

"Of course," Reynolds said. "Did he say why he wanted to see you?"

"He didn't."

"If Jaffar has anything significant, they can follow up with him."

"I understand that several of our Pakistani assets have been killed or gone missing recently," Palmer said.

"That's right." Reynolds nodded. "Some were affiliated with the nuclear program. We believe ISI is rounding up anyone they suspect of being disloyal in advance of a nuclear weapon deployment and a possible war with India. You may hear rumors that we have an internal leak who has divulged the names of some of our assets. I have no evidence of it and don't believe it's true."

"We've advised our assets to be especially cautious," Singleton added. "Those who are inexperienced or in the process of being recruited are the ones more likely to make mistakes and raise suspicion. That may be what prompted Jaffar to contact me. He might be getting nervous."

Palmer left the meeting feeling like he was finally getting somewhere. India and Pakistan were battling it out two hundred kilometers away and were on the verge of war, while he was on the ground in the world's only nuclear-capable, Muslim country.

Next step—meet his partner.

6

UNITED STATES EMBASSY
ISLAMABAD, PAKISTAN

Fifteen minutes had passed since Singleton had left Palmer in the conference room, saying that his partner had requested that no one else be present when she met him. Enough waiting. He would find Singleton and ask what was going on. He was steps away from the door when it opened. He stopped in his tracks.

"What the…?" he mouthed, staring at a woman he hadn't expected to recognize.

"Hello, Jake Palmer. Surprised to see me?"

"Alona Green," he said, indeed very surprised, though he hoped it didn't show. "Or is it Alona Kolvalyova? Or are you using a different name now?"

Green was an attractive woman of medium height, with cropped auburn hair and an athletic build and figure. She was a master of deception and disguise and held a degree in computer science from MIT. When he'd first met her, she was working as a contractor for the US Defense Intelligence Agency, although he hadn't known it at the time. He'd suspected she was some sort of con artist, as well as a person of interest in the murder of one of his best friends, a former SEAL teammate. She had said her father was a KGB agent who became a double agent, eventually moved to the US, and was given a new identity and name: Green. According to Green, both her father and mother were deceased. Of course, it was possible that Kolvalyova was not her real name either and that her entire backstory was bogus.

"Let's go with Alona Green," she said with an ear-to-ear smile. She hugged him, pressing her head against his shoulder.

Palmer disengaged from her embrace and stepped away. The last time he'd seen her, she had been wounded during their encounter with a terrorist cell in Cape Charles, Virginia. "What happened to you? I came by Portsmouth Naval Hospital to see you, but the room I'd visited you in the day before was empty. They had no record of a Jane Doe, the name you'd been registered under, or Alona Green or Alona Kolvalyova. You were gone."

"Believe me, Jake, that wasn't my choice." She flashed a smile. "I was whisked away and directed not to contact you."

"You told me you were a Defense Intelligence Agency independent contractor," he recalled, brows pinched. "No way that aligns with you being a Jane Doe at the hospital or being whisked away and told not to contact me."

Alona merely shrugged. "I did what I was told. I had no control over where they took me or how I was registered at the hospital. If I wanted to continue to work with the DIA, I had to do what they said."

"That sounds more like a full-time DIA or FBI operative. In Virginia, you handled firearms like you had some professional training and drove that boat like a pro. And going from an independent contractor to where you are now is a huge stretch."

"You can believe me or not—your choice. I'm telling the truth."

Palmer thought about what she'd said. He wanted to believe her, but his intuition prompted skepticism. If Alona *was* telling the truth, why had they been paired to work together for this initial Orange assignment? No, this was no coincidence. But he'd go along with it for now.

"That's okay," he said, unable to hold back a smile. "I'd forgotten all about you until now."

"Liar. You've thought about me walking naked out of the ocean at the North Carolina Outer Banks every day. Bet you even Googled my names on a regular basis."

"Only in your mind, Alona," he teased. "It's good to see you. And, by the way, you look fantastic."

"Training for this role got my ass into shape."

"Any residual issues from your wounds?"

"None. I was on light duty while I was undergoing rehab. After that, I was sent for training and thrown in with a group of special ops trainees. I wasn't even certain what I was being trained for. I thought it was some sort of test to confirm that I was able to do my job. It was hell. I'd heard that the training is 90 percent mental and 10 percent physical. That 10 percent almost killed me. After I survived that first stage, they called me in and told me about Orange. They asked if I would like to continue training and see if I qualified. I said, 'Hell yes.' I'm so excited. This is my dream job, so don't screw it up for me, Palmer," she added with a wink.

"I'll try not to. How do you feel about working with me?"

"Good, though I worry about your ego, arrogance, and need to control everything and everyone."

"Wait…when were you told we would be teamed together?"

"After I left Portsmouth, I was debriefed over several days on the terrorist cell operation in Virginia. They asked a lot of questions about you and your role in bringing down the cell and saving the USS George H.W. Bush and its crew. That op got us on JSOC's radar big-time. After the debrief, I never heard anything else about it or you. Then I was sent to Fort Bragg and Dam Neck for classroom, weapons, and strength and endurance training. A few weeks ago, I was told I'd be working with you and was ordered not to make contact prior to our meeting here."

Palmer studied her eyes. She was far too skilled to exhibit any clue as to whether she was lying or not. "Still an independent contractor?"

"If I wanted this job, I had to go permanent. It was a no-brainer. How about you?"

"Not me," Palmer said. "I told them the only way I would do this was as an independent contractor, although in the end, I agreed to a two-year commitment."

"They must have really wanted you." Yet again, Green's eyes yielded nothing. They were as unreadable as stone. "You asked how I felt about working with you. How do you feel about working with me?"

He took a deep breath. "You saved my life that day in Cape Charles, Alona, and I've never forgotten it. I believe you have the chops to do this work. We'll make a damn good team."

"We *both* almost died that day," she corrected. "You jumped into a helicopter, leaving me bleeding to death."

"Come on, now. You were in good hands. The Navy EMTs were there."

They both laughed.

"Whatever happened to that British woman you were seeing? What was her name?"

"Fiona Collins."

"The two of you still an item?"

"Definitely. I stopped in London and saw her on the way here." There was no point in getting into the details of his relationship with Collins or that she was with MI6. And it wouldn't be good for Green to know that he and Collins were taking a break from each other. Even though Green was strikingly beautiful, dipping one's pen into the company inkwell was asking for trouble.

"General Reynolds wants to see us at 0700 tomorrow," he went on, changing the subject before she could add to it. "He has something for us to do. Any idea what it is?"

"I haven't a clue. But I'm beyond ready to get started."

"That makes two of us. Taking on Singleton's assets has to be a cover."

"I hope so," Green said. "Don't get me wrong—recruiting and handling human assets is vital to the success of the mission. However, there are hundreds of operators more qualified than us to do that. Any of them could pick up where Singleton's leaving off. If that's all we end up doing, we've failed."

7

UNITED STATES EMBASSY
ISLAMABAD, PAKISTAN

General Reynolds looked back and forth between Palmer and Green and grinned. "I'm pleased you've met. I'd ask if you're happy with the working relationship, but I don't give a shit. You have a job to do, and I expect you will do it well. Any issues I should know about?"

"No issues, sir," Palmer said. "We've worked together before."

Reynolds looked at Green. "And you?"

"I agree, sir. We work well together."

"Good. We don't do team building and trust falls here. You were assigned to take responsibility for Singleton's assets and expand our human intelligence capabilities in the region as they relate to our spec ops teams. That's your official job, and I'm sure you would do it well in the long term. However, we're in a critical situation, and from what I see on paper and in front of me, you bring some unique skills to our team at a time when we most need a fresh-eyes approach to a bad situation. You were teamed together for a reason. You improvise. You don't play by the rules. You shake up the status quo. We have a limited time in which to identify and thwart any threat to the United States or our allies, and that includes a nuclear threat. That's your real job. Do you understand?"

"Yes, sir," Palmer and Green said in unison.

"I understand that several of our Pakistani assets have been killed or gone missing recently," Palmer stated.

"That's right. All of them were affiliated with the nuclear program or worked on bases with nuclear facilities. We believe that in advance of a nuclear weapon deployment and a possible war with India, ISI is rounding up anyone they suspect of being disloyal, including those working with a foreign government. We were concerned that we had an internal leak who divulged the names of some assets. Our investigation found no evidence to support that. However, I consider that part of your remit."

"Was Singleton read in on our role? Should we include him in what we are doing?" Palmer asked.

"Negative on both questions. He's only going to be around for a few more days. He doesn't need to know."

Palmer nodded. "Roger that."

"By now, you understand the basics of what we're faced with. Pakistan is the only Muslim nation with nuclear capability, and it shares borders with Afghanistan, China, India, and Iran. Imagine for a moment that set of neighbors. The border between Pakistan-controlled Kashmir and India-controlled Kashmir was initially a military front but became a solid boundary during the 1949 ceasefire."

"The Line of Control," Palmer said.

"Correct." Reynolds continued, "As of now, there's been no formal declaration of war between the two countries. India has conducted some ground operations in Pakistan in order to destroy what they said were terrorist sites. Unofficially, we know that the Pakistan-based terrorist groups are conducting attacks in India-controlled Kashmir, and the Pakistan government has done nothing to stop them. The US has a ten-million-dollar bounty on Hafiz Muhammad Saeed's head. He's the leader of an Islamic charity that is considered a front for Lashkar-e-Taiba, or LeT, which means Army of the Good or Army of the Pure. In spite of its name, LeT is one of the most violent and active terrorist groups in existence. Only the head of Al-Qaeda and the head of ISIS have higher bounties on them than Saeed."

"Why have tensions escalated to the point of a possible war?" Green asked.

"Two things have raised the threat level. First, Pakistani militants have attacked two Indian Army camps inside India-controlled Kashmir in the past three months, killing soldiers, women, and children. And recently, Deepak Chandra, a Kashmiri journalist and peace advocate, was assassinated in Srinagar. Chandra had lambasted leaders in Pakistan and India for their failures to keep the peace and held them responsible for thousands of deaths. Now India is moving troops, tanks, and heavy artillery to the Line of Control, and their forces are on high alert. If the current buildup at the LoC can be contained, tensions might ease, like numerous other skirmishes over the years. But that is highly unlikely."

"What happens if tensions don't ease?" Palmer said.

"The Pakistanis have made it clear that if India's Army advances across the LoC, they will consider it an act of war. If India crosses the line and pushes west toward Islamabad, all bets are off. Pakistan is only two hundred sixty-five miles wide, and Islamabad is less than a hundred miles from the LoC. Simply stated, India has a boatload of options, and all of them are bad for Pakistan."

"Pakistan has tactical or battlefield nukes that have a much lower yield than its strategic nuclear warheads. Would they use them against India's forces if the engagement was on Pakistani soil?" Green asked.

"Without a doubt. A tactical or battlefield nuke has a more limited range and is far less destructive than a strategic nuclear device. Tactical nukes are used when the forces are engaging in close proximity. So, if India's advance can't be stopped with conventional weapons, that would be Pakistan's next attempt to halt them," Reynolds replied.

"If India were to advance toward Islamabad, the Pakistanis might initially use their tactical nuclear weapons on the advancing forces," Palmer added. "Using strategic nuclear warheads, which are much more powerful, would result in radioactive fallout and considerable damage within Pakistan. But whatever Pakistan does under those circumstances, it would need to stop India in its tracks."

"Correct," Reynolds said. "Pakistan has moved from a minimum deterrence strategy to a more complex full deterrence strategy, believing that superiority in tactical weapons will trump India's superiority in troop numbers and conventional weapons."

Green pondered the statement before responding. "Because India doesn't possess any low-yield, tactical nuclear weapons, only high-yield, strategic nuclear weapons, Pakistan's use of tactical nukes would result in India launching its deadliest weapons sooner rather than later. And then Pakistan would respond in kind."

"Mutual assured destruction—the ultimate deterrence strategy," Palmer said. "It's what keeps our world safe from a nuclear apocalypse. A nuclear-capable country can't destroy another without it, too, being destroyed. So, you balance your nuclear arsenal with that of your enemy."

"Precisely. That's why no nuclear weapon has been used against another nation since the US dropped bombs on Nagasaki and Hiroshima in WWII," Reynolds said. "Even a relatively limited exchange of a hundred strategic nuclear weapons between Pakistan and India could kill over twenty million people and destroy about half of Earth's ozone layer, resulting in a nuclear winter that would affect agriculture worldwide."

"As well as innumerable other catastrophic consequences to our health and environment. So, what can we possibly do?" Palmer asked.

"Technically, both Pakistan and India are our allies, so there's little we can do except watch, continue communications with our Pakistan liaisons, and continue to gather intelligence," Reynolds said. "The Department of State has been working with the British, who are on much better terms with the Pakistanis than us, to negotiate a peace deal or at least a cease-fire. So far, they haven't had any luck, thus the order for all the nonessential personnel for the embassy and government agencies to leave Pakistan. At the moment, our major concern is the deployment of Pakistan's nukes. The security of Pakistan's nuclear weapons has always been a concern, but it is true now more than ever. If war breaks out, we cannot allow Pakistan to lose control of its nuclear arsenal. There are plenty of terrorist organizations here that would love to snag a nuke or two in the ensuing chaos, as would Iran. Your job will be to provide intel for this office that could pin down the timing of the deployment, as well as any weapon security issues during deployment."

"Are the suspected nuclear weapon sites under satellite surveillance?" Palmer asked.

"The Pakistanis have made it clear that the US is forbidden to use drone or satellite surveillance to monitor their armed forces or nuclear weapon facilities. However, much to the displeasure of our Pakistani friends, we recently resumed CIA drone attacks on terrorist sites in Afghanistan and Pakistan. There's little they can do to stop satellite surveillance, and they know it."

"This is good information. However, we need a better perspective than what's provided by reading a stack of reports," Palmer noted. "Any chance of us going to the Line of Control, General?"

A smile spread across Reynolds's face. "I can arrange that. But first, there's something I need you to do. One of our top operatives is in Srinagar. He goes by the name of Mahinder. He and his team are in deep cover within LeT and JeM, another large and active terrorist group. Communication with him has become increasingly difficult.

Go to Srinagar and meet with him. You're two embassy employees on vacation. Your objective is to find out what he knows about the current situation. He's expecting you." Reynolds handed Green a piece of paper. "Here are the details about where and when to meet him, as well as the code words. Both of you, memorize it and then destroy it. Your flight leaves in two hours."

8

SRINAGAR, INDIA-CONTROLLED KASHMIR INDIA

Palmer and Green's flight from Islamabad to Sheikh ul-Alam International Airport in Srinagar, Kashmir, India, took less than thirty minutes after takeoff. They were traveling on their US passports as a couple taking a break from their US Embassy jobs in Pakistan—Palmer as an embassy security officer and Green as a computer systems specialist. They approached passport control while smiling and holding hands. Through secure communications, Reynolds had informed JSOC and the US Embassy in New Delhi of their trip and its purported purpose.

Americans often traveled to India, but very few journeyed to Srinagar, which was in India-controlled Kashmir, near the Line of Control. The US Department of State had issued a travel advisory, citing terrorist attacks and civil unrest in the state of Kashmir, with military action and violence in proximity to the Line of Control, including Srinagar.

The immigration officer took their passports and flipped through the pages like he was shuffling a deck of cards. Palmer's only recent trips outside the US had been to the UK and Italy. Green's passport was almost full, even with extra pages added. Palmer looked at her slyly, shaking his head. She merely shrugged and smiled. The officer looked up from the passport photos to their faces and back again.

"Americans?" he surmised, with a look on his face like he had just stepped in dog poo.

"Yes, sir," Palmer said.

"What is the purpose of your visit?"

"We're taking a couple of days off from work to see your beautiful city," Green said.

"Wait here while I check with my supervisor." The officer stepped away and spoke with his supervisor, who was standing nearby.

Palmer and Green waited, glancing at each other, neither surprised by the extra scrutiny. After a few minutes, the immigration officer and his supervisor returned.

"Come with me," the supervisor said blandly, as though he'd done this a thousand times today already. The pair followed him, rolling their carry-on bags, to a room off to the side of the passport control area. The supervisor motioned for them to sit. "Are you aware of the travel advisory your State Department has issued?"

"We are," Palmer said. "We're not concerned. We're only here for a couple of days."

The supervisor, who had not introduced himself, drummed the fingers of his left hand on the table while he looked at the passports again as if the real truth was hidden somewhere between the stamps on the pages. "Where are you staying?"

"At the Ahdoos Hotel on Residency Road," Palmer replied calmly.

"Will you be leaving Srinagar during your stay?"

"No."

"What do you do in Islamabad?"

"We both work at the US Embassy," Green chimed in. "I'm a computer systems manager."

"And I'm an embassy security officer," Palmer added with a contrived smile.

Green would have no problem pulling off her position if the supervisor wanted more detail—she had a degree in computer science from MIT. Palmer, on the other hand, had only spent an hour with the real embassy security officer, but he was confident he could get by if questioned about the specifics of his duties.

"I need to look through your bags."

Palmer set the two bags on the table. The supervisor put on disposable latex gloves and looked through their belongings. Satisfied there was nothing inappropriate in them, he zipped them shut again and threw the gloves in a trash bin by the door.

"Wait here," the supervisor said before leaving.

They had anticipated everything that had happened thus far, including being left alone in a room that was almost certainly wired for video and sound. Green pulled a tourist book on Jammu and Kashmir from the outside pocket of her carry-on bag and thumbed through it. She and Palmer talked about visiting Jawaharlal Nehru Memorial Gardens and Chashma Shahi, the royal fountains, then moved on to what they wanted to have for dinner that night and other random topics related to their stay. After about ten minutes, the supervisor returned.

"You're free to go. Enjoy your stay. If you're not back in three days, we'll find you. Do not leave the city. Regardless of what you think, it is not safe here." He handed them their stamped passports and left without offering to show them out.

After checking in at their hotel, Palmer and Green, tourist books in hand, took a taxi to Shalimar, a huge garden and public park on the northeast side of Dal Lake. There, they made their way to the bench that General Reynolds had identified as the drop. They sat and talked, the map and guidebook in Green's lap. When they could see no one nearby, Palmer ran his hand under the bench until he felt a small piece of paper taped underneath. He pulled it off and put it in his shirt pocket. They walked around the sprawling garden until no one was near them. Palmer took the paper from his pocket and read it.

Shankaracharya Temple, top of the stairs, 4:00 p.m.

After checking their map, they confirmed that the temple was on the south side of the lake. They toured the gardens to kill a little time and took a taxi to the temple.

As they walked, Green read from the guidebook, "Shankaracharya Temple is named for the great philosopher Shankaracharya, who is supposed to have visited the temple a thousand years ago. It is a thousand feet up on the top of the hill overlooking Srinagar. The view of Srinagar from the temple is worth traveling the winding road to get there and the series of steps you have to climb. It was believed to have been built in around 300 Bc, although some believe the temple was originally built by King Sandiman around 2500 Bc. There have been many repairs and restorations over the years, including being wired for electricity in 1925."

Only a few people were at the site, and they were widely disbursed. Palmer and Green took the flight of steps to the top. Inside, a man who matched their contact's description stood alone, looking out at Srinagar below. He looked like any other male on the streets of Srinagar: dark complexion, about five and a half feet tall, groomed beard, and short black hair. He was wearing a beige Pheran suit, a long kurta that hung below the knees, and a salwar. They walked over and stood near him.

Palmer initiated the prearranged exchange to confirm each other's identity. "Pardon me. How old is this temple?"

The man turned and looked at Palmer and then Green. "Older than your Christ."

"We're Buddhists," Green said with a smile to acknowledge the connection.

Palmer nodded at the man. "I'm Jake and this is Alona."

"I go by Mahinder."

They deliberately didn't shake hands or do anything to suggest that this was something other than a chance encounter.

"I don't have much time," Mahinder was quick to say. "They might be watching. If anyone comes, we'll proceed down the stairs separately and meet down below."

Fair enough. Palmer got right to the point. "I understand you're working with assets inside Jaish-e-Mohammad."

"And Lashkar-e-Taiba. Both JeM and LeT have become bolder in their attacks in Jammu and Kashmir, especially here in Srinagar. You've heard of the assassination of the journalist Deepak Chandra?"

"We have," Palmer said.

"Most attacks have been small in scope—attacks on police and police stations—nothing like their 2001 attack on the Indian Parliament or their 2016 attack in the town of Uri."

"The Pakistanis are on edge and preparing for war. Is there anything you can tell us?" Green asked. "What role will JeM and LeT play?"

"JeM and LeT will not be directly involved in that decision or in the war. They will, however, take advantage of any ensuing chaos. Decisions are made within a small group of leaders who will initiate and manage the operation once they receive the order. All communication is verbal or made through encrypted messages using nontraditional platforms like message boards on electronic games or encrypted applications on mobile phones. I'm piecing together intel from several men within those terrorist organizations. Generally speaking, their stories are aligned. Their objective is for Pakistan to take control of Jammu and Kashmir through a declared war with India or for Jammu and Kashmir to achieve independence. But there is a radical element within the jihadists that wants to push the two countries to the brink of war so that Pakistan will deploy its nuclear weapons."

"Because it will make India agree to their demands?" Green guessed.

"That's been the strategy over a long period of time, and it's what most people believe now, however, there are competing priorities. The extreme elements want to acquire one or more of the warheads, either during the deployment or when Pakistan's government is overthrown in the chaos that ensues during or following the invasion by Indian forces."

"All terrorist groups want a nuclear weapon, but none have had the technical expertise, leadership, or resources to pull it off," Palmer said. "What's different now?"

"All the pieces are in place. The terrorists have acquired the financial and technical resources to do it. They have the support of the United Jihad Council. The Army is infiltrated with jihadists who are eager to die for the cause. And—mind you, I have nothing to support this—someone very high up in Pakistan's intelligence organization or military is the driving force behind it."

"Should the terrorists steal a nuclear device, what's their intention?" Green asked. "Use it against India?"

"That's illogical. It would not achieve the goal for which most have been fighting, which is to have India relinquish control of Kashmir and Jammu. If a terrorist group detonated a stolen nuclear device in India, India would retaliate in kind against Pakistan because India would believe that Pakistan supported the terrorist group that did it. Pakistan may have more nuclear weapons, but India is a vast country. Pakistan is small in comparison. Even a limited nuclear war would annihilate Pakistan."

"What's the motivation, then?" Green asked. "What's their target?"

"None of my sources know. Israel would be my bet, but there are many others—including anywhere in the US and Western Europe. Or they could simply sell it to Iran and let them do their dirty work. Hasn't the US conducted a risk analysis and developed a prioritized list of potential targets?"

"If so, I've not seen it," said Palmer. "One thing is certain—if a terrorist group had a nuclear weapon, they wouldn't waste it on a low-value target."

Mahinder nodded. "Correct."

"If this is true, someone or some group has to take the lead. Who would that be?"

"I've heard that there is a Pakistani military officer who's become a key figure. I know nothing of him other than that he's called 'The Chameleon.' He's suspected of killing the journalist, Chandra, and may have led the attack on the Indian Army camp in Kashmir. It was horrific. Women and children were murdered."

"The Chameleon?" Palmer echoed. He looked at Green. She shook her head. This was the first either of them had heard of someone called The Chameleon. "What else do you know about him?"

"Not much. There are no photographs of The Chameleon—at least none in which his face is seen. He's become somewhat of a legend. It's said he has no allegiance to any one terrorist organization and selects his men as needed for each operation. Whether he is real or simply an amalgamation of different individuals, no one knows."

"Do you believe he exists?" Green inquired bluntly.

Mahinder paused for a split second, his nostrils flared. "What I believe doesn't matter. It only matters what the people believe. Depending on their political viewpoint, people either love or fear even the myth of such an individual. The more he is mentioned as a suspect in planning or carrying out an attack, the more real he becomes. What we do know is that there are similarities in some of the attacks credited to him. Those in the terrorist organizations in which my men and I are embedded believe he is very real and is perhaps the one person who can achieve what they have only dreamed of doing for many years—obtain a nuclear weapon."

"You refer to him as a man," Green noted. "If this person is indeed a chameleon, changing appearance to blend in, couldn't they be a woman disguised as a man?"

Palmer looked at Mahinder, who was taken aback by the question. Green was right, of course. She, of all people, knew the power of disguise—although Palmer was not aware if she had ever passed herself off as a man. *Sometimes you believe you are unbiased and open-minded, and then something happens, or someone proves you wrong,* he thought.

Mahinder said, "In this culture, it's not possible. That may offend you, but it's the truth."

"Understood," Green said, pausing a moment. "Do you know anything about the timing?"

"Many believe the tipping point occurred with the most recent attack on India's Army camp and the assassination of Deepak Chandra. India will declare war and cross the LoC as soon as Pakistan deploys its weapons. Both are likely to happen within days. I'm sorry, I can't give you any more details." Mahinder looked over his shoulder. "I should go. I'm taking a great risk by talking to you, and it's placing you in danger."

"Thank you for what you're doing and for the information," Palmer said.

"Go about playing tourists, but assume you're being watched. Otherwise, they will be suspicious of why you are here. Whatever you do, be careful. Most Indians see Westerners as friends. But LeT and JeM would like nothing more than to nab two American embassy workers, and if they discover who you really are, a quick death would be a blessing. I'm sorry. I must leave. We should not go out together. Wait at least ten minutes after I go."

After Mahinder left, Green said, "There's a lot to consider. It's terrifying, but I find myself excited to be involved. It's history in the making."

"If we survive."

———⚬⚬⚬———

The next morning, Palmer dressed and went to the restaurant on the ground floor for coffee. He and Green were scheduled to leave on a noon flight to Islamabad. What seemed to him to be an unusual number of people, with luggage in tow, were milling around the lobby and at the reception desk.

"A lot of people are leaving this morning," Palmer said to the male waiter who brought him his coffee. The waiter kept looking around. His hands were shaking nervously when he set the coffee cup and saucer on the table.

"Haven't you heard? India has revoked Kashmir's constitution. This is unbelievable. How could they do that?"

Palmer left with his coffee, returned to his room, and immediately turned on the television. Many of the channels were off the air. Flipping through them with his remote, he found an English-speaking reporter talking about the situation in Kashmir. The reporter stated that the president of India had issued a presidential order scrapping the long-standing right of Kashmir to have special status and its own constitution separate from India's. Thus, Kashmir was now governed by the Constitution of India, just the same as the rest of India.

Palmer picked up his mobile phone to call Green. *No service. That's strange and serious.*

As though in response to his thoughts, the news reporter announced that all internet connections, all mobile phones, and most landlines were out of service. "Tourists are being advised to leave immediately," he said, unable to disguise the fear swelling in his eyes. "Protests are being planned and violence is certain to follow. Pakistan's Foreign Office has issued a statement that revoking Kashmir's constitution was illegal, and, following a meeting of Pakistan Army Commanders, the Army's chief is reported to have stated that Pakistan will stand by the people of Kashmir regardless of the consequences."

Palmer tried the hotel phone receiver. It was dead. He made haste to Green's room and knocked. She came to the door in her hotel robe.

"Tourists have been advised to leave Kashmir. The airport is going to be chaotic," he said. "We need to go. Get ready."

In fifteen minutes, Green rapped on his door. The line at the hotel's reception area was long, so they didn't bother checking out. They went outside, hoping to flag down a taxi, and stepped into total chaos. India's security forces were streaming by in personnel carriers, and some armed soldiers were taking up positions on the street. People were rushing by, bumping into each other and shouting. Car horns were blaring. Realizing they would never get a taxi, Palmer asked the bellman, who was assisting an elderly couple with their luggage, if he would drive them to the airport. He said he was on duty and could not leave. Palmer offered him a large sum to take them. The bellman hesitated for a moment before saying there wasn't much use hailing a taxi for them because the taxis were all full. He asked Palmer for double the amount he had offered. Palmer accepted, and the bellman left to go get his car.

Palmer invited the elderly couple to ride with them to the airport. The man and woman looked at each other and spoke in a language that Palmer recognized as Russian. Green stepped in and began talking to them in Russian. They smiled and were happy about whatever she had said.

Palmer couldn't disguise his bewilderment when Green looked his way.

"What?" she asked.

"You've never mentioned that you speak Russian."

"It never came up. My parents were Ukrainian, and we lived in Russia when I was a child. Of course, I speak Russian. Anyway, they're thrilled that we're giving them a ride to the airport."

The bellman arrived in his small car a moment later. Noting the Russian couple and their excessive luggage, he shook his head. After he and Palmer agreed on an additional charge, they crammed as much luggage as they could fit into the trunk. Palmer got in the front, while Green and the Russian couple squeezed into the back seat, holding the remainder of the luggage on their laps.

Traffic was, of course, backed up at the airport. Once inside the departure lounge, the situation worsened. Green told the Russian couple to go ahead because they had the earlier flight. They thanked Green and left. Meanwhile, the ticketing area was filled with frightened people in a panic to get out of the country. Palmer ran interference while Green followed close behind. Unable to contact the embassy or phone the airline to have their tickets changed in advance, they had no other option than to join the mass of people pushing and shoving to get to the ticket counter. All incoming flights had been canceled, and flights leaving Srinagar were quickly filling up.

When they finally got to the counter, Palmer handed the agent their tickets. She glanced at them, shaking her head. "The airline has canceled your flight, sir."

They flashed their passports and US Embassy identifications, declaring diplomatic status. Shouting to be heard, Palmer convinced her to give them priority. They had to return to Islamabad. She kept typing, looking at the computer, and shaking her head. Finally, she handed them tickets for a flight on another airline departing in two hours.

As they passed through security with their carry-on bags, Green said, "This situation is going to spiral out of control, like throwing gas on a smoldering fire. India's daring Pakistan to fire the first shot."

9

US EMBASSY
ISLAMABAD, PAKISTAN

Palmer and Green headed to the embassy as soon as they landed in Islamabad. When they arrived at the general's office, he was putting on a practice mat with a ball return. He held up his hand to silence them before they could say anything to break his concentration. "I've made nine in a row." He putted, and they all watched the ball drift right of the hole. "Damn it! Pardon me. Welcome back. You're lucky you got out when you did. Violent protests have erupted there."

"The airport was a madhouse," Palmer said.

"What did you learn?"

They told Reynolds what Mahinder had said about the intent to steal or divert a nuclear weapon during the deployment, which was expected to occur within days. They also told him about The Chameleon and asked if he had heard anything about him.

Reynolds grunted. "Pakistan-supported terrorists have been conducting incursions into Kashmir for years. We've heard rumors of The Chameleon for some time now. But they're just that—rumors. Nothing verifiable. We're continuing to gather intelligence."

"Mahinder said many believe that The Chameleon planned and led the attack on the Indian Army camp and was responsible for the assassination of Deepak Chandra," Green said. "He's become an antihero in their eyes."

"People identify with him," said Reynolds with a shrug and a slight shake of the head. "A man who has emerged from the crowded pack of jihadists and who has no allegiance to any recognized terrorist group has a lot of populist appeal. Next thing you know, he'll be riding a white horse and brandishing a sword."

"These attacks were different," Palmer insisted. "They were well planned and executed—much more so than anything LeT and JeM have previously carried out. This wasn't a suicide bomber walking into a crowd of people or a quick hit-and-run on a small army outpost. We shouldn't dismiss him as a myth. Chameleon or not, the plan to divert a nuclear weapon during Pakistan's weapon deployment seems very credible."

"We can all agree on that, as well as the fact that the deployment is imminent," Reynolds said.

"Mahinder has also heard that someone very high up in the Pakistani military or ISI is involved," Green added.

"Probably true. Pakistan's Army and its intelligence service are awash with members of terrorist organizations. I don't suppose he had a name or anything to substantiate that?"

"No," Palmer confirmed. "It makes sense, though. Diversion of a nuclear weapon would be difficult to pull off without someone senior feeding information to whoever is planning it."

Reynolds took a deep breath and said, "Other than continuing to gather intelligence, we're limited in what we can actually do. And don't forget that your trip to the LoC is scheduled for tomorrow morning. Singleton is going with you."

"Why is he going?" Green's brows furrowed. "He's leaving soon."

"You need to spend more time with him, and I believe it will do him good," Reynolds said. "The Pakistanis will drive you there and back."

Palmer asked, "Anything specific you want us to look into?"

"You asked to go, so the primary objective is awareness of the situation at the LoC. The day after you return, Singleton has arranged for you to accompany him when he meets for the last time with his new asset, Hakeem Jaffar."

10

DERA GHAZI KHAN, PAKISTAN

The night air was cool and crisp in Dera Ghazi Khan, a city of over four hundred thousand in the Punjab province of Pakistan, about four hundred miles southwest of Islamabad.

The popular Al Madni restaurant was teeming with activity. In a dimly lit corner, Shamina Ahmadi gazed across the table at her husband, Raul. He was thirty-six years old and a tad under six feet tall. His manicured beard made him look more rugged than she believed he was. She was proud of her Pakistani soldier husband and loved him dearly.

Raul and Shamina's arranged marriage ten years ago was one that they had longed for. She'd been twenty-four years old at the time and had pleaded with her father regarding her choice for a husband. At every opportunity, he reminded her that the decision was his to make. Months went by. On more than one occasion during those months, he told her he had narrowed his choice of her potential mates down to a short list. The suitors under his consideration were some of the most undesirable men she knew. He never included Raul Ahmadi, her true love. She suspected her father was playing a game—at least she prayed to Allah he was.

Now, ten years to the day after she and Raul were married, they had two beautiful children, an eight-year-old girl named Javeria and a six-year-old boy named Hammad. Tonight, the children were with Shamina's mother while she and Raul were celebrating their anniversary at a restaurant that was more expensive than the ones where they usually dined. She had taken extra care with her grooming and wore a new, beautifully embroidered salwar kameez in Raul's favorite shade of blue.

"Are you happy, Raul?" she asked, tilting her head ever so slightly.

"Never happier. Why do you ask?" Raul replied between bites.

"Because I worry about you. You're away more than you're home." Raul's time away from home on military assignments had more than doubled over the past year. Still, she had no reason to believe he had lost interest in her and the children. When he was at home, he was attentive and affectionate. She welcomed his advances, and, likewise, he welcomed hers. Their lovemaking was enthusiastic, yet soft and tender, never rushed. The problem for her was more that there were fewer opportunities to make love. She had friends who complained that their husbands had lost interest in sex. They were convinced that their husbands were having affairs. One suspected her husband had married her to hide the fact that he was gay—a crime and a sin, according to the Qur'an.

"Shamina, the Qur'an tells us that a man can have nothing but what he works for, and the rewards of his work will be complete."

"I'm just concerned about your health, that's all. The children and I would be lost without you."

"Your brow is wrinkled unnecessarily, and your worry is unfounded. My health is fine." Raul took a bite of lamb curry and chewed on it longer than needed, staring down at the plate. When he swallowed his bite, he said, "I must go away again soon. The assignment could last for several weeks."

"Where are you going? What will you be doing?"

"That's enough, Shamina," Raul snapped. "No more questions. I need to take care of some matters before I leave. I can't tell you anything else other than to say it is related to my work. Don't ask me again."

"I'm sorry. I know you can't talk about your work. Just tell me that you are not going into the tribal areas. Please…anywhere but there."

The tribal areas were a semiautonomous region of northwestern Pakistan bordered by Afghanistan to the west and north. After America's 9/11 attack, the tribal areas had become centers of militant and terrorist activity. Shamina knew this was a sensitive subject. Raul's father had been killed there. He had been driving down a street in the tribal areas when a missile from an American drone struck a house occupied by a jihadist leader. The force of the explosion destroyed the car and killed Raul's beloved father. Upon hearing the news, Raul was inconsolable in his grief. Now, he seldom mentioned his father's death, and if anyone questioned him about the renewed American drone attacks in Pakistan and Afghanistan, he would abruptly change the subject.

"I'm not. I'll be perfectly safe. It's something I've been chosen to do. I wish I could tell you more. If I could, you'd be proud of me."

His words had not assured her of the safety of his mission, but she was relieved that he was not going into the tribal areas. She still feared that this mission was far more dangerous than he could say. Shamina resumed eating her chicken karahi. In the past few months, Raul had been on other trips. He said they were related to his job at the military base, and he was not allowed to discuss them. She trusted him. He was a man of God, family, and country. His Muslim faith grew stronger every day, and she was sure he loved her and the children. He was also a dedicated soldier, serving his country. She had learned not to push the boundaries. Demanding answers from her husband would only anger him. Raul, who was normally gentle and loving, had grown increasingly short-tempered. She noticed that his cheeks were crimson, a sign to her that she needed to back off and settle the mood. After all, it was their anniversary.

Shamina rested her utensils on the plate and looked at him. "I'm always proud of you."

He smiled and reached across the table to hold her left hand. "When I return, I'll book a holiday. Just the two of us."

"I would love that. I can't remember the last time we went away without the children. At least promise me you will call when you have completed your assignment and are on the way home. Please do that for me."

"Of course. While I am away, I cannot call you. And you must not call me under any circumstance. Do you understand?" Raul said, looking her in the eyes and lowering his voice while emphasizing each word.

"I do."

11

THE LINE OF CONTROL
PAKISTAN-CONTROLLED KASHMIR

Palmer, Green, and Singleton had left early in the morning, flying in a military helicopter before transferring to a Humvee with their Pakistani Army escorts.

The armored Humvee was going too fast to avoid the potholes, although Palmer was certain the soldier driving was intentionally hitting them to make the Americans' ride as rough as possible. Humvees were armored vehicles designed to get from one place to another in a combat zone; they were neither quiet nor comfortable. Singleton flinched and braced himself with each bone-jarring pothole they hit, while Palmer leaned forward and made small talk with the driver and the other Pakistani soldier who was riding shotgun. Green wore an ear-to-ear smile like a kid on a roller coaster. The three of them were wearing battle fatigues, helmets, and flak jackets. Their orders were strictly to observe, and so none of them were armed. General Reynolds had made the rules of engagement clear: *Do not engage anyone regardless of the circumstance.*

They had traveled from Pakistan to Pakistan-controlled Kashmir and were approaching the Line of Control, a physical and diplomatic barrier that separated Pakistan-controlled Kashmir from India-controlled Kashmir. Pakistan-controlled Kashmir was a hot spot for terrorist incursions and military action, even in the best of times. The same held true in India-controlled Kashmir. The most recent skirmish had escalated to an all-out battle, garnering a little international media attention, although some speculated it could become the powder keg for the start of World War III.

Their destination was a Pakistan Army forward operating base, in order to get a firsthand look at the current state of engagement between Pakistani and Indian forces. Forward operating bases were, in general, relatively safe locations where senior officers were privy to the most current information and could direct troop movements. It was not a front-row seat with bullets whizzing by their heads but was instead a position close enough to enable them to pass information back to the top brass, who were drinking tea, safe and sound, in Islamabad.

Palmer noticed that Singleton looked a little pale, either from motion sickness, fear, or both. He leaned closer to him. "First ride in a Humvee?"

"Not my first, but not my favorite form of transportation either," Singleton admitted. "I'm leaving soon. Why the hell am I even here?"

"We're in good hands," Palmer said. "You'll see once we get there. Nothing to worry about."

"If you say so."

"How about you, Alona?" Palmer asked.

"First time for me, and I hope not the last. This is awesome."

Palmer was riding a wave of exhilaration. The familiar feel of the weight of the helmet, the snugness of the flak jacket, and the smell of diesel fuel, metal, and sweat inside the Humvee stimulated his senses and gave him an adrenaline rush. *Hooyah!*

The Humvee, including the windshield, was bulletproof. And although the vehicle would receive considerable damage if hit with a stray round fired from one of the Indian tanks on the opposite side of the LoC, they would most likely survive—depending on where it hit the vehicle. According to the intel he had, the Indians and Pakistanis were mostly behaving and staying on their respective sides of the LoC. That would all but rule out encountering a roadside improvised explosive device, commonly called an IED. That could prove problematic, again depending on the size of the IED and where it exploded relative to the vehicle's position.

The Pakistani soldier in the passenger seat turned toward Palmer. "Ten kilometers out."

The Humvee slowed as they passed through a large, semipermanent encampment where troops were staged for movement into and out of the engagement. Injured soldiers would receive emergency treatment here before being moved to trauma units staffed to treat the horrific wounds that bullets, explosions, and shrapnel inflicted on the human body. They drove by large numbers of troops, personnel carriers, tanks, and artillery.

A group of men wearing uniforms different than the Pakistani Army uniform caught Palmer's attention. He sat straight up, moved his head close to the window, and looked back to confirm what he saw. It was difficult to see through the small, thick glass, but he recognized their uniforms before he saw their faces. He looked at Green.

Green nodded, mouthing, "Chinese."

The driver said something to the other Pakistani in what to Palmer sounded like Urdu.

"Was that Chinese military I saw?" Palmer asked the driver.

The two soldiers looked at each other and said nothing.

Palmer let the question hang in the air before saying a little louder, "Any other countries involved in or monitoring the fighting?"

"Perhaps," the soldier in the passenger seat replied. "Why do you ask?"

"Just curious," Palmer said. He was not surprised the Chinese were there. He, Green, and Singleton were seven thousand miles from home. China, on the other hand, bordered Kashmir and India. Should the Chinese so desire, they could be home for dinner.

China was cozying up to Pakistan to complete the China-Pakistan Economic Corridor, giving China shorter, quicker access to the Arabian Sea and Persian Gulf. The trade route ran from China through Pakistan, ending in the Arabian Sea port city of Gwadar, which was close to the Pakistan-Iran border and the large Pakistani port in Karachi. If that were not enough to raise eyebrows, China planned to build a naval base at Gwadar. China was investing billions of dollars into completing the route and building the base. The US president declaring Pakistan a state sponsor of terrorism and cutting off aid could have been the last straw in China's replacing of the US with Pakistan as a strategic partner. As a result, the US was edging closer politically and militarily to India, while remaining in a hostile embrace with Pakistan. Regardless, the last thing either the US or China wanted was an all-out war between India and Pakistan, especially a nuclear war. China, after all, had its own border dispute with India, and there had been recent clashes on that border in the Galwan Valley.

12

FORWARD OPERATING BASE PAKISTAN-CONTROLLED KASHMIR

The Humvee skidded to a stop close to the entrance of a one-story concrete building on the forward operating base, stirring up a cloud of dust. Next to the building was a tall, fortified structure with large, open windows at the top. As soon as the Humvee stopped, the two Pakistani soldiers jumped out and motioned for Palmer, Green, and Singleton to get out and head into the building. The crack of small arms, as well exploding mortar rounds, could be heard in the distance.

"Did you catch any of the conversation between the two soldiers?" Palmer asked.

"Too noisy," Singleton said. "I only picked up a few words."

A Pakistani Army lieutenant met them at the door and introduced himself. Inside, the work area was segmented into four spaces. Most of the action was at the one closest to the door, which contained several video screens with color displays, each being monitored by one or two men. However, several uniformed men were standing around one of the video displays. One showed a low-level view, which Palmer assumed was a live feed from the top of the tall structure beside them. Other views were from higher vantage points taken by cameras on military drones. A few were low-level video feeds.

"We're five kilometers from the LoC. As you can see, we have several live feeds of the Indian forces."

"How about those?" Palmer said, pointing to the low-level, aerial video feed.

The Pakistani lieutenant smiled. "Those are from drones we purchased on Amazon. The Indians use them for target practice, so we have to replace them on an ongoing basis. It's still more cost-effective than using a military drone."

"Any military drones up there?" Singleton asked.

"Yes, but not American ones. That all but ended after we closed the Shamsi air base where the US CIA and NATO were running their top-secret drone program. Although you've renewed your drone program against terrorist sites, the US does not wish to take sides in this conflict. That would have dire consequences," the lieutenant said. "However, I'm sure you're monitoring the situation with your spy satellites."

Palmer had read the intelligence regarding the drones the Pakistanis were using. China had given Pakistan one of its large Rainbow CH-3 drones. The Chinese had also entered into an agreement with Pakistan and were coproducing forty-eight Wing Loong II armed drones. If nothing else, this trip was reinforcing the level of China's influence and involvement in this region.

A soldier rushed over and handed a piece of paper to the lieutenant, who looked at it and stepped away to speak with him. At the same time, the activity in the facility noticeably surged.

"Excuse me," the lieutenant said, rushing to one of the monitors and donning a headset. A few minutes later, he returned. "At the moment, we have an issue. I'm afraid your visit will be cut short."

"What kind of issue?" Singleton asked, eyebrow cocked.

"Follow me." The lieutenant walked over to one of the screens where a large number of soldiers were standing. "I've just learned that India has launched an air attack inside Pakistan, at a remote location they had previously deemed a terrorist training ground. During the attack, we shot down one of the Indian jets. Now Indian forces are advancing in large numbers along the LoC. You can see who the real aggressors are."

They moved closer to the screen. Deferring to the lieutenant, the others moved aside. The lieutenant pointed at the screen. A line of tanks running parallel to the LoC was advancing slowly. Armored troop carriers were a hundred or so yards behind the tanks. "Those are Russian-built T-90 battle tanks and Indian-built Arjun battle tanks."

"Have they done this before?" Palmer asked.

"In small numbers in past conflicts. Nothing of this magnitude."

"Maybe they are just probing your defenses to see how you respond," Palmer suggested, his eyes locked on the monitor. "If they were serious, they'd soften you up with artillery and a few cruise missiles before advancing."

"Neither country has ever used missiles. That would represent a major escalation. We're preparing our troops for advancement toward the LoC. You may have seen them in the staging area on your way here."

"We did. Wouldn't it be prudent to deploy your tactical nuclear weapons just to let the Indians know you're serious?" Palmer asked, casually mentioning nuclear weapons on the off chance of eliciting a response.

The Pakistani lieutenant didn't take the bait. "Both countries have policies regarding the use of nuclear weapons."

"Yes, but while India has a no-first-use policy, Pakistan does not," Green noted.

Looking annoyed, the lieutenant said, "That is because nuclear weapons might be our only defense against the overwhelming size and aggressive might of the Indian Army. It's one reason we've continued to build our tactical nuclear weapon arsenal."

Palmer did not press Green's point. The junior officer was not going to comment further. He wouldn't know at what point Pakistan would actually deploy its battlefield nukes. That decision would be made at the highest level. Policies outlining the conditions under which nuclear weapons would be used were a little gray around the edges. If the Indians advanced into Pakistan-controlled Kashmir, Pakistan would likely use their less powerful, tactical nukes—also called battlefield nukes—as a defensive measure, even if India had not used nuclear weapons first. Likewise, if Pakistan's battlefield nukes were used, India would respond with their strategic nuclear missiles, which were designed for mass destruction and would justify the move as a defensive measure. The Pakistanis would then respond in kind. That would all occur within a few minutes. The region, if not the world, was on the brink of a nuclear apocalypse.

"I'm sorry to cut your visit short. I'll have the men who brought you here take you back. I hope you understand."

"We do," Palmer said.

Before they got into the Humvee, Palmer made a quick call to Reynolds and gave him a situation report, including the sighting of Chinese soldiers. The general said he was not concerned about the Chinese observers and that the advancing battle tanks were nothing more than an Indian Army exercise intended to agitate the Pakistan Army, but he would pass the information along. However, India's air attack within Pakistan and the fact that Pakistan had shot down one of the jets was a serious escalation.

13

ISLAMABAD, PAKISTAN

The loud ring of his cell phone jarred Lieutenant General Sulayman Fahd Sarkis awake at 5:30 in the morning. He picked it up and walked out of the room so the woman stretched out beside him would not hear the ensuing conversation. Before he shut the door, he looked back at her—her leg and naked buttocks protruding from under the sheet.

The call was from Lieutenant General Khalil Ridha Hesbani, ISI's Director-General. Sarkis had expected the call. A contact in Hesbani's office had told him that the general was meeting with Pakistan's president regarding the deployment of the nuclear weapons.

Hesbani began talking as soon as Sarkis answered. "The time for deployment of our nuclear arsenal has arrived. India has carried out air attacks inside Pakistan. We shot down one of their jets. Their forces are advancing."

"Are you certain? There's no turning back from that decision," Sarkis said, dispensing with the niceties.

"Don't interrupt," Hesbani snapped. "I've spoken with the president and have his authority to deploy our nuclear weapons. We have waited long enough. Get these weapons mated and deployed. Do you understand me?"

"I should have been involved in that decision. Why wasn't I in that meeting?"

"Are you questioning the president's order? Follow the standard protocol for deployment. If India were to launch a preemptive nuclear strike, the war would be over before we had the first warhead ready to launch."

"I'll initiate the operation immediately."

"When will it be completed?"

"We anticipated this decision and have already mated some of the components. The transfer and final assembly at the bases will take a minimum of two days. Then the bases might need another day to deploy them in the field."

"That's too much time."

"It is a complex process. We have a procedure in place, and we'll execute it properly. There are no shortcuts."

"You have two days, start to finish. Report to me once everything is complete, including the final verification."

Sarkis hung up without responding to Hesbani. The man's arrogance and superior attitude annoyed him to no end. Sarkis held one of the most powerful and influential positions in Pakistan—Director-General of the Strategic Plans Division, SPD. The career soldier had served under the past five presidents of Pakistan, each of whom had considered him one of the most competent military leaders in the country. Sarkis was now nearing the end of his storied career. As Director-General of SPD, he had the responsibility of keeping the country's nuclear warheads secure and advising the president and prime minister on nuclear matters. Of the fifty Muslim-majority countries, Pakistan was the only one to have nuclear capability and had approximately one hundred sixty nuclear warheads located at high-security bases. By comparison, India had about one hundred fifty. Security of the nuclear arsenal was an expensive operation, but Pakistan had used its diplomatic leverage to secure money from the Americans in order to fund most of the costs. The American taxpayer money that supported the costs came with one important caveat: Pakistan's nuclear weapons must be kept out of terrorists' hands. However, the US president had now cut off those funds, blaming Pakistan's support of terrorist groups.

The security of Pakistan's nuclear armament had been the subject of debate in the foreign press for years. Opinions covered the full range of possibilities, from being totally secure to being vulnerable. However, since Pakistan's first nuclear tests in the late nineties, there had not been any incident in which its nuclear armament was at risk of falling into the hands of either terrorists or a foreign government. Part of the reason for this was that the components for each warhead were stored at separate facilities.

The power struggle that existed between Hesbani and Sarkis had begun several years before when Hesbani was promoted to Lieutenant General and appointed Director-General of ISI. At the time, Hesbani was considered the most ruthless general in the Army. His appointment had infuriated Sarkis, who had not only wanted the position but had also believed that his appointment was a fait accompli. It was a one-two punch of shock and anger. A year later, Pakistan's president, as a way of thanking Sarkis for his thirty years of service, promoted him to Lieutenant General and appointed him Director-General of the Strategic Plans Division.

After taking over the ISI, Hesbani was cautious in his initial interactions with the US Central Intelligence Agency but grew to despise the agency when, a year after his appointment, the US flew their secret mission into Pakistan and killed Osama bin Laden without notifying the Pakistani government or ISI. Since then, under Hesbani's leadership, ISI had become one of the most feared intelligence services since the Soviet Union's KGB. They carried out their missions with an iron fist and an almost complete lack of moral and ethical principles.

Sarkis went downstairs to his locked, windowless office and logged on to his desktop computer. He entered the required security code, confirmed by facial and fingerprint identification, and scrolled to the deployment protocols, which ran the gamut from test protocols to full-scale deployment. He selected Protocol Red, which called for the full-scale mating and deployment of the warheads at an accelerated pace. The secure military bases where nuclear weapons were stored were highlighted in red. Trucks leaving those facilities with warheads or delivery devices aboard would be monitored by GPS and show up as green lights on the map.

American spy satellites had located and identified more than fifteen of Pakistan's nuclear weapon storage facilities. The Americans monitored the movement of vehicles to and from those bases. Some were development sites, not storage sites, while other military bases had false storage facilities and existed for no other reason than to keep the international community guessing as to the location of the nuclear weapons, obviously part of a game of cat and mouse.

As furious as he was with Hesbani, the order to deploy Pakistan's nuclear arsenal played right into Sarkis's hand. This was the moment for which he had been waiting. He selected the predetermined assembly protocol that dictated the warhead components would be mated and moved to their launch vehicles that were located at several military bases throughout Pakistan. The trucks would leave the bases at irregularly spaced intervals and go along preplanned routes. A security vehicle would follow each truck, staying close enough to keep the truck in sight. The number of the operation's moving parts was such that it took a computer program to keep track of everything. Within seconds, Pakistan's president and Lieutenant General Hesbani had entered the required authorization codes.

That done, Sarkis took a laptop from his locked desk drawer. He logged on and sent a short, encrypted message to one person. Even though the individual would soon learn that the deployment had commenced through official channels, the early notice was of utmost importance. Every hour, minute, and second counted.

Over his lifetime of service in the military, the world had changed. Now was the time to act. Other opportunities had come and gone. All were too complex, risky, or expensive to pull off. Today was different. No one in the history of the world had even attempted what was about to happen, much less succeeded. The plan could only be implemented behind the veil of a massive movement of trucks, launch vehicles, and nuclear weapon components. Many—playing roles large and small—would be involved. However, only one person had the overall ability and charisma to lead the operation and see it through.

Sarkis made a cup of coffee and stepped outside onto the patio. The morning air felt cool on his exposed skin. He took a deep breath and smiled. The sky was still dark behind him, but the eastern sky was turning pink.

It had begun.

14

ISLAMABAD, PAKISTAN

Singleton's asset, Hakeem Jaffar, worked at the nuclear weapons facility Wah Cantonment—cantonment meaning military station—forty miles northwest of Islamabad. The locals called it Wah Cantt. Palmer, Green, and Singleton could have met him near there, but Jaffar felt safer in Islamabad, where the chance of running into someone he knew was small.

The meeting was at a café in Islamabad. Palmer and Green arrived at the entrance to the embassy's main building fifteen minutes early. Singleton was already there, pacing back and forth and talking to himself, which Palmer thought was odd. What did Singleton have to be agitated about? Perhaps it was simply the fact that his time in Pakistan was coming to an end, and he remained undecided about what to do next.

Singleton had expressed that the meeting was a good opportunity to introduce them to Jaffar, but Palmer believed it could be more useful than that. Even when an encounter with an asset appeared to be a waste of time, it often yielded a scrap of information that seemed insignificant when considered in isolation. But intelligence was seldom one compelling piece of information that changed everything. Instead, it was a collection of what seemed like unimportant bits gathered, compiled, and analyzed over time. Palmer looked forward to hearing Jaffar's perspective regarding what was going on inside the base; perhaps it would be another piece to a much larger puzzle.

The driver pulled up to the entrance to pick them up. Singleton said something to him and got into the passenger seat. Palmer and Green sat in the back. The driver took a circuitous route from the embassy to the café, taking multiple left turns, multiple right turns, pulling into parking spaces, and then pulling away. An exercise that when done correctly would determine if anyone was following them. What should have been a fifteen-minute drive took twice that. The assumption was that anyone leaving the embassy complex would be tailed. On most occasions, that didn't matter; however, when meeting with an asset, precautions were necessary.

The café was located on Street 1 near the Kohsar Market. As they approached it, their Pakistani driver, who Singleton said had worked with the embassy for years, pointed it out. Although parking was available in front of the café, the driver dropped them off a couple of blocks away and said he would wait for them out of sight.

Islamabad was a beautiful, modern city of over a million people and relatively safe as long as visitors followed the same precautions that any seasoned, international traveler would. Palmer, however, was not going to let his guard down. As they walked toward the café, his eyes darted from side to side, sailing along the rooftops and dropping back to street level. He had operated in areas where a large percentage of the population wanted to kill you, and being hypervigilant in this part of the world was not a sign of paranoia—it was his modus operandi.

"When did you make initial contact with Jaffar?" Palmer asked as they walked to the café.

"A few months ago," Singleton said. When they spoke, they spoke quietly, barely moving their lips, like experienced ventriloquists. "He's antiwar and is adamantly opposed to Pakistan's nuclear weapons program. Of course, he's careful not to express those opinions to anyone at work."

"Where have you met him before?"

"We mix it up. The last time was at the Shakar Parian Park near the embassy."

"How did you approach him?" Green asked.

"The initial contact was at a peace demonstration. In conducting basic background checks, we discovered that he worked at the Wah Cantonment Ordnance Complex, home to Pakistan's ordnance factories and a main nuclear weapons assembly facility. He's a civilian contractor and doesn't have access to restricted areas. He does, however, have coworkers who do. Jaffar has the makings of a good agent, hitting two of the four primary MICE motivators for foreign agents—money, ideology, compromise, and ego. Jaffar appears highly motivated by his ideology and his ego. He's also getting into the whole spy thing. I've not pitched him yet, so he's not on the payroll."

"If he's antiwar and opposed to the nuclear program, what's he doing working at Wah Cantt?" Green asked.

"Like anywhere else, a job is a job, and he may not be fully aware of what they do at the facility," Singleton said. "Think Edward Snowden and Chelsea Manning: one, a highly paid US government contractor, and the other, an Army soldier. They each had jobs to do; however, the more they saw and learned, the more concerned they became. You can't predict what people will do when confronted with something to which they are strongly opposed. The proper vetting of people—initially and on an ongoing basis—who are in jobs with access to very sensitive data and information is a big issue."

According to Singleton, Jaffar tended to rely on what he heard rather than probing for information. That would come with time and experience. Singleton said he had not pushed him yet, because if Jaffar attempted it without adequate coaching and training, his coworkers might become suspicious. Assets were often cultivated for months before becoming paid agents, and sometimes they never did, for a number of reasons.

On entering the café, Singleton looked around. "We're a little early. We have time for a coffee or tea while we wait."

The café could have been in any American or European city. Worn leather-upholstered chairs and love seats were placed around glass coffee tables in the center of the room, and rectangular wooden tables and chairs were placed against the walls. A blackboard with the specials written in English in neon-colored chalk was on a stand near the pastry counter. Palmer counted seven customers, all men: one table of two, one of three, and two sitting by themselves. The only visible exit was the front door. Another exit door was probably at the back, behind the counter and through the kitchen.

They chose one of the tables in the back of the café, sitting in chairs facing the door. Palmer and Green ordered coffee. Singleton ordered tea. They made innocent conversation while waiting, but as one minute bled into another, Singleton became visibly nervous, checking the time far too frequently and tapping his fingers on the table.

"This isn't like him," he confessed quietly. "He's never late."

Green sat a little straighter, sipping her coffee. "Maybe he's caught up in traffic."

"We have an agreement. If one of us is running late or there's a problem, we use the encryption app and let the other know. I'll text him and ask if we need to reschedule."

The last of the customers who'd been there when they arrived were now gone, and no new customers had arrived.

Green set her coffee down, pushing it aside. "We're the only ones in the café."

"What?" Singleton said, looking around the venue. It was eerily quiet, a stark contrast to the city bustling wildly outside.

"The barista's gone, too," Palmer added. "Wait here. I want to check something." He went to the door and, without opening it, looked out. A man and woman were walking toward the café. As they approached, a man, who was smoking a cigarette outside the café, said something to them. The couple turned and walked away.

Palmer stepped outside. He had taken no more than a few steps toward the man smoking the cigarette when he was spotted. The man threw down the cigarette hurried across the street. Palmer returned to their table.

"Let's go," Palmer said. "Call the driver."

Singleton was already doing just that, but after a minute of the phone ringing without any response, his face went pale. "No answer."

"Let's go out the back," Palmer pressed.

As they stood up from the table, a car screeched to a halt in the middle of the street in front of the café. They looked out the window and saw a black sedan. The car's passenger side and back doors flew open. Two men got out. They pulled a body out of the car and flung it facedown onto the street. The men stepped over the body and walked toward the café. Each was openly carrying a pistol.

Palmer pointed to Singleton. "Go to the kitchen."

Singleton was heading there but paused to see what was happening outside. Palmer and Green rushed to the café entrance. They each picked up a wooden chair from the table closest to the door. Palmer drew back his chair, ready to swing, like a batter waiting for the pitch. Green, on the opposite side of the door, clutched hers with both hands.

The men entered the café, both with semiautomatic pistols extended in front of them. They saw Singleton race into the kitchen. Both men fired. With the gunmen focused on Singleton, Palmer swung the chair, striking the man closest to him in the chest. The blow knocked him back toward the front door. The second man's head snapped around toward Palmer. As he swung his weapon toward Palmer, Green swung her chair, knocking the pistol from his hand. As he turned to look toward her, she executed a spinning back kick, striking him in the kidney. The man fell toward Palmer, who landed a punch to the side of his head, knocking him unconscious. Green grabbed his pistol from the floor. The man Palmer had hit with the chair reached for his gun, which was just out of reach on the floor beside him. But before he got to it, Palmer swung a leg cast off a broken chair, striking him in the temple. He snatched up the pistol and charged outside.

The driver of the car spotted him and sped away. Palmer raised his pistol, putting pressure on the trigger. His finger itched to fire, but shooting would only inflame an already bad situation. So he eased off, lowering the weapon, and rushed back inside.

Green had her 9mm pistol pointed at the two men, who were still down. Singleton came out from the kitchen, eyes wide. "They shot the barista," he sputtered. "While shooting at me, they shot him instead—right in the arm."

"He'll be fine," Palmer insisted, selecting a clean towel by the sink, tying it tightly around the wound to slow the bleeding. The barista merely stared, in shock.

"We need to get out of here," Green said.

Singleton, his mouth gaping, stared at the wounded man. Palmer grabbed Singleton by the shoulder and shook him. "Snap out of it. We have to go."

"What about him?" Singleton said.

"He'll be fine."

"What about them?" Singleton added, pointing at the two unconscious men by the door.

"The police will be here soon. They will take care of them. Let's get out of here." Palmer pointed toward the street. Before leaving, he rolled the two men onto their backs and took cell phone photos of them and close-ups of their faces. Palmer tucked his pistol into his waistband and took the other pistol from Green, ejected the magazine, removed the remaining bullets from it and the chamber, and put them in his pocket. He reinserted the empty magazine into the pistol and wiped it down before pressing the firearm into the hand of one of the men.

They went outside. The man who had been thrown from the car was lying facedown on the street. Palmer turned him over and felt for a pulse; there was none. "He's dead."

"Do you recognize him? Is it Jaffar?" Green asked.

Palmer rolled the man onto his side. His face was beaten and bloodied.

Singleton cringed and turned away. "It's hard to tell. I don't believe it's Jaffar. He could be another one of our assets."

Palmer took a couple of photos of the man's face. A car horn blew. It was their driver. They jumped in the car and left. Palmer looked out of the rear window in time to see two police cars, their emergency lights flashing, come to a halt beside the man.

"That was close," Green said. "Do you know where Jaffar lives in Wah Cantt?"

"I checked before we left, just in case." Singleton gave the driver the address.

"How did they know we were there? And where the hell is Jaffar?" Palmer asked, but nobody had an answer.

15

WAH CANTONMENT PAKISTAN

Palmer, Green, and Singleton drove to Hakeem Jaffar's apartment, which was about two hours outside of Islamabad. On the way, Palmer filled Reynolds in on what had happened and sent him the photos of the two assailants and the dead man on the street outside the café.

Rather than taking the elevator, they climbed the stairs to the fourth-floor apartment of the six-story building, figuring they would encounter fewer people. When they got to Jaffar's apartment, Singleton knocked on the door. When no one answered, he knocked again. Palmer tested the doorknob. It was unlocked. Moving Singleton and Green aside, he removed the pistol from his belt.

"I thought you left those pistols in the café," Singleton whispered.

"Only one," Palmer said. "Stay back and wait until I've cleared the room."

Palmer pushed open the door and moved through the small apartment room by room. There was a small living area, a bedroom with two single beds, a bathroom, and a galley kitchen. With no place for anyone to hide, Palmer was finished in seconds.

"Clear," Palmer shouted, and Green came in, followed by Singleton, who shut the door behind him.

The apartment had a cluttered, unkempt sort of look—unwashed dishes, pots, and pans filled the sink. The trash bin was overflowing. Every drawer had been pulled open and dumped. Clothes were scattered everywhere. Someone had thoroughly searched the apartment. A table in the living room was overturned, and a lamp lay shattered on the floor. Palmer pointed to blood spatter on the floor and wall.

If the dead man had been Jaffar, the men would have squeezed what they could out of him, including their names and the location and time of their scheduled meeting. Telling them everything would not have saved his life; it would have only sealed his fate as a traitor. Palmer was looking through some of the mess when he heard footsteps.

"Quiet," he whispered, nodding to the door. He moved up beside it, listening. The steps got closer and stopped in the hallway.

"Hakeem," said a woman's voice. "Hakeem," she said louder.

The door opened. A woman of moderate height, with a long scarf covering her hair, entered the apartment. She stopped in her tracks upon seeing the three of them standing there, amidst the rubble of the apartment.

"Who are you? What are you doing here?" she asked in English, with a Pakistani accent. Her dark almond-shaped eyes moved from one to the other as if memorizing their faces. "Where is Hakeem?" She spoke in a forceful, confident voice, showing no fear.

"We're friends of Hakeem's. Who are you?" Green asked.

"You're obviously Americans, and Hakeem doesn't have any American friends. I'm his sister, Aaliyah."

Palmer looked to Singleton. When he didn't respond, Palmer said, "He may be in trouble. We were supposed to meet him at a café. He didn't show up."

"Why would he contact you, three Americans?"

"We work at the US Embassy. He contacted me, saying he wanted to talk about something. We waited for him at the café where he said to meet him, but he didn't come."

"Show me your identification," Aaliyah demanded, holding out her hand.

Singleton took out his Embassy ID from his wallet and showed it to her. She studied the ID and then looked at him again. While Aaliyah was distracted, Green quickly took out her cell phone and took a photo of her.

"What are you doing?" Aaliyah barked, clearly annoyed.

"We need a photograph of you for our documentation," Green said. "Routine procedure."

"I should be taking photographs of you. Did you do this?" Aaliyah asked, motioning her hand at the overturned table and broken lamp.

"No. We arrived a few minutes before you and found it this way."

Green showed her the blood. Aaliyah moved closer and knelt, taking a tissue from her pocket and wiping some of the blood up. "It's fresh," she said, looking back at Palmer.

"Yes," Palmer said. "You should report this to the police, whether it's your brother's or not. Don't mention that we were here. You don't want the police or military probing into his relationship with US Embassy. That would not be good for him or you."

Aaliyah stood and walked around the apartment without speaking or showing emotion.

"Hakeem works at the Wah Cantt base," she said. "He has a roommate, a friend who works with him on the base. That could be his roommate's blood."

"Do you know his name?" Singleton asked.

"No. I don't. Hakeem recently took him in to help pay the rent. I hadn't met him."

"When did you last see your brother?" Green asked.

"Two days ago. He was acting strange."

"What do mean?"

"He was nervous and agitated. Something was bothering him. He was afraid. He was working with you, wasn't he? If he was, and someone found out…" Aaliyah's coffee-colored eyes locked onto Green's. "Please let me know if you hear anything." She wrote her cell phone number on a scrap of paper and handed it over. "Call or text."

"I will. I promise. You must be in shock. I would be if my brother went missing under these circumstances." Green gave Aaliyah her phone number, and Aaliyah entered the number into her phone. "If you hear from him or have any questions, call me."

The three of them said goodbye and left. Aaliyah stayed in the apartment.

As they went down the stairs, Green said, "We didn't ask for her ID."

"She's either his sister or she's not," Palmer said. "If she's not, what were we going to do, arrest her? Force her to talk? Considering her brother might have been abducted and is possibly dead, she seemed unmoved."

"What do you know about his family?" Green asked Singleton.

"He wasn't married. He never mentioned having a sister or any immediate family. Didn't even mention a roommate. That's not unusual. Assets want to keep their family and friends out of what they are doing."

"I didn't know you had a brother, Alona," Palmer said.

"I don't. It helps to make a connection. If she calls, maybe she'll call me, since Singleton is leaving. However, I'm not holding my breath. I don't believe she's his sister. At least we have her telephone number—if it's valid."

Singleton's phone buzzed. "A text from Jaffar."

I need an extraction. They are on to me.

Singleton replied to the text and received a quick reply. "He's in Islamabad. I have the address. I'll arrange for our men to take him to a safe house."

16

US SAFE HOUSE
ISLAMABAD, PAKISTAN

The sun had set by the time they arrived at the safe house. The two-story, sand-colored dwelling had a ten-foot-high concrete wall surrounding it, similar to those of the neighboring houses. Islamabad residents, those who could afford it, cherished their privacy and security.

The driver pulled up to the solid gate and spoke into a speaker, looking at the security camera aimed down at the entrance as he spoke. The gate opened. As he entered the courtyard, a motion-detector floodlight came on. He drove through to a paved area and parked beside a black SUV. Palmer, Green, and Singleton got out. Their driver told them the car was low on gas and he needed to leave and fill up.

A man, wearing an unbuttoned, casual jacket that revealed a shoulder holster and pistol, met them at the door and stepped outside to confirm their identification. Satisfied they were who they said they were, he led them inside as the gate opened for the driver to leave.

The house, like other safe houses Palmer had seen, was furnished with the bare minimum of inexpensive furniture, and the walls and rooms were devoid of any decorative items or photographs. Emphasis was placed on function, not comfort. The house was a secure location for someone like Jaffar to be kept in for a short period of time.

"How many of you are here?" Palmer asked.

"Me and one other member of embassy security, plus your asset."

"Security system?"

"Full coverage of the entrance and grounds by security cameras that we monitor from a computer. The metal doors and bulletproof windows are alarmed. The gate is opened either by code or by using the call box as your driver did."

"When did you get here?" Singleton asked.

"Late this afternoon."

"Has he said anything?"

"Nothing. We confirmed his identity and brought him here as directed."

The guard took them into the living room, where Singleton greeted Hakeem Jaffar and introduced Palmer and Green to him. The three of them pulled up chairs and sat close to him. Jaffar fidgeted in his seat, leaning forward with his elbows on his knees, rubbing his hand through his hair and over his face to wipe sweat from his brow.

"What's going on, Hakeem?" Singleton asked. "Why did you ask to be picked up?"

"I'm afraid."

Green sat closer, lowing her voice empathetically. "Afraid of what?"

Jaffar turned to Singleton. "I've never revealed any military secrets or told you anything I thought would harm my teammates. Yet, my life is in danger. I think my roommate was abducted."

Green glanced at Palmer, then returned her gaze to Jaffar. "Why do you think that?"

"When I left today, I passed two men going inside the apartment building. They did not fit in if you know what I mean. So, I waited in my car and watched. About thirty minutes later, I had convinced myself that I was being paranoid. I started the car and was about to drive off when I saw them drag a man out—one on each side of him, holding him up. He was bloodied and unable to walk on his own. A car drove up and they all got in. Then it sped away."

"What kind of car was it?" Palmer asked.

"It was black. Maybe a Toyota."

"Was the man they were holding captive your roommate?" Singleton asked.

"I couldn't be certain, but I think so. I called his mobile phone after they drove off. No one answered. They were after me. I'm certain of it."

"Did you return to your apartment and check?" Palmer asked.

"No. I was afraid to."

"You had asked to meet with me," Singleton said. "Why?"

Jaffar looked at Singleton. "You said I needed to be more assertive, yet cautious. I tried. I started asking questions. Maybe too many. I fear I've made them suspicious."

Singleton sat back in his chair, jaw tight. "Did you find out anything?"

"Yes, but it's no secret. We'll be deploying the nuclear weapons soon. Everyone knows that. In advance of it, I heard that ISI was rounding up anyone suspected of belonging to a terrorist organization or working with a foreign intelligence service. I became nervous. They must have put me on their list of people to interrogate. Seeing those men at my apartment—they know I'm working with you and came to get me for interrogation."

"People working with us often feel frightened at first. Over time, as they become more confident, that perception goes away," Singleton said.

"I am not being paranoid. You have to protect me. I overheard one of the officers at work talking on the phone. He said that the plan is in place and the timing is right. He expected it any day now."

Singleton raised his brows. "Expected what?"

Jaffar fidgeted in his seat, his gaze downward. "The deployment. I was told to be ready at a moment's notice to request security vehicles and additional trucks, the kind that haul the intermodal containers. I've seen the assignment sheets for the trucks and security details. There are rumors that someone will attempt to steal a nuclear device during the deployment."

"Do you have any evidence to support this?" Green asked.

"Nothing concrete. Just my orders and idle talk among the men. They believe it's the prelude to war with India. Some are frightened by it, while others are excited by the prospect."

Singleton's brows furrowed. "Is that something they would talk about among themselves during every deployment or was it something specific to this upcoming deployment?"

"Nothing specific, only speculation."

Palmer made eye contact with Green. She nodded and said, "You may be right about your roommate. When you didn't show up at the café, we left and went to your apartment. There had been a struggle. Does your roommate know anything about the work you're doing for us?"

Jaffar shook his head. "Nothing. I would not dare tell anyone. He was running late this morning. When I left, I told him I was taking the day off and meeting some friends for coffee in Islamabad."

"Did you tell him where in Islamabad?" Palmer asked. "It's important that we know."

"No. I wouldn't tell anyone that. Besides, he doesn't know Islamabad. Even if I told him, it would have meant nothing to him."

"Are you certain? If you did and he was abducted, he may have told the men you saw," Green said.

"I don't remember exactly what I said."

"When we were at your apartment, a woman stopped by and asked about you. She said her name was Aaliyah," Green said.

"Aaliyah? I don't know anyone by that name. Are you sure that was her name?"

"She said she was your sister."

Jaffar's eyes shot up. "I don't have a sister. I told you. They're after me. What have I done?" he asked, raising his voice. He stood and paced the length of the room.

"Excuse me. I'll be right back," Palmer said calmly.

Palmer believed that Jaffar was in imminent danger, that they all could be. It was likely that his roommate was tortured and told them where Jaffar was going. Who was Aaliyah? Was she ISI? Maybe Aaliyah came to see if Jaffar had returned. Or maybe she had been watching the apartment and saw him, Green, and Singleton enter the building. It was possible that they were followed, either when they left the café and drove to Wah Cantt or when they left there and drove back to Islamabad. *Wait … the driver.*

Palmer went into the other room to talk to the two security officers; one was reading a magazine, the other fiddling with his cell phone. The computer on the desk streamed feeds from the security cameras outside the house. Neither of the guards was monitoring them.

"What were you told about this asset?"

"We were told to pick him up at a designated time and location, bring him here, and provide security while you interviewed him. When you're finished, we will take him wherever you tell us to or stay here with him if you prefer. The house is stocked with enough food and supplies for a week or two. Is there anything we can do?"

"Your job is to provide security. See that you do. That includes monitoring the security cameras. Are you certain you weren't followed when you brought him here?"

One of the guards said, "We took precautions, but our priority was to bring him here as fast as possible. Should I call for backup?"

"Not yet. Are you armed?"

"We both have sidearms. There are two M4 rifles and extra ammo in a compartment under the carpet in the rear of the SUV." Palmer held out his hand, and the guard handed him a key ring that held an electronic proximity key and a traditional key. "The key is for the compartment."

Before exiting the front door, Palmer said to Singleton, "Call the driver and see where the hell he is."

Perhaps someone followed their car when the three of them had left the embassy that morning. Following a vehicle for a long distance without being spotted was difficult, especially when the driver was taking all precautions, as their driver had. To have followed them all day without being spotted would have been almost impossible without a trained team that switched off cars and motorcycles. Someone had to have tipped them off. Only three people knew where they'd been, as well as their present location: the driver, Jaffar, and Singleton. The driver had disappeared at the café and now again at the safe house. He was a long-term, trusted embassy employee who routinely drove for JSOC staff. Palmer made a mental note to talk to Singleton about him. Jaffar knew they would be at the café but would not have known the location of the safe house. The security men would have blindfolded him on the way here in order to keep the location secret. But why would they go to all this trouble over a contractor working in the transportation department who may have asked one too many questions? Palmer hadn't ruled out Singleton, although the driver and Jaffar were the more likely suspects.

When Palmer stepped outside, the motion detector floodlight came on, illuminating the front of the house. He hurriedly started the SUV and backed it up close to the front door. The secure compartment was under a removable carpet on the cargo floor. Using the key attached to the fob, he opened it. Inside were two M4 rifles and a case of ammo. If things went pear-shaped, they would have two choices: get into the SUV and make a run for it or call for backup and hunker down inside.

Palmer was a step from the door when all of the safe house's interior and exterior lights went dark.

17

US SAFE HOUSE
ISLAMABAD, PAKISTAN

Palmer hustled back into the house with the M4s and ammo. The two security men were standing inside the darkened front entryway. The only light inside the house was the dim light coming in from the streetlights. "Call for backup!" Palmer ordered.

One of the guards pulled out his cell phone and went into the room by the door to make the call.

"Anyone heard from our driver?" Palmer asked just as Singleton joined them.

"I called," he said. "No answer."

"That's twice today he's disappeared when we needed him. Has he done this before?"

"No," said Singleton. "Whenever I've used him, he has stayed with me or close by."

"Something's up. If we need to make a run for it, we'll take the SUV."

"It has bullet-resistant glass and tires," the guard said, "if that makes any difference."

"For now, it's safer here," Palmer said. "We can hold them off until backup arrives."

"When our driver left, did anyone come in while the gate was open?" Palmer asked the guard.

"I didn't see anyone," the guard said.

"Were you watching?" Palmer shouted in a flash of anger.

The security guard winced. "Not really," he admitted. "It opens when a vehicle approaches from inside and closes automatically when the vehicle has exited."

The guards each had 9mm pistols. Palmer looked at Singleton. "Can you use a gun?"

"I've been trained."

Palmer shook his head and handed an M4 rifle to Green and kept one for himself. Using a firearm in training and using a gun while someone was shooting at you were two very different experiences.

"Wait—what about me?" Singleton asked, eyes wide.

"No offense, but you'd be more of a danger to yourself and to us with a gun than without one," Palmer said.

The guard returned from the room. "I notified the embassy of the power outage and told them we need backup."

"How long?" Palmer asked.

"Twenty minutes out."

"Entry points?"

"Front door and rear door on this floor and a balcony door on the second floor. All windows are barred and locked."

"How about the gate?" Palmer asked.

"Standard security gate. That and the wall keep the honest people out."

Palmer opened the ammo box. Inside were six magazines for the M4s, three for him and three for Green. There were also several 9mm magazines, which the guards grabbed. In theory, they had more than enough ammo to withstand a short-term assault.

Palmer pointed at the two guards. "One of you cover the rear door. The other cover the balcony door on the second floor," Palmer said. "Stay away from the windows and doors."

The guards left to take their positions.

"Alona, you and I will take the front. I think that's going to be their focus. Singleton, take Jaffar into the room where the guards were."

"They're after me," Jaffar said, a nervous sweat running down his panic-stricken face.

"Don't worry," Palmer said. "We'll keep you safe."

"I'll never be safe again," Jaffar added hysterically.

Palmer noted the look in his eyes. It wasn't good—wasn't that of somebody thinking clearly. It was desperate, hopeless.

"They'll keep coming until I'm caught and tortured to death."

With that, Jaffar ran to the front door, unlocked the deadbolt, and ran around the SUV to the courtyard. He stood in the open with his arms stretched out to the side.

"No!" Palmer, still holding the M4, chased after him. As he lunged for Jaffar, two shots were fired, and a warm liquid sprayed Palmer's face. He pulled Jaffar back behind the SUV as another two shots were fired. Palmer looked at him. Blood was pouring from a wound on his shoulder. Palmer grabbed Jaffar by his good arm and pulled him closer to the front door. That was no spray-and-pray fire from a jihadist automatic weapon—that was the double tap of a trained sniper. He placed Jaffar's hand on the wound and told him to apply pressure. Jaffar's entire body was shaking. The door to the house was slightly ajar, left that way when Palmer ran after Jaffar. He put his hand around Jaffar's free arm. "We're going to make a run for it. We're only a few steps from the door. Are you ready?"

Jaffar nodded his head.

Palmer readied the M4. "I'm going to fire my rifle and provide cover for you. On three, I'll fire the first shot. You run to the door and get inside. I'll cover you. Got it?"

"Yes," he replied, his voice weak.

Palmer peeked around the SUV. Another shot was fired, striking the SUV. Palmer saw the muzzle flash. "Ready?"

"Yes."

"One…two…three." Palmer rose and fired. Jaffar ran to the door. Someone opened the door fully for him and shut it once he was inside, again leaving it slightly ajar. Using the SUV for protection, Palmer stayed low and kept firing until he was inside. The shooter was firing, too, but thankfully no bullets met their mark.

When he got inside, Palmer saw Singleton lying on the floor. His shirt was red with blood. Green had moved him away from the door and was kneeling beside him, trying to find where the blood was coming from. She located wounds on his abdomen and another one on the right side of his neck.

"What the hell happened?" Palmer said, taken aback.

"When he opened the door for you, the shooter shot him," Green said, peeling Singleton's shirt open to better assess the injuries.

"Is it bad?" Singleton ground out, wincing.

"Your heart's beating, and you're talking. You'll survive," Green said bluntly. "That abdominal wound on your side is a through-and-through shot, and your neck…" She grimaced. "Half an inch over and you wouldn't have survived."

Green looked up at Palmer, raising her eyebrows. Both Singleton and Jaffar were lucky to be alive. They both needed medical attention. Singleton was losing blood. So was Jaffar, who was sitting on the floor, holding his shoulder. Palmer examined Jaffar's wound. The bullet had caused a lot of damage. Was Jaffar the intended target? Or was he a target of opportunity?

"Get them farther away from the door and put them in the room where your monitors are," Palmer said, looking at the security guards, who had joined them after the exchange of gunfire.

While the guards were moving Jaffar and Singleton, Palmer spoke to Green. "I'm not certain who they're after."

"I know what you mean," Green said.

"Maybe they were the easy targets. They'll be coming at us soon. Be ready."

"Can we rely on the security guys?"

"We have no choice. You and I will cover this level."

Bullets thumped against the windows and door. The security guards returned, and Palmer told both to return to their positions. Palmer and Green took cover on opposite sides of the ground floor, away from the front door and windows, and positioned themselves to avoid inadvertently shooting each other. Singleton and Jaffar were in the windowless room where the security camera monitors were located. Once everyone was in place, the gunfire stopped.

"It's gone very quiet," Green said. "Maybe they've—"

Palmer heard a sound that he had heard hundreds of times in training and in combat. It was a thump, followed by a whooshing sound. "RPG!"

The letters were barely out of his mouth when the RPG round struck the front door, blowing it away. The detonation caught the SUV on fire. Once it was ablaze, it exploded. Smoke filled the first floor of the house. There was a gaping hole where the front door had been. Palmer shouted to Green, who was getting up from the floor, "You okay?"

"Fine. You?"

"Good. They'll be coming now. Get ready. Stay away from the opening."

Palmer and Green were on the floor, their rifles aimed at the doorway. The explosion had created a fog of smoke and dust, which would be to their benefit. Three armed men rushed through the hole in the wall, firing wildly as they entered the room. Green and Palmer fired, catching the men in a crossfire. They went down in quick succession.

Gunshots could be heard upstairs, but he and Green maintained their positions, prepared for anyone else who might come through the door. No one came. Palmer waited.

"Anyone at the back?" he shouted.

"All clear," a guard yelled in response.

"Upstairs?"

"Clear," the other guard shouted from upstairs.

Sirens could be heard in the distance. Either their backup had arrived, or the neighbors had phoned the police. Either way, the battle was over. Singleton and Jaffar were down. Three tangos were KIA.

———

US Embassy security, medics, and a representative from the deputy chief of mission—the ambassador's second-in-command—arrived first. The gate had been forced open at some point during the attack. Palmer, Green, and the two security guards met them outside. Palmer explained to the DCM what had happened. Knowing that the police were close behind, one of the security men helped the medics take Jaffar and Singleton to one of the vehicles. Jaffar's presence would be difficult to explain to the police. The DCM told Palmer and the others to stow their weapons and stay out of the way. He would speak to the police and anyone else who arrived.

The Islamabad Capital Territory Police and members of Pakistan's National Counter Terrorism Authority got there minutes later. The burning SUV and the lights on the emergency vehicles lit up the night sky. Smoke filled the house.

Palmer and the others stood back while the DCM spoke with law enforcement. It was a master class in de-escalation and diplomacy. He explained that the house was used by the US Embassy as temporary lodging for visitors. The officers looked at each other and laughed. He went on to explain that the house had been attacked and that those present had called for help and defended themselves. He gave the names and embassy roles of those present. The dialogue and negotiation continued for some time, with the DCM doing most of the talking. Eventually, the dead attackers were unceremoniously thrown into the bed of a small pickup truck and taken away.

It was late by the time Palmer and Green called Reynolds and gave him a heads-up. Reynolds said he wanted to see them first thing in the morning. Given his tone, it wasn't a meeting they were looking forward to.

18

ISLAMABAD, PAKISTAN

Green returned to her room around one in the morning. She fell onto her bed and stared at the ceiling, replaying the events of the day over and over in her mind. As mentally and physically exhausting as it had been, she felt an almost guilty twinge of excitement. She and Palmer had survived two assaults, one at the café and one at the safe house. Singleton and Jaffar were wounded but would survive. She had been in precarious situations before, like the day she and Palmer had it out with a terrorist cell in Cape Charles, Virginia. She had suffered a gunshot wound and had spent some time in the hospital. Today was different, both in its duration and intensity.

She got up from the bed and looked in the mirror, hardly recognizing herself. As she took off her clothes to take a shower, she found the piece of paper on which Aaliyah had scribbled her first name and her phone number. She stared at it. Who was this woman? She wasn't Jaffar's sister. He'd confirmed that he didn't have a sister. Was she Pakistani intelligence? There was one way to find out: bait the hook and see if anything bites. Green sent her a text.

Aaliyah, this is Alona Green. We met at your brother's apartment.
The reply was immediate.
Do you have information on Hakeem?
We need to talk. Can we meet?

Aaliyah texted the name and address of an Islamabad restaurant and said she would meet her there at three o'clock the next day. A knowing smile came across Green's face. At that time, between lunch and dinner, the restaurant would not be busy. Was it possible that Aaliyah was an ISI operative? If she was, the restaurant would be one that she had used for meetings in the past. She would arrive fifteen minutes early, and without being asked, the maître d' would seat her at her favorite table, one in a corner or near a rear exit. The waiters and waitresses would know her and know that she tipped well.

She needed to talk to Palmer and knew she couldn't sleep. She took a quick shower, threw on her robe, and went down the hall to his room.

He opened the door in his boxer shorts and a T-shirt and noted what she was wearing. "This isn't a booty call, is it?"

She walked past him into the room. "Of course not. You've been quite clear about our relationship. And please put on a robe."

"Real men don't wear robes. What is it, then?"

"I can't sleep," Green said. "Something's bothering me."

"I'd be shocked if it wasn't. It's been a helluva day," Palmer said. He walked to the kitchenette, took a bottle of scotch from underneath the sink, poured some in two glasses, and handed her one.

She looked at it and at Palmer. "Where did you get this?"

"I never divulge my sources."

Green took a long drink and said, "I've been thinking. Our working theory is that Pakistan's ISI was after Jaffar. He wasn't at the apartment, so they roughed up and killed his roommate, then attacked the café and the safe house. Jaffar thought it was his fault, saying he felt he may have been too assertive in seeking information."

"Right. So, what's bothering you?" Palmer asked.

"The attack at the café and at the safe house. What if they weren't after Jaffar? What if they were after Singleton?"

"Singleton?" Palmer asked with disbelief. "Why would you think that?"

"A couple of reasons, the first of which is Aaliyah," Green said.

"Aaliyah is not Jaffar's sister. Jaffar didn't know her. He said he doesn't have a sister."

"Exactly. When Aaliyah walked into the apartment, she looked at you and me, then her gaze locked onto Singleton, who took an almost imperceptible step back. His eyes widened slightly. I believe they know each other. I could see it in their eyes—Singleton's and hers. What if Aaliyah is ISI? What if she's his girlfriend?"

Palmer rubbed his forehead. "His girlfriend? We know Singleton was in a long-term relationship with a Pakistani woman. He reported that he was dating a local. Our team vetted her and found nothing of concern."

Green had had the relationship lecture during her training. Counterintelligence and foreign intelligence operatives were always at risk of foreign influence or moles. The CIA had a standing policy that required its operatives to report all personal relationships, both friendships and romantic involvements, with foreign nationals who were considered close and in continuing contact. For CIA staff, the guidance was straightforward: Have relationships and marry Americans, or even better, another CIA employee. On a bright note, the CIA did not require employees to report one-night stands.

"If she is deep-cover ISI, she would have had a solid backstory," Green said. "It's the perfect honey trap, using sex for the purpose of gathering intelligence or, in this case, turning a foreign operative into a double agent through sex and then coercion. Her name and identity would have been established and documented even before she met him. If you go into a relationship with the sole intent of intelligence gathering, you better damn well have your fake experience and background documented because they will check you out."

"You would know all about that, Alona. ISI could have identified Singleton and his role. Aaliyah is a beautiful, sophisticated woman. For her to establish a relationship with someone like him, a relatively ordinary-looking man, would have been easy. This would mean that not only is Singleton the mole but also that Aaliyah was his girlfriend and then his handler."

"A piece of cake," Green said. "Make contact, establish a loving relationship, and then milk him for information through coercion. You have to go slow or your mark will get suspicious. The Soviets made it an art form, creating what were called 'sparrow squads.' A female agent is a sparrow, sometimes also called a swallow. A male agent setting a honey trap is a raven. You have to admire her."

"No, I don't," Palmer replied bluntly. "If we can believe Singleton, he broke it off with his girlfriend after he found out he was being transferred. He was returning to the US, so he was of no further use to them. Maybe they wanted to eliminate him before he left."

"That would make sense," Green said. "He had access to all those files and easily could've turned over the names of other assets and agents to Aaliyah—the ones who've since gone missing. But would they really have tortured and killed Jaffar's roommate and attacked the café and safe house just to eliminate one low-level informant? I don't think so. They were after Singleton and us."

"If your theory about Singleton and Aaliyah is true, then Singleton could have told her we were taking his job and, most likely, had a much more clandestine role than our cover jobs. He could have told her that he suspected we were working for JSOC and were Orange. She would have seen it as an opportunity to kill us and him. When the attack at the café failed, they attacked the safe house where all four of us were."

"It had to have been either Singleton or the driver who let them know that we would be at the safe house and who provided the address."

Palmer downed the remainder of his scotch in one gulp. "Singleton told me that he thought we were pushing him out of his job at a time when he was most needed. It is possible that Singleton told Aaliyah who we were, and she told him to set up the meeting. Remember, he asked Reynolds if we could go along. That's how they knew we were at the café. He set up the meeting and told Aaliyah. But if they were going to attack the café, why go after Jaffar at his apartment? Why not wait until all four of us were together there?"

"Maybe their plan was to put Jaffar's body on the street and then kill Singleton and us at the café—kill the spy, and then kill the intelligence officers," Green suggested, fidgeting with the sash of her robe mindlessly. "A lesson to anyone considering working with us."

Palmer swirled his empty glass. "We need credible evidence of his guilt and Aaliyah's role."

Green caught his gaze. "I need to tell you something that you might not like."

"Hold on." He picked up the bottle of scotch and poured more into their glasses. He quaffed his down and leaned back in his chair. "Go ahead."

"I'm meeting with Aaliyah tomorrow." Green said it knowing she was blindsiding him. She had not discussed this with him in advance, and she should have. She was accustomed to working independently and taking action without asking permission or informing anyone. "Before I came over, I texted Aaliyah and said that we needed to talk. She texted the name and address of an Islamabad restaurant. We're meeting there at three o'clock. I did it spontaneously. I should have discussed it with you first."

Palmer leaned forward in his chair, a smile beginning to form. "Well done," he acknowledged calmly. "I'll go with you." When Green frowned, he added, "I'll stay out of sight."

"I'd rather you didn't go at all. If Aaliyah is Pakistani intelligence, there will be advance or protective agents watching her, and she will have described both of us to them. If they spot you, the meeting will be over before it starts."

"You're right. Tomorrow morning, see if you can find the security report from when his girlfriend was vetted."

"Do you know his girlfriend's name?" Green said.

"He never mentioned it."

———

The next morning, Green was at work early. With her top-secret access and computer expertise, she had no trouble locating the digital copy of the security investigation of Singleton's girlfriend. And there it was on the first page: her name, Jasmine Abdolahzadeh, and photographs that the investigator had taken using a zoom lens. She compared it with the photo of Aaliyah on her cell phone that she had taken in Jaffar's apartment. Unless Aaliyah had a twin sister, she and Jasmine were the same person. Green pored over the report. Jasmine Abdolahzadeh was born to an Iranian father and a Pakistani mother. She was five feet six inches tall, slender, with long black hair and a wide smile. She had a degree in international relations from the University of the Punjab in Lahore, Pakistan, and worked as an aide at Pakistan's Ministry of Foreign Affairs. She was single, had never been married, and had no children. As far as could be determined, she had no criminal record, and her only foreign travel was for holidays with her parents or friends. She was a self-described bisexual, and although Pakistan had severe penalties for being gay or lesbian, homosexuality had become more accepted in recent years. ISI would not have been bothered by Aaliyah's sexual preference because she probably used it to their advantage.

Green could not determine whether Abdolahzadeh was her real name and whether her background was true or fabricated. As she had told Palmer, any deep-cover ISI agent would have a well-documented personal and professional history. The investigator tailed her for two weeks and saw nothing out of the ordinary. Singleton was never told of the investigation or the result. However, when he reported that he was dating a foreign national, his superior had counseled him on the risks of being involved with a local. Singleton would have known she would be vetted.

Green took the report to Palmer. She watched his face when he read it and saw the photographs of Jasmine and her cell phone photo she had printed for comparison.

"You were right. Let's go. We need to see Reynolds. Prepare yourself."

"For what?"

Palmer grinned. "You'll find out soon enough."

———⁘———

Palmer and Green had barely entered the office when Reynolds laid into them.

"What the hell happened?" he asked, raising his voice. "First, the body and the shoot-out at the café, plus two unconscious Pakistani nationals. Then, on the same day, a full-on assault at the safe house with three dead Pakistani nationals. Singleton and Jaffar were both wounded, and Jaffar's roommate is dead. The only good news is that Singleton and Jaffar are in stable condition at a secure medical facility and will be released soon."

"And Alona and I are alive," Palmer offered coyly.

Reynolds wasn't amused. "We're moving Jaffar to a safer location, once he is released from the hospital. Singleton's wounds were more serious. He will not be returning to work after he's discharged. He was shaken up by the attacks and wants to pack up and leave as soon as possible."

Palmer and Green gave each other a knowing glance. Surely the reality was that Singleton wanted to get out of Pakistan before ISI killed him or he was arrested by the US. Reynolds might not feel Singleton's survival was good news after they laid out their case.

Palmer nodded. "I know. It's FUBAR, sir. We believe ISI learned that Jaffar was working with US intelligence and went to his apartment. With the deployment of their nuclear weapons imminent, he was a dead man walking. ISI takes no chances. They'd rather kill ten men suspected of working with a foreign government than take the time to identify the one who actually is."

Reynolds's face was turning red. "He's a damn transportation clerk. Why attack the café and safe house? And how the hell did they know you'd be at those locations? You two have some explaining to do."

"Any ID of those men in the photos I sent to you?" Palmer asked.

"Not yet. We should know something soon. They probably were contractors hired for the jobs. ISI wouldn't be so sloppy."

"At the safe house, Jaffar said he believed that the jihadists are planning to steal a nuclear weapon during the deployment," Green said. "He confirmed what Mahinder told us in Srinagar."

"Did he give you anything concrete?"

"No. Just rumors he'd heard."

"Well, that's not worth a damn. We've suspected the deployment for months but have no hard data on the timing." Reynolds paced the room. "The weapons are most vulnerable to theft during deployment, but usually the unmated components are transported separately. Perhaps the urgency justifies sending the components mated."

"What next?" Palmer asked.

"I'll have our other handlers press their contacts regarding current information on weapons deployment and whether there are rumblings about a theft."

"Should we step up surveillance of the nuclear weapon facilities?"

"We already have ongoing discrete surveillance of the bases. However, on a day-to-day basis, hundreds of vehicles, including trucks, come and go. Without knowledge of a specific operation to move the nukes, surveillance is not very productive. Our satellites will be redirected once we have something more concrete."

As Reynolds calmed down, his face returning to a normal color, Palmer glanced at Green in a quick exchange that as good as said, *Ready?*

Green nodded, mouth pressed into a thin line.

It was time to get this over with. "Alona and I have some information we'd like to present, sir. We believe it will answer some of your earlier questions."

Reynolds looked at them, the color already returning to his cheeks. "About what?"

Palmer and Green played tag team, filling him in on their theory regarding the attacks. They saved their findings regarding Singleton's girlfriend for last. Reynolds was quiet throughout, until they presented their findings regarding Aaliyah and Jasmine Abdolahzadeh.

That was when the general sunk into his seat, shook his head, and said quietly, "Singleton's a double agent."

"It seems so, sir," Palmer said.

"No wonder he wants to get out of the country as fast as possible. I'll contact the appropriate people about Singleton."

"Alona has a meeting with Aaliyah—or Jasmine—this afternoon. Do we have your authorization to continue working this angle?"

"Of course," Reynolds said, waving a hand dismissively. "By the way, Singleton wanted you to meet with Dr. Karen Psimas. She's a DIA nuclear weapons security specialist. See my admin. She'll schedule it for you."

On the way out, Palmer and Green shared a knowing glance. One of their remits had been to determine if they had a mole, and they had done it within a few days. Although the initial report of Singleton's relationship and the background check was done before Reynolds came on board, he would likely catch the blowback for having a double agent in his command. The fact that Palmer and Green had identified the mole so quickly would only make matters worse.

19

ISLAMABAD, PAKISTAN

Before meeting with Aaliyah, Green had one more stop—the hospital. It was time to talk to Singleton about his girlfriend and about the encounter with Aaliyah in Jaffar's apartment.

Singleton was sitting relatively upright in his hospital bed and reading a book when Green arrived. His eyes were dark and sunken in his pale face. He looked up from his book when she walked into his room.

"You're looking better than the last time I saw you," she said, forcing a smile.

"By the time I got to the hospital, I'd lost a lot of blood. I'm feeling much better." His brows furrowed. "Why are you here?"

"Seeing how you're doing," she said vaguely, sitting in a chair beside his bed. "And asking a couple of questions."

Singleton's face fell. "I've already been debriefed."

Green got straight to the heart of the matter and the reason for her visit. "Why do you think we were attacked at the café and safe house?

Surely not for Jaffar. You don't assault a café or launch an RPG raid on a safe house just to apprehend or kill a low-level informant."

Singleton closed his book and set it on the table beside the bed. "I think they were out to kill us all. A spy, his handler, and two JSOC special operators, all in one go."

"How did they know who we were and that we were there? Don't answer that." Green took a deep breath and continued. "I've spent a lot of time thinking. So, I'm going to tell you what I believe. Aaliyah, also known as Jasmine Abdolahzadeh, is your former girlfriend and an ISI agent. You recognized her when she walked into Jaffar's apartment. I saw it when your eyes met hers."

"That's ridiculous." He looked paler, drew his legs up slightly, and swiped his hand over a thin sheen of sweat on his upper lip.

"She was vetted after you reported that you were dating a Pakistani national. I've read the report and have seen her photograph. I would have never put it together if we hadn't seen her in the apartment." Before Singleton could even try to respond, she leaned closer and added, "You can't deny it."

Singleton's face went powder white. "I'm not saying anything. I want to see a lawyer."

"I feel sorry for you, Martin. We know this happens—we just never think it will happen to us. We're the smart ones. We recognize when someone is playing us."

Singleton looked down, fiddling with his bedsheet, not answering.

"Did you turn in the Pakistani assets ... the ones who have gone missing lately? What did you tell her about Jake and me?"

"I'm not saying anything," he barked. "Get the hell out of here."

Green shrugged and turned to walk out of his room. She nodded to the two men waiting by the door, who entered the room as she left. She overheard one of them say, "Martin Singleton, you are under arrest for treason against the United States of America."

—◦◦◦—

Green arrived at the restaurant thirty minutes prior to the scheduled time. She noticed a man seated near the entrance, seemingly reading a newspaper, though he distinctly turned his head to look at her when she walked in the door, his eyes taking her in from head to toe.

No matter. Let him look.

Green sat at the bar and ordered a *shikanji*, a traditional nonalcoholic limeade or lemonade drink, which she sipped while pretending to read an e-book in an app on her phone. She was still thinking about her encounter with Singleton. On one hand, she was angered by what he had done; on the other hand, she could see how easily he would have fallen for the beautiful seductress and spy. It was sickening, what Aaliyah had done. She had deceitfully sought out and entered into a romantic relationship with Singleton, a man for whom she probably had little to no feelings. She slowly drew him into her web until he was guilty of spying on his country. Once that happened, he was hers.

Ten minutes after Green arrived, Aaliyah entered the restaurant.

The waiter escorted her to a table near the rear exit and returned with a steaming cup of coffee. She spoke with him briefly, and he nodded. A few other customers were in the restaurant, none seated near her. The man near the entrance glanced up from his paper again, his attention now focused on Aaliyah. He was dressed in casual clothes, wearing a jacket that could conceal a pistol. Aaliyah never made eye contact with him.

Green took her drink, walked over to Aaliyah's table, and sat down.

Aaliyah looked up from her mobile phone. "I saw you when I came in. I thought that was you. What have you found out?"

"Hakeem is well and safe."

"Praise Allah. When can I see him?"

"A couple of things first…" Green sat patiently, waiting for Aaliyah to give her a tell, any indication of guilt or suspicious activity. But she didn't. She was good. "When we told him we met you, he said he didn't have a sister."

"Of course," Aaliyah answered naturally, though her posture seemed to straighten ever so slightly, eyes flaring a bit wider. "He doesn't want to bring me into whatever problem he has gotten himself into. He's older and has always been overly protective. Whatever he's done is very dangerous. Perhaps the blood on the floor was his roommate's, who I fear was beaten, possibly killed."

Green chose not to comment about the fate of Jaffar's roommate. "We know nothing about you, Aaliyah. But I do know about family and love. I saw no trace of shock or fear when you walked into Jaffar's apartment. Who are you?"

Aaliyah took a sip of her coffee and stared out the window, unfocused on the pedestrian traffic while collecting her thoughts. Without turning her head, she cut her eyes toward Green and said, "You know who I am, Alona, or you wouldn't be here."

Green's lips climbed into a half-smile. "Jasmine Abdolahzadeh?"

Her eyes widened slightly, and she paused before responding. "My name is Aaliyah, just Aaliyah."

"No last name?"

Aaliyah ignored the question. "Hakeem Jaffar has committed a treasonous crime and must be brought to justice. If you are hiding him, you too are committing a crime. You might work at the US Embassy, but you are not an administrative employee. You and Jake Palmer are intelligence officers, probably with the CIA, JSOC, or some other secretive American intelligence service. So many US intelligence agencies, I cannot keep them straight."

The waiter brought Green a cup of coffee, even though she had not ordered one, and set it on the table. Right. As though she'd take that bait. Green wasn't stupid, so she pushed the coffee out of reach, ignoring it.

"And what are you?" Green pressed. "Pakistani intelligence—ISI?"

"It doesn't matter who I work for. You are holding a citizen of Pakistan who is currently wanted for treason."

She made a valid point. That was exactly what they were doing. Aaliyah could get Pakistan's Ministry of Foreign Affairs involved and make an international issue of it. That would open a can of worms. There was only one way to find out.

"You're right. We are holding Hakeem for his protection. Hakeem's roommate was indeed abducted and killed. Hakeem fears he will meet the same fate. Was ISI responsible? Were *you* responsible?"

Aaliyah huffed but didn't respond.

"Pakistan is preparing to deploy its nuclear arsenal."

"That is no secret," Aaliyah said. "Anyone reading the newspaper would know that."

"The intelligence we've gathered indicates an attempt will be made to divert one or more nuclear devices during the deployment. Are you aware of this? Are you doing anything to prevent it? If your allegiance is with Pakistan, you will help us."

"Someone is always threatening to steal a nuclear weapon. It cannot happen. Our security is too tight, and our command-and-control procedure is impossible to override. Do you have any definitive proof, or are you relying on rumors and innuendos?"

"Are you Martin Singleton's girlfriend, Jasmine Abdolahzadeh?" Green knew the truth but wanted to see how Aaliyah responded.

"Your colleague?" She laughed. "You're crazy. I met him for the first time at Jaffar's apartment. He was surprised to see me, just as you were. That's all."

Green moved closer to Aaliyah and whispered, "I saw the look on his face when you walked into the apartment. The two of you know each other. I'm positive of that. Since then, I've seen the photographs of Jasmine, taken when we vetted her after Singleton informed his director that he was in a relationship with a Pakistani. Are you aware that Singleton was shot in an attack on a safe house in Islamabad? He's in the hospital."

Aaliyah slid her elbows from the table and sat up a little straighter. "You and I are a lot alike, Alona."

"We're nothing alike."

"You've used your body and intellect to get what you wanted personally and professionally. No different than me." Aaliyah paused and in a low, alluring voice said, "You are a beautiful woman. Even in your anger, I am attracted to you."

Green had never been with a woman. However, with Aaliyah's eyes locked on hers as they had in Jaffar's apartment, she felt something. Not sexual attraction—rather a feeling that, under much different circumstances, they could have been friends, worked out together, had drinks after work. Aaliyah was intelligent, confident, and strong, traits that to Green were more attractive than her flawless beauty.

Green took a breath before proceeding and leaned forward. "I may have used my feminine wiles to get what I wanted and needed. Most women do, to some extent. But I've never entered into a romantic relationship, much less a sexual one, to achieve a goal of any kind. Martin loved you. Hell, in spite of it all, he may still love you."

"He's being transferred and leaving the country."

"So, you called in a hit on him. That's not a question."

"You and I should work together. We could accomplish great things. What a team we would make, professionally and personally. Can you imagine? But first, you must turn over Hakeem Jaffar."

"Why is Jaffar so important? He's a transportation clerk."

"Whether he's a general or a clerk, he's a traitor. There are no degrees of betrayal."

"We're not giving you Jaffar. And by the way, Singleton was arrested this morning."

Aaliyah didn't flinch at the news of his arrest. Instead, she leaned over and placed her hand on top of Green's, squeezing it softly. "Be careful, Alona. Islamabad is a very dangerous place."

Before Green could ask her if that was a threat, Aaliyah stood and walked out of the restaurant.

20

US EMBASSY COMPOUND ISLAMABAD, PAKISTAN

Palmer was up and at the office early the next morning. Something was gnawing at his gut. Nothing specific, only a familiar feeling, one he got when things were about to get squirrelly. He reflected on what Winston Churchill once said: "We sleep safely at night because rough men stand ready to visit violence on those who would harm us." In today's world, it was patriotic men and women who stood ready to prevent those with evil intentions from carrying out their missions.

Green arrived at the embassy about an hour after Palmer and, over coffee, filled him in on her conversations with Singleton and Aaliyah.

"Goes to show you the extremes to which Pakistan's ISI will go," Palmer said. "Part of me feels sorry for Singleton. His life is over. The other part of me is angry with him. If he is in any way responsible for the deaths of our Pakistani assets, he'll spend the rest of his life in prison."

"How about Aaliyah?"

"As morally repugnant as it is, she was doing her job."

After coffee, they left for the meeting with Dr. Karen Psimas. Her office was located in the building adjacent to theirs. On the way there, Green said, "I did some research last night when I got back to the apartment. Psimas is a West Point graduate. She has two brothers who are doctors and one who was an Air Force pilot. After leaving the Army, she received her doctorate at the University of California, Berkeley, one of the top nuclear engineering schools in the world. Quite an accomplishment for someone whose grandfather immigrated from Greece with little more than the clothes on his back. She's the best we have regarding nuclear weapon security and the human intelligence related to it."

"How many PhD nuclear engineers work in human intelligence analysis?" Palmer said with a mirthless laugh. "That has to be a very elite club."

"She's probably the sole member," Green said. "From what I can tell, she's in high demand. She's here for only a couple more weeks before she returns to Washington."

"Single or married?"

Green smirked. "What difference does that make? Aren't you already spoken for?"

"Just curious. That's all."

"She's single."

Psimas stood when Palmer and Green arrived, taking off her black-rimmed glasses and setting them beside her laptop in a cubicle. Palmer and Green introduced themselves.

Psimas, who appeared to be in her mid-thirties, was wearing black pants and a crisp, white, long-sleeved blouse. She was about five feet, eight inches tall and slender. She had shoulder-length, dark-brown, wavy hair.

With her head cocked to one side, Psimas said, "Let's go to one of the conference rooms where we can talk in private."

They followed her to a small room with a table and six chairs. A blank whiteboard was on the wall at the far end of the room.

"General Reynolds said that you are only here for a couple more weeks," Palmer began, taking a seat at the table. "Where are you based?"

"Washington, although I don't spend much time there. Using videoconferencing, teleconferencing, satellite imagery, and intelligence reports, I could work from anywhere in the world, and that's fantastic. But in a rapidly evolving situation like this Pakistan-India conflict, where the stakes are high, the eight-hour time difference can be problematic. With a potential nuclear holocaust on the horizon, there's no substitute for looking someone in the eye."

"Roger that," Palmer said.

Green settled into the seat next to him. "The deployment of Pakistan's nuclear weapons is imminent. Our sources, including one who works in the transportation department at Wah Cantonment Ordnance Complex, believe it will happen within days."

"Will the deployment be enough of a deterrent, or do they intend to use their nuclear weapons?" Palmer asked.

Psimas shook her head and looked at Green, then at Palmer. "Deployment and use are two very different scenarios. India's air attack on an alleged terrorist base in Pakistan significantly raised the risk of an armed conflict. Based on the intelligence analyses I see and what you've told me, Pakistan will deploy their nuclear arsenal within the next couple of days."

"Nothing we can do to stop it," Palmer said.

"A diplomatic solution seems unlikely at this point," Psimas responded. "If Indian forces advance into Pakistan, Pakistan will respond with conventional weapons and tactical nuclear weapons. And if we know Pakistan will begin deployment, you can bet India knows it, too. The US has no military role in this conflict. The weapons are Pakistan's to use as they deem necessary. Even if they have no intention to use them, deployment sends a message to India that they are serious about defending their country. This is an international diplomatic crisis because deployed nuclear weapons exponentially increase the risk of an unintentional or accidental nuclear war."

Palmer nodded slowly. "How long would it take Pakistan to assemble and deploy their nukes?"

"Short answer? Probably two to three days. Pakistan has multiple protocols for assembly of the components and deployment. The components are stored in separate locations. It's an intricate, orchestrated dance of vehicles, technicians, soldiers, and weaponry. According to what they tell us, the standard procedure is to transfer the individual, unmated components—the fissile core and the weapon frame—in different vehicles. By shipping them unmated, if terrorists intercept a shipment, they would be unable to create a fissionable warhead."

"I'm lost already. Fissile core and weapon frame?" Green echoed, brows raised.

"I'll reduce this to the simplest terms. Think of a missile sitting in a silo, ready to launch. There are three components. First is the weapon frame. That is the warhead that sits atop the missile."

"Got it."

"Second is the fissile core inside the weapon frame or warhead. It's typically spherical and smaller than you would think, like a softball, and composed of highly enriched uranium 235 or plutonium 239, surrounded by a reflector, which is in turn surrounded by a highly explosive chemical."

"I see," said Green.

"And third is the missile itself. That's the delivery system or device. Because there is an imperative to deploy quickly, each device will be moved partially mated—meaning the warhead's fissile core and weapon frame will be moved in the same container. Only the delivery system will be moved separately if it's not already in place."

"Other than missiles, what delivery system capability does Pakistan have?" Green asked.

"Torpedoes, artillery shells, bombs. You name it and they have it at their disposal. Any device that can deliver large nonnuclear ordnance can be used to deliver a nuclear weapon."

"How are the components transported?" Palmer asked.

"Although the Pakistanis deny they do it, the moves are often made in unmarked civilian trucks and containers with minimum security. They believe a convoy of military vehicles would only announce to everyone what was happening and increase the risk of an attack."

"Unmarked civilian trucks?" Green repeated.

"Well, to be honest, the US moves its nuclear weapons around in unmarked trucks as well, although those trucks are specifically designed for that purpose. I suspect Pakistan's trucks will be no different than what you would encounter on a major motorway."

"Once a nuke is deployed, what security measures are in place for launching or detonating it—like the nuclear football that goes wherever our president goes?" Palmer asked.

"That's called the control framework. Pakistan's is different than ours. It may surprise you that we don't know what they actually use," Psimas said. "They don't share that information with us, even though we've paid them hundreds of millions of dollars to enhance the security of their nuclear devices. All US nuclear devices have Permissive Action Links, or PALs, which vary in type and complexity. The early ones were based on mechanical combination locks, but now they require complex digital codes. The correct codes must be entered before the device can be detonated. We offered our PAL technology to increase security, but Pakistan insisted on using their own. They believe that if they use ours, we would secretly install kill switches by which we could stop detonation."

Palmer laughed. "And we probably would."

"They might also have other security measures, like environmental sensing triggers that detonate the nuclear weapon at preset altitude, for example."

Palmer leaned back in his chair and crossed his arms over his chest. "To sum it up, then: based on our best intelligence, Pakistan will deploy their nuclear weapons—at least some of them—within the next couple of days, but we don't know what protocol they will use to move them or what security measures will be taken."

"Affirmative," said Psimas. "And we do not know how many will be deployed. It's unlikely they would deploy all of them."

"Lord help us." Palmer rolled his eyes and leaned forward. "One final question. Does the US have plans to secure Pakistan's nuclear arsenal in the event of a coup or other significant disruption in government?"

Psimas smiled. "I'm not at liberty to comment on that, Mr. Palmer. As an ex-Navy SEAL, I expect you have some insight on that. Iran, Russia, China, ISIS, the Taliban, Al-Qaeda, and numerous terrorist organizations top a long list of state and nonstate actors that I'm certain have contingency plans in the event of that happening. Win or lose, a nuclear war would have a destabilizing effect on Pakistan's government and military, if not on the entire region.

21

ISLAMABAD, PAKISTAN

The next morning, multiple US intelligence sources confirmed that Pakistan's deployment of its nuclear weapons would begin that night. The US reconnaissance satellites would be redirected from their standard orbits and made available as needed.

Pakistan was doing nothing illegal or even unethical. The weapons were theirs, and they had the right to defend themselves. The US would not interfere with the movement, deployment, or even use of the weapons. The US ambassadors to Pakistan and India, as well as the US Secretary of State, were working to negotiate a cease-fire agreement. Thus far, neither country was budging.

Except for an all-out nuclear war between Pakistan and India, a limited nuclear exchange would not directly impact the US; however, it would impact US facilities and personnel in Pakistan and was, therefore, a national security issue. The more serious concern was that Pakistan's weapons might fall into the wrong hands.

That afternoon, Palmer and Green got word that General Reynolds wanted to see them. And so, once again, they made their way to his office, gathering around his mahogany desk. The news wasn't going to be good if the general's already-reddening complexion was any indication. Palmer took a deep breath, steeling himself for what was to come.

"Martin Singleton is dead," Reynolds said abruptly.

For the first time in a long while, Palmer found himself genuinely shocked.

"Dead?" Green gasped. "How? When?"

"We don't know how. He was found dead in his room last night. Our medical examiner will conduct an autopsy and try to determine the cause of death."

"I just saw him." Green's eyes found Palmer's, as though searching for answers. "He was placed under arrest after I left and was supposed to be guarded until he was discharged from the hospital and moved to a US military brig."

"Investigators reviewed security camera footage. A blond woman of average height, wearing gray slacks and a striped blouse, visited him before his death. She was careful to avoid looking directly at the cameras in the hallways and in his room. The soldier who was standing guard outside the door said she told him she was Singleton's girlfriend. He checked with Singleton, who said it was okay for her to visit him. The exchange between Singleton and the woman appeared cordial, although there was no audio, so we don't know what was actually said."

"Aaliyah," Green said with certainty. "I'd bet my life on it."

"She doesn't have blond hair," Palmer noted.

"She was in disguise—wig, colored contacts, probably wearing American-style clothes."

Reynolds continued, "She was only in the room for a short period of time. When she got up to leave, she hugged him. After she left, he drank from a glass of water."

Green balked. "She either poisoned him or facilitated his suicide with a poison pill. If he took the pill, he would die peacefully. If he didn't, he'd be convicted as a traitor and spend the rest of his life in prison."

"Possible." The general sighed. "When she hugged him, there was a point where neither of their hands were visible. We'll know more when we get the autopsy report."

"I think she gave him a choice," Palmer interjected. "It may have been his decision to take the pill, if there was one."

"On to a more pressing topic," Reynolds went on, "the Department of State and the US Embassy are preparing additional communications for US citizens. The earlier communications had been limited to US government personnel. I expect these will be much broader, along the lines of increased tension in the region with a recommendation as to who needs to leave the country. We're not certain how many American civilians are in Pakistan, but the estimate is in the thousands. Evacuating them will be a massive undertaking."

"Can't the US say that Pakistan is deploying their nuclear weapons, and by doing so, there is an increased potential for a nuclear war between Pakistan and India?" Green asked. "Surely the international news media will speculate what's going on and may even have sources to confirm the deployment."

"We can't control the media," Reynolds said, combing his fingers through his thinning gray hair. "I just pray that cooler heads will prevail. Prepare for a long night."

22

DERA GHAZI KHAN NUCLEAR FACILITY PAKISTAN

The highly secretive military base at Dera Ghazi Khan had for years been the subject of speculation regarding its purpose. Initially, it was thought to be a uranium dioxide conversion and production facility that produced fuel rods for reactors, which in turn produced weaponizable isotopes. However, based on recent expansion of the base and satellite surveillance over time, the US intelligence community believed that it was also a nuclear weapons storage facility—which it was.

The Dera Ghazi Khan base commander received the confirmation order to transfer their nuclear armament. He gathered his senior staff officers and announced the transfer protocol they would use. His men were competent in their knowledge of all of the transfer protocols and could recite each of them without referring to the manual. They knew their role and the roles of the men in their charge. They had been trained, had practiced mock transfers, and had participated in actual small-scale transfers. There was zero tolerance for error. Regardless, the base commander reviewed the procedures for the selected protocol with them. The warheads and their fissile cores would be transferred mated. When the commander finished, he paused, looked them each in the eye, and gave the order to initiate the transfer. The men scrambled from the room, and the order was quickly passed down the line. Within minutes, the process was underway.

To avoid the appearance of a large number of escorted military trucks and containers leaving the military base at DG Khan, the deployment of the nuclear warheads would be spread over two days, using civilian trucks hauling containers that were similar to those that delivered supplies to the base. Regardless, the increased movement of vehicles and equipment to and from Pakistani military bases would draw the attention of many people.

—◦◦◦—

Raul Ahmadi was already behind the wheel of an eighteen-wheel tractor trailer at the DG Khan base when a young man named Nahib stepped up onto the truck's running board and got into the passenger seat. Both he and Ahmadi wore civilian work clothes and carried holstered pistols at their waists. An assault rifle and a shotgun lay between them on the floor of the truck.

"Who are you? Where's Rajab?" Ahmadi asked firmly, unable to hide his surprise.

"A last-minute change. I was told to ride with you, someone who is more experienced, as part of my training."

"Training is done during drills. This is not a drill," Ahmadi said, unable to hide his anger.

"And I'm not a green recruit. Whatever arises, I can handle myself," Nahib said confidently.

The operation had just begun, and already there was a problem. Was this only the first of many to come? Ahmadi's mind whirled, considering the potential negative implications of the plan. They had a long drive ahead of them—plenty of time to talk to this man and decide what action, if any, he should take.

"Do your wife and family know where you're going?" Ahmadi asked.

"No wife. My family is in Peshawar. They only know I'm serving my country and based here. They know nothing about what I actually do."

"Better that way," Ahmadi said. "Otherwise, they worry and tell you to find a different job. That's what families do."

Ahmadi drove the truck into position behind the others and waited for them to load the shipping container onto his truck. To pass the time while they waited, he quizzed Nahib on the weapons transfer procedure. Try as he might to catch Nahib giving an incorrect answer, Nahib correctly answered every question Ahmadi threw at him. After the container was secured on the truck, Ahmadi drove to a weigh station where the total weight of the truck, trailer, container, and its contents was recorded.

Ahmadi got out of the vehicle, noted the weight and lock number, and then signed a form accepting the deadly cargo. He drove toward the exit gate, stuck his head out the window, and confirmed that his security detail, in an enclosed armored vehicle, had fallen in behind him. The trucks and their security vehicles lined up past the weigh station gate. They would depart the base at thirty-minute intervals, drawing as little attention as possible to the operation. It was all part of a procedure that had been rehearsed many times before. Only this time was different. This was not a drill.

"Where to tonight, Raul?" Nahib inquired.

Ahmadi handed him a sealed brown envelope that had been given to him when he accepted the container and its contents. Nahib tore it open and extracted a sheet of paper. He read their destination aloud: "The Masroor Air Force base in Karachi. That's a long drive."

"One of the longest," Ahmadi said. "Ten hours, and that is if we don't encounter any traffic problems." *Karachi, just as planned*, thought Ahmadi.

"There are always traffic problems," Nahib commented.

Ahmadi drove the truck to the checkpoint at the gate. A Strategic Plans Division representative walked around the vehicle with his clipboard for a final check before he signed off on the transfer papers and handed them to him. He exited the gate with the security vehicle close behind him. Once they were on the highway, it would follow a quarter-mile behind the truck.

"Get some sleep," Ahmadi said. "You can relieve me later when we make our rest stop, the only one we're allowed. Hope you took a piss before we left."

They had only driven several miles before Nahib fell asleep, his head resting against the window and his chest rising and falling. Assured that Nahib was asleep, Ahmadi tapped out a coded text to Colonel Wazir Basim Ashkani, General Sarkis's aide, on the burner phone he had purchased the week before and pressed send.

—◆◆◆—

Raul Ahmadi was driving on Indus Highway, the N-55, where he would continue for two hundred miles. At 9:30 p.m., only a few vehicles were on this section of the dark road. In the large side mirror, he could see the headlights of the security vehicle behind him. Nahib was sound asleep, his mouth open, and snoring lightly. In spite of the hour, Ahmadi could not have been more awake if he had been on amphetamines. He was a Pakistani Army soldier in good standing, he had a beautiful wife and two children at home who were waiting for him to return from his assignment, and the young, eager soldier beside him had a life full of promise ahead of him.

It was all about to change.

A half-mile ahead, a truck identical to the one Ahmadi was driving was parked on the roadside. Ahmadi slowed down. About a quarter of a mile from the other one, he reached for the switch that controlled the truck's headlights and taillights and flashed them off and on twice. He leaned toward the driver's-side window so he could see the security vehicle in the side mirror.

Ahead, the parked truck's lights flashed twice, as did the security vehicle's lights behind him. Ahmadi pulled off the road and stopped alongside the truck and shipping container, both identical to his.

Nahib stirred and yawned. "Why have we stopped? Do you want me to drive?"

"I am sorry, Nahib," Ahmadi said, pointing his pistol at him. "You seem like a good man."

Nahib was wide awake now. He pushed his body against the door and held up his hands in a futile attempt to put distance between himself and Ahmadi. "What are you doing?"

Ahmadi shot Nahib twice in the chest. The impact of the bullets pushed Nahib against the door. His body slumped forward, and he exhaled his last breath.

Ahmadi, his ears ringing from the gunshots within the confined space of the truck's cab, reached over and opened the passenger door. He swiveled in his seat and, using both his feet, shoved Nahib's body out of the truck and onto the ground.

The security vehicle pulled in behind the two trucks and stopped. Ahmadi moved quickly. The progress of the trucks that left the base was being monitored. Any stop of more than a few minutes would arouse suspicion. He wiped Nahib's blood from the seat with a towel and threw it on Nahib's body.

"Take him away from the road," Ahmadi shouted to the men from the other truck, who were standing over the bloodied body. "Strip him naked and cover him with sand."

Ahmadi climbed on top of the cab, making his way onto the top of the shipping container. He rushed to the back and unfastened the GPS device, then ran back to the front of the container, jumped down onto the cab, and slid off onto the ground. He grabbed a folder from inside the truck and rushed over to the other truck where he repeated the process, this time affixing the GPS to the top of an identical container. Meanwhile, one of the men switched the trucks' license plates.

The driver of the other truck and one of the security men dragged Nahib's naked body away from the road and covered it with sand. They returned with Nahib's clothes and used them to wipe his blood from the cab of the truck before stuffing them behind the passenger seat.

All of the men were due back at the base in Dera Ghazi Khan in two days. But when Ahmadi received advance notice that the transfer would be made, he told each of the men to request a few days' leave following the transfer. Because they came from different departments, the requests would not raise suspicion. Eventually, however, when they did not return to the base after their leave, the search for them would begin.

One more task needed to be done before Ahmadi could be on the road again. The truck that had been waiting needed a security seal on the container's doors, and it had to match the one on the container of the truck that had left the DGK base with the nuclear weapons. The seals, which looked similar to zip ties, were numbered indicative seals, meaning that they were in place to demonstrate entry into the container, not prevent it. One of the men brought over the illegal security seal kit. Ahmadi watched without speaking as he created and attached an exact copy of the original seal on his container to the other container.

Once completed, Ahmadi and one of the security men got into the cab of the second truck, which now had the GPS device on the top of the container. Based on his past experience, the SPD representative and guard at the base's gate would not have a checklist of each soldier in the truck and security vehicle. They would only glance at their military IDs.

He drove away first, with his security vehicle staying enough behind so as to not look like a military escort vehicle. The truck that had left the base at Dera Ghazi Khan with the nuclear weapons inside the container would wait until Ahmadi and the security vehicle were well out of sight before pulling away. If all went well, the soldiers would meet up again the next day.

23

ISLAMABAD, PAKISTAN

Palmer and Green had just finished a late dinner when Reynolds called, telling them to get to the embassy and be prepared to leave ASAP. They left without finishing their meals and were standing in his office twenty minutes later.

"What's up, sir?" Palmer asked.

"Satellite surveillance has identified a target for investigation. On a typical day or night, our reconnaissance satellites fly prearranged routes over areas of interest. The National Reconnaissance Office—a US intelligence agency headquartered in Chantilly, Virginia—operates the satellites that conduct intelligence activity. Orbits are adjusted depending on national security priorities. Tonight, at our request, they've directed available satellites to pass over a few of Pakistan's nuclear weapons facilities. We've been monitoring the feeds and have noted a large number of trucks and light armored vehicles, probably security, staging at those bases. Those trucks and vehicles have been leaving the bases at regular, timed intervals."

"The deployment," Green said.

"Correct. The orbiting KH-12 satellites are always moving. As a result, they cover areas that are of interest to us, and in between, they fly over areas that are of little concern. But a couple of hours ago, intelligence spotted two trucks and what looked like one of the armored security vehicles that had pulled off the road in an isolated section of the N-55 highway, near Hyderabad in southwest Pakistan."

Reynolds handed them several black-and-white photographs.

Palmer and Green took a closer look. The photos were a little grainy because they had been taken with night vision technology. Each included a date and the Greenwich Mean Time stamp as well as the longitude and latitude coordinates of the location. In most of the photographs, the two trucks were parked beside each other, with several individuals standing outside the vehicles. In the last couple of images, the trucks and the light armored vehicle were moving back onto the highway.

"Do we know if they were part of the deployment?" Green asked.

"We don't know," Reynolds said. "The trucks appear to be civilian. We have no way of confirming whether they were part of the transfer or not. They were not monitored prior to being seen on the side of the road. It could simply be that a truck broke down and another stopped to help or that it's a popular spot to stop and take a piss. However, if one or both trucks are part of the transfer, the question of why they stopped becomes critical. The N-55 is the highway they would take to go from their base in Dera Ghazi Khan to the military facility at Karachi."

"We'll check it out," Palmer said, eager to do something other than sit and wait.

"The vehicles are gone, but perhaps there are some clues. It's a long drive. I've requested a helicopter to pick you up from the roof of the embassy and take you there. See what, if anything, you can find. You'll need this." Reynolds handed them a satellite phone. "The Pakistani military and ISI will probably track any helicopter leaving here now that the deployment has begun. Keep your time on the ground to an absolute minimum."

24

N-55 HIGHWAY
SOUTHWEST PAKISTAN

The helicopter lifted off the embassy roof and flew on a southwest course toward Hyderabad, using the coordinates of the location where the trucks had stopped. The helicopter had no military markings, and the pilot and crew were not wearing military uniforms. When they neared the location and began their descent, Palmer asked the pilot to touch down well off the road so as not to attract any attention and to not disturb the site with the wash of the rotor blades.

The pilot slowed, announcing that they were approaching the destination. Palmer looked out as the helicopter circled a thousand feet over the location. At that hour, few vehicles were on the road. If something sketchy had transpired, he saw why those involved had selected this isolated part of the highway with no lights within miles.

The helicopter descended fast, landing on an open area on the north side of the highway, approximately a quarter mile from the spot where the truck had parked. The pilot turned off the lights and shut down the engine. The crewman handed Palmer a couple of flashlights. "You may need these."

"Thanks. We'll be back in under thirty minutes. If not, start it up and come get us."

Palmer and Green jumped out and made their way toward the location, careful not to disturb any evidence they came across.

When they arrived at the highway, they located the spot where the trucks and security vehicle had pulled off the road. The tread marks were hard to miss, and there were numerous footprints between where the two vehicles had been parked.

"Something, or someone, was dragged from the truck parked closer to the highway." Green pointed her flashlight at what appeared to be skid marks.

Palmer nodded. "There are footprints leading away from the road and coming back."

They followed the path, swinging their flashlights in a wide arc in front of them.

"I've got something," Green said a moment later.

Palmer went over and knelt down. He put his finger on a wet spot in the sand and rubbed the liquid between his thumb and forefinger. "Blood. Still wet."

"Maybe someone was injured, and they stopped to administer first aid," Green reasoned. "Or maybe one of the trucks hit a large animal."

"They wouldn't drag an animal this far from the road. And they wouldn't drag a person away from the highway to administer first aid."

They walked into the darkness, away from the road, following the footprints in the sand and seeing more blood along the way.

"Over here," Palmer shouted.

Green hustled over. About fifty yards from where they had first seen the drag marks, in an otherwise flat area, there was a mound in the sand. It was only slightly raised, about five or six feet long and about a foot or two in height, leaving no doubt in their minds as to what they had found.

Palmer and Green exchanged a brief glance. They got on their knees and used their hands to rake the sand away, careful not to disturb or damage any evidence, keeping their flashlights off. It only took a few brushes of the sand to confirm what they suspected. A body.

Palmer stood up, sighing. "Whoever did this was in a hurry. Instead of digging a proper grave, they used just enough sand to cover the body."

They brushed away more sand, identifying the body as male. The victim, who couldn't have been older than in his mid-twenties, had two gunshot wounds to his chest.

Green's brows pinched. "He's naked."

"Why would they strip him before burying him?" Palmer asked, looking to Green for her assessment.

"To conceal his identity or delay identification?" she suggested, shrugging slightly.

"What type of clothing would tell you where to start looking?"

"Some type of uniform, like a soldier or policeman," she said. "Shot twice and buried in a hurry … What should we do?"

"Other than report it to Reynolds, I see little upside to doing anything," Palmer said. "It would be impossible to explain to the Pakistanis how we happened to stumble across a body with two gunshot wounds buried a hundred yards off the road this far from Islamabad. Although it looks suspicious, we have no evidence that either of the two trucks or the security vehicle was involved in the deployment of nukes. This man's death could be totally unrelated."

"Someone murdered him and buried his body on the side of the road. And it occurred on the night of the deployment."

"All circumstantial."

Palmer pulled out his cell phone and took several photos of the body.

"Another body, more photos," Green said, sighing. "Something tells me this won't be the last."

They heard a helicopter in the distance and saw its lights. It was headed toward them.

"Crap. Let's get out of here," Palmer said. "Now!"

The pilot had also spotted the approaching helicopter and was ready to take off when Palmer and Green arrived, having sprinted back to the chopper. Once airborne, they saw the other helicopter touch down where they had been. Palmer asked the pilot to connect him to General Reynolds. He told Reynolds what they had discovered and told him about the other chopper.

"I don't like it," Palmer told him. "Someone murdered this man, stripped him naked, and buried his body off the side of the road."

"Agreed," said Reynolds. "Let's assume worst-case scenario for a moment and say a nuclear device has been stolen. What chance would we have of finding it if we don't have the cooperation of the Pakistani military or ISI? By now, it could be in a truck headed for the Iranian border, or on a cargo ship or airplane headed God knows where. Whoever was in the helicopter you spotted probably found the body and is in the process of identifying it. I want you back here while we decide how and what to communicate to the Pakistanis and how to proceed. There are limitations on what we can do on our own."

"The trucks will blend in with other trucks on the motorway that look exactly the same," Palmer said. "The chances of locating either of them is extremely low. We need to do something. I'll send you the photos of the body."

"There's Karachi Port and Port Qasim about fifty kilometers away. Together they account for 90 percent of ship traffic in and out of Pakistan. The ports are about eight hundred kilometers from the Iranian border, which is only several hundred miles from Iran's major port in Bandar Abbas. Tell the pilot to take Green to Jinnah International

Airport in Karachi, then bring you here. Someone will meet her at the airport."

"I'm not leaving Alona."

"That's not a request, Palmer."

25

MASROOR AIR FORCE BASE KARACHI, PAKISTAN

Karachi, Pakistan, a city of fifteen million people, was the capital of the Sindh province and one of the largest cities in the world. Set on the north shore of the Arabian Sea, Karachi was home to several military installations of Pakistan's armed services, including six military cantonments that served as military bases and residential establishments. Raul Ahmadi arrived at the Masroor Air Force Base in Karachi within the small window of time in which he was expected. The main gate loomed ahead in the morning haze. The base was the largest air base operated by Pakistan's Air Force with F-16 nuclear-capable fighter jets. Inside a high-security area of the base was an underground nuclear weapon storage facility. Only those who were directly involved in the deployment would be aware that the deployment was underway.

Ahmadi took a deep breath and exhaled. The next twenty-four hours were critical. If the theft of the nuclear weapons were to be discovered at any point during that time, the entire region would be shut down, and the military would be placed on high alert. The imperative was getting the weapons out of the country before that happened.

Regret gnawed at Ahmadi's gut. He couldn't stop thinking about Nahib, the whites of the young man's eyes as he realized he was going to die. He could still feel the kick of the firearm, still smell Nahib's freshly spilled blood. He had killed many, but this one was different. Nahib was an innocent and seemed like a good enough kid, but there was no alternative. He would not have gone along with the plan. Ahmadi's orders were clear: Kill anyone that threatens the mission, no matter how trivial their offense may seem, no matter how well you know them. No rules of engagement applied. Nahib had no wife to wonder where he was, and his family lived in Peshawar. But one thing was bothering him. Nahib had not requested time off after the deployment as the other members of Ahmadi's team had. That could be problematic, but he hoped Nahib's commander wouldn't consider him an unauthorized absence for at least a day or two.

Ahmadi downshifted into a lower gear and let out the clutch, slowing the truck. As he approached the gate, he checked the side mirror. The security vehicle was behind him. He was no stranger to this base. In the past, he had moved equipment, and on rare occasions, warheads, to and from here. Most of the base security personnel knew him and waved him through after a cursory check and some banter about sports, the weather, or a few derogatory quips about life in the Pakistani Army. As was the case in all nuclear weapon transfers, a uniformed Strategic Plans Division inspector was waiting beside the base security post at the entrance.

Ahmadi leaned toward the windshield and squinted his eyes. He recognized the soldier on duty at the security gate but did not recognize the SPD representative. He turned to the man in the passenger seat and made the sign of a pistol with his lowered right hand. The man drew his pistol from his holster and screwed a silencer onto the barrel before chambering a round and sliding it on the seat until it rested against Ahmadi's leg. Ahmadi lowered the window and stuck his head outside into the cold morning air. He smiled at the soldier he recognized but received no smile in return, only an almost undetectable shake of the head.

Ahmadi stated his name and rank and flashed his ID and that of the soldier riding with him. He handed the folder containing the paperwork for the warheads and truck to the SPD representative. His nametag read Abu al-Fadl Sultan. Sultan took the file and flipped through it. He looked at Ahmadi and then at an electronic tablet he was holding in his hand.

"We've been expecting you," the SPD representative said. "You're late."

Ahmadi stuck his head out the window a little farther. "Only minutes. It's a long drive. I had to stop for a bathroom break. Hope you have some hot coffee and breakfast. I'm starving," Ahmadi added with a wide smile. He did not anticipate any issues. If any unresolvable problem arose, Ahmadi would kill the two men and run to the security vehicle. Escaping with the security detail would be their only hope. If they were captured, they would be tortured. At some point—everyone's tolerance for torture was different—they would tell them everything, and, if they survived the torture, death was a certainty. Ultimately, they had no real choice because it was better to die quickly in an attempt to escape than to die slowly and painfully at the hands of the ISI interrogators.

The soldier who was standing behind Sultan looked at Ahmadi and shrugged. Without responding to Ahmadi's mention of coffee and breakfast, Sultan and the soldier walked to the back of the truck. Ahmadi drummed on the steering wheel with the fingers of his left hand and rested his right hand on the pistol.

Sultan was in charge of the situation, and he was following the required process to the letter. He had a boyish look about him that led

Ahmadi to believe that he was new to the role and doing everything possible not to screw up this assignment. His job was to confirm the identity of the driver, inspect the integrity of the locked doors, verify the identification number on the security tags, and check the truck's and trailer's license plate numbers, ensuring they were identical to those on the manifest for the truck and trailer that left the base in Dera Ghazi Khan. The next morning, a technical inspection team, including a nuclear weapons expert, would open the containers and check the nuclear weapons against the transfer inventory and confirm there was no sign of damage before supervising the movement of the devices from the containers.

Ahmadi looked in the side mirror. Sultan and the guard were checking the military identifications of the men in the security vehicle behind him. Sultan had no checklist of each individual member of the team. He was only confirming they were Pakistani military, just as would be done for anyone coming onto the base who were not assigned there.

Ahmadi checked the side mirrors again. Sultan and the guard had disappeared behind the truck. After a few minutes, he saw them walk back from the rear of the vehicle. They were talking and shaking their heads. They came back to the driver's side, looking very disturbed.

The soldier looked up at Ahmadi, who was leaning out the window. "We are very concerned, Raul."

Ahmadi grasped the pistol with his right hand and moved it from the seat to his lap just out of their sight. His finger was on the trigger. They were easy targets—one headshot to each of them before they could even react.

"What do you think about the match tonight? Any chance that KPT FC can beat HBL FC?" the security guard asked, referring to the highly anticipated soccer match between two Karachi teams—Karachi Port Trust Football Club and Habib Bank Limited Football Club.

Ahmadi laughed a nervous laugh, removing his finger from the trigger. "It will be close, but my money is on the Portmen over the Bankers."

Sultan slapped the base security soldier on the back. "What did I tell you?" He handed Ahmadi the paperwork. "Here you go. I've already signed it. Go get your coffee."

Ahmadi reached out for the paperwork and smiled. "None too soon. I can't wait a moment longer."

The soldier waved Ahmadi and the escort vehicle through.

26

MASROOR AIR FORCE BASE KARACHI, PAKISTAN

Although Raul Ahmadi was now inside Masroor Air Force Base, he wouldn't feel completely safe until the delivery was accepted and he had the base in the rearview mirror. He had been assured that the standard protocol was not to open the container when it was delivered. He was also anxious about the large satchel full of cash behind the driver's seat. That would be impossible to explain, should anyone discover it.

Ahmadi and the security vehicle passed through another checkpoint at the entrance to the high-security area of the base. When they arrived at the underground storage facility, the security vehicle waited outside while Ahmadi drove the truck down a long ramp into the bunker. Inside, a low-ranking soldier with lighted lineman wands, like the ones used by airline ground crews on the tarmac, waved him forward onto a weigh scale. Once Ahmadi stopped the truck, the weight was recorded and compared with the weight of the vehicle when it left the base. Care had been taken to make the truck and the container identical to the one he had been driving when he left the base. Ahmadi had also texted the recorded weight of the truck and container when he left the base in Dera Ghazi Khan to the team responsible for equipping the truck he was now driving. An effort had then been made to match the weight of the two containers that were switched at the lay-by near Hyderabad. The variation of the weight associated with an empty and a full fuel tank was already taken into account in the calculation. There was also the weight difference between Nahib and the man who had replaced him in the cab of the truck, although they were approximately the same size. The soldier recorded the weight and looked at Ahmadi.

"Your weight's off. There's a big difference between your weight leaving DGK and your arrival here. Your truck and container weigh 186 kilograms more than I calculate it should be, even allowing for fuel consumption."

Ahmadi did the mental calculation. The truck had two 116-imperial gallon tanks, which were topped off when he left the base at Dera Ghazi Khan, plenty of fuel to make the trip without refueling. The trip was 827 kilometers or 513 miles. An imperial gallon of diesel fuel weighed approximately 3.86 kilograms. They had considered everything in calculating the weight of the two vehicles. *What had gone wrong?* "You must be mistaken. Run the numbers again."

The soldier was looking at some tables and the before-and-after weights recorded.

"Wait a second," Ahmadi said, "I had to piss and stopped at a petrol station. Because of the length of the trip, I decided to top up one of my fuel tanks so that I would have enough to get back to DGK tomorrow. I forgot about the weight."

"You know better than to do that."

"It was a long, overnight trip. I wasn't thinking straight."

"Let me see the fuel receipt. I'll add in the weight of the fuel to my calculation."

There was no receipt. Ahmadi attempted to quickly calculate the number of gallons and weight in his head and come up with the answer, but under pressure, he couldn't do it. A wrong answer would trigger an investigation. He couldn't be precise, so he rounded the numbers in his head to 200 kilograms difference in weight divided by four kilograms per gallon of diesel fuel. He swept his hand across the dashboard and looked down at the seat and floor, pretending to look for the missing receipt. "It was about fifty gallons. I had the receipt on the dashboard. I can't find it. It must have blown out of the window."

The soldier scribbled away on a pad of paper. "You're in for some disciplinary action when you return to your base." The soldier handed Ahmadi a clipboard with the paperwork and a pen. He signed it and handed it back to him. "The SPD rep needs to check this. After they unload the container, pull your rig outside and wait there until he arrives."

As was standard protocol, an industrial hoist lifted the intermodal container. Once freed, Ahmadi moved the truck away, and the hoist lowered the container onto the floor of the bunker, in line with a row of other containers. Ahmadi and the man with him in the cab of the truck looked at each other.

By the time Ahmadi pulled the truck outside the storage facility, Sultan was waiting with his clipboard and electronic tablet. He and the soldier who had summoned him were talking. Sultan and the soldier came over to Ahmadi.

"I understand we have a little problem with the weight of the vehicle," Sultan said, tapping his clipboard with his finger.

"I explained that to him," Ahmadi said, looking over to the soldier.

Sultan chewed on his cheek and stared at the paper the soldier had given him.

"Using the figure you gave us for the number of gallons, the fuel weight calculation is still off." Sultan exhaled and shook his head. He scribbled his signature on the paper and gave it back to the soldier and handed Ahmadi a copy. "I'll have to file a report. You'll need to explain why you stopped and topped off your fuel when you return to your base. I wouldn't want to be in your shoes."

Explaining the fuel problem when he returned to base was the least of Ahmadi's problems. He would never set foot on the DGK base again.

Although Ahmadi and the other man were eager to leave and put some distance between themselves and the base, they used the toilet and grabbed some food before leaving to avoid arousing suspicion. Other weapons would be delivered to the base. The last one was scheduled for late tomorrow. Sometime after that, the technical inspection team would arrive. They would open the containers and verify the contents. Ahmadi would love to see the look on their faces when that happened. By then, he and the nukes would have vanished.

Passing through the main gate, with the security vehicle tailing close behind him, Ahmadi waved at the guard and breathed a sigh of relief. When they were out of sight of the base, the driver of the security vehicle passed Ahmadi and turned on the emergency lights. Without the weight of the container, they would make good time. It was only a thirty-minute drive to the warehouse in Karachi where the other members of the team would be waiting, along with the truck and container that Ahmadi had originally driven away from the base at Dera Ghazi Khan—the one with the nuclear devices. They had a designated window of time within which to meet at the cargo ship for loading. Their container would be loaded onto a predesignated space at the top of the stack. The ship's scheduled time of departure was 2:45 p.m.

27

KARACHI, PAKISTAN

Earlier in the year, a Saudi shell company, using the name Global Transit & Supply, had rented a warehouse located several miles from Karachi Port for a year with the option to renew for up to five years. A large sign bearing the company's name had been erected, but the building had remained vacant. When the truck, driven by Raul Ahmadi, and the security vehicle arrived, the driver of the security vehicle went inside. One of two large, street-facing, garage-type doors opened, and Raul Ahmadi drove the truck, minus the container that was dropped off at Masroor Air Force Base, into the warehouse. The security vehicle pulled in behind him, and the warehouse door shut.

Inside was the other truck, the one that had left Dera Ghazi Khan with the intermodal container with the three nuclear devices. The men had applied transport company logos and markings to the truck's doors to make it look like one of the hundreds of trucks that frequented the port each day. Parked beside it were a large panel van and a forklift used to unload the weapons.

The three nuclear devices were on the concrete floor of the warehouse. Two nuclear engineers, who had arrived the previous day, had been working on them nonstop. The engineers came prepared to do their job. The challenges were many but nothing they couldn't resolve. The men's primary task was to bypass the current safeguards and trigger mechanisms and set new ones. They spoke only to each other and only when something was needed or when one of them had a question for the other.

Raul Ahmadi watched the engineers, one wiping sweat from his face and neck with a handkerchief. Without looking up from what he was doing, he said they were about finished.

"How much longer?"

"It's done when it's done," the engineer said. "We'll let you know."

"We're on a tight clock."

"We'll make it as long as we have no further interruptions."

Ahmadi admired the expertise and calmness with which they worked. They may as well have been working under the hood of an automobile, conducting routine maintenance. The men worked with patience and precision. He listened to them for a while before leaving. They spoke to each other, using words and terms that Ahmadi did not understand. Looking at the warhead, Ahmadi was not frightened. On the contrary, he had a sense of peace. If one of the warheads detonated, no one inside the warehouse would feel any pain or realize that it had even occurred. No one would panic. One moment, they would be living, breathing human beings, and the next, there would be nothing left of them but pink mist. There were worse ways to die.

Ahmadi waited with his men until the engineers finished and came over to him.

"Have the preparations been completed?" Ahmadi asked the engineers.

"All the requested changes have been made, including the alterations to the intermodal container."

"Show me."

The two engineers walked him through the changes to the container and the three nuclear devices. The two ten-kiloton battlefield warheads were designed to sit atop missiles. Battlefield nuclear weapons caused limited destruction and were used where the opposing forces were fighting in relatively close proximity. The lead engineer explained how the devices would detonate.

They then moved to the third nuclear device, the strategic nuclear warhead, which was in a custom-made box about the size and shape of a small casket. *A fitting comparison*, Ahmadi thought. The warhead itself was much smaller. Most people pictured a nuclear warhead in reference to its delivery device such as a bomb or missile. This warhead measured only thirty-one inches by twelve inches and had been destined to sit atop one of Pakistan's long-range missiles. It was, however, surprisingly heavy, weighing close to three hundred pounds. Add the size of the box containing it, and the total weight was nearly a half-ton. When detonated, the 150-kiloton nuclear warhead would devastate a city, killing hundreds of thousands and injuring thousands more. In a city such as New York, where the population density is 27,000 people per square mile, the death and injury toll could be in the millions. A nuclear warhead of this magnitude had never been used against an adversary or used in an actual test. Some called it a "city killer." By comparison, the atomic bomb dropped on Hiroshima in 1945 was between twelve and eighteen kilotons, and it killed over sixty thousand people and injured another seventy thousand. Combine the deaths from the atomic bomb dropped three days later in Nagasaki, and the total death toll was two hundred thousand people.

The engineers explained the alterations to the strategic weapon while Ahmadi stood by, his arms folded over his chest. Everyone was looking at him. Staring at the box, a faint smile crossed Ahmadi's face. He said, "Excellent. Allah has blessed our mission. Now load them up."

They were ready to initiate the next phase of their plan. They would leave the truck that Ahmadi had driven in the warehouse and drive the other truck with its container and nuclear devices to the port. The security vehicle would follow. They would meet up with the van later. Once the container was loaded onto the cargo ship, they would abandon that truck at the port and drive off in the security vehicle. The security seal kit would again be used to create a seal for the container, but this time, the seal number would be one that did not match the original one because it did not matter.

Ahmadi knew that in spite of the fact that everything was going well, it was only a matter of time before ISI, SPD, or Pakistani military discovered the warheads were missing and initiated an international search more widespread and intensive than any the world had ever seen. They had, at the most, two days before that happened. Photographs of Ahmadi and his accomplices would be on every television, billboard, and newspaper in the world. Every second of CCTV would be reviewed and analyzed multiple times. Ultimately, the search would include cargo ships that left Karachi on or around the date of the initial deployment.

The cargo ship carrying the container would be one of those because it would have been in port and departed during the period of time when the warheads went missing. The ship would be located and boarded before it reached its initial port of call. Raul Ahmadi was not concerned. In fact, he was counting on that happening.

28

KARACHI PORT
PAKISTAN

As the truck, the van, and the security vehicle got within half a mile of Port Karachi, the number of tractor trailers increased and the traffic slowed to a standstill. The panel van peeled off. They would meet up later after the container was loaded onto the cargo ship. Ahmadi, who was driving the truck, looked at his watch, tapped the horn, and stuck his head out the window, motioning for the security vehicle behind him to bypass the queue. The security vehicle, with the truck following close behind, pulled around the line of trucks.

At the port's security gate, the driver of the security vehicle handed the guard the false credentials for the truck. The guard glanced over the papers, directed them to Pier 8, and waved them through. Had the papers indicated that the cargo container was destined for the United States, they would have been directed to nearby Port Qasim in order to pass through a radiation screening facility.

The *Fair Winds*, a Panamanian-registered Panamax container ship, had a crew of mixed nationalities. The captain and senior officers were Greek. The ship was three hundred meters long and could carry approximately four thousand TEUs—or twenty-foot equivalent units, the term used to describe the capacity of container ships.

Ahmadi and two of his security men boarded the ship and were shown to the captain's quarters. Ahmadi introduced himself and handed the captain a large briefcase. "This is for transportation of the container to Cyprus."

Without saying a word, the captain set the case on his desk and opened it. He inspected the banded stacks of bills and flipped through three or four of them.

The arrangements had been made in advance. Ahmadi didn't know who had negotiated the fee with the captain, nor did he care. He only knew that the amount far exceeded the normal payment and purchased the captain's cooperation and silence.

The captain looked up from the case and smiled. Ahmadi reassured him that although illegal drugs were hidden in the container, the product would be almost impossible for customs agents to find. Even if they inspected the container's contents, they would not discover the drugs. With little risk of being discovered and the large payment, the captain was more than happy to look the other way.

"The container will be loaded onto the ship and placed in the requested space."

"I'll stand by until the operation is complete," Ahmadi said.

29

KARACHI PORT
PAKISTAN

Alona Green was not happy about being sent on an assignment without Jake. It wasn't that she was afraid of working alone. She had worked alone in plenty of challenging, dangerous assignments as a DIA contractor in the past. The problem was that she and Jake were a team. Not only had they established complete trust, but their abilities complemented each other incredibly well. She liked working with him. Truth be told, she liked being with him.

While he'd made it abundantly clear that their relationship was not to go beyond their professional responsibilities, she couldn't simply flip a switch and turn off the way she felt about him. Was she in love with him? She wasn't ready to acknowledge that—let alone answer it—but she couldn't deny that she was as attracted to him as she had ever been to any man.

Green was confident that given time, she could win Jake over if she so desired. She had used her charms to gain an advantage over men on many of her previous assignments, while never once becoming romantically involved or going to bed with them. That's what separated her from Aaliyah. Aaliyah had become romantically involved with Singleton, and then she had used that relationship to turn him into a foreign agent for Pakistan. However, Aaliyah was right in that attractive women have incredibly seductive power over men, and men will do almost anything if they believe it will get them what they really want. Only one thing was stopping her from making further advances with Palmer. She had worked all her life to be where she was right now, and she wasn't going to let anyone—herself included—screw it up.

A man wearing civilian clothes was waiting on the tarmac when Green exited the aircraft. He shouted to be heard over the helicopter noise, which was taking off to refuel before heading back to Islamabad. "Alona Green, JSOC?"

"Yes," she confirmed smoothly, raising her brows. "And you are?"

"Bob—just Bob. I expect this will be the only time you ever see or talk to me. No need for formalities."

"Who are you with, 'Just Bob'?" Green asked with a smile.

Just Bob didn't seem to share her humor. "The other government agency," he said bluntly.

Green rolled her eyes playfully. "Why don't you guys just say CIA?"

"Does your ID say Joint Special Operations Command?" he shot back.

"Of course not. It's a US Embassy ID." They both laughed. She was glad to have any remaining tension between them lifted, even if only temporarily.

As he escorted her away from the tarmac, he said, "In this business, Alona, we are often not who we say we are. I've been briefed and understand this situation may involve transportation of nuclear weapons, and we're going to the port to have a look-see."

"That's right."

"What's the plan?"

"There is no plan," she said. "We believe someone has diverted one or more nuclear devices during Pakistan's deployment of its nuclear arsenal last night."

"What evidence do you have? Have the Pakistanis been informed?"

"No hard evidence, only circumstantial. General Reynolds has given his boss a heads-up, and someone will contact the Pakistanis."

"Okay. I get it. It's a box that needs to be checked. But having been at the port many times, this is a massive waste of time."

Bob drove the short distance to the entrance to Karachi Port. They went by the line of trucks waiting to enter the port. He flashed his ID card, and security waved him through.

"What type of ID is that?" Green asked.

"US Customs and Border Protection. It gets me in Karachi Port and Port Qasim. Those ports are South Asia's largest deep-water seaports, handling more than fifty million tons of dry and liquid cargo a year. Unless you have a way of distinguishing the truck and the cargo ship from all of those others loading and unloading containers, this is a fool's errand. Do you have anything specific that would help us pinpoint what we're looking for?"

"Nothing," Green confessed, somewhat grimly. "But we'll have a look anyway."

"We're not going to see a couple of men carrying a nuclear missile up the gangway of a cargo ship. There are hundreds of trucks going in and out of here every day. Without having a way to identify the truck, your only chance is to identify the ship. Even that's not a simple task. At any one time, there may be several ships docked and another ten to twenty anchored offshore waiting for their turn to unload and load cargo." Bob pointed to a line of trucks away from the ships. "Those trucks are queued up, waiting for the cranes to offload their containers into a holding area. You get the picture?"

"There's one that's being offloaded directly from the truck onto that ship." Green squinted and read the ship's name on the stern. "*Fair Winds.*"

Bob looked at the truck. "You don't often see that. When you do, it's an urgent last-minute shipment or a truck that was late getting to the port."

"Are the containers screened for radiation?"

Bob shook his head. "Only US-bound containers are screened for radiation, and that's at Port Qasim."

"If someone wanted to get a nuke to the US, couldn't they ship it to a much less secure port, where there is no radiation screening, and ship it to the US from there?"

"They could. But the container would be screened when it arrived at the US if deemed a high-risk shipment. Or they could simply pay off someone to bypass the screening at Port Qasim."

"You are quite the skeptic, aren't you?" Green said, steadily getting fed up with his attitude.

"I consider myself a realist."

"Listen, I'm not stupid," Green said, turning to face him. "I know this is a crapshoot, but we're not in any position to dismiss it. If the driver produced some type of military clearance, would it receive priority and possible exclusion from screening?"

Bob looked slightly taken aback by her assertiveness. Good.

"Not routinely. But this is Pakistan. Anything's possible. You're assuming a stolen nuke would be headed to the US. There are plenty of other high-value targets that terrorists would love to blow up. Or they might put it aboard a ship headed to the Iranian Port of Bandar Abbas and let the Iranians do their dirty work for them. A cargo ship going twenty-five knots could be at Bandar Abbas in a little over a day."

"How about a major port in India?"

"The Port of Karwar, near India's largest naval base, is less than nine hundred nautical miles south. A cargo ship could be there in less than two days. Or, God help us, the Port of Mumbai, which is only six hundred nautical miles or so—easily done in one day. Can you imagine the death toll resulting from a nuclear detonation near Mumbai, a region with a population of over twenty million people? If we're wrong and a cargo ship carrying a nuclear weapon gets through the net, there are numerous potential targets where the death toll and damage would be unimaginable."

"We're not 100 percent certain a nuke has been stolen," Green said. "We're covering the bases, just in case. Let's pray to God that this is all a theoretical exercise."

They drove slowly along an access road by the loading docks. Bob explained that the port had two terminals, the three-berth Pakistan International Bulk Terminal and the four-berth East Wharf. They stopped near one of the ships.

Green watched the constant movement of cranes moving the intermodal containers from one location to another and eventually onto the ship. "There must be some method to guarantee the right container gets onto the right location on the right ship. But sitting here watching, the process looks like total chaos."

Bob laughed and pointed to a small crane lifting the intermodal containers off the trucks and placing them in holding areas beside the berths. "Those containers are mostly the international standard twenty-foot equivalent units or TEUs. Fully loaded container ships can carry between three and fifteen thousand TEUs. Containers have to be organized in the staging areas and aboard ship to make the unloading and loading as efficient as possible at each port of call."

They observed the constant flow of trucks, cranes, containers, and people but were too far away to distinguish anything of note before moving to another berth. Green noted that there was no shortage of military vehicles and personnel and shook her head. "Okay, I'm seeing the futility of this exercise." She became aware of something and looked over her shoulder. An SUV with flashing lights pulled up close behind them. "Who's this?"

Bob looked in the rearview mirror. "Looks like port security. I'm sure it's nothing. They probably want us to move along."

The driver and a passenger got out and approached them, one on Bob's side and one on Green's. Both men were in uniform and wearing sidearms. Bob lowered his window.

The man unsympathetically looked at Bob and Green and said, "IDs."

"Of course," Bob replied, though Green noted a tinge of uneasiness in his voice. He showed the man their IDs.

The guard glanced at them before bending over to peer into the interior of the vehicle. "US Customs and US Embassy," he said, clearly intrigued. "What are you doing here?"

"I'm giving our visitor from the American embassy in Islamabad an orientation tour of the port. She's only recently arrived in Pakistan."

"What do you do at the US Embassy, Ms. Green?"

"I'm responsible for the embassy's information technology system."

"Why does a computer specialist need a tour of Port Karachi?"

"I asked the same question," Green said, contriving a laugh. "My boss insisted I go on this tour. We stopped so he could explain how cargo ships are loaded and unloaded. Actually, it's fascinating."

The guard motioned to the other guard. They walked behind the car and had a powwow. One of them returned to the port security car. Green saw him talking on the car's radio. The other waited until he returned. The two of them talked briefly before returning to Bob's window.

"You can continue with your tour. Stay on this main road and keep your distance from the ships." He handed the IDs back to Bob and walked away.

"Certainly. Sorry, officer," Bob said before driving away.

Green looked over her shoulder. The men were getting into the security vehicle. She could see them talking to each other. "What was that about?" she asked.

"I'm not certain. It's never happened before. As long as you're not impeding cargo operations or placing yourself or the workers in danger, they don't care how long you stop."

"Were they legit?"

Bob shrugged. "Legit enough. Maybe they're new and being overly cautious."

"Why do you, the CIA, come to these ports?"

"I usually come when something suspicious turns up during radiation screening at Port Qasim, usually accompanying a US Customs and Border Protection officer."

Green cocked a brow. "Ever find anything?"

"I've seen a couple of false positives for radiation, but usually it's drugs, guns, knockoff designer items, or counterfeit money." Bob glanced at the rearview mirror. "Well, crap!"

"What is it?" Green looked at her side mirror.

"They turned on their emergency lights and are pulling up behind us again."

30

PORT OF KARACHI
PAKISTAN

Ahmadi had driven the truck into position near the ship and watched as one of the workmen unlocked the twistlocks and corner castings that secured the container to the truck's trailer. Once completed, the crane operator had plucked the container from the trailer and transferred it onto the *Fair Winds*, where it was secured on top of the stack of containers near the middle of the ship. As Ahmadi drove the empty truck away, something caught his attention—the flashing lights on a port security vehicle near the ship docked behind the *Fair Winds*. It looked like port security had stopped a car for some violation. He watched until the two vehicles pulled off.

Ahmadi parked the truck in a holding area among many others. He didn't bother wiping down the interior. By the time investigators located the truck, everyone would know the identities of all those involved in the plot, including his. Fingerprints would only confirm what they already knew.

Ahmadi got into the security SUV with his men and left to join the rest of his team. As they drove away, he looked back at the ship and breathed a sigh of relief. Getting the container secured on the ship was a huge step in the final plan. The *Fair Winds* would depart within the hour and be well on its way by the time the theft was discovered.

—◊◊◊—

The private marina near Port Karachi had been selected for their escape because it was small and secluded. Only a few yachts were docked there. The panel van with the other team members, including the two nuclear engineers, had proceeded from the Karachi warehouse to the marina while Ahmadi and the security vehicle waited until the container was loaded onto the *Fair Winds*. After they arrived at the marina, the men checked each of the yachts before Ahmadi and the others arrived, ensuring no one was on board. If they had found anyone, they would have killed them, regardless of whether they were man, woman, or child.

When Ahmadi arrived, he met with his men on the dock. Afterward, the security men and the senior nuclear engineer remained behind, while the other four men went with him into the panel van. Ahmadi was the last to enter and closed the door behind him.

Once they were inside the empty van, one asked, "Is there a problem?"

"On the contrary. You've all done an outstanding job. We are entering the final stage of our plan. However, we can no longer remain together. You must go into hiding."

"Aren't we going with you?"

Ahmadi looked around at the men. "That would be too risky. There are too many of us. We'll disperse now." He looked at the man who had driven the van. "Drive them back to the warehouse."

The driver seemed to hesitate. "What will we do when we get there?"

"Someone is waiting for you. He will provide you with travel documents and go over the arrangements to get you out of the country."

The men appeared to be puzzled and began talking amongst themselves. Clearly, they had assumed that they would stick together. That would've been a logical plan—if Ahmadi had wanted to spend the rest of his life looking over his shoulder in fear of capture.

Ahmadi stepped backward toward the door, keeping his eyes on the men. "I must go now. We're on a very tight time frame. May Allah bless you and your families."

Then he reached behind his back and whipped out a 9mm pistol with a sound suppressor and began firing. He shot three. The fourth rushed him—shouting as he leaped toward Ahmadi, who barely managed to get the pistol around and fire it into the man's stomach.

The man fell, crashing into Ahmadi, who shoved him off and stood up before firing another two shots: one into the man's head and one into his chest. The other three men appeared dead, but he had to be completely certain, so he systematically shot each in the head.

Ahmadi got out of the van and went back to the dock, his heart racing. First innocent Nahib, now these men—men who had worked with him for the success of the operation. He rationalized their deaths the only way he could. He had martyred them, and they would be rewarded in paradise. The other three men gawked with furrowed brows. He had to reassure them they were safe.

"We had too many men and couldn't risk leaving anyone behind to talk. You are all traveling with me to our final destination and seeing this through."

He walked up to one of the security guards. "Drive that van into the water somewhere where you won't be seen. Make certain the water is deep enough for it to sink out of sight." Ahmadi then pointed to the other security guard. "Take the security vehicle and follow him. After he's disposed of the van, bring him back. We'll wait for you. Hurry!"

31

US EMBASSY
ISLAMABAD, PAKISTAN

Palmer leaned against the closed door of his diplomatic apartment, exhausted after spending much of the night in a helicopter. He showered, then had a cup of coffee and some breakfast before rushing to the embassy for the meeting with General Reynolds and Dr. Psimas. They were waiting for him when he arrived.

"Another day, another body, eh, Palmer?" Reynolds said sternly.

Palmer was in no mood for this. He sat himself in a chair at the table the two were already surrounding, wishing he had another mug of coffee at his disposal. "Alona and I had nothing to do with this one, sir."

"Jake, I believe you've met Dr. Psimas," Reynolds said, thankfully changing the subject.

"Yes, sir." Palmer looked back to Reynolds. "Have you heard from Alona?"

"I have. Our agent met her at the airport in Karachi and took her to the port. He has a US Customs and Border Protection ID and goes there on a regular basis, so he would know if anything appeared unusual. He and Alona were having a look around when they got pulled over by port security, who questioned them, checked their IDs, and told them to move on. He drove off, but then port security stopped them again and took them in for questioning. They were released a couple of hours ago. Alona's on her way here and will arrive soon."

"Did they see anything unusual?" Palmer asked.

"Nothing," Reynolds confirmed, shaking his head. "She thinks they were detained to prevent them from seeing something that might have been, though." Turning to Psimas, he added, "Karen, I wanted you to meet with us regarding the possibility that a terrorist group has diverted one or more nuclear devices during Pakistan's deployment. As of now, we have no proof this has happened. We are only exploring the possibility."

"What's raised your concern?" Psimas asked.

Palmer interjected before Reynolds could respond. "Yesterday, during the initial stage of deployment, satellite surveillance located two trucks and a light armored military vehicle, like the security vehicles we'd seen leave the bases during the deployment. They were parked off the N-55 north of Hyderabad. Ordinarily, that wouldn't have raised an eyebrow. However, as it was on the night of the deployment, it aroused our suspicion. Green and I took a helicopter to the site to investigate. We found tread marks of two trucks and saw fresh blood puddled beside one of them. From there, we saw indications that something or someone had been dragged away from the road. The drag marks and blood trail led us to a small mound of sand. We brushed some of the sand away and discovered a body—a naked, white male, probably in his twenties—out of sight of the road where the vehicles had parked. He'd been shot twice. As we were investigating, another helicopter approached, so we ran to our chopper and got out of there."

"Interesting," Psimas said. "Is that it?"

"Our foreign asset in Srinagar, Kashmir, told Alona and me that plans were underway to steal a nuclear device," Palmer went on. "He believes a Pakistani military officer, known as The Chameleon, is leading the operation."

"That's all we know for certain," Reynolds said. "We surmise that one or both trucks and an SUV were part of Pakistan's deployment of nuclear weapons. We believe that the other helicopter was sent to investigate the location for the same reason Palmer and Green were there, or perhaps they had tracked our helicopter from the time it left here and came to investigate our interest in that location."

Psimas looked at Reynolds. "So you have no hard evidence of a missing device, only conjecture."

Reynolds leaned back in his chair. "We're simply bringing you up to speed. I'll reach out to my Pakistani contact regarding the body. It won't be a pleasant conversation, but it's one that needs to happen. Even if there is a remote possibility a nuke has been diverted, I need your insight. For example, how would they get it out of the country and what would be the most likely target?"

"Hmm." Psimas looked down at the table, considering her response. "In his book, *Nuclear Terrorism*, Graham Allison outlines the six things a terrorist would need to in order detonate a nuclear weapon in a city. First of all, a terrorist group or nonstate actor must have the finances to plan, organize, and carry out the attack. Second, the decision has to be made to do it. Third, they must acquire the weapon. Fourth, they must have the knowledge and capability to detonate it, including how to bypass any built-in safeguards. Fifth, they must transport the weapon to its destination. Lastly, they must detonate the weapon. No person or group has ever had the money, resources, access, expertise, and opportunity to pull it off. Doing so is practically impossible."

"Until now," Palmer said.

"Even if we assume they have the money, resources, and expertise, I'm not convinced they could obtain a nuclear weapon, then get it out of Pakistan, into the target country, and to the location in that country where it would be detonated. Detonating a nuclear weapon is no simple matter. It requires one or more highly skilled technicians—nuclear engineers. The target depends on which group is behind the theft and what their motivation and goal might be. Pakistan is a witch's brew of terrorist groups. And each has a country or an ethnic group that they hate. However, they all agree on two things: they hate Israel, and they hate the West."

"I understand," Palmer said. "The most pressing question now is how they would get it out of Pakistan. If a nuclear device has been diverted, we need to stop it before it leaves the country. Once it's aboard a plane, train, or cargo ship out of Pakistan, finding it becomes much more difficult."

Psimas leaned forward, elbows on the table, and looked at Palmer. "Given the countries bordering Pakistan and the location where you believe the diversion has taken place, all three of those options are possible. They could even drive it out of Pakistan. And you're right. Once the device has left Pakistan, finding it becomes an order of magnitude more difficult. As with the abduction of a person, the first twenty-four hours are critical."

"I believe they would load it onto a cargo ship," Reynolds said. "That's why I sent Green and the officer to Port Karachi."

"Is every cargo container screened?" Palmer asked.

"In a perfect world, all containers would be screened," Psimas replied. "After 9/11, the US Customs and Border Protection launched the global Container Security Initiative, requiring all incoming containers deemed as high risk be screened before arriving in the US. The only participating port in Pakistan is Port Qasim, which is adjacent to Port Karachi. Most large foreign ports do some risk-based screening, but not every container or shipment is screened. That's an extremely costly process to build, run, and maintain, and one that would slow the movement of cargo."

"So, if they wanted to get a nuclear device out of the country by ship, they would avoid Port Qasim," Palmer said.

"Correct," Psimas said. "The Secure Freight Initiative established in 2007 requires 100 percent of US-bound containers be screened for radiation through nonintrusive inspection technology. Port Qasim uses radioactivity detection portals and X-ray machines. All screening data goes directly to US Customs and Border Protection in northern Virginia. However, there are issues. For example, the screening facility isn't very effective in detecting a nuclear weapon and its fissile material, which is plutonium or highly enriched uranium. Also, there's a problem with false positives. Some common materials such as cat litter, bananas, and ceramics trigger the detector alarm."

"So, bananas might set off alarm bells and highly enriched uranium might not," Palmer said.

"Right."

"Is there any screening of cargo arriving in the US?"

"The US Customs and Border Protection can take X-ray images of a container's contents to look for dense objects that could be fissile materials or shielding for fissile materials. However, CBP screens only 5 percent of containers that have been determined as high risk—a very small number."

Palmer stood, rubbed his forehead, and walked to the window before turning back to the room. "General, can you coerce Pakistan into investigating this?"

"With what we have now, we can't even convince Dr. Psimas," Reynolds said. "I'll run this up the JSOC chain of command. Ultimately, our president needs to know that the possibility exists, even if there is no proof. The president will probably contact the Pakistani president, who will try to reassure us all is okay. However, if they know or later discover a weapon is missing, we'll declare a broken arrow or empty quiver incident."

Palmer sat back down and ran his hand through his hair. Broken arrow meant the loss in transit of a nuclear weapon. Empty quiver meant the seizure, theft, or loss of a functioning nuclear weapon. Either one was bad news. Something had to be done, but *what?*

3 2

DERA GHAZI KHAN, PAKISTAN

When Shamina Ahmadi's phone rang, she was quick to answer it. Whenever her husband was away, she never completely relaxed, in constant fear that something might happen to him.

But this call wasn't from Raul. It was from her children's teacher, who informed Shamina that her daughter Javeria had fallen from a piece of playground equipment and hurt her right arm and bumped her head. The school was usually a ten-minute walk from the Ahmadi home, but she told the teacher she would be there sooner.

When Shamina arrived at the school, she frantically looked for Javeria's teacher. She spotted her waiting at the front entrance. The young woman debriefed Shamina on what had happened and walked with her to the playground behind the school. The emergency service was already there, and a paramedic was examining Javeria, who was crying both from the pain and from fear.

Shamina rushed over to her daughter and hugged her, telling her she would be okay. Soon, the paramedic stepped away from the girl and told Shamina that Javeria needed to go to the hospital for treatment of her broken arm and a possible concussion. He told her that she could ride in the ambulance with Javeria.

Shamina wiped tears from her eyes. Raul needed to know. She couldn't phone him at the base or on his cell phone, which he switched off when he was on an assignment. Shamina telephoned the base's main switchboard. In tears, she explained the situation to the person who answered and asked to speak with the officer to whom he reported. She was transferred twice before she reached the right person.

"This is Major Amir Paratha. What do you need, Mrs. Ahmadi?"

"I'm sorry to bother you, Major Paratha, but our daughter has been injured at school. I'm in the ambulance with her on the way to the hospital. I need to let her father know of her injuries. Raul told me not to call him because he is on an important mission. Can you contact him and ask him to phone me?"

"Your husband is on a highly classified mission. Neither you nor I can call him. The use of a personal mobile phone is forbidden during certain times and at most locations, and this mission is one that includes both."

A thousand thoughts rushed through Shamina's mind. "There must be a way to contact him. He said he would be gone several days. That's too long to wait."

"Is your daughter seriously hurt?" the major asked.

"She has a broken arm and a possible concussion. If you hear from him, please tell him to call me."

"I'll see what I can do. That's all I can promise."

"I understand. Thank you."

—∽∾∽—

Major Paratha looked at the photograph of his family that was on his desk, his three children standing in front of him and his wife. How would he feel if it were one of his children who had been injured?

Ahmadi and his team had delivered the warheads late last night or early this morning. Paratha used a secure line to call him. Ahmadi answered immediately.

"Ahmadi, your wife wants you to call her. Your daughter was injured at school and has been taken to the hospital."

"Shamina tends to overreact to anything involving the children. I'll phone her. I'm sorry she's bothered you."

"I'm just passing the information along. What you do with it is your decision."

"We've delivered the container to the base. We slept in and had a late breakfast. Nahib and another of my men will return the truck and security vehicle, probably sometime tomorrow. They're going to spend the day in Karachi before heading back to the base. Believe it or not, Nahib's never been there. Remember that I'm taking some time off."

Paratha leaned back in his chair, his fingers interlocked behind his head. He recalled that Ahmadi had requested a week off following the delivery to Masroor Air Force Base in Karachi. Ahmadi's wife only said he would be away for several days, presumably on the assignment. She would not know the assignment was almost completed. Where was he now going for several days? Was Ahmadi having an affair? This wouldn't be the first time a soldier had lied to his wife, saying he was on a top-secret mission and could not be contacted. However, Ahmadi did not seem like someone who would do that. By all appearances, he was a devout Muslim who loved his wife and children.

He swung his chair around to face his computer screen and pulled up the daily absence report. Over forty soldiers were listed as absent, including Ahmadi, Nahib, and their security team. Almost all of the absentees were involved in the deployment. Only a few had returned to base, and those men had made trips to and from bases in close proximity to DGK. The remainder would be back by the end of the day tomorrow, except for those who had requested time off. Nothing looked overly suspicious. He would wait until tomorrow afternoon and check the attendance reports again.

———

Ahmadi clenched his fists. He had told Shamina not to contact him for any reason. He waited a few minutes, collected himself, and called her. "Major Paratha said you were trying to reach me."

"Oh, Raul, I'm so relieved to hear from you. Javeria was injured at school. She has a broken arm that is being set, and she's being evaluated for a concussion."

"How did that happen?"

"She fell from the playground equipment. The doctor said she'll be okay. They set her arm. Because of that and the possible concussion, she'll have to remain in the hospital overnight for observation. Hammad is staying with the family next door tonight. They will take him to school tomorrow morning. When will you be home?"

He loved his daughter and hated that she had been injured. Nothing he could do or say would make it better. The stark reality was that he would never see his family again. He would be killed, arrested, or in hiding for the rest of his life. On the other hand, Shamina and the children would be shamed and punished for what he had done.

"I'm sorry. You know I can't be there with you. I have to complete my assignment. Tell Javeria I love her and will be home soon. I'll check in with you again. Please do not try to reach me or phone the major again. My assignment is important and very secret. Your call jeopardizes our entire operation."

Shamina didn't question Ahmadi any further but murmured, "I'm sorry to have bothered you about Javeria's serious injuries." Then she hung up, apparently angered by his lack of concern for Javeria and for her.

Ahmadi was indeed concerned, but not because of Javeria's injuries.

How had Major Paratha reacted when Shamina called? Had he told her I had signed out for the next several days? If he had, she would have been angry and asked where I was going without her. Perhaps the major had forgotten until I reminded him.

The mission was exceedingly complex and as such was subject to change. Extensive effort had been put into identifying the problems that may arise and the steps that would be taken for each one if it did. Yet no one had anticipated Shamina contacting the major, certainly not Ahmadi. He thought through the possible scenarios. None of what he foresaw led to altering the plan as it existed. Everyone had requested time off so that no one would investigate why they were not back at the base. The alternative, simply being away without authorization, would draw immediate attention. If all had gone as planned, no one would be looking for them until the inventory of deployed nuclear weapons was conducted or until someone reported that Ahmadi's truck and his security vehicle were long overdue. He had lied to Major Paratha about Nahib and another one of his men spending some time in Karachi before returning the vehicles. Hopefully, that would allay any concern he might have about the delay in the return of the vehicles.

Having thought it through, Ahmadi assured himself that everything was on track. Death was coming, and he was the horse it was riding on. Or, as it was said in the Qur'an, *the angel of death, who is set over you, will take your souls.* Nothing could alter his destiny.

—◦◦◦—

The next afternoon, Major Paratha checked the records again. Nahib and the other soldier should have returned their truck and security vehicle. He reviewed the daily attendance reports, which had been updated earlier that day. The absentees were spread across several departments and transfer teams. There was no apparent pattern.

In another window on the screen, he pulled up a list of the teams that had transferred the nuclear devices and found Ahmadi's. All of his transfer team members who went with him to the Masroor Air Force Base in Karachi were absent; however, all had requested time off except Nahib, who had been assigned to the team at the last minute.

Paratha then reviewed the vehicle log. Neither Ahmadi's truck nor his security vehicle had been returned to DGK. Normally, the vehicles would be returned the next day, but there was still time. The return trip to Karachi was one of the longest, and Ahmadi said that the two men driving them back had spent yesterday in Karachi before leaving for DGK. They should have returned them this afternoon at the latest, even if they stayed out late and left this morning.

Paratha sat back in his chair, puzzled. He couldn't stop reviewing the time off requests over and over again. The afternoon before the warhead transfer began, each of Ahmadi's team, except for Nahib, had requested time off. How would his entire team have possibly known of the order to transfer the warheads prior to their orders for the deployment to commence?

Although everything he considered could be explained away, he decided to err on the side of caution and report it. A sizzle of alarm ran through Paratha's body. He printed the team assignment and absentee reports and grabbed them off the printer.

Paratha was rushing to the door when he stopped himself.

Before alerting the base commander, he called Ahmadi once more. *No answer.*

The last thing he wanted to do was raise a false alarm. He decided to wait until after his next meeting and then phone one more time. When he returned from the meeting, he sat down at his desk and again checked to see if the truck and security vehicle had been returned. They had not. He called Ahmadi. Again, there was no answer. He found Nahib's cell phone number and called it next. *No answer.*

Where was Ahmadi? Had he already left for whatever he was planning to do for the next few days without his family? Had he returned to be with his injured daughter?

Major Paratha hurried to the base commander's office. "Sir, we may have a problem."

Standing in front of the commander's desk, he told him about the call from Ahmadi's wife and then showed him the absentee report. "The day before the deployment was initiated, each of Ahmadi's team assigned to the warhead transfer to Masroor Air Force Base in Karachi requested time off. The only exception was Nahib, who was a last-minute reassignment to the team meant to replace Rajab. Rajab had requested a few days off, too, but the records show he did not take them. I spoke to him. He said that his wife was ill, and they had to cancel their holiday. But now, Nahib has not returned either, and the truck and security vehicle have not been returned yet."

The commander studied the report Paratha had given him. "On the surface, this looks troubling, but until we have actual verification, I am not going to raise an alarm. The consequences would be severe."

"As would the consequences for not reporting this if there is a problem," Paratha countered.

"I'm not escalating this until you show me evidence of a real issue, Major, instead of these absentee reports and lack of documentation that the vehicles have been returned to DGK. You know these reports always contain errors."

Paratha returned to his office, calling in his DGK Strategic Plans Division representative the moment he sat down at his desk. Together, they called the Karachi Port SPD representative, a soldier named Abu al-Fadl Sultan. They explained it was a spot check to ensure the delivery had been made.

"Let me pull up that report," Sultan said, "so that I have the information in front of me." After a brief pause, he added, "Ahmadi and his team delivered the container from Dera Ghazi Khan on the day and at the time expected. The only issue was a slight weight variance related to an unauthorized fuel stop."

"Fuel stop?" the major echoed, bewildered. "Every truck left with enough fuel to get them to their destination. We can't have vehicles that are carrying nuclear devices stopping to top off their fuel tanks. They refuel on the return trip, if necessary, when they *aren't* carrying nuclear weapons."

"He said he had to use the toilet and stopped. I thought that was odd, too, but given the length of the trip from your base to ours, the stop was not surprising. The approximate weight of the additional fuel that Ahmadi estimated he purchased accounted for the variance in overall weight. I signed off on the delivery and told him I was obligated to file a report."

The major had a decision to make. This was yet another issue that was out of the ordinary but could be explained. Should he drop it or go around his commander and escalate his concern? If he was wrong, there would be consequences for him and his career. He decided to go around his commander. He called SPD Director-General Sarkis's office and was transferred to a junior officer who told him that Sarkis was temporarily unavailable. However, he would notify Sarkis, and someone would be back in touch.

Thirty minutes later, Sarkis phoned Paratha, who was careful to qualify his concern by stating nothing out of the ordinary had actually been reported. Sarkis said, "Thank you for reporting this. I will investigate immediately. Take no further action."

—◦◦◦—

Director-General Sarkis called in his aide, Colonel Ashkani. The two of them had been involved in the planning of this plot for years. He brought Ashkani up to speed on the call from the major at the DGK base. "We need to give Ahmadi and his team more time, at least a day or two. Take three of your men with you to Masroor Air Force Base—soldiers that have no connection with SPD and that you can trust to do what needs to be done. I'll phone our SPD rep and order him to keep it quiet and lock down the underground storage facility."

33

DERA GHAZI KHAN PAKISTAN

Sarkis found SPD representative Abu al-Fadl Sultan's cell phone number on his contact sheet. There was no answer. If Sultan was in the bunker, there would be no mobile phone reception. He then phoned the number for the nuclear weapons bunker at Masroor Air Force Base. A soldier answered on the second ring. Sarkis identified himself and demanded to speak to Sultan immediately. He heard the soldier shout, "It's Director-General Sarkis."

A moment later Sultan answered.

Sarkis said, "We have an issue we need to resolve regarding the delivery from DGK. My aide, Colonel Ashkani, is on his way there. I want you to secure the bunker. Who is with you now?"

"Only a few soldiers who work at the storage facility."

"Allow no one to enter or leave the bunker until Colonel Ashkani and his team arrive. Also, do not remove the security tag or attempt to open the container."

"Yes, sir. Consider it done."

—◦◦◦—

Sultan told the others that an SPD team was on the way and that no one was to enter or leave the bunker until they arrived. The soldiers looked at Sultan, their eyes filled with concern. Sarkis had not explained this highly unusual situation to him, and Sultan had not asked, hesitant to question the Director-General.

Soldiers on the base were unarmed unless they were standing security watch or there was a general alert to carry their weapons. As a precaution, Sultan ordered his men to arm themselves.

"I have the keys to the weapons locker," said one of the soldiers, pointing to a locked gun case on the wall of the bunker.

"Unlock it," Sultan ordered, and the soldier with the keys nervously unlocked the case, quickly distributing the rifles and ammunition. Sultan inserted a loaded magazine into his rifle, as did each of his men.

Almost three hours later, a buzzer sounded. Someone was requesting entry to the secure bunker. Sultan studied the security camera. Three uniformed men were outside. He pressed the intercom switch, speaking into a microphone. "Identify yourselves and state your business."

A man stepped in front of the camera, held up his ID, and identified himself as Colonel Wazir Basim Ashkani. He said that Director-General Sarkis had sent him to investigate an issue. Sultan hit the switch that opened the door, letting in Ashkani and the three armed soldiers. Sultan, who was also a trained soldier, noticed that their weapons had sound suppressors attached to the barrels.

This is wrong… all wrong, he thought. *These men don't look like they know a warhead from a warthog. There's not a nuclear weapons expert among them.*

One of Ashkani's men closed the bunker door behind them and locked it. Colonel Ashkani conferred with Sultan about what had happened and again asked if anyone had entered or left the bunker.

"No, sir. No one has entered or left since I spoke to Director-General Sarkis."

Ashkani and his men walked behind Sultan to the container. Ashkani compared the number on the security tag with the one he had entered on his phone. It was the same.

"Cut the security tag," Ashkani demanded.

Sultan cut the tag and swung the doors open, stepping aside. He looked inside the container with a blank stare, speechless.

"What's the problem, soldier?" Ashkani asked.

"See for yourself, sir."

Ashkani walked inside. Sultan's high-lumen LED flashlight lit up the dark container. Inside, where the nuclear weapons were supposed to be mounted onto fixed supports inside the container, were only sections of concrete pipe. There were no nuclear devices.

Sultan's gaze was fixed on the concrete pipes. *How could this happen? Where are the nuclear devices?* The security tags on the doors were secure, and the numbers checked out. Sultan recalled the weight difference and Raul Ahmadi's explanation. He had signed off on it. What if he were charged for not investigating the weight issue further? He would be executed. Sultan flicked the safety off on his rifle.

At that very moment, Ashkani's men began firing.

Sultan whirled, returning fire. He wounded one man before Ashkani fired, striking Sultan in the back. He collapsed onto the container, blood flowing from his bullet wounds. Sultan's men were no match for the highly skilled soldiers who had accompanied Ashkani. Within seconds, they were dead.

Ashkani directed his men to put Sultan, the dead soldiers, and their weapons into the container and close it. They exited and secured the storage facility. Ashkani's wounded soldier had been helped outside and was leaning against the door.

"I'm not going to make it, sir."

Ashkani stood close beside him and looked at the wound before his gaze shifted back to the soldier's face. "Nonsense. We'll get you out of here. You'll be fine."

"No. I'll stay and make sure no one enters."

"As you wish."

Ashkani and the remainder of his men left and were off the base within minutes.

———〰———

A short while later, someone passing by the facility discovered the dead soldier at the entrance and sounded the alert. When a response team entered the storage facility, they saw blood on the floor and followed the trails to the container. When they opened it, they found Sultan and his men, all of whom were dead. But their attention quickly turned to the sections of concrete pipe placed on the supports and realized that the nuclear devices were missing.

3 4

INTER-SERVICES INTELLIGENCE AGENCY ISLAMABAD, PAKISTAN

When Director-General Hesbani heard that a soldier's body had been discovered outside the high-security underground bunker at the Masroor Air Force Base—and that several more bodies had been discovered inside—his first call was to Sarkis, only to be told that Sarkis had left for the day and could not be reached. He asked to speak with Sarkis's aide, Colonel Ashkani. He, too, was unavailable. Hesbani slammed down the phone. Moments later, he learned that three nuclear weapons were missing from the container in the bunker at the base. Investigators found and questioned Major Paratha at the Dera Ghazi Khan base, who explained his earlier concern and his telephone call with Sarkis.

After the ISI investigators spoke with the major, they took Shamina Ahmadi into custody and subjected her to intensive interrogation. Ultimately, she was released because it had been her call to her husband's manager that inadvertently alerted the military to a problem.

ISI concluded she could not have been aware or supportive of her husband's actions, but they wanted to know every detail of her recent telephone conversation with him and his prior actions and movements before she last saw him. At the point of exhaustion and showing signs of physical abuse, Shamina was allowed to return home. An ISI team would keep her under surveillance and monitor her computer and telephone communications in case her husband contacted her.

Hesbani informed the president and established a crisis room to manage the catastrophe. In addition to the fact that two tactical weapons and one strategic warhead were missing, Raul Ahmadi and his team, who had transported the nuclear devices, were missing, as well as two nuclear engineers. The missing nuclear engineers were a significant concern.

Had Ahmadi and his team been abducted, or were they participants in the scheme? During the ensuing investigation, a report surfaced that described a helicopter leaving the US Embassy and landing at a location on the highway between DGK and Karachi. When ISI investigated it that night, they found a poorly hidden, naked body near the location. The fingerprints were those of Nahib, a soldier from Dera Ghazi Khan, who had been assigned to Ahmadi's team. The pieces were falling into place but not quickly enough.

The possibility that other warheads and strategic weapons were missing could not be ruled out. Hesbani accelerated the inventory of all nuclear device components that was already underway, whether they were included in the deployment or not. Done properly, the job would take the better part of two days. But with more men assigned to the task, they could complete the investigation in approximately twelve hours.

Meanwhile, ISI operatives were searching for General Sarkis and his aide, Colonel Ashkani. Scenarios played out in Hesbani's mind. Had Sarkis and his aide been abducted and forced to participate? Perhaps he was the mastermind behind the operation. Was he hiding somewhere in Pakistan? More likely, he either had left the country or was trying to leave the country. The longer Sarkis was missing, the more Hesbani was convinced he was involved. Sarkis had always said it was safer to transfer nuclear weapons in unmarked civilian containers and vans. Had this been part of his plan all along?

An ISI team reviewed the surveillance footage recorded from outside the bunker at the Masroor Air Force Base. Unfortunately, no security cameras were located inside the bunker. This footage showed Ahmadi and his team arrive and leave. They also saw Colonel Ashkani and three men in Pakistani Army uniforms enter the bunker later and leave soon afterward. One had stayed behind to guard the entrance— his was the body found outside the bunker. The team concluded that, because nobody else had approached or left the bunker, it had to have been Ashkani and his three men who had slaughtered SPD representative Abu al-Fadl Sultan and the other soldiers.

The ISI team was also reviewing video footage from each of the bases where the weapons had been transferred. Thus far, no irregularities had been found.

Lastly, CCTV videos from every railroad station, airport, port, and border crossing were being scrutinized. Ships and trucks that had departed Pakistan were being identified, located, and inspected visually and with radiation detectors. Planes that had departed within the time window were boarded and the cargo holds inspected for residual radiation. Airport security alert status was set to the maximum, especially for flights departing Pakistan. Ships that were docked the previous day were being located, and plans were being made to inspect them. Particular attention was being paid to the cargo ships that had departed from Karachi Port and Port Qasim due to their proximity to the air base where the weapons should have been delivered.

The president of Pakistan held telephone conferences with heads of state to discuss the crisis, stressing that the risk was minimal because of the built-in protections on the weapons, which would prevent them from being detonated in their current state. He withheld the fact that the two nuclear engineers they had hired were missing, believing that it would not alter the actions each head of state would take to prevent the weapons from entering their country. The priority was to contact the United States, China, Russia, Israel, India, Great Britain, France, Italy, and Germany. He had to contact all the heads of state prior to any release of information to the news media. The heads of state for less significant countries would be contacted by other members of his cabinet. A script had been written for each of those callers, with instructions not to vary from the script, and not to answer any questions. The script read:

Alert: Pakistan has discovered that during a transfer of nuclear weapons from the base at Dera Ghazi Khan, two tactical nuclear weapons and one nuclear warhead are, as of now, missing. The weapons cannot be detonated in their current state. Intense efforts are underway to locate the weapons and identify those responsible. Heightened vigilance is recommended, as is increased security at all ports and airports. Updates will be provided through the press as more information becomes available.

Most governments agreed on increasing security at their borders and requested frequent status reports on the search, as well as information on the type and size of the missing weapons. The US insisted on involvement in the search for the missing warheads. China had a vested interest and began flexing its powerful muscles, acutely aware of the fact that the development of the economic corridor through Pakistan was at risk. However, China's biggest concern was that the warheads would be detonated in India, resulting in a nuclear war between the two countries. They had no intention of getting involved in any potential war but would assist in the discovery of the missing warheads in whatever way possible. Most vocal of all was India's president, who accused China of joining forces with Pakistan to the detriment of his country. He made it clear that if one or more warheads were detonated in India, they would consider it a first strike and respond in kind. Meanwhile, Russia thanked the president for the information without requesting future status reports or volunteering assistance, and Iran was predictably quiet.

On the nuclear war countdown calendar, it was a minute till midnight.

35

US EMBASSY
ISLAMABAD, PAKISTAN

General Reynolds and the senior embassy staff learned of the missing nukes soon after Pakistan's president informed the US president. Reynolds called an urgent meeting of his staff, including Palmer and Green. He told them that Pakistan's president had specifically denied the US president's request for involvement in the search. As frustrating as it was, there was little they could do.

After the meeting concluded, Palmer and Green cornered Reynolds before he could leave.

"I'm afraid to ask," Reynolds began, sighing. "What do you want now?"

"Well, frankly, Green and I aren't the sitting-on-our-hands-doing-nothing types," Palmer said, stuffing his hands in his pockets. "Any chance we can do some digging?"

Reynolds scoffed. "What do you have in mind?"

"On one of my missions to the region, I worked with Pakistan's version of our Navy SEALs. I became friends with one of the young officers, Zahir Sabri. We worked out together and spent time at the shooting range. I went on a couple of missions with him and his team and developed an appreciation for his leadership style. I recall that we argued over politics. He was strongly opposed to our involvement in the region. We stayed in touch for a while after my assignment, but I've not heard from him in years. If he's still in the service, he may have some information he's willing to share with me."

"He shouldn't be too difficult to locate," Green said. "I'll work on it with one of our analysts."

Reynolds passed a hand through his thinning hair. "What have we got to lose? Just try not to kill anyone else."

———～～～———

Palmer was reading intelligence reports when his cell phone rang. It was Green.

"Your naval officer friend, Zahir Sabri, is now Commodore Zahir Sabri with Pakistan's Naval Strategic Forces Command, based at the Naval Headquarters here in Islamabad. They have responsibility for the defense and protection of Pakistan's naval nuclear assets. Prior to that, he was base commander of PNS Iqbal, the operational headquarters of Navy Special Service Group. PNS Iqbal is their submarine base near Karachi."

"Contact information?"

Green gave him the primary phone number for the command. "Good luck. With everything else going on, it may be difficult to get through to him."

Palmer rang the number from a phone in the embassy, hoping the caller ID might get the attention of whoever answered and avoid the typical runaround. He was partially right. Someone answered on the second ring.

"Naval Strategic Forces Command."

"This is Jake Palmer calling from the US Embassy in Islamabad. I need to speak to Commodore Zahir Sabri."

"Your name again?"

"Jake Palmer. I worked with him when I was in the US Navy."

"Hold, please."

After a few minutes, an aide answered the phone, wanting clarification of who he was, his current position within the embassy, and the purpose of his call. Palmer explained that he was the head of embassy security and wanted to reconnect with his old friend. He was again asked to hold.

Palmer wasn't about to hang up. After almost ten minutes, the aide was back on the line. "The commodore is in a meeting and asked if you would be able to have tea with him in his office at four o'clock this afternoon."

And so their date was set.

An embassy driver took Palmer to the Naval Headquarters building at Defense Road, E-9, in Islamabad. The headquarters was a thirty-minute drive west of the Diplomatic Enclave. Commodore Sabri's aide met Palmer at the entrance and took him through security and straight to Sabri's office.

36

PAKISTAN NAVAL STRATEGIC FORCES COMMAND ISLAMABAD, PAKISTAN

Sabri smiled when Palmer entered his office and was quick to stand and shake his hand. "Well, well, well ... Jake Palmer. Welcome back to Pakistan."

Sabri was in uniform and looking as fit as he'd been when Palmer last saw him, despite the gray highlighting his temples and the new wrinkles accentuating his eyes.

"Thank you for seeing me. You must be incredibly busy with the missing nuclear devices."

"There's not much that I can do. However, some of my men are involved. It's good to see you. I would say you haven't aged a bit, but I'd be lying," he joked with a half-smile. "How long have you been in Pakistan?"

"I only recently arrived and am trying to feel my way around. I'm on a two-year assignment as head of embassy security. I had some time and thought I would see if you were still alive. Based on what I saw back in the day, I figured you'd either be dead or running the show," Palmer said with a sly, offset grin. "I am happy to learn it's the latter."

Sabri canted his head facetiously. "I, too, have on occasion thought about you—wondering how you died. You were a bit of a cowboy. I never thought you'd live long enough to run the show."

The men laughed.

"Please," Sabri said with a genuine smile, gesturing to an ornate table stationed at the center of his expansive office. "Have a seat."

As though awaiting this cue, a steward entered with a service of chai tea. The Pakistani version was known as *doodh patti* and made with black tea and milk instead of water and usually contained sugar and aromatic Indian cardamom. Palmer would have preferred a cup of strong, black coffee. He took a sip and set the cup down.

The men talked about the time they'd served together, retelling a few of their on- and off-duty exploits. Palmer gave him an elevator speech of what he had done since leaving the Navy. He told him that he took the opportunity to lead embassy security, including an in-depth review of current security policies and procedures and enhancement of them where necessary.

"Head of embassy security," Sabri said, spitting the words out like a piece of bitter fruit. "That seems like a terrible waste of talent and not a job that you, Jake Palmer, would drop everything to take on." He paused then, studying Palmer in a way that indicated a drastic shift in demeanor. "I'm aware of your recent exploits—saving the US aircraft carrier, taking down a terrorist cell, and breaking up a counterfeit medicine operation."

Palmer didn't break eye contact, taking care in his response. "Those were the assignments that garnered the most attention. Believe me, the vast majority of my work was mundane." Lying now would not set the tone for an honest dialogue, but still, he had to stop short of the complete truth. "Although we worked together for only a short time many years ago, I have great respect for you, Zahir. I'm not the least bit surprised you have advanced to your current position. My security role is broader than the title would imply and includes any and all threats to the embassy and to US personnel in Pakistan. I'm sure you had someone research my activities, especially those since I entered the country. You'll know, for example, that I recently visited a military facility at the Line of Control, where I witnessed India moving its battle tanks as if they were preparing to cross it and enter Pakistan."

"I appreciate your honesty and directness, Jake." Sabri sat back in his chair, his gaze highly analytical, scrutinizing. Palmer didn't flinch. "I would expect nothing less from you. And yes, I do know you've been busy since you arrived."

Surely, Sabri knew about the shootings at the café and the attack on the safe house. Whether he did or didn't, Palmer wasn't going to mention those incidences. If Sabri knew about them, he would likely say so in an indirect way and let Palmer explain what he and his colleagues were doing there. Of course, it was possible both were ISI operations and not widely communicated.

When Palmer continued, he chose his words carefully. "I have indeed, although I did have some time to visit Srinagar with my attractive colleague for a short break." Palmer offered that information freely as it would have been easy for Sabri to have had his aide check his travel. "On to a more serious topic. We're concerned about the deployment of Pakistan's nuclear weapons. Mind you, not your right to deploy them. We fully support that. You're on the brink of war with India and must defend yourself. Our primary concern is that during that deployment, which began within the last couple of days, three nuclear devices were diverted. We know only that one strategic and two tactical weapons are currently missing. We're not privy to the type or power of those devices. However, we believe that they were destined for one of the military bases in Karachi, perhaps the naval base. We have communicated our concern through normal channels. However, as you are responsible for the security of your navy's nuclear assets, I wanted to speak with you to offer any assistance we can."

Sabri took a slow, deliberate sip of his tea.

"I'll let you in on something we haven't communicated," he began.

Palmer felt a rush of relief. *Now, we're getting somewhere.*

"The devices were destined for Masroor Air Force Base in Karachi, not our naval base. The air base has a secure, underground storage facility. Our navy's nuclear weapons are stored there until deployed on our ships. Other than the communication from our president and his discussion with yours, what information do you have that relates to the nuclear devices that were diverted?"

Palmer informed him of the tread marks left by two trucks and the body that he and Green discovered buried in a shallow grave by the road—although he specifically did not mention her by name. He also told him that another helicopter was approaching when they left, and based on the sound, he assumed it to be a military helicopter.

Sabri nodded knowingly, taking another sip of his tea. He took the opportunity to summon the steward to top off his cup. It was as though he was stalling, contemplating his response.

Eventually, he said, "We are confident we will resolve the situation within the next day or two and locate the weapons. As you are aware, our president has contacted heads of state regarding this. He spoke to your president earlier today. Security posts have been established at all land routes out of Pakistan, particularly those into India and Iran. We have identified the cargo ships that were in port at or near the time of deployment and inspections are underway. A team of our Navy Special Service Group, including explosive ordnance disposal experts, are flying out to inspect each ship. None will be allowed to enter another port until they have passed our inspection. Would you like to observe the first one or two of the inspections?"

"Absolutely," Palmer said, surprised by the offer.

"I will allow you and whomever else you select to observe from one of your helicopters, but you must not interfere. Take your EOD guys if you like. If ours need assistance, which they should not, it would be reassuring to know they are available. I'll inform our team so they will know who you are and can establish communications with yours."

"I will pass that along, but I'm certain we will accept your offer to observe. We will include US Navy EODs as requested."

"Your attractive colleague, Ms. Alona Green, might be interested in going. I understand she is working with you."

Sabri's mention of Green by name—and his suggestion that she was his partner—caught Palmer off guard. No doubt that was Sabri's intention. Palmer wasn't going to take the bait and acknowledge it. "Do you have any idea who is responsible for the missing weapons? A terrorist group, perhaps?"

Sabri did not reply.

"The Chameleon?" Palmer was as interested in Sabri's reaction as his answer.

Sabri laughed. "The Chameleon is a myth that many gullible people are embracing. He does not exist. I'm surprised you would even suggest it."

Sabri provided Palmer with the details regarding the timing and the exact location where the Pakistani team would depart Karachi. His aide escorted Palmer to the front entrance.

—✺—

Before Palmer got into the car, he phoned Reynolds and told him about his conversation with Commodore Sabri. Palmer relayed the details of when and where Pakistan's inspection teams would depart for the cargo ships. Reynolds said he would get the ball rolling so that they could leave immediately. He wanted Green and Psimas to accompany him. The timing was tight.

On the ride back to the embassy, Palmer reflected on the meeting. Sure, it had been cordial enough, but something wasn't right. Sabri was caught up in the chaos of the situation and extremely busy, regardless of what he said. *Yet he had taken time to meet me on what was a purported social call. Why would he do that?* Sabri also had not pressed him about his activities since arriving in Pakistan. Regardless, the invitation to observe the inspections of the cargo ships was a win. Best to take it for what it was and run with it.

37

THE ARABIAN SEA

Two Navy Explosive Ordnance Disposal team members were loading their gear onto the US Navy MH-60 Seahawk helicopter when Palmer, Green, and Psimas arrived at PNS Mehran in Karachi, home of the naval aviation branch of Pakistan's navy. Commodore Sabri had authorized the US helicopter and personnel to use it as a base for flying to and from inspections of the cargo ships. The Pakistani helicopters and teams were also flying out of the air base.

The EODs were members of a secret team that had been on station in the region for years. One of the team's roles was to seize control of and disable Pakistan's nuclear weapons in the event of a jihadist coup. The EODs on the team worked with all types of explosives, including chemical and nuclear, and were fully trained and qualified in nuclear weapon render safe procedures—a military term for seizing or disabling a weapon of mass destruction. One of the men, grinning from ear to ear, who had a master EOD badge sewn onto his uniform and a senior chief insignia on his cap, walked toward Palmer.

"Well, son of a bitch, if it isn't Jake Palmer." They laughed and man-hugged, slapping each other on the back.

"Well, I'll be damned," Palmer said with a broad smile. "Great to see you, Cole."

"I heard you were on contract with JSOC. Or more specifically Orange, right?"

"Let's leave it at JSOC."

"Whatever the reason, we're honored to join you."

"The honor is all mine," Palmer said.

Palmer introduced Senior Chief Petty Officer Nick Cole and his teammate to Green and Psimas, explaining that Green was his JSOC partner and Psimas was a nuclear engineer. As they were getting on board the Seahawk, Green asked Cole, "How do you know Jake? He hasn't been on active duty in years."

"We ran a few joint missions back in the day. That man has some serious cred among SEAL and EOD team members," the senior chief said. "His exploits, on and off duty, are legendary. Remind me, if we have some time, and I'll tell you a few."

"Oh, I definitely will," Green said, flashing Palmer a devious grin.

Palmer, Green, and Psimas strapped themselves side by side into three jump seats with the EODs sitting across from them. One of the US crewmen gave each of them a headset so they could communicate with each other and the crew. As they lifted off, Palmer asked, "Do the Pakistanis know what they're doing?"

"We'll find out soon enough," Cole said.

"Initial success or total failure, right?" Palmer said, citing the motto on the EOD patches.

"Damn straight. No middle ground or second chances," Cole replied.

The Pakistani helicopter took off first with the American Seahawk following close behind. Once airborne, the helicopters flew over the Arabian Sea, heading west toward the Gulf of Aden. The cargo ship was on a course for the Suez Canal and on to the Mediterranean Sea and Cyprus. This was a Pakistani operation, but Sabri had given the US permission to observe and to provide technical assistance if required.

The Seahawk helicopter hovered near the cargo ship, *Fair Winds*, close enough to see what was going on but not close enough to interfere. Palmer, Green, Psimas, and the EODs watched with binoculars through the open side doors. Their headsets connected them to the internal communications aboard the helicopter so that they could talk to each other. They could also switch channels and communicate with the helicopter's pilot, copilot, and warfare systems operator, who were in communication with the Pakistani helicopter pilot and copilot. The Pakistani soldiers, including their EODs, were wired for communication with both helicopters and the RHIBs. Everyone communicated in English.

About twenty miles from the container ship, Palmer spotted a small warship below them and asked the pilot about it. He said it was one of their new corvettes, the smallest class of warships. It was capable of carrying two rigid-hulled inflatable boats or RHIBs. The cargo ship was too far out for the RHIBs to get there and back from Pakistan on their own. Using his binoculars, Palmer saw the RHIBs rapidly approaching the container ship on the port and starboard sides. They were backup in the event that extra muscle was needed.

"I remember the *Fair Winds* at the dock at Karachi Port," Green said. "A truck pulled up to off-load a container. Bob, our CIA guy, said you didn't see that very often. It usually occurred when a truck was late or was carrying an urgent, last-minute shipment. We were watching the ship when port security pulled up and questioned us."

"All ships in port during that time will be inspected," Palmer said. "The *Fair Winds* was one of several ships the Pakistanis have identified for boarding and searching for the missing nuclear weapons." He looked at Psimas, who could hear the conversation through her headset.

With a nod, Psimas told the pilot to stay a minimum of five miles from the ship. The pilot banked the helicopter and set up at that range from the ship.

"Have you worked with nuclear weapons, Senior Chief Cole?" Psimas asked.

"Only in simulations. We're trained on a wide variety of devices and the mechanics of disarming them. Have you had hands-on experience with nukes? If so, we might need your assistance."

"I know a great deal about how the devices are designed, built, function, and detonated, but I've never been called upon to actually disarm one," Psimas said. "How about you, Palmer?"

"SEALs are trained in the basics—just in case. But we rely on our EOD teammates to do the heavy lifting when it comes to explosive ordnance, especially nukes."

3 8

THE ARABIAN SEA

Captain Michail Dimitrios stood on the bridge of the *Fair Winds*, looking out at the horizon. The sea, buffeted by a ten- to fifteen-knot wind out of the west, was choppy with four- to five-foot swells, which was of little consequence to a container ship the size of the *Fair Winds*.

Dimitrios was glad to be underway and rid of Ahmadi and his drug-dealing friends. He would be even happier once their container was off-loaded in Cyprus. Ahmadi had told him that his representative would meet the ship there. Limassol, Cyprus was a small port and an unlikely terrorist target, so the obligatory customs inspection was superficial at best. He made a good living as a ship's captain, more than enough to live on. The money he received from people wishing to transport illegal cargo enabled him and his family to live well. Responsibility for examination of international cargo lies with customs inspectors at the ports of call, not with the ship's crew. The shipping companies can't be held responsible for every item they transport. Therefore, the risk to him was low, and the reward was great. Still, knowing the drugs were in the container made him uncomfortable.

Dimitrios was still on the bridge with two of his officers when the Pakistani military radioed that they were inspecting ships that had left Karachi Port on the day the *Fair Winds* had departed. They requested permission to come aboard to inspect his records and the containers that were loaded in Karachi. They ordered him to slow the ship to the lowest speed that still allowed for control of the vessel. They would approach the vessel from the south and would be landing a team on board.

Captain Dimitrios told them he needed to clear it with the shipping company. He was concerned that it was an elaborate hijacking, but to his knowledge, there were no pirates claiming they were Pakistani special forces, who operated with helicopters and boats. He was in international waters in a Panamanian-registered ship. The Pakistani military had no jurisdiction and no authority to board the ship. However, there would be implications for the shipping company if he refused their request. He was aware of the missing nuclear weapons and was not concerned about that. His thoughts went immediately to the drugs in Ahmadi's container.

Dimitrios stepped out onto the exterior wing bridge and scanned the skies with his binoculars, locating the helicopter and boats approaching from the south. He radioed the shipping company and was connected to the director of shipping operations. After Dimitrios explained the situation, the director approved the inspection and instructed the captain to keep him informed. Next, he radioed the Pakistanis, informing them that they had permission to come aboard and inspect the containers loaded in Karachi.

This was trouble he didn't need. If the soldiers found the drugs, the shipping company would launch an investigation. What should he do?

"Sir, we have two helicopters and boats approaching from the south. ETA approximately five minutes," one of his junior officers shouted. "Another military helicopter is in position approximately five miles off our starboard bow. It appears to be American."

It would be impossible to open the container and dispose of its contents without being noticed. He would claim ignorance if they discovered the drugs. They had no proof he knew about them.

The Pakistani helicopter hovered over the bridge of the ship. Because there was no helicopter landing platform on the ship, any boarding would have to be by fast-roping down or by boarding from one of the approaching boats. The RHIBs took up position on each side of the ship.

The ship's first officer went to a small, flat area behind the bridge of the ship and waved self-illuminating wands back and forth, guiding the helicopter. The captain shielded his eyes from the sun, watching the helicopter hover over the wing bridge, maintaining the ship's precise course and speed. A rope dropped from the door.

Seven men fast-roped from the helicopter onto the ship. Captain Dimitrios waited at the bridge door to meet them. He gave the senior officer of the Pakistani team a listing of the containers loaded onto the *Fair Winds* at Karachi Port, highlighting the fact that one was loaded late—just prior to departure. The officer scanned down the list and said he wanted to start with the ones loaded last. After some discussion, the captain gave them the locations of the four containers to be searched, including the one Ahmadi delivered just prior to departure. The first officer escorted them to the location.

—◁∿▷—

Five miles away, downwind from the *Fair Winds*, the captain of a luxury cruise ship stood on the portside bridge wing, looking through binoculars at the helicopters and boats that raced toward the cargo ship they had just sailed by. The duty officer on the bridge had summoned him after receiving a communication from a Pakistani officer that they should steer away from the military activity. The Bahamian-registered ship, carrying seven hundred and fifty passengers and a crew of four hundred, was on a fourteen-day Indian Ocean cruise. They had been cruising at ten knots, timing their speed to arrive at the next port of call on time.

The captain ordered an increase to twenty knots, near their maximum speed, to put distance between them and the container ship. He had witnessed military boardings in the past, mostly practice exercises, but this was different. The company had announced that a Pakistani nuclear device was missing and ships were being searched. The captain had assessed the wind speed and direction, deliberately changing course to position his ship away from being directly downwind of the container ship. As a precaution, he went on the intercom and made an announcement.

"This is your captain. You may have noticed the military helicopters near the cargo ship we've just passed. There is no need for immediate concern. However, they have advised us to steer clear of their exercise. As a precaution, if you are outside, I ask that you go inside until you are advised that it is safe to resume normal activities." Knowing that cruise-ship passengers were not quick to respond to requests, he added, "To compensate for this inconvenience, all beverages, including alcoholic drinks, served at our inside bars and restaurants will be free of charge."

—∿—

Palmer and the others aboard the gray Navy MH-60 Seahawk watched as the Pakistani soldiers made their way to the containers of interest. Their procedure, as they had explained before the helicopters departed from Karachi, was to inspect the exterior of the container, take a radiation reading, and check the security seal. The first two passed without an issue that would warrant further inspection. When the soldiers moved on to the third, the last one loaded before departure, one of the soldiers shouted that the security seal was intact and was not the same number as the one on the container that had left DGK. At that same moment, the EOD with the radiation detector said he had detected radiation. Another shouted there was a wire, possibly an antenna, extending along the side of the container, near the top. The team leader ordered him to stop and get down.

When Psimas and Cole heard that Pakistani soldiers were reporting radiation detection, as well as an antenna on the side of the container, they looked at each other with wide eyes.

Cole shouted to the pilot, "Get the hell out of here. Go! Go! Go!"

The pilot needed no further urging. He banked the helicopter hard to the left and flew away from the cargo ship.

The US Seahawk helicopter was accelerating to its maximum speed of 170 miles per hour when the sky brightened. Seconds later, the helicopter shook wildly, as though an invisible giant had just tried and failed to pluck it out of the sky.

The shock wave was followed by a heart-stopping boom.

Green grabbed ahold of Palmer's arm, looking to him—in a rare moment of vulnerability and desperation—for reassurance. He found himself squeezing her hand, breathing heavily. A look at Psimas and Cole confirmed what he already knew. This was no conventional weapon explosion; it was nuclear.

When Psimas and Cole determined they had reached a safe distance, Cole told the pilot to turn and give them a view. A cloud hung over the point of explosion and was trailing to the east. Psimas urged the pilot to remain upwind of the explosion to minimize radiation exposure. She had radiation-detection and air-quality-measurement devices on board. They scanned the area with their binoculars. The cargo ship was gone, as were the Pakistani helicopter and two RHIBs.

The sea was littered with debris. Psimas took photographs and collected radiation and air-quality readings from their position. The photos and data would assist in confirming if, in fact, the blast was from a nuclear device and, if so, help to determine its size.

Palmer cleared the tremble from his voice. "Opinion, Dr. Psimas?"

"Definitely nuclear—probably a tactical device," she said. "We won't know if it was an atomic or hydrogen warhead until all the data are analyzed."

"Can you be sure?"

"Pakistan doesn't release information on the number, type, or yield of their warheads, so there's no way to pin down the exact size. It's usually expressed in kilotons or megatons. A kiloton is a thousand tons of TNT. A megaton is a million tons of TNT. Distinguishing between a tactical and strategic nuclear weapon is difficult. But whether it's a hundred-kiloton strategic weapon or a ten-kiloton tactical weapon, they all have the potential for massive destruction and death. If it were one of their large strategic warheads, we might not have survived. We'll know more when we look at the data."

Cole and the other EOD nodded in agreement, their faces still quite pale. At Palmer's side, Green was staring out the window, unspeaking—though her hand still gripped his forearm as though her life depended on it.

He kept his focus on the matter at hand. "Will the data define the number and size of the devices that detonated?"

"Detonation of a nuclear device is a complex engineering feat. It requires a precisely timed and perfectly symmetrical explosion that surrounds a solid ball of plutonium called the pit. You remember, we talked about that. The pit being small, like a softball. For example, even if a tactical device were to detonate next to one or more nuclear warheads, it would not result in the detonation of the other devices because those explosions would not be symmetrical. They might also explode, but the explosions would be significantly weaker or not nuclear at all. It's called a fizzle yield. Let's say, for example, that all three stolen nuclear warheads were in that container. One might be an actual nuclear explosion. The other two would explode, but the explosions would either not be nuclear or produce very low yields. Still, plutonium-oxide aerosol would be released from the plutonium pits, which itself would be a substantial public-health risk."

"We're low on fuel," the Seahawk pilot interjected through their headsets. "We've got to leave for Karachi. Do you have all you need, Psimas?"

"Yes," she confirmed, sitting back in her seat. On their way back, they spotted the Pakistan Navy corvette on a heading back to Karachi.

When they landed at the air base in Karachi, a Pakistani military hazmat team, outfitted in hazmat suits with self-contained breathing apparatus, was waiting for them. The passengers and crew were whisked away to a hanger and scanned for radiation. A small amount was detected on everyone, but nothing significant enough to be worthy of concern. Regardless, they showered, scrubbed, and were given clean military work uniforms to wear. In addition, they were given potassium iodine tablets to protect the thyroid gland from radiation injury.

—*∽*—

The cruise ship captain and crew on the bridge had taken their own advice and were inside the bridge when the sky brightened. It was as if a photographer's flash had gone off inches in front of his face. The shock wave came next. Although invisible, the effect could be seen on the surface of the water, and the air seemed to shimmer, like a curtain of hot air in the desert, as the wave approached his ship. It came so fast that there was no time to sound an alarm beforehand.

When the captain saw a distinct mushroom cloud rise from the place where the cargo ship had been only moments before, he suspected he had witnessed a nuclear explosion and sounded the alarm for all passengers and crew not already inside to go inside and remain there. He increased the speed of the ship to maximum, changing course to one that would take the ship away from the downwind drift of any radioactive fallout.

Many of the passengers were enjoying their free drinks at one of the inside bars or were taking a stroll around the inside before getting ready for their next meal and had stopped to watch the helicopters and boats approach the cargo ship in the distance. Some, however, had ignored the announcement from the captain and had remained outside. Crew members were attempting to herd all remaining passengers inside. One passenger, a German amateur photographer, had a Nikon SLR camera and 200–500mm telephoto lens zoomed in on the action and took photos at various stages of the operation, occasionally taking bursts of several photos in less than a second. He was taking one of those bursts when the light almost blinded him. His vision had not yet cleared when the shock wave hit. He had grabbed for anything attached to the ship and held on as the ship shuddered and swayed.

Passengers who were on deck said later that the intensity of the heat that accompanied the blast wave was like opening the door to a hot oven. Then came the tidal wave, extending out from where the cargo ship had been. The rise and fall of the ship over the wave was negligible; a greater effect would be felt when the wave struck the coastline.

Cruise ship passengers with a Wi-Fi connection fueled speculation as they sent messages to friends, family, their hometown television stations, and posted their photographs on social media. The German passenger who had taken photographs of the explosion posted one he had taken with his mobile phone on Instagram and was swamped with requests for interviews and any other photographs he had. The captain quickly shut down the ship's Wi-Fi, announcing that it had been overloaded and would be back up soon. At first, the passengers and crew aboard the ship did not suspect it was a nuclear explosion, but they became alarmed when the captain had all the doors to the exterior of the ship closed and locked.

Rumors as to why no one could go outside centered around the military helicopters and boats near the cargo ship at the time of the explosion and the earlier news coverage of the lost nuclear devices in

Pakistan. Many of the passengers deduced that it was from fear of radiation exposure. To reduce the risk of panic among the passengers and crew, the captain eventually announced that there was no proof that the explosion was nuclear, therefore, no proven risk of radiation exposure. However, as a precaution, they were headed to the nearest port, where the passengers, crew, and ship would be checked and treated if necessary.

39

US EMBASSY
ISLAMABAD, PAKISTAN

Palmer, Green, and Psimas arrived at the embassy and rushed to see General Reynolds.

The phones were ringing off the hooks. Reynolds was in a meeting, which he promptly ended the moment he'd heard the three had returned. Waving them into his office, he asked, "What the hell happened?"

"Everyone is still trying to sort that out," Palmer replied, proceeding to tell the general everything that had taken place from the time they took off in the helicopter to when they landed and were processed.

"Let's make this quick. I need to get to my computer and a phone," Psimas said. "I have colleagues around the world assessing the explosive power of that blast, as well as poring through data related to the air content, radiation, and seismic activity. I was there. I can contribute my firsthand experience."

Reynolds nodded. "This won't take long. First of all, Dr. Psimas, do you believe that was a nuclear detonation? Could it have been one of Pakistan's missing nukes?"

"I'm 95 percent certain it was a relatively small nuclear device, a tactical or small strategic weapon. However, it's possible that there was one nuclear blast and the other two warheads exploded at a nonnuclear level."

"That aligns with what the Pakistanis are saying," Reynolds said. "Their position is that all three warheads were in that cargo container."

Psimas shook her head and leaned forward. "How would they know this soon? I'll admit it's possible, but it's also possible that only one was aboard the *Fair Winds* and the other two are still missing and in transit. The data are still being collected and analyzed."

"Maybe the terrorists want us to believe it was all three nukes," Palmer said.

"That makes sense," Green added. "If we bought into that, we'd stop looking for the other two."

"The Chameleon, or whoever is behind this, would like nothing more." Palmer sighed, his mind racing. "It gives them time to position the other two."

Reynolds glanced back and forth between Palmer and Green. "Our handlers are contacting and interviewing their assets, including those Singleton managed." His gaze settled on Palmer. "You look like you want to say something. What's on your mind?"

Palmer stood and walked around the office with his hands deep in his front pockets like a professor in front of an auditorium full of students. "Let's assume one of the two trucks that stopped on the highway, near where we found the body, was transporting the nuclear weapons as part of the deployment. We know from Pakistan's president that the shipment originated in DGK, and Sabri told me that the destination was Masroor Air Force Base in Karachi. That's where the nukes were discovered missing. If that's true, then what was the other truck doing there, and why did the truck carrying the nukes stop? Certainly not to assist a disabled vehicle. The satellite images did not show any forklifts or means of moving the device from one truck to the other. And Alona and I didn't see any tread marks other than for the two trucks and a smaller vehicle. Perhaps they didn't need to move the weapons."

Reynolds stared back at him, eyes wide. "What are you saying, Palmer?"

"Perhaps the other truck was identical and they simply switched them. They would have taken the empty truck to the base and the other truck with the nukes to Karachi Port. We know that at least one device was on the cargo ship en route to Cyprus and then Haifa, Israel. I find it difficult to believe that the device just randomly detonated. Something or someone triggered it. The fact that it detonated at the moment the inspection team was at the container would be an almost impossible coincidence. Just before the blast, the Pakistani soldier said there was an antenna attached to the container. Was that the trigger? Or was it detonated by someone close enough to watch what was going on and who could see when the team was inspecting the containers? If so, where were they?"

"Maybe it was a jihadist crewman who was willing to give his life," Green offered. "There are more than enough crazy jihadists who would sacrifice themselves for an eternity in paradise. Or maybe it was a motion sensor that triggered it."

"That's possible," Psimas said. "But why didn't the movement of the container as it was loaded onto the ship detonate it?"

"Damn good question," Reynolds acknowledged.

Psimas shook her head slowly, thinking fast. "They needed one or more persons with the nuclear weapon expertise to alter the preset triggering mechanisms and bypass any controls. That would have taken time. If what you're suggesting is true, and the trucks were switched, the one with the weapons would have gone to a concealed location where engineers could make those changes. They couldn't do it in a truck moving down the highway."

"Of course," Palmer said. "They would have needed a warehouse or someplace they could make those changes before the container was loaded onto the cargo ship. That window of time would be from the time we saw live feed from the satellite showing the two trucks until the time the last container was loaded onto the *Fair Winds*, just prior to departing the port…less the time it would take to drive from the meeting point to the ship."

"Exactly," Psimas said. "We need to locate that facility, perhaps a warehouse at or near the port."

"I've been chewing over something else," Palmer said. "The meeting with Sabri."

"Why is that?" Reynolds's asked. "We got exactly what we wanted. He invited us to observe the inspection."

"He was too quick to extend that invitation. Had Dr. Psimas not told our pilot to keep a minimum of five miles away and stay upwind, we might have been destroyed along with the other helicopter and boats."

"Maybe he knew our EODs would give our pilot the same warning," Green said. "If he wanted to ensure we were killed, he would have asked us for hands-on assistance or for us to provide close-in support."

"Perhaps." Palmer shrugged, staring at the ceiling. "Still doesn't feel right. If it were hands-on assistance, only the EODs would have participated. You, Dr. Psimas, and I would not have been invited to observe." He paused briefly before adding, "He mentioned Alona's name during our meeting, even though I had not."

"It's obvious that there's a lot we know and much more that we don't," General Reynolds said, leaning forward with his elbows on his desk. "The three of you get out of here and get to work. You'll have access to all the information available to us and will be in the loop for any information we receive from the Pakistanis." He addressed Palmer and Green. "Make full use of Psimas as long as she's here."

"Are you leaving?" Green asked Psimas. "I thought you would be here longer."

"Washington wants me back. I'm going to try to convince them that I need to stay. I'll make the case that if I'm in Washington, I can't serve as the intermediary with Pakistan's nuclear weapons experts."

"One more question before we leave," Palmer said to Reynolds. "Did you ID the men in the photos we sent? The body beside the highway, the two gunmen in the café, and the body that we believe was Jaffar's roommate that was dumped in the street outside the café?"

"Our team was unable to identify the men," Reynolds said. "We're working with a trusted ISI contact. He said he would get back to us. Don't hold your breath."

40

INTER-SERVICES INTELLIGENCE, CRISIS ROOM ISLAMABAD, PAKISTAN

ISI Director-General Hesbani learned of the explosion of the *Fair Winds* moments after it occurred. Upon hearing that the explosion was most likely nuclear, he fell back into his chair and closed his eyes, letting the news sink in. How had this happened? Who was responsible?

The implications for Pakistan were far-reaching, but as tragic as it was, detonation at sea was a gift from Allah. Had the ship been at Karachi Port or elsewhere, the human and material losses would have been much worse. The loss of life had thankfully been limited to the crew of the cargo ship and the relatively small number of Pakistani military men who were aboard it, as well as those in the Pakistani helicopter and in the RHIBs nearby.

Commodore Sabri had authorized the Americans to observe the operation. But *why?* The ongoing concern was the potential for radiation exposure to thousands of others, perhaps hundreds of thousands of others, as the wind carried the radiation cloud toward land.

Was this the work of a terrorist group? Perhaps Al-Qaeda or one of its affiliates? Pulling this theft off required meticulous planning—the hallmark of an Al-Qaeda operation. Or perhaps it was ISIS? ISIS had the sort of power and money to plan and execute the operation but lacked the finesse or expertise. No, it wasn't their style, and after their defeat in Syria, they were likely incapable of pulling it off. It was possible the culprit was one of the Iranian terrorist groups. Whoever it was, someone inside the Pakistani military and intelligence operations community must have been involved. Was it The Chameleon? The meticulous planning, the expertise, and the financing were typical of other attacks attributed to the man—if he even existed. Whoever it was, why destroy a cargo ship? Nothing politically significant could be gained from that. Had the device exploded prematurely? The navy's corvette had been on station miles from the container ship. Its officers had been in communication with the two RHIBs and were also monitoring the communications from the team that had boarded the *Fair Winds*. Their last transmission regarded radiation detection and an antenna extending from the container.

The American military and CIA would demand an explanation of the theft of the weapons and the detonation at sea, as would every country in the world. Hesbani hated the Americans' condescending attitude and arrogance. Were it not for their money and expertise, he would have nothing to do with the United States. They used money like a weapon, wielding amounts so large and so freely that, like a powerful opioid, one became physically and emotionally dependent on it. Then, when they threatened to reduce or eliminate funding, men became desperate to do whatever was necessary to meet America's demands.

American and Pakistani nuclear weapon experts were analyzing the explosion data. As a result of the 1996 Comprehensive Nuclear-Test-Ban Treaty, global monitoring stations had been set up around the world to monitor compliance. Based on the available data and the eyewitness accounts of the cruise ship crew and passengers, experts were in agreement that at least one nuclear device had detonated. However, a debate raged on as to the number of nuclear devices that had been in the container and the number that had detonated in a nuclear versus a fizzle manner. Because the blast had occurred on the Arabian Sea instead of on land, the data from seismic monitoring stations that differentiated between earthquakes and nuclear explosions were imprecise and therefore inconclusive.

In addition, data from over eighty monitoring stations built to detect radionuclides released following detonation of a nuclear device were analyzed. Although radionuclides were detected, experts still could not agree on the actual number of nuclear detonations.

The *Fair Winds* had been en route to the Port of Limassol, Cyprus, one of the busiest ports in the Mediterranean. There was always tension between the Greek Cypriots and the Turks. However, neither was stupid enough to use a nuclear weapon against the other, and the close proximity of the two meant that both would suffer the ill effects of a nuclear explosion on the other's soil. According to the men interviewed at Karachi Port, a container bound for Cyprus was loaded onto the ship an hour or so before departure. Was that the container that exploded? After Limassol, the next port of call for the *Fair Winds* was the Israeli Port of Haifa, the country's largest commercial port. Haifa was the most obvious and desirable target for an attack. Had the intention been to detonate the warhead there and something had gone wrong, resulting in a premature detonation? If so, what caused the warhead to explode? Had it been detonated intentionally because the Pakistani military was boarding the vessel? Or was it an unfortunate coincidence? Many questions remained unanswered.

Hesbani contemplated the possible circumvention and apparent breach of Pakistan's command-and-control structure for control of its nuclear weapons and the individual weapon's internal security measures. Pakistan's weapons were not usually mated, but Sarkis had said the urgent movement of weapons required both components be moved.

One component was useless without the other. Still, the operation required the technical expertise to override the security measures, arm the weapons, and detonate the warheads—an extremely complex task. The terrorists would need to override the assigned triggers—like altitude—and create a type of trigger to detonate the warheads remotely or by a timer. Such nuclear weapon expertise was difficult to come by and exorbitantly expensive to buy.

And what of the two-man rule that required that two people authorize use of the warheads by providing the required warhead-specific codes within a defined window of time? Pakistan's military had absolute control and authority over the use of nuclear weapons. Even the most senior civil leaders did not know where the nuclear weapons were stored. The need to minimize the number of people authorized to launch a nuclear attack or counterattack meant that, as far as he knew, all men on the two-man list were high-ranking members of Pakistan's military. Either two of the men on the list were complicit in the plot or someone had the technical skills and access necessary to overwrite the requirement.

41

FOUR WEEKS AFTER THE EXPLOSION OF THE *FAIR WINDS*

Four weeks had passed since the cargo ship explosion. The general consensus was that all three devices were aboard the *Fair Winds*. The media still provided periodic updates on the investigation, but the reports no longer dominated the news. The loss of the nuclear weapons and the explosion had fallen off the news cycle. The media provided daily updates, but with nothing new to report, people lost interest. Tourism rebounded in locations considered nuclear terrorism targets like the Vatican, New York City, and the Holy Land.

Now was the time for finger-pointing. Much of the attention focused on Pakistan's nuclear weapon security procedures and its command-and-control process. The media had reported every detail of Pakistan's investigation, the men involved in the theft, and the steps to prevent the theft of a nuclear weapon from ever reoccurring. Thus far, Raul Ahmadi and his men had not been found. Some speculated they may have been aboard the *Fair Winds* and perished in the detonation.

Psimas was in Washington and in constant contact with her colleagues around the world. After weeks of data analyses, the experts' consensus opinion was that one device had accidentally or intentionally detonated, causing the other two to explode in a nonsymmetrical manner, producing fizzle yields. Not everyone was convinced.

Pakistan also agreed with the consensus opinion and issued a statement that all warheads had been aboard the *Fair Winds* when it was destroyed. Pakistan was under tremendous international pressure to be more open about their nuclear weapon security and their command-and-control process.

When the president of Pakistan initially notified the president of India about the theft, the Indian forces crossed the Line of Control. With the two countries on the brink of a nuclear war, China sent troops to the Line of Control, which prompted India to pull its forces back and agree to a temporary ceasefire. Had China not intervened, India and Pakistan would have been at war, perhaps a nuclear one. Tension between India and Pakistan remained at an all-time high; however, neither was prepared to anger China, least of all Pakistan. India had implemented rigorous screening of incoming ships and planes and showed no signs of easing up.

Similar enhanced screening continued in most major ports around the world. The result was a worldwide slowdown of cargo into and out of ports, causing huge backups at the ports in terms of ships and trucks. Cargo companies complained that the threat had passed and so cargo operations should return to normal. Lastly, security at all transit points from Pakistan was tightened, none more so than at the border with Iran.

A thorough review of soldiers and personnel who were away without leave was conducted by the Pakistani Army. The final list was short and accurate. Raul Ahmadi, who the media had begun calling The Chameleon, was almost certainly the leader. In addition to several soldiers, two nuclear engineers remained missing, along with General Sarkis and Colonel Ashkani. A worldwide manhunt was underway.

42

ST. KATHARINE DOCKS
LONDON

Fiona Collins's team in the counterterrorism branch of Britain's Secret Intelligence Service, more commonly known as MI6, had been putting in such long hours that the director invited everyone out for an appreciation dinner.

Collins would have preferred a day off to sleep and reboot, but she couldn't refuse. They deserved a celebration, a chance to let their hair down, laugh, and have some fun. She enjoyed the team and had made a few friends during her relatively short time with MI6. Dinner would be at the Dickens Inn at St. Katharine Docks, which was on the Thames River and adjacent to the Tower of London. The vibrant waterfront was home to several businesses and restaurants, and its marina had one hundred eighty-five berths, accommodating vessels up to forty meters long.

The three-story, wood-framed Dickens Inn dated from the 1700s and had balconies on the top two floors that ran the length of the building. Both balconies were adorned with hanging baskets of flowers, making it appear more like a country pub one might see in rural Cornwall rather than in London. The director booked tables at the inn's tavern bar rather than its pizzeria, which was too informal, or its grill, which was too formal. Collins had not been to the Dickens Inn in years but had eaten at another St. Katharine Docks restaurant the month before.

Collins and a coworker, Carol Baxter, who also lived in Clapham, took a taxi to the restaurant and split the cost. Baxter, a tall brunette in her late thirties, was one of the most energetic, dedicated people she had met at work. Because she held a much more senior position than Collins, who was a junior intelligence analyst, Collins considered Baxter her mentor.

On a personal level, Baxter had confided to Collins that she and her significant other had broken up a few months before, and she was enjoying the freedom of being unattached. Collins wondered if her total immersion into work was part of her strategy to keep her mind off her ex.

"This is going to be a fun night, Fiona," Baxter said. "We deserve a break."

"I'm so looking forward to it. I can't remember the last time I had a night out. I love the Dickens Inn. Next time Jake's in town, I'm going to take him—"

"Stop!" Baxter interjected, rolling her eyes.

Collins balked. "What?"

"No Jake Palmer talk tonight. Two gin and tonics, and you'll go all melancholy on me and want to go home straight after dinner and have a good boo. No, no. We're going to eat, drink, and dance."

Collins tilted her head skeptically. "You know it's not a good idea to drink too much at a company event—too easy to speak your piece, kiss someone you barely know, and say and do things you'll regret while staring down at your cup of coffee the next morning."

Baxter looked at Collins as if she had lost her mind, and then they both broke out in loud laughs. "Seriously, I need this," Baxter said. "And I have a feeling you'll watch out for me."

They indeed had a grand time. Collins had never seen this side of Baxter, who always maintained a serious demeanor at work. Baxter lived up to the adage of "work hard and play hard." It had been a long time since Collins had laughed so much. Most of the team was ready to leave around ten o'clock. She and Baxter stayed a while longer and then walked around the marina, talking about the evening and their coworkers. The sky was crystal clear, although London's light pollution hid all but the crescent moon and the brightest stars and planets.

"Wouldn't you love to go out to sea on that one?" Baxter asked, pointing at a magnificent, white yacht. "I can see myself basking in the sun on the upper level, my top off, a cold drink in my hand, and the warm sun on my face and tits. The light is on. Maybe they'll invite us in for a drink."

They turned and walked toward the yacht. The yacht's name, *Medicine Man*, was displayed on the stern, and underneath the name was its home port, London.

Collins stopped in her tracks and gasped.

"What is it?" Baxter asked. "What's wrong?"

"I know who owns that yacht. Or at least who owned it at one time."

"Brilliant! Let's go aboard and knock on the door."

"That's not a good idea." She proceeded to tell Baxter about her and Palmer's involvement in the investigation of Richard Moore, who was convicted of selling counterfeit medicine through his pharmaceutical distribution company and laundering the proceeds. A Saudi sheikh had a large stake in the company and had donated much of his earnings to fraudulent Arab charities that were fronts for terrorist organizations.

"That's interesting," Baxter replied halfheartedly, as though she'd only half paid attention to Collins's story. "But I'm serious, let's knock on the door and see who's home. We can pretend we're two silly women who've had far too much to drink."

"That's not going to be much of a stretch on my part," Collins admitted. "And no, we're not doing that."

They looked up at the yacht as they strolled down the docks, stopping as they neared it. The light was on in the main cabin. Shadows were visible through the sheer curtains on the windows. *One—no, two men. Who are they? I wonder who owns this yacht now?* Collins thought. Her concern was probably nothing but her imagination running wild after a few drinks. If she still felt this way in the morning, she would pursue it.

———

Collins rolled out of bed, heading to the kitchen with no small amount of desperation for a strong mug of coffee. Her head was pounding. While the coffee was brewing, she popped a couple of over-the-counter painkillers to combat her raging hangover. *Why did I allow myself to drink so much? Never again.*

Once her coffee was finished brewing, she made her way to the living room, slumping onto the nearest couch, where she proceeded to reflect on the previous night. It was the first time since she'd been hired that she had spent time with her colleagues outside of work. Baxter was a hoot and quickly becoming a good friend.

Collins's thoughts soon drifted to the *Medicine Man* yacht. She did not remember seeing it when she was at St. Katharine Docks the previous month. She would have noticed; it was almost impossible to miss. *When did it arrive? Where had it been?*

———

Once she'd gotten dressed and had breakfast, Collins was feeling much better. She phoned the office and said she would be a little late. The admin she spoke with confided in her that she wasn't the first who had called saying they were running late or weren't coming in at all.

Collins took the tube to St. Katharine Docks. The *Medicine Man* was still there, looking more luxurious in the sunlight than it had the night prior. She located the marina office and went inside. A man sitting at a desk near the door stood and asked if he could help her. She introduced herself and flashed her MI6 identification card.

"I have a couple of general questions to ask about one of the yachts, the *Medicine Man*," Collins said. "Can you tell me if it has been out of port recently, and, if so, when did it return?"

"Is this an official inquiry, or are you just curious?"

Collins had made a living getting information from people when she was a pharmaceutical company research auditor and later head of the clinical auditing group. A key skill she had honed over time was her ability to make people comfortable. She suspected she would be speaking with a man, and thus, before she'd left the house, had applied makeup and done her hair. She'd put on a nice outfit for good measure, something casual but not too much so.

"Let's just say I'm officially curious. This is a routine inquiry, nothing more," Collins said.

"The yacht has been docked here for a long time. Off the top of my head, I'd say two to three years. But it's been away for months for some engine maintenance and interior refurbishment. Rich people like to update the interior every couple of years. For something that significant, they usually return it to the manufacturer or take it to a marine facility that specializes in that specific type of boat."

"Do you know where the work was done?"

"They didn't say, and I didn't ask. None of my business. They told me it would be out for an extended period and said they wanted to retain that specific space at the marina. Expensive to have such a large slip and keep it empty. Again—rich people." He shrugged and rolled his eyes.

Collins kept her smile intact. "How long has it been back?"

"It arrived yesterday morning."

"Will it be leaving soon?"

"Didn't say." He paused and took a step back. "You're making me nervous, Ms. Collins. If you want any more information, I'll need to contact my manager."

"No need. But before I go, one more question: Do you know who's on board? Names? The number of people?"

"That's more than one question," he countered slyly. "I've never seen them. The captain contacted us by marine radio when they were a day or two out and gave me their ETA. I told them which lock opening would meet their needs and told them to contact us either by phone or on VHF Channel 80 when they were in sight of Tower Bridge, which they did."

"Thank you for your assistance. The agency really appreciates it, and I do as well."

Collins walked to the station and took the tube to MI6. On the way, she thought about what she'd learned. It was probably nothing. She hesitated to file an official report. An MI6 junior analyst raising an alarm where there was no evidence that anything was wrong— and on top of that, investigating the situation without any prior authorization—would not sit well with her management. On the other hand, what she knew was intelligence, actionable or not. Only one person had her complete trust. He would understand and know what to do.

I need to phone Jake.

43

US EMBASSY
ISLAMABAD, PAKISTAN

Jake Palmer was at the Embassy gym working out when his cell phone rang. He toweled the sweat from his face before answering.

"Jake, it's Fiona. Can you talk?"

Palmer's heart, which was already beating fast from the workout, seemed to skip a beat. He had missed her and had thought about calling her several times. The change in their relationship and the awkwardness of their parting had made him hesitant to make the first call. He had texted her with his new cell phone number but received no reply. As work consumed his days and nights, time passed by, one day bleeding into another. Now, weeks later, she was calling him?

"Yes, I'm at the gym working out. It's great to hear from you. How are you?"

"I need your advice on a business matter."

"Oh, business." His heart sunk a little. "Nothing classified, right?"

"Of course not. Regardless, I'm at the office and on a secure line. Do you recall the yacht that Richard Moore had in London, the one the Saudi sheikh who invested in his pharmaceutical distribution company gave him?"

He flipped through his memory. "The *Medicine Man*, right?"

"Yes. I was at a business dinner last night at St. Katharine Docks and saw it. There were at least two people aboard. This morning, I went by and spoke with the marina manager. He said the yacht had been out for maintenance and refurbishment for months and had returned yesterday morning. He had not seen or spoken to anyone since it docked. The owner kept making payments on the marina's slip while the yacht was away."

"Moore's still in prison, isn't he?"

"He is."

"Do you know who owns it now?"

"I went by my office and looked into it. Sheikh Khalifa Isma'il El-Hashem had given it to Moore. Apparently, when Moore went to prison, ownership of the yacht reverted to him."

"And El-Hashem was funneling money from his investment in Moore's distribution company to Arab charities, some of which were fronts for terrorist organizations. I know where you are headed. Could the missing nuclear devices possibly be on the yacht?"

"It's a long shot and probably nothing," Collins said. "I considered discussing it with my director at work but wanted to run it by you first. The consensus is that all three nuclear devices were destroyed in the explosion of the cargo ship."

"That's correct. For lack of anything definitive to the contrary, Pakistan has taken that position. However, governments around the world continue with stringent inspections of vehicles, vessels, and aircrafts entering the country. That may go on for months, if not years, to come."

"What do you think, Jake?"

"There are other theories. One is that the explosion was a diversion and that one or two of the devices are still missing. That's my belief, too. With the missing nuclear engineers involved, the detonation aboard the cargo ship would not have been accidental. Whoever planned this is smart. They would not waste the time and money on blowing up a cargo ship unless that was a cover for a much more important target."

"Do you believe a nuclear warhead could be hidden aboard a yacht the size of the *Medicine Man*?"

Palmer's mind spun into full gear. "Yes, of course." Inspections were conducted of mega-yachts that were at or near Karachi Port around the time the devices were diverted. The authorities used the yachts' transponders to locate and identify them. "Where was the maintenance and refurbishment work done?"

"The marina manager only knew that it was not done locally. He believes it was done somewhere outside the UK. He told me that repairs and major refurbishments on mega-yachts are usually performed by the manufacturer or by a company specializing in that make of yacht."

"If the vessel entered British waters from outside the EU, customs inspectors would have asked for documentation and may have conducted an inspection. A yacht that is known to authorities and is homeported in London would not typically be boarded, but under the current circumstances, it might be. Can you find out if customs inspectors inspected the yacht?"

"I can try. I'm not certain where to look."

"I see red flags, Fiona. If the owner of the yacht had not been suspected of funding terrorist organizations in the past, I wouldn't think twice about it. You need to report this as soon as possible."

"I will. Thank you for listening and for your advice. I needed it before filing an official report."

"Let me know what action they take. I want to know before I report it here."

"I've missed you, Jake." Her words took him entirely off guard, especially after all of the work-related talk.

"I've missed you, too," he confessed. "Does this mean you're taking me back?"

"Let's talk about that the next time I see you."

———

After speaking with Collins, Palmer finished his workout, showered, and went to his office. First, he checked a public website that tracked nonmilitary marine traffic worldwide to confirm that the *Medicine Man* was at St. Katharine Docks. The site showed the location of every ship and registered vessel in the world. He zoomed in on London and found St. Katharine Docks Marina, and then was able to locate the *Medicine Man*, which meant its transponder was on. He looked at photographs of the yacht and for its past track. No past track was shown.

Later that day, Collins called him again. She had not yet found whether the *Medicine Man* had been inspected when it entered British waters. She said that she'd met with her director, who told her to file a formal report and chastised her for speaking with the marina manager. He reminded her that she was not a field officer and that it was not her role to conduct an external investigation, especially one that was potentially dangerous. She had written and filed the intelligence report and would wait and see what action, if any, was taken.

Palmer told her he would speak with General Reynolds and let her know what transpired.

———

The general listened, waiting until Palmer finished relaying his MI6 girlfriend's concern about a yacht in a London marina before commenting.

With his arms crossed and eyebrows lowered, he asked, "So, what did MI6 think of her concern?"

"Her director told her to file a report, which she's done, and chastised her for going to the marina and talking to the manager. He said she was not authorized to conduct external surveillance or investigations."

"Rightly so. If a junior analyst did that on my watch, I would have done the same thing. That aside, I want to know what *you* think should be done."

"If I were completely objective, a report of this type raised by a typical junior analyst would not be a priority. However, Fiona is not a typical junior analyst. I trust her instincts. And having been involved in the investigation of Richard Moore with her, I believe someone should follow up and determine when and where the maintenance and refurbishment work was done and where else that yacht might have been."

"Should that someone be us or MI6, the equivalent of our FBI and Homeland Security rolled into one?"

Palmer's eyes narrowed. "The Brits, of course."

"You've answered your own question." Reynolds expelled a sigh. "Now, it's up to her to see that this gets the attention it warrants. Anything else, Palmer?"

"Yes. Now that things here have wound down a little, I would like some time off to see Fiona."

"Wound down? Just because most everyone thinks the nukes all blew up or were destroyed in the Arabian Sea does not mean things have wound down."

"I'm not requesting a leave of absence, only three or four days off."

Reynolds drummed his fingers on his desk while his eyes were fixed on Palmer's. "Okay. You have four days, including travel there and back. But let me make one thing perfectly clear: The Brits do not appreciate us pissing on their tree. You are not authorized to conduct any investigation or intelligence work in the United Kingdom. You are off the clock. Understand?"

"Copy that, sir."

"Repeat what I said."

"I will not conduct any investigation or intelligence work in the United Kingdom. I'm off the clock."

"Does Green know you're taking some time off?"

"I'll tell her before I leave. May I ask a favor? Earlier today, I checked the flights to London. There are no nonstop flights. It'll take me almost a day to get there and a day to get back. I'll have only two days, at best, in London. The situation with Fiona has reached critical mass. Our relationship is at stake."

Reynolds shook his head. "Damn it, Palmer. I'll authorize you to fly military both ways. That way you can squeeze out an extra day. Now, get the hell out of here. And don't forget to tell Green."

44

US EMBASSY
ISLAMABAD, PAKISTAN

After General Reynolds approved his request for a few days off in London, Palmer's first call was to Senior Chief Nick Cole. He invited him to tag along, suggesting he bring his kit—just in case they stumbled upon a nuclear weapon that needed diffusing.

Cole laughed before realizing that Palmer was perfectly serious.

With the international consensus being that all three weapons were destroyed in the explosion on the cruise ship, and with China stepping into calm tensions between Pakistan and India, Cole admitted he was bored sitting around waiting for something to happen.

Palmer then headed to Green's office, preparing for her possible reaction to his going to London for a few days. Earlier, he had wondered why she hadn't checked with him before she texted Aaliyah and asked to meet. Now it was his turn to be honest with her about the trip and the reason for it. He caught up with her in the Embassy's computer services department and told her he was going to London for a couple of days.

"Spending some time with Fiona?"

"Yes. We have some issues we need to talk through. I'll be back in few days."

Green looked at him, brow furrowing. "This isn't like you. Trouble in paradise? No. You're not the forlorn-lover type. Why are you really going?"

"Things have slowed down. I need to get away for a couple of days."

"I don't believe you. Don't you dare go off on a mission without me. I'll never throw you under the proverbial bus, but don't lie to me."

Palmer paused before he responded. Green was his partner. She had once saved his life. If he couldn't trust her, he couldn't trust anyone. Besides, he had only recently questioned Green's calling Aaliyah before running it by him. *Time to read her in. We're partners and I need to be honest with her.*

"Fiona and I worked on a counterfeit-medicine case in the UK a while back. The perp, Richard Moore, kept his yacht at a marina in London. A Saudi sheikh named Khalifa Isma'il El-Hashem, a coconspirator, had given him the yacht. El-Hashem funneled the counterfeit medicine through Moore's drug distribution business and used the profits to fund Arab charities, some of which were fronts for terrorist organizations. El-Hashem was never charged or convicted in any crime. When Moore went to prison, ownership of the yacht reverted to the sheikh. The yacht left London for maintenance and refurbishment work months ago, most likely outside the UK. Two days ago, it reappeared at the London marina and Fiona saw it."

Green looked at Palmer, absorbing what he had said. "Really? That's all you've got?"

"I admit it's a long shot, but the timing fits. If not for the fact that El-Hashem is involved, I wouldn't give it much thought."

"So, you're going to the UK because your girlfriend suspects there is a nuke on board the yacht. Why hasn't she reported it to the British authorities?"

Palmer had not told Green about Collins working for MI6. If he was going to be honest with her, he had to tell her. She was his partner, and she would have his back on this. "Fiona now works for MI6 ... "

"She *what?* A minor point you failed to mention before."

"She's an intelligence analyst. She spoke with the marina manager and submitted a report to her boss at MI6. He said it would be entered into their intelligence system but that no further action was necessary. I suggested that she check to see if the yacht was inspected when it entered British waters, and if so, what was found."

"Her boss must be a man. Typical male reaction," Green said, scoffing. "As insignificant as it appears, someone should have at least followed up. What's your plan?"

"To be honest—"

"You'd damn well better be, Palmer."

"I don't have a plan," he finished. "I want to see the yacht and monitor what's going on for a day or two. Remember the EOD, Senior Chief Cole?"

"How could I forget him?" she said, shaking her head. "He was on the helicopter that day."

"I'm taking him along. If there's a nuke on that yacht, I'll need someone who can disarm it."

Green paused for a second, chewing a lip. "Anything I can do here?"

"Commodore Sabri—"

"The one who almost got us killed?"

"That's the one," Palmer said, grinning mirthlessly. "Use those computer skills of yours and see what you can dig up, and keep an eye on him while I'm gone. It still bothers me that his offer to observe the inspection of the cargo ship came without me even asking."

"You don't really think he's involved, do you? You seem to hold him in such high regard."

"He's changed. And he knew more about you and me than he was letting on. I never mentioned your name. My only reference to you was when I told him I had visited Srinagar with my attractive colleague."

Green smiled, feigning coyness. "You said I was attractive?"

"All part of the cover story for why we were in Srinagar."

"And he mentioned my name?"

"He said that my colleague Alona Green might be interested in going and said he understood we were a team."

Green's eyes widened slightly. "That's a little unnerving."

"Why would he suggest that you, officially a computer specialist, go along? Or for that matter, why invite me, the head of embassy security?" Palmer raised his brows in emphasis. "He already knew about us and our actual roles here. That's why."

"Why haven't you told me this before?"

"I should have. It caught me off guard at the time. I told myself he was probably privy to ISI reports and had seen something. Nothing more."

"Do you suspect he's The Chameleon?"

"I don't know. But if he is, and there's a nuke in London set to go off, he'll want to see it through. See what you can find out. If he leaves for London, let me know. That would be very useful information."

"Have you told Reynolds?"

"I told him about Fiona's suspicions about the yacht. He's approved me taking some time off to see her, even authorized me to fly military so I could get there quicker. However, he ordered me not to do any investigation or intelligence work while I'm there."

"Was that said with a wink-wink?"

"No. He was dead serious."

"I'll check on Sabri. And, Jake... thanks for reading me in on the op. If you hadn't and lived to come back here, I would have kicked your ass."

"I would have deserved it."

45

UK SECRET INTELLIGENCE SERVICE, MI6 LONDON

Collins had hit a brick wall in her investigation of the *Medicine Man*. She'd researched the requirements for private vessels entering and leaving the UK, and as Palmer suggested, she would need to find out if the *Medicine Man* was inspected by customs. But she had no information that proved it had even left British waters. The marina manager only said he didn't believe the maintenance and refurbishment had been done locally. If it had been inspected, she wanted to review the documentation and perhaps speak with the customs inspector. None of her work to date at MI6 had involved the UK Border Agency or customs authorities. She still had much to learn, but her inherent drive to solve the puzzle and find the answer had served her well in her audit role at B&A Pharmaceuticals and was paying dividends now. In this case, she had done all that she could on her own. She needed someone who was familiar with customs and border control procedures and processes. *Carol.*

Baxter wasn't in her office, so Collins went to the break room and found her there, having a late afternoon cup of tea.

"I need your help," Collins said.

"Anything. Well, almost anything."

Collins explained what she was trying to learn regarding the yacht they had seen.

"I told you. All we had to do was go on board and knock on the door," Baxter said. "What man in his right mind wouldn't have invited two stunners like us in for a drink?"

Collins rolled her eyes and patted her hair, laughing.

She sat down across from her friend. "Seriously, I'm hoping you have a contact within the customs authority that can help me."

Baxter cocked an eyebrow. "Is this official or off book?"

"Off book, I'm afraid. I've spoken with the boss and filed a report. Now I'm following up on a hunch and will file a supplemental report. Anything you tell me will be confidential. I won't mention I even spoke with you."

Baxter nodded. "A while back, I was gathering intelligence on a group we believed were smuggling firearms into the country. I worked closely with someone at Her Majesty's Revenue and Customs, Bradley Caldwell. He was in the customs arm of HMRC and was a handsome young man, I might add. We went out a couple of times." She sighed. "Quite a kisser, as I recall."

"Carol!"

"I digress … " She chuckled. "Follow me to my office."

Baxter gave Caldwell's contact information to Collins. "You probably shouldn't mention me when you speak with him."

Back at her desk, Collins phoned Caldwell. He answered on the second ring. She explained the situation to him and asked if he could help her. He said it would take a little time. He would finish what he was working on and get back to her before he left for the day.

About an hour later, he phoned.

"I've read the customs inspection report. Rather than go over it with you, I prefer that you speak with the one who inspected the yacht and filed the report. If you still need a copy of his report, he can send it to you."

"Without going into detail, is there anything of note in the report?"

"That depends on what you're looking for. By the way, did Carol ask you to phone me?"

"Carol?" Collins was caught. She couldn't lie. "Oh, yes. She's one of my coworkers. I asked her for a contact, and she gave me your name and number."

"Tell her I said hello. She owes me a drink."

Caldwell gave her the inspector's cell phone number, saying he was seldom in his office. Collins phoned straightaway, but the call went straight to voicemail. She left a brief message, stating that she needed to speak with him urgently.

She was about to leave for the day when he returned her call. Relieved, she answered and shut the door of her office. After a brief introduction, she got straight to the point. "I'm with MI6 and am following up on a routine inquiry. Could you tell me about a yacht named the *Medicine Man* that entered British waters a couple of days ago?"

"The *Medicine Man*... Yes, I saw it early yesterday morning. Quite impressive. Vessels registered in the UK that are reentering UK waters after repairs or modifications—other than routine maintenance— must check in with us. The captain of the vessel complied with the requirement to phone the National Yachtline. He said that they would be returning the yacht to her home port in London and that he and two other crew members would need immigration clearance. They completed the necessary form in advance and sent it to the UKBA, the UK Border Agency. When they entered British waters, the vessel was flying the Q flag, a yellow flag meaning the occupants are not under quarantine and the vessel needs customs clearance."

"Did you board the vessel?"

"Of course. I checked that they had filed the paperwork with UKBA well in advance, and then I met the crew and checked the men's passports."

"What nationality were the men and how many of them were there?"

"Three Saudi Arabian citizens. A captain and two crewmen. The captain said they were representing the Saudi sheikh who owned it. They had flown into Heathrow several months ago to transport it to Dubai for the work to be done. The proper immigration stamps from that visit were on their passports."

"What work had been completed on the yacht?" Collins pressed.

"I reviewed the invoice for the repairs and refurbishment. The captain explained that the ownership of the vessel had recently changed, and the new owner intended to sell it. He wanted it checked out and made ready for sale. This same captain and crew that flew to London several months ago took the vessel to a repair facility in Dubai, where it was purchased initially. The work had been completed, so the yacht was being returned to London and would be turned over to an international broker to sell. The captain said he and his two crew members planned to fly back to Saudi Arabia within the week. Being more curious than anything, I asked for a walk-through. He pointed out the interior decorating upgrades. If the upgrades had been substantial enough to increase the value of the yacht significantly, they would have been required to pay a value-added tax on the vessel. He also took me to the engine room and went over the maintenance that was performed. All of that was routine and did not increase the value of the yacht. I saw nothing out of the ordinary and signed off on their reentry."

"Could you send me a copy of the report for my files?"

"Certainly. I'll send you the form C1331 they completed as well." A brief pause before he asked, "Why are you so interested in this vessel and crew?"

"Because of the recent nuclear incident, we are following up on vessels that entered the UK from the Middle East. The information you provided will allow us to close the inquiry on this one. You've been most helpful."

Collins breathed a sigh of relief after she hung up. The inspector had convinced her that everything was in order. Although her initial fears were unfounded, she was still glad she had filed the report. She needed to tell Palmer what she had learned.

—⁂—

Collins phoned Palmer and told him about her conversation with the customs inspector, including that the yacht had been in Dubai. He told her that General Reynolds had already authorized him to take a couple of days off and fly on a military flight to London. He would be arriving at RAF Northolt and would be accompanied by Navy Senior Chief Petty Officer Nick Cole, an old friend of his. Collins knew not to ask any questions. Palmer had a reason for coming, and it wasn't only to see her. And why was Cole accompanying him? Palmer wouldn't bring him along unless he thought he might need help. She would learn more after they arrived. Meanwhile, she would see what she could find out about Cole and then talk to Baxter.

46

UNITED STATES EMBASSY ISLAMABAD, PAKISTAN

Green hurried to General Reynolds's office. His aide had phoned and said the general wanted to see her immediately. What could she have possibly done? Was it the overdue chewing out for what went down at Karachi Port? That had been Bob's fault for being a smart ass.

She saw that his door was open and kept walking, coming to a halt just before entering, as if she had suddenly reminded herself that she should request permission to enter. She cleared her throat and tapped lightly on the open door. Reynolds was at the window. When he looked around and saw her, he grimaced, shaking his head slowly.

"You wanted to see me, General?"

"Come in, Green," he said dully, waving her inside. She did as requested, closing the door at her back and meeting him beside his office's window. "Did Palmer talk to you about where he was going?"

She wasn't about to lie to him. "Yes, sir. He said he was going to London to spend some time with his lady friend, Fiona."

"Did he mention anything about a yacht and a nuclear warhead?"

"He did. He said Fiona had some far-fetched idea that one of the stolen warheads might be on a yacht at a marina in London."

"Palmer talked me into getting him on a priority military flight there. Ten minutes ago, I got a call from the head of our regional EOD group saying he had authorized one of his chiefs to accompany Palmer to London on the condition he could be reached while there."

Green held back a smile.

"Did Palmer contact you again after he told you he was going to London?" Reynolds said.

"He didn't. Before he left, he asked me to find out all that I could about Commodore Zahir Sabri and let him know if he leaves the country, especially if he's heading to London."

"When the three of us met with Psimas, Palmer said that he was suspicious that the offer for us to observe the boarding and inspection of cargo ships had come too easily. He believed Sabri may have set up the two of you to be in close proximity to the detonation."

"It's possible. Sabri told him I might want to join him in observing the inspection of the cargo ship. He mentioned me by name, even though Jake had not told him my name or told him that I was working with him. In fact, Sabri even knew our official job titles."

Reynolds swore under his breath. "Singleton!"

"Quite possibly," Green said. "I've been working with Dan Adams, one of our information resources specialists. We've gathered a lot of information about Sabri, personally and professionally. This is going to sound strange, but…"

"The two of you are full of surprises. What did you find?"

"Jake could be right."

"About what?"

Green kept her voice steady. "Sabri may be The Chameleon."

"You can't be serious," Reynolds said, balking.

"We've mapped out the time and location of major terrorist attacks that have been attributed to The Chameleon and compared those to where Sabri was when they occurred. It's far from conclusive, but there are too many instances where they match up for it to be coincidental."

"How about Raul Ahmadi? He led the team that stole the nukes. The media have speculated he is or was The Chameleon, depending on whether you believe he was killed when the *Fair Winds* went down."

Green bit her lower lip and shook her head. "No. I don't think so. Ahmadi led the ground operation. But he wasn't senior enough to have access to the information needed to pull off such an intricate diversion or the resources to pull together the financing and logistical support, nor did he have the right skills, frankly. We know Director-General Sarkis is missing. He may have provided the strategic knowledge and planning, but the killing of the journalist in Srinagar took detailed planning and tactical skill to pull off. Ahmadi may have been involved, but he couldn't have planned and led the operation. On the other hand, Sabri is a charismatic leader and former head of Pakistan's Navy Special Services Group. And because of his current position, he would have been in the loop on the deployment of the nukes. With your permission, I'd like to continue to research this angle, sir."

"You're treading on dangerous ground, Green. You're investigating a senior Pakistani military officer. Keep your head on a swivel. And if you hear from Palmer, let me know immediately."

—◈—

Green left General Reynolds's office and walked straight to the computer intelligence support office. Dan Adams—an overweight, prematurely balding, twenty-eight-year-old wearing a Hawaiian print shirt—was sitting in front of a semicircular array of LED computer screens in the corner of the room, away from the other analysts. Without looking up, he said, "Hi."

Green moved close, looking over his left shoulder. "Anything new, Dan?"

"As a matter of fact, there is." He spun his chair around to face her. "In recent years, Islamabad introduced CCTV surveillance throughout the city. The police call it the Intelligence Video Surveillance and Vehicle Management System. The cameras have number plate recognition, and the CCTV feeds and data are retained for months. Fortunately, or unfortunately, depending on your perspective, Islamabad is not concerned about the privacy of its citizens and has rules regarding how long the data are retained. I've also learned that our friend, Commodore Sabri, has three vehicles: a Range Rover, an Audi A8, and a classic 1968 Mercedes-Benz 300SEL. In my humble opinion, that is the number one classic Mercedes," he added offhandedly as he was prone to do now and again. He smiled. "I have the plate numbers for them."

"Quit teasing me," she chastised. "What have you done?"

"I've hacked into the system and have been able to track Sabri's movements, including the route he takes to and from work."

Impressive. "Are you kidding me?"

"I'm not," he said. "And I have, with a high degree of certainty, determined which days he did not travel to work, and to some extent, where he went. At least where the car went. I took the dates and times of attacks attributed to The Chameleon. There's an 87.5 percent match."

"Where is he now?" Green asked. "There is a rapidly developing issue in London."

"He left home this morning and drove to his office. Nothing on any of his vehicles since then. I can't rule out that he left by another means of transportation."

"The Chameleon appears to be very hands-on. If there is a potential attack brewing in London, he would be there," Green said.

"That's not my area of expertise."

"I know. I'm talking to myself. Which car did he drive this morning?"

"The Audi A8. That's one sweet ride," Adams added with a wide grin. "I can't say who drove the car—only which car made the trip from Sabri's home to his office."

Green smiled, shaking her head. "Are you a car aficionado, Dan?"

"It's in my DNA. My father owns an auto repair shop as did his father before him. I worked there in the summers from the time I was in middle school through college."

"I thought so. If I go to Sabri's office now, could you let me know when his Audi leaves? I want to follow him."

"No problem," Adams said. "It's early. He usually doesn't leave until late."

She glanced at her watch. "That's okay. I don't want to miss him. When I leave here, I'll grab one of the embassy loaner cars and drive to his office. I'll call you when I'm on the way."

"Oh, one more thing," Adams added. "I've reviewed the various CCTV video footage from the time period when the nukes were taken. I narrowed my search to the area at or near the port in Karachi."

"So, you hacked into that system, too."

The tech nodded his head and laughed. "I thought you might be interested in what I found. This is the CCTV footage from a camera at a small private marina a short drive from the port."

He ran the footage on one of his screens. Green watched a somewhat grainy video of some men loading a large rectangular box onto a large yacht. "You don't think…"

"It's impossible to say. Within an hour after the box was loaded, the yacht pulled out."

"Wouldn't Pakistani ISI have seen this and investigated it?"

"It's an older system. The video is low-res and in black and white with no interactive feature. It was probably installed years ago and not monitored by the Pakistan government or a security monitoring service."

"Send me a copy of that now. I'll send it to Jake."

—◈—

Green phoned Adams when she was in position near Sabri's office. Adams kept watch on his screen. In less than an hour, the Audi pulled out of the parking lot. He phoned Green, who said she saw it and was following at a distance.

47

THE RIVERSIDE RESTAURANT AND PUB LONDON

Collins shoved the open files and reports into her desk drawer, locking it.

She needed to find Baxter. As fun as Baxter was to be around, she took her job seriously and often worked late. But her office was dark, and she wasn't in the break room. Angry with herself that she had waited too late to catch her, Collins left for the day—only to spot Baxter in a crowd of people walking in the direction of the underground station and rushed to catch up.

"Carol!" Baxter looked over her shoulder and saw Collins. She stopped and waited for her to catch up. "Got a minute?"

They resumed walking in the direction of the Vauxhall underground station.

"No," Baxter admitted, "I'm done for the day. Time to get home and have a glass of wine. Oh, did you speak to Bradley Caldwell?"

"Yes. Thank you. He connected me with the inspector who went aboard the yacht when it entered British waters. Bradley told me to tell you that you owe him a drink."

Baxter's head snapped around, and she stopped walking. "Did you tell him I gave you his name?"

"He asked if you did. I couldn't lie."

"Hmm… He remembered me, did he? Maybe I'll call and tell him I always pay my debts," she schemed, only to catch onto Collins's silence. "You need something again, don't you?"

"Yes, I do. This may take some time to explain. May I buy you a glass of wine at the Riverside?"

"If it's only one glass, the answer is a hard no."

The Riverside, a trendy restaurant and bar on the Thames, was a short walk from the Vauxhall underground station and made full use of the windows overlooking the river and the London Eye. The popular bar was already filling up with the after-work crowd when they arrived. The two of them chatted until they were seated. Collins ordered a French Chablis and Baxter an Argentinian Malbec.

"Jake is flying in tomorrow," Collins began. "He's bringing a friend."

"Is that what this is about? You want me to go out with his friend? Is he married? Is he handsome?"

"I don't know. I've never met him. It's not about that, anyway." Collins's expression grew more serious. "This is really important, Carol."

Collins brought her up to speed on her conversations with the customs inspector and with Palmer. She told Baxter that she believed Palmer's friend was a special warfare operator with the US military.

"I'm not sure I like where this is going," Baxter said after taking a long drink of her glass of wine. "You still believe there's something sketchy about that yacht, don't you?"

Collins fidgeted in her seat. Baxter had been with MI6 for years and held a senior associate position in the counterterrorism directorate. She knew everyone worth knowing and had seen a lot during her tenure with the agency.

"Tell me I'm crazy, and I'll stop right here."

"You're crazy. But proceed. You've piqued my curiosity, and I'm enjoying this wine."

Baxter flagged down the waiter and ordered two more glasses of wine even though they weren't even half-finished with their first.

"I'm not sure what they intend to do when they arrive. I suspect Jake and his friend will reconnoiter the yacht. Maybe that's all that will happen. But I know Jake. Even if they see nothing unusual, he will want to do more than look. I fear this might get out of hand."

"Have you told the director?"

"I gave him my initial report and the follow-up report. He said I'd done a good job and the information would be entered into our intelligence database. He stopped short of patting me on the head and saying, 'Well done, girlie. Now get back to work.' You know—junior analyst gets excited about something insignificant."

"What do you want me to do?"

Collins looked around to ensure no one was within earshot and lowered her voice. "This is a massive stretch. Please don't laugh. If they ... If we find evidence that there was or is a nuclear device aboard that vessel, what should I do if we need help? Who would I contact? Is there an MI6 hotline, sort of like an emergency 999 number?"

Baxter looked out the window toward the London Eye Ferris wheel, watching it slowly go around. "MI6 is foreign intelligence."

"But one of our core areas of focus is counterterrorism, stopping terrorist attacks in the UK."

"True, but much of that is achieved by gathering foreign intelligence, which is what we do. MI5 have primary feet-on-the-ground responsibility for threats against our national security, including foreign and domestic terrorism. And we, MI6, definitely don't do bomb disposal in central London. For that, we'd work with MI5 and the

Army's Explosive Ordnance Disposal and Search Squadron. I believe the closest EOD&S unit to us is based at RAF Northolt."

"That's the airport Jake and his friend are flying into tomorrow."

"Bloody hell, Fiona." Baxter held her hand over her mouth, looking at Fiona as if she were an alien who had just stepped off a spaceship. "You're telling me that two American special ops types are landing on British soil to investigate and possibly thwart a terrorist attack involving a nuclear warhead that could potentially take out the entirety of Westminster."

Collins nodded grimly. "That pretty much sums it up."

"The director should have sent your report straight to MI5. It's probably in a pile of other intelligence reports waiting for some junior analyst to enter it into the database. No offense."

"None taken. Remember, Carol, at this point, there is no evidence that a nuclear weapon is on that yacht. Also, the customs inspector found nothing suspicious with the yacht or the crew. All we have to go on is my gut feeling. When I briefed the director, he didn't seem concerned. He just wanted me to document what I had learned."

Baxter took a deep, calming breath and exhaled slowly. She put her elbows on the table, leaned in toward Collins, and whispered with a clenched jaw, "You're assisting two Americans, one of whom is your part-time lover, in a preliminary investigation of whether a problem exists and warrants action. What could possibly go wrong?"

"I'll meet them there and see how it goes. If at any time we confirm there is a problem or even a potential problem, I'll call or text you, then you can notify the appropriate people."

Baxter nodded. "That's good. But text me regularly and let me know what going on."

"I will," Collins said. "I promise. Should I tell Jake? Should we give MI5 a heads-up?"

"Put your relationship with him aside for a moment. If this were any other American JSOC officer, how would you handle it?"

Baxter was right. Collins was letting her feelings for Palmer interfere with her ability to approach the situation objectively. Collins nodded. "We need MI5 informed and involved as they see fit. And I need to tell Jake."

"What time are Jake and his friend arriving at Northolt?"

"Late afternoon."

"Good. I'll contact MI5 and EOD&S tomorrow. I'll say we're pursuing a soft lead and confirm the names and contact details of people I need to call if the lead pans out. I'll be surprised if MI5 doesn't require that someone join you."

"Tomorrow is going to be a busy day for both of us," Collins said. "Call if you haven't heard from me by tomorrow evening."

48

ROYAL AIR FORCE BASE NORTHOLT

Palmer and Cole boarded a C-20B, the military version of the Gulfstream III and IV used by the Navy and Air Force, at Pakistan Air Force Base near Islamabad. The base had a small US military presence and was used by US government personnel. Other than the pilot and copilot, they were the only two on board.

They were taxiing out when Palmer's phone chimed. It was a text from Green.

CCTV video from a small marina near Karachi Port, taken the day after the nukes went missing. Probably not your yacht but thought you would want to see it.

Palmer showed Cole the text and clicked on the video link. They watched the thirty-second video and played it several more times. The yacht was similar to the *Medicine Man,* perhaps the same. However, the CCTV video had been taken from a distance, and the camera lens must not have been cleaned since the camera was installed.

Yachts of this make and size were not so rare as to make this one unique, but how many like it would be in a marina near Karachi Port at the same time the nukes were taken? That was the question. Regardless, he and Cole agreed the video was inconclusive, one more piece of circumstantial evidence.

He texted back, *Thanks for sending. Difficult to tell if that's the yacht. Taking off soon.*

The plane sped down the runway and pulled up and away from Islamabad.

"Nice ride, Palmer. Beats the hell out of riding in a C130 jump seat. How'd you pull this off?"

Palmer laughed. "I know people. How did you manage to get some time off?"

"Oh, my CO wasn't happy. He approved my request on the condition that I could be contacted while I was away. I said I was accompanying you to London as backup. Told him you needed a wingman. Oh, I forgot to say something on the chopper—too much else going on that day. I was sorry to hear that your former teammate, Wade Jansen, was killed a while back. I know you two were close."

The SEAL and EOD community was a tight-knit group. Although it had expanded and grown, he and Wade had come to know each other over the years and during countless missions. The bond had been strong. Palmer took a deep breath. "Wade had contracted me to work on a case in Virginia Beach. While we were working on it, he was murdered."

"All those missions, only to get killed sitting in your office," Cole said, shaking his head.

"Fiona helped me on that case, too. She was working for a pharmaceutical company in the UK then but provided me with some valuable information about one of the perpetrators." Palmer filled Cole in on his relationship with Collins, her role at MI6, and the *Medicine Man* yacht.

"Sounds to me like the Brits did everything by the book," Cole said. "If the yacht and crew checked out, why the concern?"

"Call it a hunch on Fiona's part and mine. I want to see the yacht and monitor what's going on for a couple of days."

"You and Fiona could do that without me," Cole noted.

"If we find a nuclear device, would you trust me to disarm it?" Palmer asked. It was a rhetorical question and they both knew it.

"No way in hell."

"Precisely. After I spoke with Fiona, I asked myself, 'Why would someone bring a mega-yacht back to London to sell?' It was in Dubai for maintenance and renovation. Why not sell it there? The Middle East is one of the biggest markets for multimillion-dollar yachts. There's also the timing of its arrival back in the UK. Give or take a few days, if it was in or near Karachi at the time the weapons disappeared, it would be arriving in London about now. I know that's a stretch in a number of ways, and this might end up being one big boondoggle. If it is, we'll make the most of it and enjoy ourselves, my treat."

"I'm not so sure Fiona will enjoy having me hang out with the two of you. Based on what you've told me, the tension between you two may be more difficult to mediate than the Pakistan-India conflict," he said with a half-laugh. "Wait a damn minute. Does Reynolds even know I'm with you?"

"There's no tension, just a rough patch in an otherwise loving relationship, a simple bump in the road," Palmer answered, deliberately ignoring his question.

"That's not what I asked," Cole barked. "Does the general know I'm here with you on this clandestine mission?"

"Not exactly. He told me to take a couple of days off and catch up with Fiona. He also mentioned that I was off the clock and should not conduct an investigation on British soil or get in any trouble."

Cole gaped at him. "How in your twisted mind do you interpret that as authorization?"

"He comped a nonstop flight on this jet. He wouldn't say or do that unless he knew what I intended to do."

Cole laughed. "What the hell … Not only does he not know I'm here but he also specifically told you not to do what we're planning on doing, didn't he?"

"Sounds about right."

"Screw it." Cole shrugged. "I'm just happy to get out of sand land for a couple of days."

"By the way," Palmer began, scratching his scalp, "have you ever actually disarmed a nuclear warhead?"

"Sort of. It's not like they roll out a live hundred-megaton weapon set to explode in five minutes and tell you to disarm it. If you want to see that, go to a James Bond movie. In training, everything is exactly like a nuclear device, except there is no plutonium core or explosive charge. We have mandatory Render Safe training on disarming all types of devices and real-world experience disarming many of them. The problem is that Pakistan is so damn secretive about its nuclear weapons that we can only speculate about the details. So, our training focuses on the types of triggering mechanisms we believe they use. Disable the triggering mechanism, and you've disarmed the warhead."

Palmer knew Cole was a member of a JSOC Render Safe team that included Delta Force and SEAL Team Six special operators. The Render Safe teams were trained at a secret facility in Nevada in what is called "Deep Underground Shelter" penetrations. They used sensitive radiological detection devices to detect the presence of trace amounts of nuclear material and locate where the devices are stored. They also built a replica of a Pashtun village complete with a mock nuclear storage facility on the US East Coast. The concern was that now Cole was operating solo. Without a team to support him, they had a mammoth task ahead of them.

"I wouldn't have asked you to come along if I wasn't confident you could handle anything we encounter. When we land, it could get busy fast," Palmer said. "The yacht arrived a couple of days ago. If there's a nuclear device on board, they'll want to get it into position as soon as possible."

"What are they waiting for? Why not detonate it in the marina now?"

"Good question. If that was the plan, they would have docked and got off the boat on the first day, having set the device to detonate once they were out of harm's way. Fiona said they are still on board. One thing is for certain: if the device is on that yacht, they won't wait much longer."

Cole said, "I assume these tangos are well-armed. Just how do you see this playing out? All I have is my render-safe kit. Nothing to use in close quarters combat except a couple of screwdrivers."

"To be honest, I haven't thought that far ahead. Let's start with a little recon and see where that takes us."

Palmer tried to get some sleep on the long flight. The days ahead would be long, with little time for rest. He was awakened when the pilot announced they were on final approach to Northolt Royal Air Force Base in the London Borough of Hillingdon. In the past, the airport was only used by the RAF and, because of its relative privacy, the royal family. Although small commercial and private flights now used the airport, it was still much more private than other London area airports.

Palmer looked out the window on the right side of the plane as it descended below the gray clouds just east of Harrow on the Hill. He spotted Harrow Boys School and the eleventh-century St. Mary's Church where he and Collins were reunited after her abduction. He had met Collins on that case. She was a clinical research auditor for B&A Pharmaceuticals, and he was an independent investigator. B&A had contracted him to work with her on the investigation of the mysterious deaths of a physician and nurse in Cornwall in southwest England. Fiona Collins was an intelligent and strong-willed woman. She would demand involvement in whatever happened during this operation.

—*◇◇*—

Collins was waiting when they got through immigration and customs. She and Palmer embraced before he introduced her to Cole.

Cole looked at Collins and nodded. "Jake neglected to tell me you're gorgeous."

"You're too kind, Senior Chief Cole," Collins said with a broad smile.

"Feel free to call me Nick."

They threw their bags in the trunk and got in her car, Palmer in the passenger seat and Cole in the rear seat. Collins drove out of the airport onto the A40 headed into London.

"This may be a rhetorical question, Ms. Collins, but does MI6 know we're here?"

"Other than me and one of my trusted colleagues, no one else knows the details. I saw no reason for anyone else in MI6 to know as long as this is a social visit—which I understand is the same rationale Jake used for coming to London. However, just to be safe, my colleague is alerting MI5 and EOD&S about the investigation and asking that they be on standby."

"Let's go to St. Katharine Docks and have a look," Palmer said. "If at any time we determine things aren't as they seem or we run into trouble, you'll need to let your team at MI6 know what we're doing, and your colleague can alert MI5 and EOD&S. This thing could get ugly in a heartbeat."

49

ST. KATHARINE DOCKS
LONDON

Traffic from Northolt was flowing freely until Collins exited the A40 and hit central London, then it crawled. By the time they arrived at St. Katharine Docks, the sun was about to set. Fiona parked in the City Quay Car Park near the Dickens Inn, which was on the south side of the marina near where the *Medicine Man* was docked.

They walked around the marina with Collins leading the way and playing tour guide. She explained that St. Katharine Docks was built in the early 1800s as one of the commercial docks of the Port of London when the Thames River was the beating heart of London's industrial shipping business. In recent years, the area had expanded to become a popular mixed-use district called Docklands, which included the marina, housing, the hotel where they would be staying, shops, and restaurants including the Dickens Inn.

They continued around the three-basin St. Katharine Docks Marina on the Thames River. She explained that it was renovated in 2017 to accommodate one hundred eighty-five vessels up to forty meters long and was Central London's only marina. Because the coastal tide caused the River Thames water level to rise and fall as much as twenty-three feet twice daily, a lock was built at the marina's entrance. The lock operated for approximately two hours before and one and a half hours after the high-water tides each day to equalize the water level and allow boats to enter and leave the marina.

"I'm impressed," Palmer said, looking at her with a surprised expression.

"I needed to have my act together if I was going to educate you about the marina, so I did a bit of research." She smiled. "I'm afraid I've exhausted my knowledge on the subject."

They slowed their pace as they approached the *Medicine Man*. By anyone's standards, it was a magnificent vessel. The tall, totally white yacht had a contemporary, streamlined appearance. The cost to purchase, maintain, fuel, and crew such a vessel made them affordable only to corporations or the super-rich. The multimillion-dollar yacht was tied up in one of the long berths. Some interior lights were on, but it was impossible to tell if anyone was on board.

They maintained their slow pace around the marina, stopping at a Starbucks that had outdoor seating and a view of the marina, including the *Medicine Man*. After they got their coffees and tea and sat at one of the outdoor tables, Collins pulled a document from her handbag. "I found the brochure for this yacht online. It's 30.9 meters or 101 feet long. Built in 2009 in the United Arab Emirates. Here's the layout of each of the decks and compartments as they existed when it was built."

Palmer and Cole pored over the brochure. The open-air upper deck was primarily a sun lounge, except for the forward wheelhouse, which was covered to provide shade for the instruments and the captain. Atop it was a domed radar. The upper deck wheelhouse had only the essentials for steering and navigation and was used in good weather conditions. Situated between the upper and main decks and several steps below the exterior wheelhouse was the interior wheelhouse, which had the full array of high-end electronics, navigation, radar, and all the bells and whistles required to pilot the yacht in any weather condition. Aft of it was the mostly enclosed main deck with a small galley, dining area, bar, and lounge. The owner's suite was all the way forward. At the rear of the main deck was an exterior entrance and port and starboard stairs, leading down to a platform from which a person could board or leave the yacht and which was used as a swimming platform when anchored out. The lower deck contained the engines, guest cabins, and the crew's quarters, which were cordoned off from the guest area.

"This is going to be invaluable," Palmer remarked. "You said the captain told the customs and immigration inspector that the yacht had been in Dubai undergoing maintenance and renovations. We need to get on board somehow and have the captain show us what those renovations were. Now that we've seen the yacht, let me show you something."

Palmer showed Collins the grainy video Green had sent him, explaining where and when it had been taken. As it played, she looked back and forth between the phone's screen and the *Medicine Man*. "It could be the same yacht," Collins said.

"That's what Nick and I concluded. It's impossible to say. It does, however, support the case for checking it out."

"Fiona," Cole began, "I've not spent much time in London. Give me some perspective. Would this marina be an ideal location in London to detonate a nuclear device? What's near here?"

Collins took a moment to consider the question. Thinking through the scenario of a nuclear weapon detonating in London made the possibility seem more real. "Because London is densely populated, the death toll from a nuclear detonation would be massive anywhere. I suppose the worst impact politically, emotionally, and in terms of death toll would be if it were detonated near the Lambeth Bridge, which is between the Westminster Bridge and Vauxhall Bridge. The detonation of even a relatively small nuclear device could destroy or significantly damage the Houses of Parliament, Westminster Abbey, MI6 and MI5 headquarters, the new US Embassy, Big Ben, and Buckingham Palace. They are tightly grouped within a mile or two of the bridge."

"One blast that would take out the Houses of Parliament and the US Embassy—talk about an ideal target. They would need to leave here and take the yacht to Lambeth Bridge," Cole said. "How far is that?"

"About three miles," Collins replied. "But I don't believe a yacht the size of the *Medicine Man* could do it. Coming westward on the Thames from the North Sea, they would have passed under only one bridge, the Queen Elizabeth II Bridge, which has a very high clearance. Continuing on the Thames from the marina to Westminster, they would encounter bridges that would be too low for them to pass under, and a yacht like this would certainly draw a lot of attention, which they would not want."

"If they wanted to move the device, the only choices would be by truck or a smaller boat," Palmer noted.

Collins brought her hands to her head and took a deep breath. "Oh my God."

"What is it?" asked Palmer.

"Tomorrow is the State Opening of Parliament. The queen will be there to address both houses and officially open parliament. It's the only time the three elements of legislature come together—the House of Lords, the House of Commons, and the queen."

Palmer's eyes widened slightly. "What time of day does it occur?"

"Late morning, around eleven o'clock or so."

"Will boat and vehicle traffic be restricted? Will there be security boats on the Thames?" Cole asked.

Collins chewed a lip. "Security in general will be tightened. I'm not sure about boat traffic. A few years ago, security officers conducted a mock terrorist attack at night to check on possible flaws in the security from the river at the Houses of Parliament. They used a boat to approach and enter the Palace of Westminster. Within minutes, the mock terrorists targeted about a hundred members of Parliament that they could have killed."

Cole's eyes narrowed. "What security measures were implemented as a result?"

"As I recall, they installed a boom or something that prevents boats from docking or stopping next to the Houses of Parliament. Of course, that doesn't prevent boats going past Parliament. On the other hand, a truck could easily get stalled in London traffic, especially if streets are cordoned off."

Palmer pointed toward the yacht. "Look."

Two men had walked out onto the deck of the yacht's seating area. One of them lit a cigarette. They were having an animated conversation.

"They look Middle Eastern," Cole commented.

"The marina manager said they're Saudis. And the customs inspector I spoke with said there were three Saudi men on board, the captain and two crewmen. The captain gave the inspector a tour of the yacht. He saw nothing out of the ordinary."

Cole shook his head. "I seriously doubt those three yahoos have the skills to make the necessary changes and detonate a nuclear warhead. One or both of those missing nuclear engineers would have to be on board."

"Couldn't it be preset?" Collins asked.

"Yes," said Cole. "They would need to override the weapons security and delete the preset mechanisms, and then set new ones. They could use manual, timed, or environmental triggers, or trigger it by electronic signal from halfway around the world. We need to get on board. I have equipment that can detect trace amounts of radiation."

"Photographs of Raul Ahmadi, along with the others who Pakistan believes were involved, have been all over the media and internet," Palmer said. "The police, military, and intelligence communities are still searching for them. No one has seen them. With all the CCTV monitors in London, if they were out and about, they would have been spotted by now."

"Pakistan's official position is that all of them were on board the cargo ship and were killed when the device detonated," Cole said.

"That's possible. It's also possible they weren't." Palmer looked at Collins. "Have you heard of The Chameleon?"

"The name pops up on our intel reports. But nothing solid to confirm whether The Chameleon is real or imagined. Why do you ask?"

"Just curious. The theft of the nuclear warheads was a complex operation. Because of that, and because it was successful, some believe he led the entire operation."

Collins looked at her watch and interrupted. "Sorry, I should check with the marina manager to see if there has been any activity since I spoke with him."

Palmer waited until she was far enough away before he said, "Any idea how we can get on that yacht?"

Cole shook his head. "Whatever we do, we need to exercise caution. So far, everything is based on your and Fiona's hunch that there's a nuclear device on board. Don't get me wrong, I'm happy to be here, but no actionable intel supports that position. If we shake the tree and there's no nuke, we're in deep shit. You're a JSOC contractor. They'll terminate your contract, and you can go about your business. I'm active duty Navy with two years left before I have my twenty in and can retire. And don't forget Fiona. MI6 would probably fire her for going rogue."

Palmer was asking a lot of Cole and Collins. Why would The Chameleon attack London? The previous attacks attributed to him were all directed toward India and Pakistan's annexation of Kashmir or Kashmir's independence. If that was the objective, why would he not take a nuclear device to Mumbai? The *Fair Winds* wasn't going to Mumbai; it was bound for Cyprus and Haifa. Perhaps the strategic objective of the previous attacks was to escalate the tension between

Pakistan and India to the point that Pakistan deployed its nuclear weapons, which would provide the opportunity to steal one or more warheads. Collins was right. If London was the target, the biggest impact would be to detonate a nuclear device near Westminster. And because of the low bridge clearance, the only way to move the device to Westminster by water would be to transfer it to a smaller vessel.

Palmer turned and looked at Cole. "I have an idea."

50

THE OLD TOWN BAR & RESTAURANT CLAPHAM

Carol Baxter was out having dinner and drinks with friends at the Old Town, a lively, neighborhood bar and restaurant overlooking Clapham Common, when she remembered. Fiona had said to contact her if she hadn't heard from her by the end of today. Maybe Fiona had called, and she hadn't heard the ring. She fumbled through her handbag and grabbed her mobile. No missed calls or texts. Fiona had told her about Jake and the EOD specialist coming to London. They planned to stake out the yacht, *Medicine Man*, at St. Katharine Docks Marina to see if they noticed anything suspicious. Why hadn't she talked Fiona out of it? If Fiona's boss and the higher-ups got wind of what she was doing, they'd sack her on the spot. She wasn't a field operative. On top of that, cooperating with two American special warfare operators on an operation in London—madness. She excused herself and stepped outside. She looked through her contact list on her mobile and found Fiona's number. After several rings, the call went to voicemail.

"Fiona, this is Carol. Are you all right? What's going on? Call me immediately unless you're having a shag—I can wait a couple of minutes."

It was 7:15 p.m. Too early to sound the alarm. Baxter told herself that she would phone Fiona again when she left to go home. It was a work night. She wouldn't stay out late. Baxter walked toward the entrance to go back into the bar and stopped just before she got to the door. She had drunk two gin and tonics on an empty stomach. She shook her head back and forth like a dog coming in from the rain, as if that would make her think more clearly. *Get it together, girl.* She had dismissed Fiona's concern about a nuclear device being on the yacht, but what if there was one? Or, even if there was no nuclear weapon, the men on the yacht could still be terrorists. No hard evidence proved that either was the case, only Fiona's suspicions that something nefarious was happening based on the shady history of that boat and its owners. Had Fiona's imagination gone off the rails? Had hers?

The 7/7 terrorist attacks in London on 7 July 2005 had inspired Baxter to apply for a junior analyst position at MI6 when she was in her early twenties, just after graduating from college. She had been at work on 22 March 2017 when the terrorist Khalid Masood drove his car into pedestrians on Westminster Bridge in London. Fifty people were injured; four of them were killed. Masood had sent a text before the attack, stating he was waging jihad. She was also at work when, less than three months later, on 5 June 2017, an Islamic terrorist drove his vehicle into pedestrians on London Bridge, and then the driver and two other terrorists ran from the car into Borough Market and began stabbing people. Eight people were killed, and forty-eight were injured. They claimed to have been inspired by the Islamic State, ISIS. She had seen a great deal during her time at MI6 and had progressed up the ladder to her current position. Somehow, she had agreed to be a participant in this operation, the one and only link between Fiona's team and MI6 and MI5.

Baxter had contacted MI5 and EOD&S earlier that afternoon. After being transferred a few times, she finally spoke with someone in authority. She had downplayed the situation, not saying anything about a possible nuclear device being on board the yacht. She understood Fiona's concern, however; now was not yet the time to raise the threat level with the person to whom she was talking. After all, she didn't know Fiona, a junior analyst, that well. She needed a contact and assurance that if she called, their response would be immediate. The MI5 officer was helpful and said she should contact him, day or night, in case of an imminent threat or emergency situation. Though when Baxter inquired about any situation involving an explosive device, he said her priority, in that case, would be to contact EOD&S. She had spent another hour or two calling, getting transferred, and awaiting a call back before she spoke with someone with EOD&S who would serve as her contact. He also committed to an immediate and rapid response should it be warranted.

Baxter could feel her heart pounding in her chest. She called Fiona again. Still no answer. If Fiona didn't turn up for work in the morning, she'd … Well, what would she do? Why hadn't they allowed location access to each other's phones? If they had, she would know exactly where Fiona was. So stupid. She could take a taxi and go to St. Katharine Docks. What would she expect to see? What would she do if she didn't see Fiona, Jake, and the other special operator?

Maybe Fiona's mobile battery was dead. Maybe she put her phone on mute while they were on the stakeout and forgot to take it off. They never discussed what to do if she didn't answer. *Where are you, Fiona? Call me.*

51

ST. KATHARINE DOCKS
LONDON

When Collins returned to the Starbucks, she told Palmer and Cole that the marina manager said the captain of the *Medicine Man* had requested a time for marina entry of a boat arriving early on the morning high-water lock opening and leaving before the morning closure. The captain had told the manager that the boat would be delivering some supplies to the *Medicine Man*, and they would offload items onto the boat that were not to be sold along with the yacht. Not unusual, the manager told her, when a vessel of that size is on the market. As with a house, you take out anything that you're not planning on selling with it. He said, however, that vessels normally offload items onto the dock and into a van or truck instead of bringing a boat alongside.

Palmer and Cole looked at each other and then at Collins.

"What time is the opening?" Palmer asked.

"It begins at 7:32 a.m. and ends at 11:02 a.m.," Collins said. "Once boats enter the lock from the Thames, the outer gate will be raised. The water in the lock will be leveled to the water level in the marina. At that time, the inner gate will be fully lowered, and the boats can proceed into the marina. The entire process takes about thirty minutes. The reverse is true for vessels leaving the marina."

"Good information. I have an idea, Fiona," Palmer said. "And it involves you."

"Let's hear it."

"We need to get on board that yacht and see who's there. Cole and I could conduct a nighttime op."

"Or," Collins replied, "the three of us could go aboard in the morning, flash our MI6 and JSOC IDs, and say we're conducting a joint British-American inspection of boats and ships that entered British waters since the nuclear weapons were stolen. If the captain was confident enough to show the customs inspector around, and the inspector didn't find anything suspicious, why would the captain balk at doing the same for us? But if he refuses to allow us inside, we have no official paperwork authorizing us to inspect it."

"I don't believe they will. If they do, you say you'll phone it in and ask for an order for immediate seizure of the vessel," Palmer said. "Tell them that an MI5 team will be dispatched straightaway to secure it."

"I have a device that can detect trace amounts of radiation," Cole said.

Palmer gave him a pointed look. "Don't show them the device until we start the tour. We'll see how nervous that makes him."

Collins thought a moment, letting the scenario play out in her head. She looked at Cole, who nodded his approval, seeming to know what she was thinking. "One of us must stay behind."

"Why?" Palmer asked.

"What if there are others on board and they are armed? We have no weapons."

"She's not wrong," Cole said, looking at Jake.

"Okay," Palmer reasoned. "Nick and I will go."

"I have to go," Collins asserted. "I'm the one with the British MI6 ID. They wouldn't believe two Americans have authorization to inspect the yacht."

Palmer's eyes flashed, knowing where this was heading. "Well, I'm definitely going. Nick, you stay behind. I'll take the radiation detector."

"No way," Cole interjected, scoffing. "There's more to interpreting the results than looking at the screen. I have to be there. We could bring in the Brits to assist."

Palmer shook his head. "No. The only evidence we have is what Fiona's already reported, and that didn't set the wheels in motion. If we find nothing, she'd be guilty of circumventing the chain of command and would be sacked, or worse. If we don't find anything and walk away, no one's the wiser."

They looked at each other in silence, their eyes darting back and forth. Collins knew she was right; so did Palmer and Cole. Jake would detest being too far away to protect her if anything went wrong, and a part of her worried about that, too. But the reality was that there wasn't any other way of going about this.

After an extended pause, Palmer's downcast eyes appeared to accept defeat. He clenched his jaw, hardly able to look at them as he growled, "Damn it all, I'll stay behind."

With that agreed, they discussed the plan.

If the inspection detected no issues, they estimated it would take ninety minutes at the most. If issues were detected, Cole would not say anything to Collins, only note the location on the ship and the reading on the radiation detector. They would thank the captain, rejoin Palmer, and contact MI5 and EOD&S. Collins did not have names or contact details, but Carol Baxter did. She would text Palmer, and he would contact Baxter, who would alert MI5 and EOD&S. Collins gave Baxter's mobile phone number to Palmer. If Palmer didn't hear anything from them ninety minutes after they boarded the yacht, he would call Baxter immediately.

"What do you think, Nick?" Collins asked.

"As crazy as it sounds, I like it. Hell, it might even work."

"What about the timing?" Cole asked Palmer. "It's getting dark now. Should we wait until morning?"

"We'll make our move at seven o'clock tomorrow morning," he decided. "A half-hour before the lock opens."

"I booked two rooms at the Tower Hotel," Collins said, pointing over her shoulder to the four-star, eight-hundred-room hotel, which sat adjacent to the marina. While most requested rooms with a view of the Thames or Tower Bridge, Collins had booked two overlooking the marina.

———

On the walk to the hotel, Collins checked her phone. Somehow, she'd missed a call from Baxter. After listening to the voicemail Carol had left her, she returned the call.

Her colleague answered on the first ring and lit into her. "Where have you been? I've been worried sick. Why didn't you phone me earlier?"

Collins let her finish ranting before responding. "I'm sorry. It's been manic ever since Jake and Senior Chief Cole, the EOD, arrived. We're going aboard the yacht tomorrow morning. Were you able to get contacts at MI5 and EOD&S?"

"I did. They are prepared for a rapid response when I contact them. There is a lot riding on this. I'll text the names and numbers to you, in case something unforeseen happens and I can't be reached."

"Perfect. If there is any problem, or if we locate the warhead"—a zip of horror and thrill in equal measure spiked through her body at the thought of it—"Jake will call you, okay? I gave him your contact details."

"Okay," Baxter said, though her voice was quiet.

"Carol, the marina manager said that a small boat would be coming alongside the yacht tomorrow morning to deliver supplies and to offload some items from the yacht. *The Medicine Man* is too large to go under the low bridges between here and Westminster. A small boat wouldn't have a problem. To top it off, tomorrow is the State Opening of Parliament."

Baxter didn't respond.

"Carol? Are you still there?"

"I'm here. Just thinking. This is sounding more plausible, Fiona. Why don't I come there tomorrow morning? I could wait nearby."

"No. It's critical you're at the office where you have access to the appropriate people. What would happen if one of your contacts was unavailable when you called?"

"You're right," Baxter said with a nervous sigh. "What time in the morning are you going to the yacht?"

"Seven o'clock. We agreed that only two of us should go on board, and since I'm the only one with an MI6 ID, it will be me and Senior Chief Cole, because he has the radiation detection kit. If it's all for naught, I'll phone you."

"You'd better."

———

The three of them checked in and had a quick bite at the hotel restaurant before reconvening in Collins and Palmer's room for their rehearsal.

"Every op must be rehearsed and practiced," Cole said. "We need to think through our response to any anticipated action. Our words and actions should leave no doubt in their minds that we are on official British government business. Hesitancy or uncertainty will only plant doubt in their minds, causing them to second-guess our legitimacy."

For the next hour, Collins and Cole practiced what each would say and how the dialogue would change based on what the captain and crew did or questioned. They stood side by side and faced Palmer, who played the part of the yacht's captain. They rehearsed every possible scenario, including what they would do if confronted by armed men.

"Remember, if I detect radioactive material, I'll not say anything. If we're near the end of the tour, I'll suggest we've seen enough. At that point, we thank them and get the hell off the yacht."

"And we'll phone it in, right?" Collins said.

"Of course," Palmer replied, glancing over to Cole.

"It's getting late. I'll take the first watch and call you when I need a break," Cole said while walking toward the door to return to his room. He paused to flash a grin over his shoulder. "You kids catch some sleep or whatever it is you may have planned."

"I'll relieve you when you're ready," Collins volunteered, cheeks reddening slightly.

"Please don't be offended, ma'am, but we need one of us on watch at all times," Cole said, pointing to himself and Palmer.

"I'm not offended."

"I believe we're ready. We have a good plan, but…" Palmer hesitated, looking to Cole.

"No plan survives first contact with the enemy," Cole said, completing the Navy SEAL saying.

"Or as Mike Tyson once said, 'Everyone has a plan until they get punched in the face.'"

"You two are not funny," Collins said, shaking her head.

———

After Cole left, Palmer and Collins sat on the edge of the bed with the shade open so they could see the yacht. Although their view was somewhat obstructed, Cole would be positioned outside to monitor the yacht. Still, they wanted the shade open.

Palmer spoke first. "Fiona, this plan puts a lot of pressure on you. The last thing I want is for it to cost you your job. Do you really believe there's a nuclear warhead on that yacht and that there's no alternative to the three of us taking action?"

"I can't be absolutely certain, obviously, but I am certain that there's enough circumstantial evidence to create concern. The risk of not doing anything far outweighs the risk of taking action and finding nothing, even if it costs me my job. I can't even imagine our thinking there might be a nuclear device on board that yacht and doing nothing about it. Even if London survived the attack, the city would be forever changed. And it would all be our fault—although, chances are we wouldn't be around to know it."

"Cole and I feel the same. We have to do something." Palmer's expression hardened at the reality they could no longer deny. This was far riskier than any of them had anticipated, but it was what was right. "If everything checks out, at least we did our jobs."

Collins nodded solemnly in agreement.

"Now, I have something to say," Palmer began. He moved closer to her and paused, looking deep into her eyes.

His sudden switch in demeanor caught Collins off guard. Typically, he was so cavalier, so carefree. She became nervous, almost fearful of his next words. Somehow, she knew that what he said next would have nothing to do with tomorrow's plans. It was going to be about them—their future together, or not. Their entire relationship hinged on this moment. Suspecting the worst, she bit her bottom lip and her shoulders slumped as she edged away from him.

"I don't know what tomorrow will bring, Fiona. I don't want to go forward with our plan without telling you that I love you. I've thought a great deal about the conversation we had before I left for Islamabad.

You were right. We can't continue like this. I want to be with you, wherever that might be or wherever it takes us."

Flooded with relief, Collins threw her arms around him and hugged him as tightly as she ever had. As tears ran down her face, she knew this was what she wanted, too. "I love you, too, Jake." With that, she walked over to the window and lowered the shade.

52

ST. KATHARINE DOCKS LONDON

Palmer stared across the darkness at the yacht. A front had eased in, casting a light fog over the area. The lock opening for the high-tide entry into the marina from the Thames was a couple of hours away. The crew of the *Medicine Man* had three and a half hours to transfer a nuclear weapon onto the boat if that was indeed what they were doing. If it was, Palmer doubted any supplies would be arriving, as the captain had told the marina manager. There would be no need for them. Once the transfer was complete, the captain and crew would leave and get as far from London as they could. Timing was critical.

Cole met Collins and Palmer in their room.

"We're prepared and ready," Palmer said. "Just like we rehearsed last night. The two of you will go on board. Fiona will flash her MI6 ID, and Nick, you'll flash your JSOC ID. Fiona, you'll take the lead and explain that MI6 is conducting an inspection of all vessels that entered the UK since the date the nuclear devices were diverted in

Pakistan. If they refuse the inspection, you argue the point. If that fails, tell them you will phone in their refusal and a team will be dispatched immediately."

Collins nodded. "Who would I call?"

"Call me," he said. "Say you've been denied access to a vessel and require backup to carry out the inspection. Tell them that the request is urgent and that the crew may be armed. They'll cooperate. They were confident enough to give the customs inspector a tour. I expect they will offer you the same. Nick will have the radiation detector. If you complete the tour, and there is negative indication of radiation and no evidence of hidden compartments or anyone else hidden on the vessel, then it was all for naught, and we're done. If Nick detects radiation, get off that yacht. Either way, one of us will phone Carol. You have the detector charged and ready to go?"

"Checked it out in the room," Cole confirmed. "It's ready, and I'm ready."

Palmer glanced at the small case he was holding. "What type of radiation detection device are you using these days?"

Cole opened the case and produced a small, handheld device. "The technology is advancing so fast that I upgrade every couple of years. This one can locate, measure, and identify a radioactive source even when the source is in a container or behind a wall."

Cole took it from the case and handed it to him.

Palmer examined it and said, "Amazing what they're doing nowadays. I recall when you needed a suitcase to carry one around."

Palmer looked at Collins. If she was nervous, she wasn't showing it. She was one heck of a woman. It wasn't the time for a hug and kiss goodbye. She'd understand. "Any sign of trouble, get off that yacht, even if you have to jump in the water."

53

ST. KATHARINE DOCKS
LONDON

C ollins and Cole walked toward the yacht. Collins hadn't seen another person the entire time. In fact, the marina was exceptionally quiet. The height of tourist season had passed, and as a result, most of the shops and businesses had not yet opened. The only exception was a small café called White Mulberries.

It was as though no time had passed before they were stepping onto the yacht and venturing up the starboard-side steps to the main deck. The interior lights were on, but there was no sign of activity.

Cole knocked on the sliding glass door that led to the main lounge, where Collins had seen the men when she was with Baxter. No one came. This time, he banged on it. A man yelled something from inside. In a moment, the door slid open. A young, dark-skinned, Middle Eastern man looked at them, an angry scowl on his face. He was wearing a pair of jeans and an untucked, long-sleeved work shirt. He was unshaven and long overdue for a haircut.

"This is a private vessel," the man said gruffly. "What do you want?"

"Request permission to come aboard," Cole said, complying with naval protocol.

"You're already aboard. Now get off."

Collins cleared her throat. "My name is Fiona Collins. I'm with MI6." She held up her MI6 identification. The man looked at the card and at her, confirming she was the one whose photo was on the ID. "This is Nick Cole. He's with the US Joint Special Operations Command."

Cole held up his ID. By then, an older man had joined them.

She continued, "We're conducting a joint inspection of all vessels that entered the UK after the recent theft of nuclear devices in Pakistan."

The older man came to the door and said, "I'm the captain of this vessel. We already passed inspection by your customs and immigration as we entered British waters."

"We're aware of that," Collins said. "I have a copy of the inspection report." She held it up for the captain to see. "Today is opening day of Parliament. We're taking no chances."

Shaking his head, the captain muttered something in Arabic to the other man. From the tone, Collins assumed it was not complimentary.

"I am sorry. We have a busy day. We have no time for this. Come back tomorrow."

"Are you refusing our request?" Collins inquired in a stern voice.

"No. I'm simply asking that you come back at a more convenient time when we can give you our full attention."

"That's not possible," Collins said, addressing the captain. "We're here today, and this vessel will be inspected now. Refuse, and I'll phone in your denial of our request, at which time a team will be dispatched to secure this vessel."

The captain appeared to think this over a moment, his lips pursed. Surely, he knew he was screwed if he didn't comply. "It appears I have no choice. Come inside."

Collins noted the change in the captain's tone. He obviously had concluded it was better to maintain a more polite and respectful demeanor as they could cause him serious problems. If there was a nuke on board, he would want them off the vessel as quickly as possible.

—⁓—

Palmer staked out a place at the White Mulberries café. It wasn't an ideal location because he had only a partial view of the *Medicine Man*, but it was one where he would not raise suspicion if someone on the yacht spotted him. The yacht was backed into the slip, the bow facing toward the open marina. He had a good view of the bow and starboard side of the yacht. The aftmost portion, where one boards the yacht, was blocked from his view. The slip on the near side of the *Medicine Man* was empty, leaving more than enough room for the other boat to tie up alongside.

Palmer sat at a table outside, tapping his foot as he looked for Collins and Cole. As they walked onto the main deck, he saw them. He watched as Cole banged on the sliding glass door, prompting a man to open it. They hadn't talked for more than thirty seconds before another man appeared, and after a brief conversation, they all went inside. It was 7:00 a.m.

Palmer reminded himself that the chance of a nuclear device being on the yacht was extremely small. Still, he was nervous, mostly for Collins's safety. If there was a device on board, there were probably men who had hidden from the immigration and customs inspector. They would be extremely dangerous, even willing to lose their lives for their cause.

He tapped his foot a little more rapidly.

He should have gone with Collins and had Cole stay behind. The radiation detector couldn't be that difficult to read and interpret. A brief instruction from Cole would have been all he needed. He took a deep breath and sipped his sixteen-ounce cup of black coffee, which did nothing to steady his nerves or calm his anxiety.

Collins and Cole stepped inside the yacht's large, open, and luxuriously decorated main deck, a space befitting the multimillion-dollar yacht.

"How many are on board?" Cole asked before the captain could comment further.

"The two of us and one other."

"Small crew for such a large yacht. You've had a long journey from Dubai to London. I would expect you to have a first mate, bosun, deckhand, chief engineer, and chef—a minimum of four or five crewmen."

"Normally it's me and four men. All of my men are qualified and cross-trained. We all multitask when we're deadheading a vessel, and we don't need a cook or steward."

Collins said, "We need to see everybody's documentation. Then we need a tour of your vessel."

"Wait here. We'll get the other man and come back with our documents."

Collins was calm, considering the circumstances. She was acting on her own, without the support or knowledge of MI6. And she was the only one with the credentials to request to see the crew's documentation and demand the captain allow them to inspect the yacht. Had the captain been more knowledgeable, or perhaps in a better position to stand on his legal rights, he could have questioned why someone from the MI6, Britain's foreign intelligence service, along with a US JSOC operative, were conducting an inspection. The only things they had going for them were that they had caught the captain off guard and the fact that he did not want to rock the boat.

In a few minutes, the captain and two crew members returned. The captain handed Collins their Saudi Arabian passports. She reviewed them and confirmed that the names were the same ones the customs inspector entered on his report. The two crewmen were both in their thirties, under six feet tall, and slender. Neither of them said a word while she compared the photographs with the men standing in front of her, much as the captain had done with her and Cole's IDs. The three men looked and acted like who they said they were—a captain and his grime-under-the-fingernails crew of a luxury yacht. They looked nothing like terrorists about to blow up London, and they certainly weren't nuclear engineers. But, like the poor souls who have been brainwashed into believing that wearing an explosive vest and detonating it to kill innocent men, women, and children was their one-way ticket to paradise, they would know what they had signed up for.

Collins handed the men their passports. "Everything looks in order," she said, looking at the captain. "Now, show us around the vessel."

"Before we begin, you should know that this vessel is for sale, and the broker who is listing this yacht told us to remove anything not intended to be sold with the yacht. A boat will be pulling alongside soon. We'll be loading those items onto the boat. It's also bringing us some supplies. Is it possible to conclude your business by then so we can get our supplies and load the items onto the boat in time for it to leave before the morning lock operation ends?"

"If there are no issues, that should not be a problem. Let's get on with the inspection. The sooner we begin, the sooner we'll be on our way." Then, without breaking eye contact with the man before her, Collins added, "We'll need to see the items you're transferring to the boat."

The captain's eyes narrowed. "Most of them are already boxed."

"Have your men stand by to open the boxes if required," Cole chimed in, backing her up.

Collins sent a quick text to Palmer: *Captain and two crewmen. Immigration checked. Starting tour.*

"Pardon me. I need to give them some instruction before they go." The captain spoke to the crewmen in Arabic, and they rushed out. The captain then said, "Follow me," and led the way, with Collins and Cole close behind.

"Captain, according to the inspection report, the *Medicine Man* has been in Dubai for maintenance and some renovations," Collins said.

"That's correct. The owner wanted to have the yacht in shape to fetch a top price."

"What renovations were done?" Cole asked.

"Cosmetic, mostly. The vessel is ten years old and was showing its age in terms of its dated appearance and overall wear and tear. The sun and saltwater take their toll. I'll point out some of the renovations as we go along."

Cole was at the rear of the group as they walked through a passageway. Collins glanced back and saw him pull the radiation detector out of his bag and turn it on. Cole saw her and gave her a quick wink.

The captain showed them around the interior lounge, dining area, and galley on the main deck. Collins remembered it from the layout. The next stop was all the way forward, which took them to the massive master suite. It occupied the entire width of the yacht and had a king-size bed with lots of pillows and other extravagant furnishings. There were also his and her bathrooms, or heads, as Cole reminded her. The captain highlighted some changes in the furnishings and updated furniture, fixtures, and appointments in the master suite, including a settee imported from France.

"Nice couch," Cole commented.

"It's a settee," Collins corrected him with a grin.

"What's the difference?"

"In this case, a few thousand euros."

Cole made a show of scanning the room with the radiation detector. The captain saw him but said nothing.

With their backs to the captain, Cole whispered to Collins, "Nothing here. He'll show us what he doesn't want us to see last, after we're feeling comfortable that everything's fine and are overwhelmed by the extravagance of the filthy rich. Something's up, though. I can feel it."

Collins pulled out her phone and tapped out a quick text to Palmer: *Main lounge, dining area, and master suite checked.*

"What are you doing?" the captain barked.

"Just making some notes as we proceed," she replied smoothly, pocketing her phone. "I'll use them to write up a report later."

The captain escorted them up a few steps to the enclosed, main wheelhouse that was located between the main and upper deck. Cole walked around checked out the electronic navigation system and controls. It was all state of the art, as complex as the cockpit of an airplane.

The captain checked his watch and tapped his foot. "We need to move on if you're finished."

Cole responded, "Lead the way, Captain."

The captain went down the stairs back to the main deck. Collins and Cole lagged behind for a moment.

"I don't like it," she whispered to Cole.

"The yacht?"

"No, the situation. I've conducted a lot of facility inspections in the past. I know when I'm being led away from a problem."

"I agree. He's nervous."

She tapped out another text: *Wheelhouse checked.*

The captain took them up another set of stairs to the sun deck and lounge. In the forward section, there was an exterior bridge used for steering the boat when the conditions were favorable. The exterior bridge was located directly above the enclosed main wheelhouse they had seen earlier. They had a quick look around and moved back down two sets of stairs to the lower deck and into the engine room.

Interior wheelhouse and upper deck checked.

The captain explained that the engines had been completely overhauled and proceeded to tell them about the propulsion systems and the maintenance that had been completed in far too much detail. Earlier he had wanted them off the yacht as quickly as possible, but now he was killing time.

The captain had not taken them on a direct route during his tour. Collins wondered if the customs inspector was given the same tour. The captain used a walkie-talkie device to communicate with the crewmen, always speaking in Arabic. They finished up the engine room and moved on.

Engine room checked. Yawn.

"Where are the crew's quarters?" Cole asked.

"Sorry. I forgot. Follow me." The two guest cabins were just forward of the engine room. They were not nearly as extravagant in terms of size or furnishings as the master suite. Each had a sitting area and small head. Cole walked the perimeter of the rooms, glancing at his radiation detector.

They exited to an exterior passageway and moved toward the bow where they went through a nondescript door and saw the crew's quarters, ship's laundry, small crew's galley, and dining space. It was a cramped, efficiently laid out space containing a refrigerator, stove, and pantry. The captain showed them his cabin, which looked like it had not been occupied, and then the two crew cabins, each of which had a bunk bed for two. A head and shower that he and the crew shared were at the end of a narrow passageway.

"Very nice," Cole said. "Have you been using the owner's suite on this trip?"

"Of course not. I make the bed and clean everything at the start of each day. It's my military training."

Cole looked at him. "Where did you serve, Captain?"

"I was in the Saudi Navy."

"Doing what?"

"Small boat captain. After I got out, I worked until I passed all requirements for a civilian captain qualification."

That seems like a rehearsed response, Collins thought. She texted Palmer another quick update before proceeding any further. *Guest quarters, crew's quarters, galley, laundry checked.*

"Where are the items to be offloaded?" Collins asked.

"We'll go there last. Let's swing back by the bar and lounge," the captain said, appearing much chirpier than earlier. "By the time we finish, the men should have the items staged and ready for your inspection."

"That would be nice," Collins said.

A coffee service was on the dining table when they got back to the lounge. The captain poured three coffees into the cups. Collins sipped on hers, noticing that Cole didn't touch his. She took the opportunity to send another text to Palmer: *Back in the bar and lounge for coffee before going to the staging area. Almost done.*

One of the crewmen entered the lounge. Sweat was dripping from his face. He said something to the captain in Arabic.

The captain smiled. "The items we are offloading are ready for you to see."

When Cole got up, he saw a boat tied up in the slip beside the *Medicine Man.* He nudged Collins and motioned his head in that direction. She looked at him, her face tense, and nodded.

The captain and crewman led the way out of the lounge, descending the stairs on the starboard side down to the platform of the yacht, where Collins and Cole had first come on board.

Collins was following close behind and had just reached the top of the stairs when Cole whispered, "Fiona, wait."

54

ST. KATHARINE DOCKS
LONDON

Too jittery to sit any longer, Palmer took his coffee and walked toward the lock. He and Cole had arrived too late the previous day to observe the opening. He paused before a sign, which described the lock and the process behind it. The original lock had opened in 1828 and had been modernized over the years. The lock was thirty feet wide and one hundred feet long, with an inner and outer gate that would open and close to allow vessels to enter.

Today, the lock would open at 7:32 a.m., two hours before high tide, and as Collins had described, boats would enter and leave the lock as the gates were raised and lowered to equalize the water level between the Thames and the marina.

Collins had sent him a text at 7:15 a.m. saying that she and Cole had examined the captain and two crewmen's passports, and the tour had begun. So far, so good. The captain might easily confuse Collins as they wound from port to starboard and forward to aft on the yacht.

However, Cole had spent years on boats and ships of all shapes and sizes; he would notice any attempt to avoid specific areas.

Collins sent periodic texts during the inspection, stating where they had been, along with a simple checkmark. Following the engine room tour, she had sent a text with "*Yawn.*" It made him smile. He made his way back to the White Mulberries café, went to the toilet, bought another coffee against his better judgment, and took a seat outside with a good view of the yacht.

A boat had gone through around 7:45 a.m., not long after the lock operation first began. He watched its slow, no-wake progress as it remained on course toward the *Medicine Man* and then saw it tie up in the slip beside the yacht. He had seen one like it before when he lived in England. It was a Smelne Vlet—an unusual boat, and not the kind he expected to see. Was this the boat that was supposedly there to deliver supplies and pick up some items that would not be sold with the yacht? The marina manager had not given Collins the type of boat or an exact time it was coming, only that it was scheduled to come through the lock early in the three-and-a-half-hour window of time. This was a cruiser or trawler, approximately forty feet long and twelve feet wide. But unlike the trawlers in the US, which were slow-moving and sat tall in the water, this boat sat low in the water and would have no difficulty passing under the low Thames River bridges. Based on its style and condition, Palmer judged it to be about twenty years old. The aft portion above was open. He could see the man at the helm.

Palmer looked at his cell phone, as everyone does when there is the least bit of dead time. He checked Baxter's number and was tempted to call and give her an update. Most of all, he wanted to be certain she was standing by and prepared to make the appropriate calls. After giving it some thought, he decided to wait. The inspection would be over soon.

Another text from Collins. They were in the lounge having coffee, finishing up the inspection. He breathed a sigh of relief.

55

ST. KATHARINE DOCKS LONDON

Collins turned and looked back at Cole. Without speaking, he pointed to the radiation detection device and nodded. She looked down at the captain, who was waiting below. "We need to discuss something. We'll be down in a moment."

The captain nodded and stood at the bottom of the stairs.

"What is it?" Collins asked Cole.

He showed her the reading on the radiation detector and spoke softly, even though they had moved away from the stairs so the captain would not see or hear them. "When we got to this stairway, I saw this low reading, nothing too serious, maybe a false positive. We came on board this way, but I didn't turn the radiation detector on until the tour started."

Collins, arms crossed over her chest and biting her cheek, looked back toward the stairwell. "We agreed that if you had a positive reading, we should leave and call Jake."

"The captain's standing on the platform where we came aboard," Cole said. "We can't leave without walking by him. I'll take another reading at the bottom of these stairs to determine whether this reading is a false positive."

"We've made a big deal out of seeing those items. If we leave without inspecting them, they'll know something is up," Collins reasoned. "Let's go ahead and have a quick look. We'll then tell the captain everything looks good and thank him for their time. You can get another reading from the detector while I'm talking." She glanced at her watch; it was 8:30 a.m.

"The three of them do not appear armed. If this goes badly, I'll overpower them long enough for you to escape," Cole said, jaw tight. "Then, run like hell and call Jake."

"Right. On the way down, check the detector and confirm the reading. We'll say we've seen enough, thank the captain, and get off this yacht."

When they were almost at the bottom of the steps, Collins glanced back at Cole, who was looking at his detector. He put the detector in his bag and whispered, "Hot."

They moved down the remainder of the stairs onto the platform. The captain and two crewmen were waiting. The crewmen, sweat dripping their foreheads, were standing so that Collins and Cole's exit onto the dock was completely blocked.

Collins's mind was racing. The boat tied up in the slip across from them was less than half the length of the *Medicine Man*. Its engines were idling, and a man, who was wiping sweat from his face with a rag, was standing on the aft end. This was the boat they were expecting, and those men had not worked up a sweat staging the few small items that were on the platform. Her gut led her straight to an alarming conclusion: *They've already transferred the device to the boat. It had all happened while we were on the tour.*

The back section of the yacht between the port and starboard stairs that went from the platform to the main deck was raised. When they had boarded, Collins had noted the name of the yacht on that section and gave it no further thought. Inside was a small dingy. Her mind raced through the layout of the yacht that she had shown Palmer and Cole. According to the layout, a dingy and two jet skis were stored in this space. Inside the compartment were some random pieces of furniture and accessories, but nothing worth taking off the yacht before it was sold.

Her heart was pounding in her chest. She quickly tapped out a text to Palmer and sent it.

SOS

———◠◡◠———

The captain saw Collins texting and yanked the phone from her hand.

In an instant, Cole charged him. She heard a muffled sound and saw Cole grab his leg and fall to the deck.

A man was standing inside the storage compartment. He had been hidden just out of sight and was wielding a rifle with a sound suppressor, which was now pointed directly at Collins. Three others approached, flanking him.

Collins immediately recognized Raul Ahmadi and gasped. She recognized them all, and was certain Cole did, too. Ahmadi and his men hadn't attempted to disguise their appearances, although their hair and beards had grown out. Most everyone had concluded that these men were aboard the *Fair Winds* and had died alongside everyone else on or near the ship when the nuclear weapon detonated in the Arabian Sea. Their photographs had been distributed to all intelligence and law enforcement agencies and published in national and international media for weeks just in case any or all of them had not perished. No one had suspected the captain and his two crewmen were involved; therefore, no one had been looking for them.

"Raul Ahmadi. What hole did you crawl out of? We thought you were dead," Cole ground out, putting his weight on his good leg and standing up.

Ahmadi pointed to one of his men. "Hurry! Move them inside. Check them and take their phones and anything else they have on them."

The man took Cole's bag and patted him down, finding his mobile phone. Another patted down Collins and said, "They're clean."

The captain looked through Collins's recent texts. "These are not your notes," he shouted. "Who were you texting? Who is Jake?"

"My colleague at MI6," Collins said, her voice angry. "The notes are related to our progress on the inspection."

The captain held up the phone to her and Cole, showing them the "SOS" text. "And this one? What was that about?"

Cole spoke before Collins could respond. "My radiation device detected a low level of radiation, perhaps a false positive. No big deal."

The captain tapped out a text and sent it to Palmer from Collins's phone. "Let's see if this calms the situation," he said, holding the phone out for her to read the text: *False alarm. Everything okay. We're done and moving on to the next inspection.*

Her heart sputtered in her chest.

He then went into the phone's settings and reset it so that the phone would not lock when unused and he could read and reply to any messages she received.

Cole limped closer to Ahmadi. "So, that's where you were you hiding. How about the nuclear device? You wouldn't have brought it down the stairs and ladders. It was in there with you."

"We were in there whenever we needed to stay out of sight. The device and its container were concealed behind a false wall."

Ahmadi, who was standing near the entrance of the compartment, pointed to a wall located at its rear. The others had fanned out, further blocking any chance of escape, even by jumping into the water. Cole was only a few feet away from Ahmadi. He lunged at him and reached for the rifle.

But Cole's wound slowed him down, and Ahmadi was ready. He struck him in the abdomen with the butt of the rifle. Cole folded over himself, dropping to one knee. Ahmadi then swept the butt of the rifle around like a baton, striking him in the head. Cole fell over, dazed but still conscious. Collins screamed.

"Either of you make another move and you're dead," Ahmadi threatened, and the edge to those dark eyes of his spoke to the legitimacy of it. This man was a killer. The fact that they hadn't died already, frankly, was miraculous.

Collins found her voice. "Aren't we all going to die soon anyway?"

"I want you to die not knowing when your time will be up. I want you to hear the detonation and know we have succeeded. You'll be so close to ground zero that it will happen within a couple of seconds, but you'll know we did it. One moment you're living and breathing—the next, you're burning in hell with the rest of the infidels."

Cole summoned a laugh. "You're done. You have no place to hide, Ahmadi. You've been cooped up on this boat, so maybe you've not seen or heard it. You are the object of an international manhunt. Every law enforcement agency in the world is after you and the others. Your photographs are all over the internet."

"I'd be surprised if they weren't," he countered. "It doesn't matter now."

"Some people think you're The Chameleon." Collins took a step toward Ahmadi inside the compartment. "But not me. I think you're just one of his expendable lackeys." Perhaps jabbing at his ego would elicit a response.

Ahmadi shook his head, scoffing through clenched teeth. Then, without warning, he threw the back of his hand against her face, nearly knocking her clean off her feet. "Infidel whore!"

Collins hadn't ever been struck like that in her life. The swelling was instantaneous, as hot as a fever, throbbing to the beat of her heart.

Cole tried to get up but stopped when Ahmadi pushed the barrel of the rifle into Collins's abdomen.

"Stop," he growled, motioning for his men to leave. He kept his rifle trained on Collins as he backed out of the storage area, and then lowered it out of sight by his leg after pushing her into the compartment with Cole. Collins heard him tell the captain, "Close the door and lock it. We need to go."

The captain took a set of keys from his pocket and went around the starboard side. A couple of seconds later, the door shut, and there was a loud click. She and Cole were locked in the dark with no way out.

56

ST. KATHARINE DOCKS
LONDON

Palmer finished his coffee, got up to throw the cup in the trash, and sat back down. He looked at his watch; time seemed to be standing still. He had received a text from Collins that they were in the lounge and finishing up. What was taking so long? The plan was to leave as soon as they completed the inspection or Cole got confirmation of radiation on his detector. He would wait another ten minutes. If he didn't hear from her, he would make his way to the yacht. Just as the thought crossed his mind, his phone dinged.

SOS

Palmer stood straight up and looked at the yacht. They were in trouble. His first inclination was to get to the yacht as fast as he could, but he needed to alert Baxter first. They needed backup. *No answer. Damn it.* Before he could leave a voicemail, there was another text. He disconnected the call.

False alarm. Wrapping up now and moving on to the next inspection.

Palmer's eyes were fixed on the text. Something didn't feel right. *Next inspection? Fiona?* He thought for a moment before texting back, *Well done. Advise when you begin the inspection of the next vessel.*

The reply from Collins's phone came quickly: *Affirmative.*

Palmer's eyes widened. *Affirmative? That is not Fiona.*

Palmer called Baxter again. No answer. He left a message, saying there was a problem, and he was going to investigate. He told her he might not have a chance to contact her again and that she should alert the team.

Collins and Cole were in trouble.

They had all agreed that if Cole's device detected radiation, they would thank the captain and leave immediately. Where were they? He put his phone on vibrate and rushed toward the yacht. As he neared it, he saw the Smelne Vlet boat pull out of the slip.

57

ST. KATHARINE DOCKS
LONDON

Palmer stepped quietly onto the yacht's rear platform and began to go up the portside stairs when he heard a thumping sound. He stopped and listened. His thoughts reverted to the deck plans that Collins had shown them. At the aft end of the yacht, there was a storage area for the dingy and jet skis. He hadn't paid it much attention at the time. The entire bulkhead between the port and starboard raised and lowered to allow access. Someone inside was banging on the bulkhead. He didn't want to shout, so he struck the bulkhead twice and heard a faint voice, "Who is it?"

He said in a normal voice, "Jake."

"It's us," he heard Cole say, his tone more serious. "They have a nuke."

"I need to get you out."

"There's a switch on the starboard-side bulkhead," Cole answered.

Palmer found it enclosed behind a small, watertight access panel. He opened it. A key was required to access the switch. He went back around and said, "It's locked."

Collins shouted, "It's disabled. The captain has the keys. He also has our phones."

"I'll find him. I've notified Carol to alert the team. How many men are on board?"

"The captain, two crewmen, Raul Ahmadi, the nuclear engineer, and two of the missing Pakistani soldiers that we know of," Cole said. "Ahmadi and the two soldiers were armed when we saw them. The others may have weapons, too."

"I'll be back."

"You'd better be," Collins said.

Palmer quickly texted Baxter. *Backup needed now. URGENT.*

He went up the steps to the lounge door on the main deck. Out of the corner of his eye, Palmer saw the boat. It was about to enter the lock. Two other boats were queued up in front of it, waiting for the inner gate to lower and the boats inside the lock to exit into the marina. He had some time, but not much.

Palmer entered the large lounge and dining area. He walked quietly forward until he entered the owner's cabin. No one there. Where were they? He approached the steps that led to the lower deck and heard movement below—footsteps, and they were getting louder. Someone was coming up the stairs. He stood with his back against the wall and moved to the side, where he would be out of sight until the man entered the room. The only weapons he had were his physical strength, close-quarters combat training and experience, and the element of surprise—perhaps the biggest advantage of all. He wasn't certain who, if anyone, was still on the yacht. Ahmadi and the two soldiers were well-trained Pakistani military. They would most certainly be armed.

Whoever it was, the man was making no attempt to be quiet and was near the top of the stairs. Knocking him down the stairs would temporarily disable him but would also make a racket. And if the man wasn't knocked out or didn't lose his weapon in the fall, he could fire at Palmer, alerting everyone on the yacht and possibly wounding him.

When the man took his initial step at the top of the stairs, Palmer moved quickly in front of him. The man's eyes widened, and he reached for Palmer. His movement was impaired by the fact that he had a canvas bag slung over his other shoulder. Palmer grabbed his shirt with his left hand, drew back his right, and punched him square in the nose. The man was stunned but conscious and dropped a rifle he had been carrying. As he began to fall backward from the force of the blow, Palmer jerked him into the lounge and threw him onto the floor. His head hit the hard deck with a thud. Palmer wasn't certain if he had killed him or just knocked him out. Either way, he was out of action.

Palmer moved him behind a sofa and looked inside the canvas bag, which resembled a large gym bag. Lying on top of some clothes was a military handgun—a 9mm German Sig Sauer P226, one of the pistols used by the Pakistani Army. He felt around the clothes and found two extra magazines, both of which were loaded with bullets. The weight and feel of the pistol felt very familiar. It was the same make and model of pistol as he had used when he was a Navy SEAL. He ejected the magazine; it was loaded. Palmer pulled back the slide, loading a round in the chamber, and put the extra magazines in his pocket. A pistol would be more practical in close quarters than the rifle.

He moved down the steps the man had come up, grasping the pistol with both hands in a firing position. With the device off of the yacht, everyone was making a hasty escape. At the bottom of the stairs, he stopped and peeked around the bulkhead. About fifteen feet down the passageway, another man was exiting a cabin. He also had a bag and was smoking a cigarette—a popular habit among Pakistani men. The man was an easy target. Palmer thought through the alternatives and made a decision. He heard the man walking toward him. Palmer stepped into the passageway, the P226 up and in the firing position. They were less than ten feet apart.

"Stop where you are," Palmer shouted. "I'm US special forces working with MI6. Drop the bag. Hands behind your head."

The man took the bag off his shoulder. His eyes were fixed on Palmer.

"Put it down!"

The man had both hands on the bag and began to lower it when he shoved it directly toward the pistol and charged him. Palmer fired a shot that hit the bag before the bag hit his pistol. The man barreled into him, knocking him down. Palmer's grip on the P226 was firm, and he held on to it. The man was on top of him. He was strong, and using both hands, grabbed Palmer's arm that was grasping the pistol. Palmer struck him in the ear with his left fist. The man seemed groggy but didn't release his arm. Palmer's second punch was to the man's throat, causing him to fall away. Gasping for breath, he came at Palmer again, but not before Palmer shot him in the chest. He fell to the floor, mumbling something in Arabic.

Palmer checked his pulse. He was dead.

When he searched the man's bag, he found clothes, a Sig Sauer P226, and extra loaded magazines. Palmer shoved the pistol into his belt behind his back, placing the spare magazines in his other pocket. Anyone else on the yacht would probably have heard the gunshots. The element of surprise was gone.

Instead of going up the stairs, Palmer went out the door and walked down the narrow exterior passageway toward the bow. He climbed on top of the bow portion of the yacht and walked on top of the front, crouching as he made his way toward the exterior bridge on the top deck. He peered inside the enclosed wheelhouse, which was just below the exterior bridge, and saw the two men he had seen smoking outside the night before. They saw him, too, and shouted in Arabic.

Palmer stood and ran up toward the roof that covered the exterior bridge above it and a portion of the sun lounge area. He leaped onto the roof as rifle shots rang out. Palmer ran toward the rear, dropped to his hip, and slid like a baseball player beating out a throw into second base.

Bullets penetrated the roof behind him. The shooter was directing fire at the sound of his footsteps. Palmer's slide carried him to the edge, and he went off, turning as he fell and getting off a shot before his feet hit the deck below. One of the bullets struck the man in the arm, and he turned and disappeared down the short set of steps that ran between the exterior bridge and the enclosed wheelhouse just below it, where the two crewmen were hunkered down. Based on the man's age and somewhat portly appearance, Palmer deduced he was the yacht's captain.

"Give it up, Captain," he shouted.

"You're too late."

Palmer had no time for negotiation. He aimed his pistol at the steps and fired once, then stepped out of sight, rolling behind a wet bar. The captain appeared again on the steps, holding his rifle at hip level while pointing it toward Palmer. Before he could shoot, Palmer fired twice, and the captain fell backward and was down. Palmer rushed to him and reached in his trouser pockets, finding two cellphones and some keys on a key ring. He took the rifle and went down to the enclosed wheelhouse where the two crewmen had taken shelter.

Palmer shouted for them to come out, which they did slowly. He made them put their hands on their heads and marched them down to the platform at the aft end of the yacht, keeping the pistol aimed at them. He opened the panel and used the captain's key to activate the motor that opened the fantail door. Collins and Cole spilled out, exhaling sighs of relief.

Palmer heard sirens and the unmistakable sound of a British Royal Air Force HC Chinook helicopter. He handed Cole the captain's rifle.

"Nick, keep an eye on these two. The captain and one other man are dead. Another is out cold on the main deck lounge. I have to catch that boat before it leaves the lock. If either of them so much as farts, shoot him."

"Was Ahmadi one of the dead?" Cole asked.

"No. Ahmadi's too invested in this. He would want to see it through and fulfill his final destiny. He wouldn't trust it to anyone else. He and the nuclear engineer must be on that boat."

"I need to go with you, but I'd slow you down," Cole admitted, shaking his head. "Who's going to disarm the nuke?"

The sirens were getting close, and the helicopter was dropping down. "If I don't stop the boat, it's irrelevant. I need to leave now."

"Go. We've got it," Cole said. "I'll join you as soon I can. Wait!" Cole pointed inside the compartment to his equipment bag containing the tools needed to disarm a nuclear device. "You might need it."

Palmer retrieved the bag. "I'm not sure this will be of any use to me. Come as soon as you can. Oh," he added, handing Collins and Cole their phones, "and you'll need these."

Collins looked at him, her face a stew of relief, fear, and anger. He knew she was dying to tell him to be careful, but it wasn't the time. Instead, she said, "Kill the bastards."

Palmer sprinted around the marina toward the lock, the P226 in his hand. The marina had been quiet before the shooting started. Gunfire in London was a very rare sound. After that, anyone near the marina had run in the opposite direction. The Smelne Vlet was almost in the lock. A man stood at the rear of the boat, watching him. As Palmer got closer, he recognized the man—Raul Ahmadi.

58

ST. KATHARINE DOCKS
LONDON

Palmer sprinted back past the White Mulberries café and across a narrow footbridge. The inner lock gate was open, and boats were entering the lock to exit the marina. The Smelne Vlet was waiting for the boats in front of it to move into the lock. No boats were behind it, although a cabin cruiser was moving quickly through the marina toward the lock.

Ahmadi stood beside the man piloting the Smelne Vlet, holding a rifle in firing position.

Palmer scrambled behind a tree, using it as a shield. Two loud thumps confirmed the rounds meant for him had been buried in the wood instead. There had been no other perceptible sound. *The rifle has a sound suppressor.* He peered around the tree and saw the rifle barrel extended slightly from a break at the bottom of the bulkhead at the rear of the boat.

The midsize cabin cruiser, which had been headed toward the lock, came to a stop near the tree where Palmer was hiding. The man at the helm had been watching the helicopters and observing the Smelne Vlet—he had apparently decided to hang back. The boat was about five feet from the bulkhead. Palmer had one of the pistols in his hand and had the other tucked in his belt. He held on to Cole's bag and took off like a sprinter out of the blocks. Ahmadi fired two more rounds at him during the short run. Both missed.

Palmer leaped toward the cabin cruiser. As he was in midair and preparing for the impact of hitting the deck of the boat, he lost his grip on Cole's bag. It fell, as though in slow motion, into the water below, sinking rapidly out of sight. *Shit.* He landed hard on the deck, rolled over, and knelt for a moment, gauging if the coast was clear. When he popped up from the deck and put weight on his feet, a sharp pain in his ankle caused him to wince. He waved his pistol in the direction of the cruiser's cabin and shouted at the man at the helm, "MI6. I have to stop that boat. Get below and hold on to something."

The man, his mouth gaping in fear and shock, went below without saying a word.

Palmer got behind the wheel and pushed the controls down to full power. The cruiser's bow rose high in the water as the twin inboards responded to the controls, which blocked Ahmadi's view of him. Ahmadi fired a burst of bullets, which struck the hull.

Palmer knew exactly what he needed to do; he played it out in his head. But it had been years since he had driven a boat anywhere near the size and power of this one. He wasn't certain how it would react. He relied on his past experience and instincts. The boat was still accelerating the thirty yards to the Smelne Vlet. As it neared it, rifle shots struck the windshield. Palmer fired three shots at the spot where the shooter had been, and then pulled back the port throttle and steered hard to port. The cruiser rolled to the left, just short of capsizing. He then straightened the wheel and switched both controls to reverse at full power. The actions combined threw a wall of water onto the rear of the Smelne Vlet as the cruiser slid toward it.

Palmer cut the engines just as it appeared a collision was inevitable. The cruiser settled down into the water, and as the two vessels touched, he jumped from the gunwale of the cruiser to the railing of the Smelne Vlet.

Palmer pulled himself up and over the railing with the pistol in his hand. When his feet hit the deck, he flinched. The ankle sprain was painful. Ahmadi's rifle was on the deck. The man he had seen steering the Smelne Vlet was also gone, perhaps hiding in the cabin below. Palmer reached over and cut the throttles, stopping the boat's forward motion. Both boats were now inside the lock, and the inner gate was raising. As he turned away from the boat's controls, Ahmadi rushed from the cabin, lowered his head, and ran hard into Palmer's abdomen, knocking him into a large box covered with a tarp. Palmer's pistol flew out of his hand and slid across the deck. The tarp was dragged off the container in the scuffle.

Palmer was still down and gasping for breath when the man who had been steering the Smelne Vlet came up from the cabin, hands shaking as he nervously gripped a rifle. Ahmadi was a few feet away now, holding his bloodied right shoulder. One of Palmer's shots had hit him.

Palmer groaned. "It's over, Ahmadi. We're not going anywhere."

"Not ideal for it to detonate here … yet the world will see the damage and death that will result. It will be the worst since your country dropped nuclear bombs on Japan, killing thousands of innocent civilians."

"We were at war with Japan."

"As the West is now with Islam. Many innocents will die in order for us to prevail."

Palmer grunted, reached down, and slowly pushed up just far enough off the deck to reach the second P226 from his belt. He whipped it around, shot the man with the rifle before he could react, and then aimed it at Ahmadi's chest.

Standing slowly, Palmer said, "I want you alive to face justice for what you've done."

Ahmadi laughed. "None of us will be alive." He raised his hands up to the sky, looked up, shouted, "Allahu Akbar!" and then charged at Palmer.

Without hesitation and with the skill and instinct that years of training had instilled in him, Palmer's aim shifted from Ahmadi's center mass to his heart. He pulled the trigger and fired two shots in rapid succession into his chest. The force of the 9mm bullets at close range propelled Ahmadi backward. He struck the deck hard, lifeless.

Palmer moved over and knelt beside the mortally wounded man who'd been behind the wheel of the boat earlier. He kicked his rifle away.

"Nuclear warhead?" Palmer asked, pointing his pistol at the container that had been covered by a tarp and was now exposed.

The man, who was close to death and couldn't speak, nodded.

59

ST. KATHARINE DOCKS LONDON

Collins helped Cole get to the yacht's lounge. He was in a chair, a pistol pointed at the three surviving men. The two Saudi crewmen were sitting on the deck, fingers interlocked on the back of their heads. The Pakistani soldier, who Palmer had knocked out, was lying facedown next to them, fading in and out of consciousness. Except for the mumbling of one of the crewmen, there was only silence.

Collins had a hard time getting her head around what had happened and the unfathomable fact that a nuclear warhead was on that boat. If it wasn't disarmed, the weapon would detonate and flatten much of London, killing and injuring hundreds of thousands. Palmer was their only hope to stop that boat from leaving the marina until the others arrived.

Collins's phone rang. It startled her, and she jumped slightly.

"ETA five minutes, four if I keep shouting at the driver to speed up."

Collin's voice quivered. "Carol?"

"Of course, it's Carol. Who were you expecting, Mary Poppins? I got Jake's message and alerted the teams. They're arriving soon—very soon. Status report."

Collins quickly collected her thoughts. "The device is aboard a boat headed toward the lock and will detonate near Lambeth Bridge if not disarmed. Jake is in pursuit. Nick Cole has a gunshot wound. He and I are still on the *Medicine Man*, with two dead and three captives."

"I'm in a taxi. Can't talk. I see the marina. Meet me on the dock."

Collins got to the dock beside the yacht in time to see the taxi drive off and Baxter run up to her. They had a quick embrace and went up to the lounge.

She introduced her to Cole and gave her a high-level, fast-talking summary of what had occurred from the time they came on board the yacht. In the distance, they could hear the sound of a helicopter.

"Are you sure it was Ahmadi?" Baxter asked.

"Positive," Cole said before Collins could respond. "We IDed the others, too, including one of the nuclear engineers. Ahmadi and the nuclear engineer left with the boat. Who's coming and when? I hear sirens and helos."

"MI5, MI6, and the British Army's 621st EOD&S. And probably some London police."

They heard several gunshots coming from the direction of the lock. Collins turned toward the sound, sensing her face draining of color. "Oh, no."

"Jake?" Baxter asked, eyes wide.

"He has two 9mm pistols he took from the soldiers," Cole reassured her, though he couldn't disguise the tinge of worry in his voice.

Baxter looked at Cole's leg and said, "Both of you, stay here. I'm going to the dock to flag down whoever arrives. I'll bring them up to speed and put some sense of urgency and priority to the situation. I don't want them charging aboard. We can't have twenty or more people in your face and asking questions all at once."

"There's only one priority," Cole said. "We have to disarm that device. If we don't do that, we're all dead."

"I called the EODs first, even before my MI6 colleagues. That should be them in the helicopters we hear. I'll send them straight up."

"No. I'll go with you," Cole said. "That'll save some time. Every second we have to disarm that nuke is critical."

"Your wound—"

"I'm okay. Let's go."

Cole stood and handed Collins the pistol. "Safety's off and a round's in the chamber. If anyone moves, blow their head off."

—◦◦◦—

On the dock, Baxter and Cole waved their arms, guiding the British Army helicopter pilot to their location. The chopper swooped in low and dropped off the 621st Explosive Ordnance Disposal and Search Squadron team. Other military helicopters were circling high overhead. An Army major approached Baxter and Cole even before all of his men were on the ground.

"Are you Carol Baxter?" the major shouted over the noise.

"I am." She introduced herself and Senior Chief Nick Cole.

The major looked at him. "Where's the device?"

Cole explained that it had been transferred to a boat that was now heading toward or already in the lock. Before he could finish, they heard the crack of another gunshot from the direction of the lock.

"We need to go," the major ordered his men.

"I'm going, too. I'm up to speed on nuclear weapon disarmament. And Jake Palmer, who's with US Joint Special Operation Command, is the one trying to stop that boat before it's too late."

The major looked at Cole and his wounded leg. He didn't have time to argue, and he needed Cole to identify the boat and possibly assist in disarming the nuke. He sent a soldier up to the lounge to guard the captives and posted one with Carol at *Medicine Man's* gangway. They rushed toward the lock, with one of the soldiers practically carrying Cole.

—◆◆◆—

Collins felt each of the gunshots she heard as if they had struck her instead of their intended target. But as long as the gunfire continued, she knew Jake was alive and fighting.

Everything had rapidly descended into chaos. It was hard not to get overwhelmed by the commotion outside, the pulse of helicopter rotors, people talking—some shouting. She wanted to look out and see what was going on, but that would distract her from guarding the three men. The one who had been semiconscious was now sitting up. The heavy pistol in her hand required her full attention. The men weren't constrained and might rush her given the slightest opportunity.

Collins breathed a sigh of relief when a British soldier entered the lounge. She handed him the pistol. Although he had his own weapon, she didn't want the firearm in her hands one moment longer.

MI5 and MI6 arrived next and spit out a burst of rapid-fire questions. *What had happened? Who killed whom? Where were the bodies? Was there a nuclear device? Where was it?* Although the men were far senior to her, Collins remained calm and spoke with confidence. They hung on to her every word.

6 0

ST. KATHARINE DOCKS LONDON

Palmer hobbled toward the opening that led down to the cabin, the pistol in his grip, a round in the chamber, and the hammer pulled back. By his calculation, the only person left was the nuclear engineer. At the top of the few open steps that led to the small cabin, he stopped and peered down inside.

Commodore Zahir Sabri was standing in the center of the cabin, holding a pistol to Alona Green's head, his left arm tight around her neck. It appeared her hands were tied behind her back. Sabri could have shot it out with Palmer, but in doing so he might have been killed himself. Sabri knew Palmer would not risk harming Green, his JSOC partner.

Another man was cowering in the corner of the cabin, possibly the nuclear engineer.

Palmer was standing with most of his body behind the bulkhead next to the steps to the cabin, his gun hand pointing down at Sabri.

"So, you're The Chameleon," he said. "That's why you were so eager to have us observe the inspection of the cargo ship."

"You were supposed to die that day, along with Ms. Green here. Casualties of war. Put down your gun, Palmer."

"Don't do it, Jake," Green pleaded. "Shoot, even if you have to shoot through me to kill him."

Palmer considered what Green had said. Her life for thousands of others if the EODs could disarm the nuke in time. Was that really the only option? Palmer's aim was by her head. He saw no fear in her—only anger and determination. She wanted Sabri dead.

Sabri was of average height for a Pakistani man, about as tall as Green, who completely blocked Palmer from having a clear shot. At the range he had, a 9mm bullet would go through Green and into Sabri's chest. Even if it didn't kill him, Palmer would fire another round into him. Sabri knew there was no escape; he was stalling. Palmer lightly squeezed the trigger. He tried to look through Green and only envision Sabri's head. As the pressure on the trigger increased, he saw her face and relaxed his finger.

"It's over, Sabri. Let her go. You hear the choppers. What difference does it make? We'll die anyway when the nuke explodes."

"Shoot the son of a bitch!" Green shouted.

"Why are you doing this?" Palmer asked Sabri. "Your battle is with India, not the British."

"That was only a ruse to escalate the tension with India to the point that we would deploy the nukes, which gave us the opportunity to acquire the devices we needed."

"Why the British?"

"They are an easier target than your country. America has disrespected Pakistan for years, including running a black op to kill Osama bin Laden without giving us any notice. That device will take out your extravagant new embassy in London along with the British government—Parliament, the queen, MI5, and MI6."

Sabri pushed Green forward slightly, bringing them closer to the steps. Now Palmer's angle of attack had changed. He had a shot at part of the top of Sabri's head, but the margin of error was still too narrow, perhaps only an inch. The risk was too great.

Sabri saw the slight lowering of Palmer's pistol and fired at him. Green had apparently sensed that he was going to shoot and nudged him, causing him to miss. Sabri quickly put the gun back on her head, pressing the barrel hard against her temple.

"Throw your weapon down, Palmer."

"You're finished, Sabri. You're not able to take the boat and weapon to the place you want it to be, near the Lambeth Bridge and the targets you mentioned, especially the US Embassy."

"If that's the case, it will detonate here, and there's nothing you or anyone else can do."

The device had to be on a timed detonator, which meant time was running out. The more time Sabri killed, the less time the EODs would have to disable it. Where were Cole and the others? With Green's hands behind her back and Sabri's arm around her neck, there was little she could do. He just couldn't bring himself to shoot through her to kill Sabri.

Then, Palmer's eyes met Green's. Her face was bruised, and her auburn hair was a mess; however, the look on her face said it all. She was angry. Sabri or his thugs had roughed her up in their attempt to extract information.

Palmer had no doubt that she would not have told them anything of value. Time was up.

He took aim and again put pressure on the trigger. With his eyes still locked on hers, she smiled, winked at him, and nodded her head ever so slightly.

What does she have to smile about?

He watched her take a deep breath, look down, and then back up. On the exhale, she suddenly raised her legs off the deck, bringing her knees to her chest. Because Sabri had his arm tight around her neck, her weight pulled him forward and down. It happened too fast for Sabri to react. Palmer fired a single shot. The round struck Sabri in the top of his head, and he collapsed on top of Green—dead.

61

ST. KATHARINE DOCKS LONDON

Palmer rushed down the ladder, ignoring the acute pain in his ankle. He pushed Sabri off Green and knelt down beside her. The round had blown the back of his head off. She was a bloody mess. He untied her hands and helped her up. She was trembling.

"That was a bold move," he said.

"Someone had to do something. You two were like rams with horns locked. Why didn't you shoot him through me like I told you? I might have even survived."

"I didn't want to harm your beautiful face, Alona. Are you okay?"

"I'll survive. I need some fresh air."

Palmer helped her topside and sat her down in the captain's chair. "I'll be right back."

With pistol in hand, Palmer went back into the cabin and limped over to the nuclear engineer, who had watched the encounter from a few feet away. He was a slender, middle-aged man wearing thick glasses.

"Stand up!" Palmer ordered, motioning with his pistol. The man stood with his head lowered. Palmer recognized him from the photographs he had seen but asked anyway, "Who are you?"

"I am a nuclear engineer."

"Is that a nuclear device?" Palmer asked, pointing at the box outside.

He smiled. "It is a 150-kiloton nuclear warhead," he said, almost with a sense of pride.

With his pistol pointed at the engineer's head, Palmer asked, "What is the triggering mechanism? Timer? Location? Manual?"

"I will tell you because you cannot stop it in the time you have left," he said with smug satisfaction. "A timer."

Just as he thought. "Can you stop it?"

"Would you trust me to do it? I could intentionally detonate it."

"You're right. I don't trust you."

"The West will feel the pain and suffering it has imposed on Muslims worldwide."

Palmer looked at him and shook his head. Engaging in even a brief discussion of terrorism and Muslim extremists was a waste of breath. The engineer was prepared to die. He knew when he got on the boat that he would become a martyr. Not only did he volunteer for the mission, but he believed it was his destiny, that his reward would be eternity in paradise. It wasn't something that was open for discussion or something that could be forced through threat of pain or death.

"Nothing you can do will stop it," the engineer said with a nervous laugh.

"How long do we have?"

"Eleven o'clock."

Palmer looked at his watch. It was 9:45 a.m. "If you're not going to help, I can't have you interfering."

The engineer's eyes widened as Palmer moved closer. He might not fear death, but like all men, he feared the act of dying. Palmer swung the pistol and struck him in the side of the head. The engineer fell over, unconscious.

Palmer went topside and examined the container. He needed to speak with Cole and Collins. He used his secure phone's video chat function to call Cole, who answered on the first ring. Cole told him a soldier was holding him up as they walked.

"We heard the gunshots," Cole said. "Are you okay?"

"Yes. Alona is here, and she's okay, too. Sabri was holding a gun to her head."

Palmer told him that he had killed Sabri, Ahmadi, and the boat's captain. The nuclear engineer, who was currently unconscious, had said the device was a 150-kiloton device and set on a timer for 1100 hours. "To make matters worse, I dropped your tool bag in the water."

Cole said, "I'm on the way there now with a British special forces escort. If the nuclear engineer is on board, he has tools to handle any problem with the device. Find them."

Palmer went inside the cabin, holding the phone in front of him. He found the toolbox in the fourth cabinet door he opened.

"What now?" he asked.

"We're almost there. A British nuclear weapons specialist is with me. Did you believe him when he told you the device was on a timer?"

"Yes. He said he would tell me because there was nothing that we could do to stop it."

"We'll see about that." Cole told him that British special forces had arrived on the Chinook. They were almost at the lock. Two British Apache helicopters were circling the marina. Palmer looked up and saw the Apaches, each armed with seventy-six CRV-7 rockets and sixteen Hellfire missiles. He didn't have to ask. They were going to fire at the boat if Cole and the British EOD were unable to dismantle the warhead.

"Where's Fiona?" Palmer asked.

"She stayed behind on the *Medicine Man*. She's bringing the soldiers up to speed on the situation. Carol and a few of her MI6 colleagues arrived. They'll fly her out if we can't shut this down."

"What are their plans?"

"They're locking down the yacht and checking on the killed and wounded. They briefly considered stringing the warhead up under the Chinook and heading out to the English Channel."

"And what? Let it explode underwater? That's madness."

"That's what they concluded, too. They decided to give us a chance to disarm it."

Palmer's mind went into overdrive. If he could get the boat out of the lock, he could get it downriver four or five miles to a less populated area before the Apaches would fire at it. It would put some distance between Central London and the blast area, which included the Tower of London, Tower Bridge, Houses of Parliament, Buckingham Palace, and the MI6 and MI5 headquarters. He had to get out of the lock first.

"We're here," Cole said. "We're coming aboard."

Palmer heard shouting and saw several special forces soldiers on the dock. Cole was with them, still holding his phone. Palmer shouted at them to finish opening the lock so that he could move the boat downriver. The lockmaster had abandoned his post when the shooting began. One of the soldiers threw Palmer a line, which he grabbed and tied to the boat. They pulled the boat over to the dock wall, and a British Army major came on board with Cole and two Army medics. The EOD was wearing a large backpack. He briefly introduced himself as an ammunition technician with the 621st Explosive Ordnance Disposal and Search Squadron.

Palmer looked at Cole. "Are you well enough to do this?"

"The medics applied a tourniquet to stop the bleeding. It'll have to do. No way in hell I'm going to miss this. You know what they say, it's all mind over matter—"

"—if you don't mind, then it doesn't matter," Palmer finished. "How about you?"

Palmer was limping from a badly sprained ankle. "I'm good to go."

Cole looked at Green, a grimace on his face. "Alona?"

"I'm way better than either of you," she said with determination. "I'm staying on the boat. End of discussion."

Palmer and Cole looked at each other and shrugged.

Cole was pale and moving only with assistance from the medic. He and the British EOD immediately kneeled beside the device with heads down, using the tools that the EOD had brought on board and the Pakistani's equipment that Palmer had located. They were like surgeons hovering over a critically ill patient who had moments to live. Palmer watched them and understood. When you train in your craft all of your life and there is an opportunity to do something no one else has ever done, your mission overcomes the pain and you do what needs to be done.

One of the medics began working on Green while the other tried to examine Palmer, who said, "Now's not the time. If we survive the next hour, we're all yours."

The soldiers on the dock had finished opening the lock's outer gate. Others had come aboard and taken the bodies of Sabri, Ahmadi, and the captain off the boat and zip-tied the nuclear engineer's hands behind him in the cabin.

The British major glared at Palmer and barked, "Prepare to depart."

"What about him?" Palmer said as he pointed at the nuclear engineer, still lying on the floor in the cabin. "He's the Pakistani nuclear engineer. He confirmed the device is on a timer set for 1100 hours."

"Let's keep him on board."

Palmer handed Green his pistol. "Watch the engineer. If he moves, you have my permission to kill him."

The major spoke into a communicator and then turned to the medics. "You two go ashore. Now," he shouted.

No need to ask twice. In seconds, they had packed up and were off the boat.

The major cast off the last line and said, "Let's get this boat out of here and head east at full speed, Mr. Palmer."

"Aye, aye, Major."

Palmer pulled the boat out of the lock and into the River Thames. He turned to starboard, heading east toward the English Channel, although he would get nowhere near that far. There was not enough time, and that was not the goal. The goal was to get the device away from Central London.

62

THAMES RIVER
LONDON

It was 9:55 a.m. Palmer pushed down the engine controls to full speed. He noticed the major's helmet had a built-in communicator. "Are you talking to the helo pilots?"

"I am," responded the major.

"Fizzle yield?"

"That's correct, sir. If they can't disarm the nuke, the pilots have orders to fire once we abandon ship and are a safe distance away or at 1045 hours, whichever comes first."

Palmer looked up at the two British Apache helicopters overhead and recalled Dr. Psimas telling him about a fizzle yield. Detonation of a nuclear device is a complex engineering feat that requires a precisely timed explosion—a perfectly symmetrical explosion—that surrounds a solid ball of plutonium called the pit. If the warhead is hit by a missile and explodes, the resulting explosion will not be symmetrical, and therefore significantly weaker or not nuclear at all.

That type of explosion, called a fizzle yield, would release plutonium-oxide aerosol from the plutonium pit. Although it would still present a significant public health risk, it would cause nowhere near the death and destruction that would follow the detonation of a strategic nuclear warhead.

Cole was not James Bond, stopping the detonator at 007 seconds. This was real life, and the Pakistani engineers who had bypassed the security system and switched the triggering mechanism might have built in a booby trap or two.

The Pakistani nuclear engineer had regained consciousness and saw Green standing over him with a gun pointed at him. He looked up the ladder and saw the EODs and shouted, "Give up. You'll never figure it out in time, even if ten of you were working on it."

Palmer heard Green shout at the engineer, "If we don't, we'll cram your sorry ass inside the case with the warhead before we get off this boat."

Palmer glanced at his watch. It was 10:05 a.m. At full speed, the Smelne Vlet cruiser was putting out a significant wake. With two British Apaches flying overhead, no marine policeman was about to challenge him for speeding in a no-wake zone. Palmer could see people walking on the riverbanks. Many were looking up at the helicopters, which appeared the focus of their attention, oblivious to what was really going on. His gaze refocused downriver. This close to Central London, there were no broad swatches of pasture, but he hoped they at least found a much less populated area.

The Smelne Vlet was not a speedboat; it was built for long cruises. He wasn't familiar with the boat's specifications but sensed that the boat had reached maximum speed, which he believed was about ten to twelve knots—about twelve to fourteen miles per hour. The tide had turned and was going out. That added a couple of miles per hour to their speed. With a disembark time no later than 10:45 a.m., he calculated they had forty minutes or less before they had to abandon ship. At the current speed, that meant they would get six or seven miles away from St. Katharine Docks. Far enough.

Cole and the British EOD were bending over the device and talking to one another. Palmer could not make out what they were saying over the noise of the boat's engine and the helicopters. He wished he had had the chance to speak with Fiona. Even so, there would have been no time to talk. Every minute—every second—counted. Had he seen her for the last time? Like these terrorists, who were willing to give their lives for their cause, Cole, Green, the British EOD, the major, and he were on a potential suicide mission. Not all lives would be saved, but thousands, perhaps hundreds of thousands, would be.

Seven Special Boat Service craft, fast-moving riverine boats of the British Navy's special forces, sped up to them with lights flashing and UK flags flying. Three of the boats hung back two miles behind the Smelne Vlet. Another three continued until they were about two miles ahead, serving as an escort and clearing the way. The seventh boat pulled alongside the Smelne Vlet, just off the starboard side. Alerts had been sent out on the marine channel to all commercial and pleasure boat traffic, warning them of a possible explosion in the area.

The major was standing by Palmer's side, his eyes moving back and forth ahead of them, scanning the river for anything in their way.

Palmer shouted to the major, "Are you familiar with the Thames? I calculate that at this speed we can get six to seven miles from the marina before we need to abort."

"I grew up in London's East End. We need to get around the Isle of Dogs, or at least past the south end of it, well past Canary Wharf and Greenwich. To be honest, there is no good place. We should try to get between Greenwich to our right and London City Airport on our left, just before the Thames Barrier. That should be about the right time and distance—assuming they are unable to disarm the device."

The Isle of Dogs was not an island but instead a large peninsula protruding south from the northern bank of the river and surrounded on three sides by the Thames. It was a rapidly expanding part of Greater London, dominated by tall buildings, housing, office, and retail space. The Thames Barrier was a tidal barrier that prevented London from being flooded by exceptionally high tides and storm surges.

They continued on, passing the Royal Observatory in Greenwich on the south side of the Thames near the southernmost part of the Isle of Dogs. In the distance, he could see the O2 Arena, the former Millennium Dome, a vast dome-shaped structure that was the ninth largest building in the world by usable volume.

The major saw it, looked at this watch, and said, "We're running out of time. There's the O2 Arena. Let's get just past it, somewhere between it and London City Airport."

Palmer continued on without saying anything further. Air traffic had been stopped at the airport, but he could see the tower. The British major looked at his watch and said, "This is good enough. Let's shut her down and drop anchor. That will give us enough time to get away from this boat." He spoke into the communicator, advising the helos and boats of the decision.

The boats in front of the Smelne Vlet sped farther away while the ones aft of the boat stayed farther back.

Palmer backed down the engine, hit reverse to slow it almost to a stop, and then hit the windless anchor release switch. It was 10:30 a.m. He looked over his shoulder at Cole and the ammo tech. "How are you two doing?"

"Getting close," Cole said.

"Close is good only in hand grenades and horseshoes, not nuclear warheads. The major's called it."

"What do you mean?" Cole said.

"We're out of time." Palmer pointed at the boat pulling up to them. "That's our taxi home."

The Royal Navy high-speed workboat pulled up to their starboard side, and one of the crewmen threw a line. The major grabbed it and tied up.

Palmer looked up at the Apaches. They were hovering in position for a missile strike. They had moved upwind and on opposite sides of the Smelne Vlet boat, their noses down and pointed toward it.

Cole shouted, "We're damn close. We need more time. I'm staying. You go."

The British EOD looked up and said, "Me, too."

63

THAMES RIVER
NEAR GREENWICH

The Smelne Vlet was motionless now that the anchor had taken hold. Sirens were blasting from the British boats.

"We're not leaving you behind," the major said. "The Apaches will fire no later than 1045 hours regardless of who's on here. We need to put some distance between us and this boat."

Green had stepped up from the cabin. "What about him?" Green said, pointing to the Pakistani engineer sitting on the deck in the cabin, his arms wrapped around his legs.

"We're taking him with us. He may have some useful intel."

The major spoke into his communicator, telling the boats and the helicopters what they were doing. The major went below and grabbed the Pakistani engineer by the arms and jerked him up. The engineer resisted and said he wasn't going. The major struck him in the face with his fist, picked him up, threw him over his shoulder, and carried him up the steps.

Palmer looked at Green and smiled. "Ladies first."

Green went over the gunwale and boarded the Navy workboat. A crewman assisted her. The major lowered the Pakistani engineer over the side, telling the crewman to keep an eye on him. He then looked at Palmer, Cole, and the British EOD. "Sorry men, time's up. Let's go."

Palmer stood within a foot of Cole and shouted to be heard over the noise of the helicopters and sirens. "If you cannot disarm that device in the next two minutes with absolute certainty, you need to get the hell out of here. They *will* fire, whether you're on this boat or not. It's suicide. We've done all we can do."

Cole glanced at his British colleague, who looked up, dejected, and nodded. With that, the three of them rushed off the boat. Palmer was last, taking a final look before he jumped aboard the waiting Navy workboat. As soon as his feet hit the deck, the major communicated to the helicopter pilots that they were all off the boat. The workboat turned and sped away, heading back into the wind toward St. Katharine Docks at about twenty-five knots. The other boats moved a safe distance fore and aft of the Smelne Vlet.

In theory, the missile strikes would almost immediately result in a fizzle yield but a massive explosion nevertheless. Except for the crewman steering the boat, everyone's eyes were glued in the direction of the Smelne Vlet, even though they were out of sight of it. At precisely 10:45 a.m., the Apaches fired their Hellfire missiles, which impacted the boat. The resulting sound was deafening. The explosions were appropriate to the missiles' name. During training and his many deployments, he had seen all types of explosions up close, including IEDs, missile strikes, and even conventional bombs. This was different; this was London, not Kunar Province in Afghanistan.

Palmer turned to Cole and his British counterpart. "Fizzle yield?"

"Without a doubt," said Cole, not taking his eyes off the smoke rising in the air. "A 150-kiloton device would have produced a fireball of half a kilometer, a heavy blast radius a little less than a kilometer, and a moderate blast radius of about two kilometers. That's been avoided, but with the moderate westerly wind, radiation will carry through England to the east of us and into Europe."

"I'm glad you got off that boat," Palmer said to Cole. "I couldn't have watched for that explosion knowing you were still on board."

"If we'd had fifteen more minutes, we could have disarmed it." Cole looked toward the Pakistani nuclear engineer. "He's in for some intense interrogation."

Palmer nodded. Cole was right. In the weeks and months ahead, all of the individuals who had been involved in funding, planning, and carrying out the operation would be identified. The investigation into the theft of the weapons had been underway ever since it happened. Blame was being cast around like a massive fishing net, bringing in fish big and small. Palmer considered the other fallout, the nonnuclear variety. How would Fiona and her friend Carol fare? Fiona, a junior British MI6 intelligence analyst, had worked with foreign special forces operators to avoid a nuclear disaster beyond anything the world had ever seen. Would they be congratulated or vilified and fired?

64

THAMES RIVER
LONDON

The Royal Navy boat continued away from the site of the explosion at maximum speed. Palmer and Cole watched the cloud of smoke and debris in the sky behind them. The choppers rose and continued flying in a circular pattern over the point where the Smelne Vlet had been. The other Royal Navy boats had moved even farther away from the site, their objective being to prevent any ships or boats from approaching the location. The crews had gone into the enclosed wheelhouses to mitigate radiation exposure risk. The River Thames was, for the foreseeable future, closed to marine traffic.

When the boat with Palmer, Cole, and Green aboard approached St. Katharine Docks, the area looked like a carnival was in town. Blue and red emergency vehicle lights were flashing, and news and military helicopters filled the sky. The sound of sirens seemed to be coming from every direction. The lock was closed. The boat would tie up nearby at the Hermitage Community Moorings.

Palmer stood and looked for Collins as they slowly motored by. It was impossible to spot her—too far away and too many people. He took out his cell phone and called. The cell lines were overloaded; everyone was calling someone about what had happened.

The major had radioed ahead. Two British medics were waiting and boarded once the boat was docked. One medic cleaned Cole's wound, put on some butterfly strips, and wrapped a large bandage around the leg. The other medic wrapped Palmer's ankle and checked Green's bruises from the beating Sabri's men had given her. He also gave her a blanket, not so much to keep her warm as to hide Sabri's blood and brain matter that had splattered on her. The past twenty-four hours had been harrowing for Green. However, Palmer was confident that she would recover. She was a strong woman. He walked over and sat beside her.

"I won't ask if you're okay."

"Good. I'll slap the next person who does. One of the medics asked if I needed anything. I glared at him and said a hot shower would be nice. If I don't get one soon, I'm jumping in the river."

Palmer laughed and pointed at the blood in her hair. "They will need a sample of that for DNA testing."

"They already took some for evidence. They can have all my clothes, too. I'll never wear them again."

An American man approached them and introduced himself, showing them his Defense Intelligence Agency identification. "The three of you need to come with me."

"I need to find someone at the marina," Palmer said.

"Sorry. I'm afraid I can't let you go."

"Where are you taking us?"

"The embassy."

"Which one?"

"The US Embassy."

Green said, "Thank God. They'll have showers."

65

THE UNITED STATES EMBASSY & CONSULTANTS LONDON

The DIA agent whisked Palmer, Cole, and Green away in a black SUV with heavily tinted windows. The SUV's emergency lights were on, as were those of the two London police vehicles accompanying them, one in front and one to the rear of the SUV. As they approached the embassy at 33 Nine Elms Lane, the three of them stared at the peculiar building in front of them.

The US Embassy was located near the center of London on the south side of the River Thames, at 33 Nine Elms Lane in the London Borough of Wandsworth. The embassy had moved from Grosvenor Square, a posh area of Central London, to its new location in 2017. The architect had envisioned a crystalline cube. The British media had referred to it by less flattering names, like a "glass box covered in shite" and a "high-security Travelodge." The move to Nine Elms was the subject of much criticism, including that of the president of the

United States, both for the billion-dollar cost and for the giveaway price received for the previous building at Grosvenor Square.

The DIA agent guided them to a clinic in the building. The doctor further checked out Palmer. He removed the bullet from Cole's leg and redressed it. Green finally had her hot shower and changed into a pair of hospital scrubs. The DIA agent then escorted them to a conference room adjacent to the ambassador's office, where an assortment of sandwiches and nibbles were laid out for them. The US Ambassador, the Deputy Chief of Mission, and a JSOC Army colonel dressed in a suit and tie were waiting. General Reynolds was linked in by video, which was projected to a screen on the wall.

Following introductions, the ambassador began by saying, "I apologize for the haste in getting you here. We needed to get you away from the chaos before the newspaper reporters and television crews descended upon you. We intentionally kept this meeting small. The fewer people who know, the better."

"Thank you for that," Palmer responded. "We neither wanted nor are we in the mood for media interviews. Before we get started, I need to talk to Fiona Collins, an MI6 analyst who worked with us. She's my…" Palmer searched for the right word before finishing. "Fiancé. She was on board the yacht at St. Katharine Docks."

Green cocked her head and looked at Palmer, hearing him refer to Collins as his fiancé for the first time.

"We'll see what we can do," the ambassador said with a nod. "I'm certain that Ms. Collins will be tied up for a while, as are you. You've had a horrific day, including suffering injuries. And if what I know is true, the three of you—four, counting Ms. Collins—are heroes. What you've done is incredible, though from a public relations perspective, we will give the British the credit, saying that our role was only supportive."

"Quite right," Palmer said. "Fiona's the heroine. Her concerns regarding the *Medicine Man* yacht were reported through the appropriate MI6 chain of command and were minimized and dismissed. Had Fiona not pursued her investigation and alerted me as to her suspicions, I'm certain this building would be rubble and each of you would be dead, along with hundreds of thousands of others, including the queen. That boat and the nuke with a timed detonator set for 11:00 a.m. were bound for Lambeth Bridge."

The colonel blurted out, "Oh, shit."

Reynolds chimed in. "Also, Palmer and Green are JSOC Orange. We would not want that to get into the media."

The senior staffer said, "There were many witnesses, onlookers in the offices and buildings surrounding St. Katharine Docks, who saw what was going on and took cell phone videos. The media will dig further and might eventually identify the key players. For now, let's focus our immediate attention on learning what actually happened."

The ambassador nodded. "I suggest you three give us a high-level summary of what has occurred in the past twenty-four hours and then get some rest. We can complete this tomorrow morning when you're fresh."

"It's early," Palmer said. "Let's get started and see how far we get."

Palmer took the lead and described how he, Green, and Cole had gotten involved and the salient points of what had occurred that day. Reynolds spoke of the events leading up to Palmer's going to London with Cole. He didn't mention that he directed Palmer not to get involved in an operation on British soil or that he was initially unaware that Cole was accompanying him.

Green told them about their concern that Sabri was involved in the operation and that she was tracking him when she was abducted in Islamabad. She said she was interrogated, avoiding going into the details of the aggressiveness with which she was questioned. They then put her on a private jet to London with Sabri and gave her an injection. She woke up on the boat before dawn, having no idea where she was.

The interview went on for about three hours before they called it a day and were shown to individual VIP guest rooms. Palmer mentioned they could use a drink, and within minutes a minibar was rolled in with more than enough beer, wine, champagne, and liquor for the three of them, plus more sandwiches and snacks. Green and Cole came to his room, where they discussed the interviews and their current situation over drinks, assuming all the while that the room was bugged.

Green set her drink down and leaned back, looking at Palmer. "Was Sabri The Chameleon?"

"We'll never know. Perhaps The Chameleon was, as some have suggested, a myth, an amalgamation of people, like Sabri, Ahmadi, and others. Regardless, now that a void has been created, someone else will fill it. Evil will always find a home and have those who are unwise enough to follow him or her. But there will always be those who are willing to stand up to evil and risk their lives to fight it."

When they were done and Green and Cole had returned to their rooms, Palmer called Collins, left a long message, and sent her a text. He could only imagine what she was going through.

—◦◦◦—

At a quarter past two in the morning, Collins called Palmer. Although she said she was exhausted, she talked a mile a minute when describing everything that had occurred from the moment she and Cole walked on board the *Medicine Man* until now. He let her talk, interrupting only to let her know he was awake and paying attention. He had seen it before, after successful missions. Everyone was physically drained but full of emotional energy. Inside they were elated with the outcome and relieved that they had survived. Collins would be awake most of the night until the point at which her body said enough was enough. Then she would sleep.

Palmer asked her how she and Baxter were being received by her superiors at MI6. She said that so far, the emphasis had been on determining what had happened and who had been involved. She had not seen or spoken to her director, the one who had brushed off her initial concern. Baxter had arrived early and had been a big help in getting her through the day. Their ultimate fate was unknown.

Collins asked what happened after he and Cole left the *Medicine Man*. He summarized it and told her about Sabri and Green.

"She told you to shoot through her to get to Sabri?" Collins asked.

"She was willing to give her life to assure we had time to disarm the nuke."

Collins paused before asking, "That's incredible. Would you have done it? Would you have shot her in order to kill him?"

"Time was running out. Thank God I didn't have to decide. When she lifted her feet up and the two of them toppled forward, I took the shot."

Collins was quiet for a moment. "Will I see you before you return to Islamabad?"

"Doubtful. We have interviews scheduled tomorrow. We're not allowed to leave the embassy. They checked us out of the hotel at the marina and brought our things here. The news media are camping out at every exit from the embassy. I expect we'll be going directly from here to a military flight to Islamabad."

"I don't know how long I'll be here before I'm allowed to go home," Collins said.

"This will be a very long news cycle, and you're the prize catch for the BBC and every other news outlet."

"I doubt my name will be mentioned. There will be the usual politically and diplomatically correct press release—joint mission between MI6, MI5, and the British Army with no names given."

"Don't count on it. The British press aren't so easily deterred."

"When will I see you again?" Collins asked.

"Soon. I promise. Even if we have to meet on an island in the Mediterranean to escape work and the media."

66

SIX MONTHS LATER

International intervention and pressure had resulted in a temporary cease-fire between Pakistan and India. Both had withdrawn their troops from the Line of Control. China, in turn, withdrew its troops from the Galwan Valley, ending its conflict with India over that disputed border for the present. With the US facilitating the discussions, the countries agreed upon some basic policies and principles regarding the first use of nuclear weapons, nuclear weapons security, and the long-term destiny of Kashmir. Most believed that if the latter was not agreed upon, compliance with the agreements would last only several months before the conflicts reignited.

Much attention was on Pakistan to explain their lapse in security and the circumstances under which the nukes were stolen. The evidence left no doubt that senior members of Pakistani military were instrumental in the diversion of the nuclear warheads during the deployment and in the plot to detonate a nuclear warhead in London. Officials explained the elaborate terrorist plan that had been executed from within their military. To quiet the worldwide outrage, Pakistan agreed to an independent international review of its security and command-and-control structure for nuclear weapons.

Without fanfare, MI6 gave Fiona Collins what amounted to a battlefield promotion to a senior analyst position with a path to becoming an operational manager within a year, and she was awarded a Distinguished Intelligence Medal by both the CIA and MI6. She and the British major who was on the boat with Palmer were invited to meet Queen Elizabeth, who thanked them for their contribution to the security of their country. The media eventually determined that Collins was involved, but they were not allowed to interview or photograph her or anyone from MI6. That didn't stop the press from using old file photos and videos of her. As for Fiona's boss who dismissed her concern, he was transferred to the British High Commission in Bangladesh.

Alona Green remained with JSOC in Islamabad and took over directorship of the computer technology intelligence service. Reluctant to be tied to a desk, she accepted the position with the agreement that she would continue special operations assignments.

Cole returned to his EOD role and was promoted to Master Chief Petty Officer, the US Navy's highest enlisted rank. He planned to retire in a few months after completing his twenty years of military service. He had already been promised a position with a government contractor, providing explosive ordnance training, including nuclear weapon disarmament training, to NATO and other US allies.

The autopsy report on Martin Singleton revealed that he had been poisoned. No one was charged in his death. The woman who visited him in the hospital was not identified.

Sarkis and Ashkani had escaped before the hunt for them had even begun. Ashkani was found dead in a villa on the coast of Argentina five months later. He had been tortured to death. A week later, Sarkis was found dead in a house in a remote location on the Italian Isle of Capri. Traces of the deadly Novichok nerve agent were found on the front door handle of the house where he was staying. The method was the same one that had been used in the attempted assassination of a Russian double agent in England in 2018 and a Russian dissident in 2020. The fact that Sarkis's death followed so soon after Ashkani's led to speculation that Ashkani had given up Sarkis's location during his torture.

67

ISLAMABAD, PAKISTAN

Green had recovered from her injuries, at least the physical ones. The others would heal with time, she hoped. Her mind flashed back to the showdown with Palmer and Sabri. It was a few minutes of hell that she could not get out of her head. She had been willing to die and supposed that was a good thing—the *right* thing to do. She had told Palmer to shoot through her to kill Sabri. He'd had the pistol aimed at her head, a shot he would not have missed, and a shot she would not have survived. She remembered closing her eyes, and when she had, it was as if a voice told her what to do. Palmer said she'd smiled and winked; she didn't remember that. She did remember raising her feet off the deck and moving her head and chest forward and downward. Every special operator probably has at least one story like hers, a near-death experience when life and death hung in the balance and training kicked in to save the day. This was a career she chose. No other would fulfill her.

One thought she couldn't shake was what Aaliyah had said to her at the restaurant and the feeling that had rushed through her. A little voice was speaking to her. She had to see this through, and now was the time. Green pulled her phone from her purse and texted Aaliyah. A few hours later, Aaliyah responded: *Surprised to hear from you.*

Green texted, *Just surprised or pleasantly surprised?*

Curiously surprised.

I want to see you.

Why? Aaliyah replied.

Personal interest.

Where?

Monal 8 p.m. tonight.

Monal Restaurant sat in the Margalla Hills, almost four thousand feet above sea level, with a spectacular view of urban Islamabad below and an outdoor hillside dining area from which to enjoy it. It was five and a half miles on a hairpin-turn road from urban Islamabad and had the reputation of being an expensive, special occasion restaurant, one where lovers went to create a memory. She wanted to send an unsaid message to Aaliyah by her choice of restaurant.

Green tucked her auburn hair under her medium-length black wig and applied makeup, including dark-red lipstick. She dressed in a blue lace, Pakistani couture outfit and matching shoes that she had recently purchased.

Green arrived early and sat in the car with her driver until they saw Aaliyah enter the restaurant. She waited before getting out of the car and going in. The large, contemporary Monal Restaurant was divided into seven open-air terraces that took full advantage of the view of the valley below and Islamabad. Reservations just prior to sunset were highly sought after. The hostess showed Green to the table where Aaliyah had been seated. Aaliyah stood as Green approached.

Green said, "As-Salam-u-Alaiki," which meant "Peace be unto you"—the greeting to a Muslim from a non-Muslim.

Aaliyah responded, "Wa Alaikum Assalam wa Rahmatullah," which meant "May the peace, mercy, and blessings of Allah be upon you."

Both sat down at the table. "I didn't recognize you, Alona. You look tantalizingly beautiful. Even more so than when I last saw you."

"As do you, Aaliyah."

"Congratulations on saving the world," Aaliyah said sarcastically. "The ISI Director-General was grateful that a horrific disaster had been avoided. Although it was not in the media, my sources tell me that you were abducted and abused."

Green looked down, trying to ignore the upsurge of negative memories. With a deep breath, she forced a smile she didn't quite feel. "All in a day's work."

Aaliyah studied her for a moment before saying, "At least The Chameleon is dead."

"Enough about work." Green leaned in and rested her elbows on the table. "You've been on my mind."

Aaliyah's eyes sparkled. "You've been in my thoughts, too, Alona."

They talked throughout dinner, making mostly polite conversation about their backgrounds and how they each came to work in similar areas.

Green eventually changed the subject. "You mentioned The Chameleon earlier. At first, everyone thought it was Raul Ahmadi. Now, everyone seems convinced it was Commodore Sabri, a high-ranking, charismatic officer with special operations and nuclear weapon experience. Did you know him?"

"We interacted on military and intelligence issues over the years."

"Why was he on that boat?" Green asked. "He had no way out. He would have died when the bomb detonated. The Chameleon had a reputation for being directly involved, as in the assassination of the journalist, but he always had an exit strategy."

"You're talking about The Chameleon like he actually existed. Perhaps this was simply Sabri's 'bin Laden' moment. His name and the attack will live forever in history. You spent some time with him. Did you ask if he was The Chameleon?"

"Funny. As they were beating and drugging me, the subject never came up."

"Regardless, we've seen the last of The Chameleon—if he ever existed."

They talked for a while longer. When it was time to go, Green paid the bill. Aaliyah offered to give her a ride home. Green refused, saying she had a private car waiting. She quickly texted her driver, asking that he meet her at the door.

Before Green got into the car, she placed her hands on Aaliyah's arms and kissed her lightly on the lips, a practice not condoned in public, but no one was watching. Aaliyah pulled her closer, holding the kiss for a moment longer.

"Goodnight, Alona," she said softly, pulling away. "This was lovely."

"Goodnight, Aaliyah. When will I see you again?"

"I'll set up something more private soon."

Green smiled. "I look forward to it."

Green got in the rear seat of the car and leaned forward as the driver pulled away.

"Thanks for being my driver tonight, Dan. How did it go?"

"Piece of cake."

———

The next day, Green had coffee in the break room with Dan Adams, the computer specialist who had helped her locate and track Sabri's car and who had been her driver the previous evening. Two of their colleagues walked in. Green and Adams overheard the two men talking while they were pouring their coffees.

"Did you hear about the wreck on Pir Sohawa Road, near the Margalla Hills viewpoint?" one of them asked the other.

"I did. That's one dangerous stretch of road, full of twists and hairpin turns, and it's the only way to and from Monal Restaurant."

"Single car accident. A woman ran off the road. The car flipped."
"So sad. Well, it couldn't be because of drunk driving."
"Not in this country."
Green and Adams looked at each other and smiled.

68

ISLAND OF SKIATHOS, AEGEAN SEA
SKIATHOS, GREECE

Palmer sat at the rear of a small boat, his hand on the motor's tiller. The boat made slow, steady progress as it cut a path in the Aegean Sea. A beach mat, umbrella, a couple of towels, and a cooler of wine, beer, bread, and cheese were stowed between him and Collins, who was on the beach seat at the bow. They were renting a seafront house on Achladies Beach, a water taxi ride from the town of Skiathos. Until today, they had been happy spending time on the beach, coming up to the balcony of their bougainvillea-draped house for lunch. They ate dinners at a nearby taverna on the beach and took a water bus to the town of Skiathos one evening for dinner and to walk around. Today, however, Palmer was in search of an even more peaceful place, a small, uninhabited island they could see a few miles from the house.

Collins sat facing backward on the bench seat at the front of the boat. Once they were too far from the shore to be seen by anyone, Collins looked around and, seeing no one in sight, untied her bikini top and laid it on top of the cooler. She leaned back slightly, letting the sun warm her face and breasts. Baxter had once mentioned being on a yacht and taking her top off. Collins thought her crazy at the time. This was a far cry from a yacht, but the feeling of the warm sun on her was just the same.

Palmer smiled and shook his head. "Need me to apply some suntan lotion?"

"You are kind to ask, but I already have."

"You're supposed to reapply every hour. Sooner, if we swim."

Collins laughed and sighed. "I needed this. I hadn't realized how much of a toll the stress of the last few months had taken on me."

"*We* needed this," Palmer said. "This is our first trip where neither of us is working."

"And at a place where neither of us has ever been. It's heaven."

As he approached the island, he spotted a cove, raised the motor, and coasted onto the sandy beach. They unloaded the cooler, set up the umbrella, and spread out their beach mat. Their only company was the birds overhead and the goats feeding on the vegetation growing on the rocky hillside behind them. Collins poured some white wine, and Palmer popped open a beer.

"Have you ever skinny dipped?" Palmer asked.

"No," Collins said, casting him a devilish grin. "But I've never been to an uninhabited island before either."

With that, Collins got up and walked into the water. When she was deep enough, she took off her bikini bottom and threw it onto the gunwale of the boat. Palmer joined her after removing his swimming trunks. The water was warm and refreshing.

When they got back onto their beach mat and covered themselves with a towel, Palmer reached in the cooler and took out a small box.

"Jake…" Collins's voice softened. "What's that?"

"See for yourself."

Collins opened it. It was a gold ring with an intricate Greek key design. Her eyes sparkled in a way that dulled every diamond the world had ever seen. She glanced between the ring and him, lips parted but smiling. "It's beautiful, Jake."

"I know it's not a proper engagement ring. We can pick one out in London on my next trip there. Will you marry me, Fiona?"

"Yes!" she shouted so loud that the birds took flight and the goats stopped grazing to stare down at them from their lofty perches.

"Where and when did you get this?"

"I bought it when we were shopping in Skiathos town. You were in the dressing room trying on clothes."

Collins hugged and then kissed him, and they made love before going back into the water.

—◦◦◦—

Palmer sold his condominium on Rittenhouse Square in Philadelphia. During his visits to London to see Collins, they spent time with an estate agent searching for a place in the London area for the two of them to live. He was serving out the remainder of his two-year commitment with JSOC, splitting his time between Islamabad and London as a liaison to British special forces, with a focus on Pakistan and South Asia intelligence. JSOC asked him to extend his contract, but he refused. After the end of his two-year commitment, he would resume his role as an independent contractor and investigator.

At least, that was his plan.

ACKNOWLEDGMENTS

W riting seems a solitary effort, but numerous others are involved in ways big and small in order to bring a book to its final published form. I'm indebted to each of those who have contributed their time, insights, and constructive feedback.

I would like to express my sincere gratitude to my wife, Mildred, who reads and edits countless versions of the manuscript as it makes its way from rough draft to the final, publisher-ready version. She is truly my editor-in-chief. Beta readers provide invaluable feedback. My beta readers for *The Chameleon* were Judith Armfield, Robert Armfield, William R. Anderson, Lynn Bauer, and Henry Pittman. Special thanks to William R. Anderson, who, in addition to being an outstanding saxophone player, is a US Customs Service Special Agent and member of the Joint Terrorism Task Force (retired). As with *The Envelope*, he provided important information related to customs enforcement and inspection of international cargo and the processes federal agents use. Finally, I want to thank my readers, who encourage and motivate me to continue writing.

Lastly, I would like to thank Kathy Meis, Founder and CEO of Bublish, and Shilah LaCoe, my project manager, as well as others who encouraged me and provided their creative skills and experience to bring this book to publication.

The Chameleon is a work of fiction and all characters are fictitious. Resemblance to anyone living or dead is unintended. I have used the actual names of one person I know, Karen Psimas. Karen has been one of my most avid readers and supporters. I hope she likes her fictional namesake. Also, the assassination of Deepak Chandra in the book is based on the real-life assignation in 2018 of Shujaat Bukhari—founding editor of *Rising Kashmir*—and his two police officer bodyguards.

ABOUT THE AUTHOR

R on McManus is an award-winning author of *Libido's Twist, The Drone Enigma, The Envelope*, and *The Chameleon*. The Charlotte, North Carolina native is a former US Navy lieutenant, combat veteran, and corporate executive.

Following graduation from the University of North Carolina, where he was a Naval ROTC midshipman, Ron served aboard the USS San Marcos (LSD-25) and later volunteered for in-country service in Vietnam where he provided support to the Navy's patrol boat riverine operations throughout South Vietnam. After completing his active-duty obligation, he became director of Program Integrity at the North Carolina Medical Peer Review Foundation in Raleigh, where he established NC's first Medicaid fraud and abuse investigation unit. Over twenty-five years of Ron's professional career was in research and development with a British pharmaceutical company, including an expatriate assignment in England where he and his wife Mildred worked and maintained a residence for several years. He retired from the company as the global vice president of research and development quality and compliance and began studying creative writing and authoring novels that reflected those that he enjoyed reading.

He is a past president of the board of the University of North Carolina's Naval ROTC Alumni Association and was a member of the Board of Visitors for the university's Health Sciences Library.

Ron and Mildred reside in Virginia Beach, Virginia, on the shore of the Chesapeake Bay where he is currently working on his next Jake Palmer novel.

IF PROBLEM.

1-800-780-0256

Made in the USA
Middletown, DE
16 December 2021

56108240R00213